Stellar Endorsements for Mary Mueller

WOW! Don't start to read *The Redemption of Matthew Ryersen* unless you have some time. When you start it, you won't be able to put it down. But it's more than a great story. It's a story about you and me, God and what it means to be loved and to love. Life is messy and not for sissies, but out of the messy dirt God grows beautiful flowers. Don't just look at the mess...smell the flowers. This book will help you do that and, not only that, but after you read it you will "rise up and call me blessed" for having recommended it to you.

– Steve Brown
President of Key Life Network, Inc.
Professor, Reformed Seminary –

Mary Mueller's *The Redemption of Matthew Ryersen* is a beautifully penned narrative from a master storyteller. Sweeping in its scope yet simple in its story, Mary Mueller paints the concept of family with many different strokes while taking the reader on an emotional journey through somber valleys and soaring mountaintops. Through laughter and tears, triumphs and tragedies, Matthew Ryersen must face the demons of his past and learn to love in a world that never loved him. With *The Redemption of Matthew Ryersen*, Mary Mueller is at her absolute best. Not only is the narrative flawless, but it speaks to the places of the heart that need it the most. This is one that must be read.

– Josh Clark,
Author of The McGurney Chronicles
and Dakota Divided –

After reading *Stargazer*, I was excited about another novel by Mary Mueller. She is a master at creating living, breathing characters with the precision of a honed and abundant vocabulary. *The Redemption of Matthew Ryersen* takes us back to another time when people knew how to trust, to give, to set others above themselves. She reminds us how it feels to be all alone and entirely naked apart from Jesus. We have all been Matthew Ryersen.

– Kathy Frias
Author of Rumors of Eden –

Mary Mueller's smooth narrative grabs you instantly in *The Redemption of Matthew Ryersen* and signals that you are in for a special ride. Matthew Ryersen is a man in a desperate struggle to simply survive from one day to the next. It is said that sometimes God lets us hit rock bottom to get our attention. This is exactly where we find Matthew at the beginning of this fine story. At this lowest of points, Matthew not only manages survival, he stumbles into a second chance. This book is something special. Do yourself a favor and read it.

– J. Keith Jones
Author of "In Due Time" –

The first time I heard Mary Mueller speak for a brief five minutes, I was enthralled with her manner of expression. This lady is interesting to listen to if she is only speaking of finding a parking place! Her writing follows in the same vein. I often am guilty of the thought, "I wish I had said it like that!" Mary Mueller is, without doubt, one of the most interesting writers of our modern times, whether it be about the kid next door or the president of the world.

– Will Riley Hinton, Author of
The Rocky Mountain Odyssey Series –

The Redemption of Matthew Ryersen

Mary

Mueller

Published by White Feather Press. (www.whitefeatherpress.com)

ISBN 978-1-61808-016-5

Printed in the United States of America

Cover design created by Ron Bell of AdVision Design Group (www.advisiondesigngroup.com)

All scripture quotations in this book are taken from the New International Version of the Holy Bible.

White Feather Press

Reaffirming Faith in God, Family, and Country!

Dedication

To Abba, our "Daddy" God, in Whom we are never father-less.

On behalf of all the Muellers, to John and Barb Horning, for Matthew 25:35.

And to Carl T. Wilson, who loved much, gone too soon.

Acknowledgements

The problem I have with acknowledgments is knowing when to stop, and never more so than with *Ryersen*. When I wrote the first draft, almost fifteen years ago, many people were involved in my life who are gone now, and so many more have come to help with the final product.

You know that blurb in the front of many novels which says, "...no resemblance to actual persons...?" Well, that's a lie to avoid lawsuits. Writers of fiction are cannibals who steal bites of people they know – and people they don't know – and turn them into "material." So each character in this book reflects some good part(s) of a real person who has helped me on my journey. Please accept my gratitude and blessings as you find yourself in our story.

My special thanks and blessings to:

Skip Coryell, White Feather Press, publisher, cheerleader, outstanding example of a man who lives his dreams.

Author and radio personality Steve Brown, of Key Life Network, for endorsing this book. Few professionals will consider the pleas of an unknown author, but you never hesitated. God bless you for your generous spirit!

Barbara Bolsen and the staff of The Night Ministry, for allowing me to use the ministry's name and part of their story, and for taking time to be sure I got it right on behalf of those they serve. May God prosper your work so much it puts you out of a job.

Will Riley Hinton, friend, brother in Christ, voice of my conscience, for holding me to a higher standard and never letting me quit.

Mike Salsbury, King of Commas, beloved brother in Christ and adopted son, for encouragement and editing and, with Sandy and Kate, for loving friendship and family.

Gene, Kevin and Wauneta Meller, for a wonderful afternoon with the dairy herd and a wonderful evening of hospitality and fellowship. Any errors about the dairy are mine.

Jodi, Dawn and Linda, for being first readers and giving feedback to make this a better book.

Members of the Writers' Forum, for encouragement, loving criticism and, always, a godly perspective.

Josh Clark, friend and colleague, who had the guts to tell me to scrap the last quarter of the book and rework the whole story. You were right, and I'm grateful. Your presence in my life is a gift.

PART ONE

SALVATION

October, 1990 - December, 1993

"I was a stranger,

and you took me in..."

Matthew 25:35

One

The Grayson County Sheriff padlocked the door on the first Monday in October. "Take what you kin carry," the Sheriff told him. There wasn't much, so Matthew Ryersen slung on his jean jacket over a long-sleeved green-plaid flannel shirt and waded into a raw north wind, tossing shaggy, straw-blond hair out of slate-blue eyes to look back at the little house his grandfather had built on the side of Rough River Ridge before World War II. Gray mares' tails of cloud raced by overhead and black ice formed on the pavement as he reached the highway, far too cold for October in Kentucky. Matthew didn't feel it much, except where his left knee ached.

That first night, he found an abandoned barn and slept in some moldy straw. In the morning, snow had sifted through the cracks in the roof to cover him, but he took no harm from it that he could see. He kept on walking north, wandering from farm to farm, seeking work, or even a handout. Every day was cold, and many days were icy. Sometimes the snow was deep. He began to feel the cold as his rangy frame grew thinner; his knee ached all the time.

As winter advanced into spring, the air remained icy, the ground stayed frozen and the crops which dared to sprout were drowned by torrential rains. He stole an occasional shirt or pair of jeans from some farmwife's clothesline and patched one pair of jeans with a piece of feedsack found in an empty barn. He ate whatever he could find in the edges of fields, thanking his mother's mother for his knowledge of flora, his mother's father for his knowledge of snares.

Summer came on with hot, brassy skies. As the corn grew, the ground dried out until it cracked. He found a day of work here or there, baling hay, raising a barn, slopping hogs. The copper sun sucked his breath, burned his back; thirst cracked the corners of his mouth like the fissures in the earth. He was *always* thirsty! No one ever refused him a drink of water; he gulped their lukewarm offerings gratefully from tin cups, never lost the metal taste on his tongue. As he held the ragged tail of his stolen shirt under a pump to sponge his sweaty face, he longed to plunge into a trough, a pond, a lake of cold, fresh water, to stay submerged until his skin shriveled and his thirst was slaked and all the dirt finally soaked out of his skin and from under his fingernails.

Summer ground on relentlessly. Nights brought scant relief. Matthew lay spread-eagled on the dying grass by some farmer's field, gasping for breath, aching for rain, wishing for someone to come - anyone, *anyone* - who would bring him a cold drink, a hot meal, a clean shirt, a laugh, a touch... And he slept, at last, alone. And he woke alone. And summer ground on relentlessly.

At last, by some mercy he didn't know, the heat receded grudgingly; the light no longer glared. He found more work as bountiful crops cried out for harvest. He bought a new shirt and a bar of soap in Jamestown, Ohio, and bathed in a small creek. At night he slept in barns, burrowed into the straw like a kitten as the air grew chilly. His left knee began to ache again, predicting winter. Farmers paid him well for the harvest work and farmwives fed him, but no one asked him to stay, so he kept on walking north.

Despite the frost, it was a lovely day in Fulton County in Northwest Ohio, a hard blue sky and pleasing warmth from the winter sun. Matthew's jacket kept him comfortable and his knee stopped aching after a few miles. He thought he was not unhappy as he was. He could go on this way for a long time.

But why?

A cold sweat broke out across Matthew's hairline. His hands trembled until he clenched them and crammed his fists into his pockets. He increased his pace until he was almost running down the road. His errant thought echoed in his ears and pounded in his chest. For the first time in that long, sad, lonely, incomprehensible year, he knew he was afraid.

He couldn't outrun that fear, but he could exhaust it. Finally his heart rate slowed and his feet followed, until he stood still, quivering, suddenly aware of the dropping temperature and lengthening shadows, of his empty belly and dry throat, of a blister on his heel and the lights of a farmhouse not too far off the road. He limped up the drive, watching for a mean dog, watching the figures he could see through the windows.

No dog appeared; he was grateful for that! He had lost skin and the cuffs of his jeans to several dogs along the way. Inside the house a family was getting ready for dinner. He saw some of them touching affectionately as they passed one another. He was suddenly so cold, so tired, so hungry - desperately lonely - unable to leave and afraid to ask to come in.

A tall farmhand came loping up the drive and almost passed by him as he stood yearning in the shadows. The hand stopped, grinning, and beckoned. "C'mon in! I'm Ed Yoder. This is the Abbott place, and you're just in time for supper!" Yearning warred with fear - and lost. He couldn't move, was sure his shoes had been nailed to the stones. The farmhand just grinned again, took his arm and led him in to the kitchen, asking his name as they went.

Light and steam, odors and voices, the symphony of pots, pans, silverware, china and glassware, all clinking and rattling and chiming, assailed him. He had been alone outside so long he couldn't take it in. His head ached, his muscles quivered; he turned toward the door looking for escape, but several giggling children blocked his way. They were singing and rowing an imaginary boat and snitching radishes from the relish tray. He clenched his teeth so hard his jaws ached. Ed introduced him and indicated a chair at the dining room table. Matthew sank into it, only because his knees wouldn't hold him upright a moment longer.

A short, stocky old woman bustled in carrying a loaf of hot homemade bread. A wicked sparkle in her dark eyes softened the brisk, no-nonsense manner to which everyone deferred. As she looked Matthew over thoroughly, he remembered suddenly both his grandmother and his grade-school principal. "Of course you'll stay for dinner," she said. "You've been very hungry, and now you'll be fed." He nodded helplessly.

Outside the farmhouse, a winter night clamped down. Inside, Matthew was warm and sated and exhausted. He forced himself to his feet and headed for the front door. They flocked around him like guinea hens, touching him gently, clucking anxiously over his efforts to leave, urging him to stay, leading him upstairs to a small bedroom. One of the little boys clung to his leg and hitched a ride on his worn shoe. He briefly touched the boy's hair. He had never felt anything as warm and silky as those pale strands weaving themselves around his fingers.

The Abbotts gave him pajamas, a toothbrush, a razor, a comb, a new bar of soap. They showed him his bed, his dresser, his closet, his towels in the bathroom. They showed him the nightlight, the extra blankets; they told him to raid the refrigerator, to call if he needed anything. The little boy tugged at his pants-leg. "Bend down, man, bend down so I can kiss you good-night."

As he bent to the velvety little mouth and received the blessing, he distinctly heard something in his chest snap like a frozen branch. He assumed his heart had broken and was confused to feel no pain, to find himself continuing to stand, to breathe, as the family left him alone in the room.

The farmer, John Abbott, came back to the door to say, "There's plenty of work for you here, and you're welcome to stay as long as you want."

§ § §

He heard that snap in his chest again, and felt it, too, as John spoke. He met the farmer's eyes for the first time, unable to believe this man could be offering so easily so much more than he had hoped for all that long year. John was smiling, saying something as he turned away whose sense was lost in the brittle crash of shattering ice under Matthew's skin, behind his eyes, inside his heart. Alone, Matthew lay down on the bed, shaking, rattling inside himself.

Gentle light came in from the hall, and the murmur of gentle voices. Outside, snow began to fall. The wind picked up. The last oak leaves clattered into the driveway. Inside, Matthew slowly thawed. All the broken pieces melted and warmed until they flooded up and over and ran down his cheeks. He straightened out at last and lay easy under the quilts.

I could put up a shelf on that wall, he thought. *A cherry-wood shelf. Buy a few books, and maybe a plant, to put on it. Just a small plant.*

Then he thought, *I could make a little boat for that little boy.*

He imagined carrying groceries for the old woman and the farmer's pretty wife, repairing the farmer's tractor, helping to sow the farmer's fields – and being there next fall to help with the harvest. He fell asleep with a smile on his lips and dreamed of the silver-gold glint of ripe wheat in the summer sun.

Two

He dreamed, or thought he was dreaming, that he slept on sun-dried sheets, warm under heavy quilts, in a soft white room. In the dream, if it were a dream, a tiny little boy with hair like dandelion fuzz pulled at his sleeve, insisting, "Man, wake up! Wake up! You're missing the morning!"

Slowly he gave up the dream, expecting to feel frost-stiffened stubble against his back and emptiness in his heart and belly. And there was the boy.

"I'm David," the boy said, grinning. "Who'd you say your name was?"

"I'm Matthew Ryersen."

"Then get up, MatthewRye! Mama cookeded pancakes."

Matthew took in the room, the boy, remembered the night before, the ache in his knee and the ache in his heart as he stood paralyzed and freezing in the driveway, the overwhelming warmth of the house and its inhabitants. He wanted to lie there just a few moments more, remembering, before he had to go out into the cold.

"Come on!" David insisted. "My mama's pancakes are good! And my daddy's already in the barn a long time now. Don'ch'a want to see the cows?"

"Sure," he agreed. "I'll be right down."

David scampered away, tiny shoes clattering down uncarpeted stairs. With a luxuriant stretch, Matthew rose from his haven into the real world. At least he had been gifted with one hot meal, one night of safe, warm sleep, and now, if he dared, a hot shower.

At the end of the shower, he found a slightly worn pair of jeans, cuffs intact, and a blue plaid flannel shirt which couldn't have been washed more than once or twice hanging over the ladder-back of his chair. Folded on the seat were new white briefs, tee-shirt and socks.

At the bottom of the stairs, Matthew found so much more than a stack of pancakes and a brisk farewell. The Abbott family was determined to take him in.

Ed Yoder, the farmhand, who was a shade taller and heavier, loaned him a few changes of clothes and introduced him to the routine. He learned that they rose at four a.m. to milk and feed the small Jersey herd John Abbott kept "because he likes 'em" and to gather eggs from the sleepy hens. He learned that no matter how quickly he dressed and hurried downstairs, John's wife Carolyn was already there, pouring him a mug of strong coffee to chase the dawn chill. He learned that they were "those people," who went to church and prayed before meals and talked about Jesus as if He were one of the family.

After coming to breakfast for several days with hands red and chapped from cold, Matthew found a pair of leather gloves by his plate. On Friday John paid him, cash, more than he could believe he had earned. *Why are they being so nice?* He wondered. *When it seems too good to be true, it usually is.*

Ed filled in the blanks for Matthew as they worked side by side. Matthew asked, "Do you have family around here, too?"

"Nope," Ed answered. "Most of my family's passed on years ago, and the ones that's left give up on me a long time ago."

"You mean they don't want anything to do with you?"

"Yep." Ed avoided meeting Matthew's curious glance.

"But... I mean, you're a nice guy, and-"

"Maybe you see Jesus in me now, Matthew, but it weren't always so. You ever wonder how come I ain't married?"

Surprised, Matthew looked up. "Well, yeah."

"Was once. She divorced me - because I couldn't have kids, and we started fighting about it something fierce, and I started drinking. That's when she left me, and that's when I done the worst of my drinking, drifted around, couldn't hold a job. I remember being drunk at the bus station in Indinap'lis - and coming to at the bus stop here. Sobered up and went looking for work so's I could buy a bottle and a bus ticket out of here. Boss heard me asking about work at the feed store - and here I still am. Ain't proud of my past. Figured you ought to know, though, that you ain't the first drifter the boss took in. Probably won't be the last. I figure it fills in the gap. Figured you was wondering about how you got in so easy, so I thought I'd tell you."

"Oh. What gap?"

"Eh?"

"You said 'to fill in the gap.'"

"Oh, yeah. Well, long time before David they had another little boy, Johnny. He died when he was a baby, and they thought they'd never be able to have any more. They don't talk about it much, so don't bring it up."

"I won't. So, anyway, how long you been here?"

"Ohhh – let me see. Maybe thirteen, fourteen years."

"Wow. Long time. Don't you ever think about leaving or about having your own place?"

"Nope. Might if I was married, but that ain't happening."

"You don't want to remarry?"

"Don't seem right. Most women want kids. Naw, I'm all right the way I am. Got a good job, got a little house, got some friends – got my Lord now – don't need no more."

"Do you ever think about drinking again?"

"Nope. Well, least not like I done before. The Lord took that all away from me."

"Oh." *That God thing again. What is it with these people?*

§ § §

The next afternoon, in the barn, helping Ed muck out the stalls, he asked, "So whose mother is Pearl? Who are the Gundermans? How does she fit in with all these people?"

"Pearl? A widow with no kids. Not related to this family by blood."

"But she's in and out of here all the time. She helps with meals and laundry and eats dinner here and bosses people around..."

"Ain't that the truth!" Ed laughed. "Yep, she'd probably boss Peter and Paul in heaven if they didn't do something to suit her." He wiped his face with a clean but wrinkled blue bandana and returned to his work.

"So who is she?" Matthew persisted.

"Why, she's part of the family, same as me and you." Ed's voice held a certain amazement, as if he couldn't believe the answer wasn't obvious.

"But where did she come from?"

"Son," Ed said slowly, "she's a member of the church, just an old lady with nobody to do for and nobody to take care of her. She's got a whole lot to give, a whole lot of wisdom, and nobody to give it to. So she gives it to us. And we give stuff to her. That's how family does."

He cast a hard eye on Matthew. "Now, the fact is, in this family we don't ask a lot of questions about where people come from or who they used to be. You need us, you want to be here, you're in. Might be, some of our stories wouldn't stand up too good to close inspection. Notice nobody's asked you any questions, like how come you got a hillbilly accent."

Matthew looked at his worn, steel-toed work shoes, their coating of manure and straw, thought back over the miles they had traveled and the things he had done along the way.

"You're right," he said. "I didn't mean to pry."

"No problem. But there *is* gonna be a problem if you fork that stuff onto these boots."

Genuinely intent on being careful, Matthew almost immediately tripped over his own feet and dropped his pungent load right onto Ed's boots. He blushed from the roots of his hair to the soles of his feet and cried, "I'm sorry, Ed, honest! It was an accident!"

Ed, face turned toward the ceiling, was busily reciting: "Genesis, Exodus, Leviticus, Numbers, Deuteronomy!"

"What?"

Ed's dusky blush nearly rivaled Matthew's. He gave a sheepish grin as he knocked the filth from his boots. "I used to have a real good string of cusswords to use when the wrench slips or the stuff gets all over my boots. But I got on speaking terms with the Lord, and I read in the Bible where he don't like us using those words. So I decided when I just had to use strong language, why, I'd recite the books of the Bible instead. Went through the whole Old Testament when the cow stamped on my foot a few years back. Covered most of the New while they were x-raying and setting it."

"How many books are there?"

"Enough for most occasions," Ed laughed.

Sharing the laugh, they went back to work. *I wonder how many*

books there really are in the Bible, Matthew mused, *and what's a "book,"
and how he remembers them all. And why he'd want to.*

When Pearl came over for dinner that evening, she had a brown
lunch-bag with her. She beckoned Matthew aside into the living-
room and stood closer to him than she usually did. "I have something
for you," she said quietly, holding out the bag.

Matthew took it, surprised by the weight. "Thank you, ma'am."

"Well, open it, Matthew!"

"Yes, ma'am." He opened the bag to find a heavy book inside.
Drawing it out, he frowned in confusion. It was titled *Collected Works
of Robert Frost.* "Uh, thank you..."

"It's poetry, Matthew. I know you don't want to be reading the
Bible yet, but you need to read more than seed catalogues!"

"We didn't study poetry much in school, and I don't know-"

Pearl gave him her gimlet stare. "You must not reject anything
prior to consideration. This poetry is not too difficult for you, and it
will speak to your spirit if you let it. Come to dinner now." Turning
on her heel, she left him standing there.

*Huh. Poetry... Well, why not? If I don't like it I don't have to read
it.* He opened the book to one of the early pages and read, "I'm going
out to clean the pasture spring... I won't be gone long, You come,
too." *I know how that feels. It was a short poem. Maybe this will be
good...*

§ § §

Finally the suspense became too much for Matthew. "Can I talk
with you?" he asked John after dinner one evening.

"Sure. C'mon into the living room." John led the way and sat
down in his chair by the fireplace. Matthew gingerly took the couch
facing the fireplace.

After the silence had become too uncomfortable to bear, Matthew
ventured, "Why are you doing this?"

"Doing what?"

"Being so nice. Giving me all this. Not just a job, but a place, and
things - "

"Oh." John relaxed back into his chair, its leather creaking. "Want
some coffee? There are a couple of parts to that answer."

"No, thank you." He was poised on the edge of the couch, fingers clutching the cushion-seams on either side of him.

"All right, then. First, and most important, we believe God calls us to help people when they need it. So if you need it and we have it – it's yours."

Matthew just looked at him.

"Next, you have farm experience and we have work. Seems logical to me. I'm not *giving* you anything if you look at it that way; you're *working* for it – and hard.

"Carolyn and I, we both had pretty easy lives growing up. Good parents, good school, good friends, good church. Got to do what we wanted with our lives... mostly." A shadow crossed John's face and lingered in his eyes until he seemed to push it away. "Anyway... we saw we were blessed with so much, and we decided we ought to share it. So when Ed came along, when Pearl came along, we just opened up our – our family and let them in. Now, here's Matthew. We have the space, we have the job, David likes you – so why not?"

"People don't just do that."

John smiled. "Well, they do sometimes." He rose slowly, stretching. "I can see why you'd maybe think this is too good to be true, but hang around a while and check us out. You can leave any time you want to, but we want you to stay."

"Thank you," Matthew said softly, standing as well.

§ § §

Matthew's words had been polite; his quirked eyebrow and compressed lips had suggested to John that he was continuing to reserve judgment.

Oh, Lord, John thought, scarcely calling it a prayer, *I want to do this right. But every time I look at him, I think about Johnny. Johnny would probably have looked a lot like that when he grew up. I'm surprised Carolyn doesn't see it. She would have said if she sees it, wouldn't she?* He rubbed a hand across his face, scraping on the stubble of his end-of-the-day beard. No matter how many years passed, the pain could still surface in an instant. *I won't think about that,* he told himself sharply. *No. Gone. Over and done with. I'm not substituting Matthew for Johnny. I want to help him for himself – and for You.*

"What's wrong with Matthew?" Carolyn asked her husband later in the privacy of their room. "Doesn't he like us?"

John lay back against the pillows, hands behind his head, banishing dark thoughts by enjoying the sight of his wife getting ready for bed. He never tired of the line of her body through her nightgown, the soft, blond curls at the nape of her neck, the intense blue of her eyes.

"He just doesn't trust us yet," John said. "We need to give him more time."

"He's so thin! I can practically count his ribs through his shirt. And I never see him smile, except at David."

"The boy's our secret weapon, I think," John smiled. "He's too little to understand walls, so he goes right through 'em."

"Do you think Matthew will stay?"

"Do you want him to stay? I didn't ask – just kind of took it for granted you'd feel the same way I do."

Carolyn laughed lightly, crawling into bed and turning on her side to face him. "Lucky for you, I feel exactly the same way. Matthew needs a family even more than he needs a job. Of course I want him to stay! I want to put a few pounds on him and find his smile and help him to know the Lord – But do you really need him? Can we afford another hand?"

"Darlin'," drawled the farmer, gathering her into his arms, "I really can use him. He's pretty good at what he does, and he catches on fast. Can we afford him? Well, almost." He kissed her hair and worked his way toward her mouth before adding, "Do you mind having him in the house? I could make other arrangements with Ed."

She rose up on her elbow and poked his chest in indignation. "Don't you dare! That poor man hasn't had a place to call home in God only knows how long. Well, now this is his home, and that's his room!"

John laughed gently, drawing her back into kissing range. "All right, okay, I surrender! The room is his for as long as he wants it." He kissed her thoroughly.

Undistracted, Carolyn returned to the original question. "But do you think he'll stay?"

John ran his fingers absently through her hair, considering. "I hope he will. I hope he'll come to trust us and love us and feel at home with us. But we have to give him space and time to get used to us. And we have to leave him free to choose."

"Just love him and let him be, hmmm?"

"Exactly right," agreed the farmer, turning off the light.

§ § §

Across the hall, Matthew lay on the edge of sleep, mentally examining a block of pine John had given him when he expressed an interest in woodcarving. In the workshop, far back in a cluttered drawer, Matthew had uncovered a cache of woodcarving knives and chisels wrapped in greasy rags. "What are these for?" he had asked John.

"These were my father's," John had said. "He really liked working with them. Said it relaxed him. I honestly never had the knack or the interest he had, so they've laid here since - oh, I guess since a few years before he died."

"Was he good?" Matthew asked. "At carving, I mean."

"Yes, he was. I thought so, anyway. He did simple things, like boxes and some little cars for me when I was a kid... I think he was disappointed when I didn't want to do it, too." John sighed. "I hated to disappoint my dad, ever."

"Did he get mad at you?" Matthew asked.

"For not wanting to carve? No, he just looked sad for a minute when I refused for the second or third time. Then he said something like, 'Never mind, son, we can't all be just the same.' He never brought it up again after that. He was proud of me for other things."

"Oh." Matthew turned away, then turned back to the tools. "I think – I might like to try it some day."

"Well, why not? These tools have just been waiting for someone to come along who would care enough to use them. I can show you how, but I'm no artist. That part has to come from inside yourself."

Three

As weeks went by, Matthew eventually sorted out the rest of the Abbott family. The four little blond boys he had met the first night, Teddy, Stevie, Andrew and Greg, were David's cousins; their parents were John's sister Olivia, called Livvie, and her bearded brown bear of a husband, Carolyn's brother Ted Seibenek, who farmed a few miles down the road. The four adults still lived on the two families' adjoining farms, and they had all gone to school together. Ted and John were both two years older than their wives.

"Picked her out when she was ten and I was twelve," Ted declared. "Told her I'd marry her on graduation day."

"Did you?" Matthew asked.

The brother-in-law's laugh boomed in the crowded room. "Nope! She made me wait for years. Thought I'd probably die waiting for her to get the travel bug out of her system."

Livvie radiated the same steady peace her brother did. Matthew tried to imagine her flying off to exotic places, speaking strange clicking languages, sleeping in grass huts or on mountainsides, but he could not.

"What did you do?" he asked. "Were you a photojournalist or something?"

Everyone burst out laughing. Matthew blushed and looked down at his hands. Livvie, seated next to him, put a sympathetic hand on his arm.

"We're not laughing at you," she said. "It's me. I wanted to see the world, all right, but I wanted to do it as a flight attendant. I was really good at the training, and I think I looked great in the uniform. But every time I went up in a plane, I threw up. *Every* time. So I went to school to be a travel agent. I worked at an agency in Toledo."

"Well, go on," her husband urged, grinning. "Tell him the rest." The little boys were giggling uncontrollably; they had obviously heard this story before.

"Oh, all right," she huffed. "I sold so many big trips I won a seven-day cruise for two to the Caribbean. So I invited this big lug to go along..."

"And I had to drive her to New York to catch the boat because she couldn't fly, and Dad was ticked at having me gone two weeks from the farm, and her family was sure I was gonna - and the wench refused to make it a honeymoon cruise..."

"Wench?" Livvie interrupted, raising both eyebrows.

Ted smiled at her sheepishly, but his eyes glinted with mirth as he continued, "But as it turned out, I'm glad she said no, because I spent the whole seven days either holding her head while she upchucked or holding her up because she was too drunk on Dramamine to walk straight!"

Matthew joined shyly in the general laughter, marveling to himself at the easy unselfconsciousness with which these people laughed at themselves and teased each other. No one stormed out or burst into tears or raised a fist... not like anything he had ever known.

§ § §

Leaning against a beam, waiting for the milking machine to signal the end of its cycle, Matthew let his mind drift back to a brindle cow and a three-legged stool and a galvanized bucket. He could feel the warm, leathery teats in his hands and hear the hiss and ping of milk into the bucket. Her name was Posy and she had had all the patience in the world with an eight-year-old boy. So had his granddaddy. A faint smile lit Matthew's face as he remembered, wiped away in an instant by a harsh voice behind him.

"Matthew! What're you doing? Pay attention!"

He spun around to face John.

"Never turn your back on these cows. You need to pay attention all the time!" John turned on his heel and stamped out of the barn.

Ed came in moments later, laughing. "What'd you do to them

cows, boy? Boss sure was testy!"

"I – I was daydreaming when it was time to finish up." He used his hip to nudge the last cow back into the yard. "I had my back turned, and I didn't see they were finished. Do you think he'll fire me?"

Ed laughed. "Shucks, no! He just has a short fuse sometimes. He'll be back saying he's sorry in a bit."

"He was so angry! He was yelling."

"Yep." Ed began to hose down the concrete floor as if nothing had happened.

"I never heard him raise his voice like that before."

"Nope." Ed rehung the hose. "He don't do it all that often. But, whoo-ie! When he does...!"

"All that Jesus stuff – "

"Huh?"

"Well, aren't you people supposed to be all kind and gentle like Jesus was?"

Ed sighed. "Yeah, we are. But, Matthew, just think. Jesus was a man, too, not just God. He got mad and tired and scared and all them things, just like we do. God don't say, 'Don't get mad.' He says, 'When you're mad, don't sin.'"

"Oh, *that* makes sense." Sarcasm laced Matthew's voice and twisted his mouth. "People who get mad like that are dangerous. Does he ever act like that to David?"

"No, he don't get mean with David, and he ain't dangerous. He's just human. Let it go, Matthew. Your job's safe, and you are, too." Ed made a snorting sound and stalked out of the barn.

You don't know, Matthew thought, *but I do. I know how an angry man can treat a little boy. I know how one mistake can mean no more chances. Maybe I'd better pack.* He headed for the house, mentally cataloguing his few possessions for what he could carry on the road again.

As Matthew washed his hands and arms in the utility sink on the back porch, John came out from the kitchen.

"Ready for dinner?" John asked.

"I'm not very hungry."

"Ham loaf and buttered noodles," John said. "Carolyn will be hurt if you don't even try them."

Matthew studied his cuticles.

"Listen, let me just say this, okay? I'm sorry I flew off the handle out there. I know you wouldn't mess up on purpose. Just keep an eye out from now on, and don't worry about it."

"Sure."

John reached out to put a hand on Matthew's shoulder but drew back quickly as Matthew flinched. "Whoa!" He put his hands into his pockets. "Please believe me, Matthew, I really am sorry."

Still unwilling to meet John's eyes, Matthew said, "Thank you. It's okay."

"Let me – I've been working on the books all day, and I have a headache and I keep thinking about – well, that doesn't matter. I just – sometimes I get to the point where I'm about to explode, and then – you know. It wasn't you. It's my own – stuff. So will you have dinner with us?"

Matthew nodded but waited for John to go through the door ahead of him, unwilling to turn his back on the farmer.

Four

With one finger, Matthew traced a healing cut on his thumb, where one of the knives had slipped. So far he was just practicing on scraps, learning what the tools could do. But his mind, far ahead of his fingers, was imagining the block of pine as a boat for David for Christmas.

As he lay there, a tiny shadow appeared in the half-open doorway. A tiny voice whispered, "Help!"

Matthew sat up abruptly, swinging his feet over the edge of the bed. "What's wrong?"

The boy edged into the room. "I wet my bed." His little voice quivered. "It's cold now, and there's monsters under there."

C'mon, kid, go get your mom. But Matthew stood, shivering at the cold wood under his feet, and found himself saying, "I'll go back with you and change your sheets."

The boy edged closer. "They're really BIG monsters." A tear glinted in the glow of the nightlight. "C'd I come in with you? Please?"

His treacherous heart rolled over in his chest. He sat on the bed and held out his arms to the boy, who scampered over to him with the tiniest of bare-foot sounds and clung to his neck. The boy was warm and damp, with a sharp-sweet odor rising from his pajamas. It didn't matter.

When John roused him with a knowing smile at four the next morning, Matthew found David burrowed into his armpit and his own pajamas and sheets soaking wet.

Having decided to claim ownership that first night, David wouldn't leave Matthew alone. With three-year-old innocence, he assumed the man would share his devotion. While no one else would consider violating Matthew's boundaries, the boy charged across them every day, occasionally bursting into Matthew's room and bouncing on the bed to wake him, hitching a ride on his shoe whenever the fancy struck, following him around as he did chores and asking endless questions he knew fascinated Matthew as much as they did him. Despite the warnings he gave himself, Matthew was falling into the trap. *You know this isn't a good idea. You know it isn't safe*, he told himself over and over. Then he would think, *Just this once...*

Plump as a grape in his dark blue snowsuit, cheeks blazing from the cold, David turned soulful eyes on Matthew to lure him out to throw snowballs and build a snowman in the first real snow. Drying out in front of the fire in the living room afterwards, he climbed into his man's arms and fell asleep.

Matthew sat there on the floor in front of the flickering flames, warm, almost dry, sated with graham crackers and hot chocolate, cradling the sleeping child carefully. He rubbed his lips against the silky, pale blond hair and breathed in the boy's tangy, sweet scent. He felt a strange expanding feeling in his chest, and a sweet contentment. Knowing he was safe because David was asleep, he kissed the flushed little cheek and said softly, "I love you."

§ § §

Watching Matthew and David silently from the doorway, John had not been able to regret his spying. That night as they knelt together by the bed, he told Carolyn what he had seen and heard. "Lord," they prayed, "thank you for sending Matthew to us. Please help us to help him to find his relationship with You, to realize how much You love him and want the best for him – and we do, too."

Five

"**I** don't *go* to church," Matthew growled.

"Well, Titus and Philemon, boy!" Ed exclaimed. "I was just asking. If you don't want to come, that's your business. Hand me that biggest crescent wrench." He extended his hand without looking or withdrawing his head from the guts of the John Deere.

Matthew gently slapped the wrench into Ed's rough hand and gazed idly around the large pole barn they called "the shed." Barn swallows had made nests in the corners of the ceiling, but they had gone south for the winter, leaving only the messy little funnels behind.

"Lookit here," Ed said, drawing Matthew's attention back to the tractor. Matthew obediently peered at whatever Ed was trying to show him. "You just don't care much for engines, do you?" Ed laughed, shoving lightly to move Matthew so he could ease back and straighten up.

Matthew laughed a little, too. "No, I guess not. I'm pretty good with mules, though. That's how I learned to plow."

"Oh! Sorry we don't have no mules, son, because I'd purely love to see that."

"Why do you all keep asking me to go to church anyway?" Matthew persisted, handing Ed a rag to wipe the grease off the wrench. Ed's hands would need a little more attention.

"Church is a good thing," Ed said slowly. "Bible says Christians're supposed to get together to pray and praise the Lord and such."

"You already do that at home. And I'm not a Christian."

"Yeah, we do that some," Ed agreed, avoiding the second half of Matthew's statement, "but it means more than just the immediate family. Here, put this wrench back in the kit."

Matthew began nesting wrenches into their designated slots in the box. "Okay, but you get together with John's sister Olivia and Ted and their kids pretty often, and you always pray, and somebody always talks God-stuff before the day's over."

Ed sighed. "Yeah, but we don't have a choir and we don't have a preacher. If you'd hear Pastor Miles preach, you'd know for sure you was getting fed."

"Maybe I'm not hungry," Matthew said. "Maybe I just want to be left alone."

Ed sighed again. "We ain't exactly dragging you behind the bumper of the car, Matthew!" He paused, wiping his hands on his already greasy blue bandana. "Let me say just one more thing, okay?"

Matthew nodded.

"It's like – say you found this really great diner, with the best food you ever ate, the best cup of coffee, pie better than Pearl's – and a whole lot of great people who're always glad to see you whenever you come in. And say you had this friend. Wouldn't you want him to come with you, when you knew it'd be the best meal he ever had?" Matthew nodded, half-smiling. "Well, that's how we feel about church, and that's why we want you to come. Jesus, he's the best thing we know to share with a friend."

Matthew looked up from careful examination of his ragged cuticles into the clear, open face before him. "I get what you're saying, but, trust me, I have my reasons for staying home." He paused. "Mama said my granddaddy was a church-goin' man when he was young, he and my gramma both. Granddaddy went away to the war in the South Pacific in the 40's; and when he came home, he never went to church again. So my gramma stopped, too. Mama said my granddaddy said there couldn't be a God, because no God could have allowed the things he saw. Or if there was a God, he was a monster and Granddaddy didn't want any part of him. Thing is, everything I've seen my whole life pretty much says my granddaddy was right. So – no church."

Sadness in his eyes, Ed nodded. "Got it," he acknowledged. "No church."

§ § §

"MatthewRye," David said, pulling at his shirtsleeve, "please put me in my chair."

Matthew picked up the tiny boy and hoisted him into the booster seat which let him see over the edge of the dining room table. "There you go."

"David," John's voice came from behind them as he carried in a heavy platter laden with roast and vegetables, "what do you say to Matthew?"

David smiled, showing tiny white teeth and two dimples just like his father's . "Thank you," he sing-songed.

"You're welcome," Matthew laughed, heading for a seat on the other side of the table.

The smile turned into a ferocious frown. "No, MatthewRye! Sit by me!"

Matthew froze, looking at John.

"That's your mama's chair," John said.

David squinted his round blue eyes at his father and pushed out his lower lip. Matthew imagined the sound of rapidly approaching thunder. But David had gauged his opponent. He released the frown, widened his eyes again and turned on his smile. "Please?"

John and Matthew simultaneously turned their backs to hide suppressed laughter. It had been a brilliant, blatant performance. Finally John cleared his throat and managed to say, "Matthew, it's fine if you want to sit with David."

Matthew silently took his place beside the three-year-old fledgling thespian, a place that would be his thereafter. When David leaned over and patted his shoulder, Matthew felt as if he had been knighted.

Unaware of the dining room drama, Carolyn and Pearl came in from the kitchen with side-dishes of corn, fresh rolls and gravy. The mingling aromas were almost overpowering to Matthew, spurring his appetite and killing it at the same time. He swallowed hard.

Ed popped in through the kitchen door to take his seat beside Pearl. "Sorry I'm late. Didn't like the looks of Blanche. Way too early to drop that calf."

"We need the vet?" John asked.

"Already called him. Be by after dinner."

"All right, then," John said, "let's pray." He bowed his head over folded hands, eyes closed, and all the others followed suit – except Matthew, who kept his eyes open, watching.

What's the point? Matthew wondered. *Why thank God for food John raised and harvested himself? And why ask God to take care of a cow? Why would he think God cares about cows when He doesn't care about people?*

"Amen." John said.

"Amen," they echoed.

The food passed from hand to hand. Matthew put small portions on David's plate. He cut the meat into tiny bites and mashed the vegetables with his fork. David dug in with more enthusiasm than skill as Matthew began the same process on his own plate. He had managed one bite of meat and two of the unbuttered roll when David spoke.

"MatthewRye, how come you keepeded your eyes open when Daddy was praying and you didn't say 'amen' when he was done?"

Matthew stared at his plate, hearing Ed – and possibly Pearl – snort, feeling a hot flush rise up his neck to his ears and his cheeks.

"David..." John warned. "That was a rude thing to say. We don't question people about how they pray, because it's private. You remember we talked about what's private?"

David nodded enthusiastically. "Yes! Like when you have to go to-"

"Exactly right," John cut him off.

Carolyn was biting her lip. "You've just made a very interesting association for him, John."

David leaned over to Matthew, speaking confidentially in his best "inside" voice. "Since it's private, you can tell me later, okay?"

"David!" John snapped, startling everyone. The boy's lip began to quiver. "I'm sorry, son," John said, patting his little arm. "I didn't mean to scare you. 'Private' means Matthew doesn't have to tell anyone."

"Oh." David considered that.

"David," said his mother from the other end of the table, "how did you know Matthew's eyes were open unless your eyes were open, too?"

David considered for a moment, and then the answer dawned across his face. "I heard that his eyes were open, so I had to look to see was he all right." Satisfied with his own cleverness, he shoveled a large bite of potato and gravy into his mouth to forestall any further conversation.

Matthew continued to stare at the food congealing in cold gravy on his plate. He cleared his throat and washed down rising bile with a swallow of water. Finally, he said, "I didn't mean any disrespect. I just – don't pray."

"No problem," John responded easily. "It should never have come up. What's for dessert, Pearl?"

§ § §

When the trying meal was over, David insisted Matthew be the one to get him down from his chair. As Matthew lifted David, his rolled shirtsleeves showed the bones in his arms and the shirt pulled across the prominent blades of his shoulders. The child held him captive with one small hand to lead him out of the dining room.

"This is ridiculous!" Carolyn fumed as Matthew and David left the room. "I can see all his bones!"

"He's not stupid," John mused. "He's got to see there's more than enough for him."

Pearl gave them both her patented no-nonsense look. "What do you do when David is acting picky?"

"Tell him to eat."

"Exactly."

§ § §

The little face was deeply serious; David had been thinking as he led Matthew into the living room. He turned to look up at Matthew and asked, "Where's your little boy?"

Matthew froze. "What?"

"Where's your little boy? And your mama?"

"I don't have a little boy. And my – mama? You mean my wife?" David nodded vigorously. "Yes! Wife!"

"I don't have one of those, either."

"But everybody gots 'em. My daddy, an' Uncle Ted - "

"What about Ed? He doesn't have a wife."

"He used to had one. She went away because she wanted a little boy. Don't you want a little boy?"

Matthew turned away, unable to bear the piercing blue stare any longer. "No, I don't."

"Don't you like little boys?" He could hear the quiver in the reedy little voice. "Don't you like me any more?"

He turned back and squatted to be on eye-level with the boy. "Aw, David, of course I like you! You're a *great* kid!" He gently bracketed David's shoulders with trembling hands. "See, the thing is – some people just – they just wouldn't make good daddies. So they don't deserve to have little boys."

"But you do. You'd be a good daddy. You know how to do all kinds of daddy things, like chase monsters out from under the bed."

"You need to go find your mom now. *Right* now. She needs you. Run!" He gave the boy a spin toward the door and a shove which startled both of them. Alarmed, though not frightened, David ran; and Matthew watched him, grieving.

Oh, David, you don't get it. Sometimes the daddy is the monster under the bed.

Six

October had been perfect, except for one early snow on David's fourth birthday, clear and sunny, crisp in the mornings but warm across his shoulders like a hand-knit shawl by afternoon. November seemed inclined to copy-cat, and everyone said they were all right with that. Matthew didn't mind if the sunny warmth lasted all winter. His knee didn't ache so often on these days, and he loved to see the hard blue sky above him.

This particular Saturday afternoon Carolyn gave him a huge bag of pecans and a nutcracker piled into a large plastic bowl and sent him out to the back steps to shell the nuts.

"Do the best you can to keep the halves in one piece," she instructed. "And don't eat more than you keep!"

"Yeah, yeah," he teased as he went. He settled on the steps and began the chore.

"Whatcha doing?" David asked, coming to him from the vicinity of the barn and standing close.

Matthew looked up, grinning. "Spinning straw into gold."

David giggled. "Are not!"

"Am too. And I remember now who you are – your name is Rumplestiltskin!"

David laughed. "No, it's not! I'm David – not Rumpleskin. You're silly!" He reached into the bowl and winkled out one of the few pecan halves in there.

"Hey! Your mama said not to eat the nuts. She's going to make something with them for Thanksgiving."

"Yeah," David mumbled around the nut in his mouth, "she makes pies and stuff. I don't like 'em."

"Well, if you don't like them, why are you eating them?"

"To see if they taste better than last time."

"Do they?"

"No." David spat the pasty mess onto the grass. "Guess what?"

"Okay. What?"

"Mama says we're having comp'ny for dinner for – uh – for Thanksgibing."

"Yeah, sure. Uncle Ted and Aunt Livvie and their gang always come for holidays."

"No! I mean, yes they do, but that's not it." David sat down beside Matthew and eyed the nutcracker. "It's Pastor Miles and Mrs. Penny and their kids."

Matthew removed the nutcracker from temptation's way and applied it harshly to a pecan. The brittle shell collapsed in a shower of fragments and the nutmeat was crushed. Matthew bit his tongue on a curse-word. "That's nice," he said.

§ § §

The family seemed concerned with preparing Matthew for the pastor's visit. "They come once in a while," Pearl said, "when their own families can't make it from out of town."

"You'll like them," Carolyn enthused. "They're such nice people."

"They don't bite," Ed reassured, "and he won't try to hit you over the head with his Bible."

Right, Matthew thought. *Like a preacher won't try to preach. Or at least to tell me what a sinner I am and how I'd better get with the program if I don't want to go to hell.* He rubbed the nagging ache in his knee.

Suddenly November seemed less hospitable, even though the unseasonable warmth and sunny skies continued. Matthew walked through his days with a hard lump in his stomach which made eating difficult and his rest at night unhelpful.

"What're you chewing on now?" Ed asked as they milked.

"Nothing." Matthew examined a feeder-hose.

"Could you at least have the courtesy not to lie to me?" Ed sputtered. "I may not be educated, but I ain't stupid. Any fool can see you got a problem."

"I *don't* have a problem! I was just thinking about Thanksgiving. Maybe I'll – just – take a trip somewhere."

Ed gaped at him. "You nuts? Where you going to go, Matthew? You told us you don't have no family left. Why would you want to go off by yourself on a holiday when you got all of us right here?"

"Maybe that's just it." Matthew met Ed's eyes. "I'm not comfortable with all those people."

"Esther and Ruth!" Ed swore. "It's the Corrigans coming, right? You don't want to break bread with a pastor."

Matthew looked back at the cows. "No, I don't. I don't want anyone to sell me anything."

Ed laughed, but not unkindly. "They ain't like that, son, I promise. Besides, with Ted and Livvie's bunch going on, you won't even hear them."

§ § §

On Thanksgiving, it snowed. They woke at four to do the milking and found several inches of powdery white over everything. After breakfast, John took David out to play, dragging Matthew along as usual. They tried to build a snowman, but the snow was too dry to pack. Matthew showed David how to make snow angels, but the steady fall filled in the impressions too quickly to please the boy.

John hoisted David onto his shoulders and tramped around the near edges of the farm, singing "Over the River and Through the Woods." David liked especially the line, "Trot fast my dapple gray!" "Trot fast, my dapple Daddy!" he yelled, pounding on John's head and arm with his mittened fists. John laughed and went faster.

Yeah, Matthew thought, watching father and son cavorting in the snow. *That's how it's supposed to be. I guess that's even how it can be. I've never seen him lose it with David yet.*

"We'd better go in and dry off so we can help Mama," John told David.

"No. I don't want to go in." His lip puckered as John lifted him down.

"None of that," John said sternly. "Your mother needs us. Men take care of their women-folks, son."

"Let Matthew do it," David sulked, but he took his father's hand on one side and Matthew's on the other for the short walk back to the house.

"About today," Matthew said.

"Yes?"

"About the Corrigans –"

"Yes?"

"Oh – nothing." Matthew opened the back door for John and David.

"Thanks. Don't worry. I told Miles you're skittish and he should save the talking in tongues and Bible-thumping for another time."

Matthew was horrified on several fronts at once. "He's going to think I'm some kind of – of – I don't know what! And does he really talk in tongues?"

"Not that I've ever heard, and he just thinks you're skittish. Forget about it and have a good time. I know you like Ted and Livvie, so just enjoy them." John finished stripping David out of his snowsuit and began hanging things up to dry. "Go to your mother," he told the boy, "and see what she wants you to do. Oh, and blow your nose."

David rushed off, calling for his mother, wiping his nose on his sleeve.

"Are you okay?" John asked.

"Yeah." *Yeah, right. Maybe I'll get pneumonia by two o'clock. Maybe I'll break out in a terrible, contagious, ugly rash and have to stay in my room.*

§ § §

Sadly bereft of rash or fever, Matthew put on clean jeans and a blue-and-green plaid flannel shirt, rolling back the sleeves. He brushed his teeth again, sternly suppressing his gag reflex, and brushed thick hair back from his forehead.

Sidling down the stairs, he found himself engulfed by David and the four Seibenek boys. Following David's lead over the past year, they all assumed Matthew was theirs for whatever purpose they had in mind at the moment. Today, with the snow, it was forts and a snow-ball fight.

"No," he said, "I don't think your moms will want you to play outside." *And I don't want anything to do with a bunch of kids.*

"Uh-huh," Stevie Seibenek challenged. "They said we should use up some energy outside."

"The snow won't pack, remember, David?"

"It will now," Stevie countered. "We tried it on the way in."

Matthew recognized being out-maneuvered and helped them all to bundle up for the trip to the back yard. Within minutes, the older children and Matthew had mounded up small hills of snow opposite one another while the younger boys made slap-dash snow-balls to stock the forts. They divided three and three, Matthew and David with the youngest Seibenek boy. A rousing few rounds of wildly inaccurate pitches and disintegrating missiles was nearing an end as they ran out of ammunition, but Matthew had a couple of good ones left. He reared up and let fly without aiming, just intending to get one over the top of the other fort.

However, Matthew's wild pitch became a solid hit, slamming into a black-clad shoulder and spraying up into a laughing face.

"Good one!" the tall, skinny man yelled.

Oh, no. That has to be the pastor in that black suit. Oh, great.

"I came out to tell you guys it's time to come in for dinner," the man said. "Boys, run on in and get out of your wet stuff."

The boys decamped immediately, giggling as they went. Matthew and the man looked at each other. Matthew cleared his throat.

"I'm really sorry about that." He gestured to the snow clinging to the man's shoulder. "I should have looked before I threw."

"No harm done – didn't hurt a bit. Well, maybe just a bit. You have a pretty good arm. I'm Miles Corrigan." He grinned again and held out his hand.

Matthew pulled off his wet glove and shook, cold hand to cold hand. "I'm Matthew Ryersen."

"Yeah, that's what I figured. Let's go on in. Food smelled great!"

They went in together, Matthew hanging back just a little.

Penny Corrigan, almost as tall and skinny as her husband, presided over the five little boys and her own three daughters, seating and provisioning them with seemingly effortless grace and good humor. David balked at being seated apart from Matthew, but she persuaded him to share and averted a tantrum. Matthew was impressed.

Children served, the adults sat down together. Penny sat in David's usual place next to Matthew and Miles sat across the table. Matthew cast stealthy glances at the man from lowered eyes as John prayed over the food and gave thanks for all the blessings of the past year.

Miles was all bones and angles, knobby shoulders and wrists inside his starched white shirt and black jacket. His long, thin face was punctuated by a large, beaky nose, giving him a vague resemblance to a stork.

Matthew was hard-pressed to endure the meal without leaping up and escaping to his room. He tried to ignore the Corrigans' attempts at conversation but couldn't without being obviously rude. Yes, he told Penny, he was from the south, from Kentucky. No, he told Miles, he hadn't played sports in school and wasn't particularly interested in the Ohio State-Michigan rivalry. Yes, he told Penny, he would like gravy for the potatoes. No, he didn't care for peas, but he would eat them to please Pearl. He did appreciate Miles's laugh at that one and approved as Miles hid some of his peas under his stuffing.

With unsalesmanlike sensitivity, the pastor backed off and concentrated his conversation on the rest of the family. Matthew was able to relax enough to eat his dinner and avert Pearl's evil eye. He even began on a piece of pecan pie, but David shouted from the children's table: "No, MatthewRye! Don't eat that!"

"What in the -" John looked down the table to David. "Is there a problem, son?"

Matthew sat there, fork half-way to his mouth.

"I told you," David insisted, eyes only for Matthew, "it's nasty! It tastes like poison!"

Out of the general laughter, John said, "David. It's not nice to call your mother's cooking nasty. It's all right to say you don't want any pie, but it's not all right to insult the cook." David hung his head, mouth quivering. "Please apologize to your mother."

"Sorry, Mama." The fair little cheeks flushed red with embarrassment. Then he lifted his head defiantly. "Just don't eat it, Matthew!"

"You have quite the little champion there," Penny said quietly under the second wave of laughter.

"Yeah." Matthew carefully put the fork, with its poisoned bite, back onto the plate. "He's a great kid." He pushed the plate away. Oh, well. It was a small price to pay for such devotion.

"I watched you with him earlier," Penny continued. "You're good with him. Do you have kids of your own?"

"No, ma'am." *And I never will. Unless I already do. Unless Dinah wasn't lying.* Once again the people, the room, began to press in upon him. As the men adjourned to the living room to watch football, Matthew made a break for it.

Safely closed into his room, Matthew removed his shoes and lay down on the bed. Hands behind his head, he studied the ceiling and listened to the cheers and groans carrying up the staircase from the living room.

Well, I guess she's okay, he decided. *But he's – I don't know. So formal. I wonder if he sleeps in that necktie. Can't imagine him in jeans or coveralls, that's for sure. Must have had an off-day, though, because he didn't try to "save" me. Thank God! I mean, if there were a God...*

Why'd she ask me about kids? Do I look like a guy who has kids? Do I look like a guy who even likes kids?

All at once he smelled it again, the stale, yeasty odor of beer-breath whispering in his ear, "Don't think you can get away, you little brat!" He felt the meaty hand squeezing bruises out of his arm and heard the swish of the belt through the loops. He saw the skinny girl with over-bleached hair and a very low-cut top coming into his arms in the front seat of his grandfather's pick-up truck.

A light tap on the door distracted him. "Come in."

Carolyn said through the door, "Please open for me, will you? My hands are full."

As he flung open the door, Carolyn stepped in, a coffee mug in one hand and a dessert plate in the other. "Don't tell David, but I brought you your pie." She put mug and plate on the bedside table. "You'll need the coffee to cut the sweetness, but I promise nothing is poisoned."

Matthew made himself grin at her. "Thanks! I did want to taste the fruits of my labor. Thanks for dinner, too. It was great."

"Thank you, sir! So what do you think of the Corrigans?"

Matthew froze in the act of reaching for the plate. "Nice people. Cute kids."

"Did you and Miles have a nice chat?"

"Yeah, sure."

"I'm so glad!" She headed out the door. "I knew you'd be friends. Enjoy the pie!" And away she went, gently closing the door behind her.

Matthew shook his head as he picked up the pie. *Most naïve woman in the world.* He placed the first bite of pie on his tongue and wallowed it around in his mouth. David was right – so sweet it did taste like "poison." He gulped hot, bitter coffee to cleanse away the taste.

Having flushed the evidence, Matthew drank his coffee standing at the window, looking out at the snow-covered farm. Under the deep white layer all rough edges seemed smoothed and rounded; anything ugly was disguised in beauty.

That's life, Matthew thought, remembering Baltimore, remembering Kentucky. *Nothing ever is the way it seems. Every time something looks good, there's something bad or ugly underneath. The pie – looked great, tasted like "poison." People, too. Seem nice enough until you make a mistake or say something they don't like, then they turn on you. That pastor – for sure he's not who he seems to be. It's not possible. He likes the Abbotts because they're good church-goers. Pearl and Ed, too. But not me. If he knew me –*

The coffee suddenly rose up the back of his throat like battery acid. He put the half-empty mug back on the table and picked up his volume of Frost. "'Good fences make good neighbors,'" he quoted aloud, then added in his own words, "so do good walls."

Seven

Startled by the Victorian burr of the front-door bell, Carolyn snatched up a dishtowel to dry her hands as she abandoned a sink full of dishes to hurry toward the summons. No one ever used the front door or came calling at three in the afternoon the day after Thanksgiving. She flung open the door.

"Good afternoon, ma'am. I'm lookin' for Matt Ryersen? Lady in town said I might find him here?"

Carolyn took in the young woman standing on the porch, her brassy-bleached, spiky haircut, poor skin, thin figure well-displayed in tight jeans and a low-cut tank top under a thin pink nylon jacket. She held a large denim purse in one hand and the wrist of a young boy in the other. He looked to be seven or eight, too-long dirty-blond hair flopping over slate-blue eyes as he looked up at Carolyn anxiously. He was shivering in a Cardinals sweatshirt.

"Well, hello!" Carolyn said. "Come in out of the cold! I'm Carolyn Abbott, and Matthew does live here. Was he expecting you?"

The woman huffed a short laugh. "No, ma'am, not hardly. Me and Will here come a long ways to see him, though. Is he here?"

Carolyn stepped back, still smiling, saying, "Please come in! I think he's around here somewhere."

The woman entered, dragging the reluctant boy behind her.

"Why don't you come into the kitchen," Carolyn offered. "I have fresh coffee ready for the men and I just finished making cookies a few minutes ago. Oatmeal-raisin-chocolate chip – Matthew's favorite."

Settling the visitors at the table with coffee, milk and cookies,

Carolyn gazed out the kitchen window for a glimpse of Matthew. "It's too early for barn chores yet," she said, "but I thought maybe I'd see... Oh, there he is!" She went quickly out the back door, down the steps and across the yard, signaling to Matthew, who was just parking the tractor in front of the barn.

He turned off the motor so that he could hear her. "What's up? David up from his nap?"

"You have a visitor – well, two, actually." She gestured toward the house.

"Yeah? Who?"

"I really don't know. She hasn't told me her name..."

"Guess we'd better go see," Matthew grinned, escorting Carolyn through yesterday's snow back into the warm kitchen. He stopped abruptly, dropping her arm, and turned so white Carolyn thought he might faint.

"Hey, Matt," the woman said.

"Carolyn," Matthew said without inflection, "this is Dinah Boone. From Rough River."

"And this is my boy Will," Dinah added. "We come to see you, Matt. To talk about old times."

"Old times," he mimicked. No color had returned to his face.

"Matthew," Carolyn asked, "are you all right?"

"Fine. Carolyn, would you mind givin' the kid some more cookies while Dinah and I step into the livin' room for just a minute?" He jerked his head at Dinah and walked out, clearly expecting her to follow.

"Mom?" the boy's voice rose anxiously. She neither looked back nor answered.

"It's all right," Carolyn soothed. "They're just going into the other room for a minute." She smiled and sat down across the table from him. "Your name is Will?" He nodded. "That's a good strong name. Please have another cookie, Will."

In the living room, Matthew gestured Dinah to the couch – but he remained standing. "What do you mean by comin' here like this? How'd you find me?"

Dinah crossed her legs and smiled up at Matthew, showing sharp little teeth behind her dark red lipstick. "Why, I went home to visit Mama and paid a call on Miss Evvie at the post office. She knew right where to find you from that letter you wrote her. Aren't you glad to see me, Matt, after all these years?"

"Don't play games, Dinah. I told you I never wanted to see you again."

"I was hopin' you might have changed your mind." She swung her leg restlessly. "Matt, we need to talk about Will."

"No. I told you – he's not mine - "

Exasperation wiped the smile from Dinah's face. "Oh, get real, Matt! Anyone can tell he's yours. Why, I'll bet that nice lady in the kitchen has it all figured out by now. He looks just like you, and just like your granddaddy."

Matthew dropped into John's chair because his knees refused to hold him upright any longer. "And if he was mine...?"

"It's time for you to face up to your responsibilities. I never came after you for child support - "

"Because he's not mine! And because you married a guy with enough money that you didn't need me. Where is he now?"

"Well – uh – we're divorced – for a few years – I'm with some-body else now. And the thing is, Matt, I didn't love Jesse, but I really do love Clete. And he wants to marry me - " She paused.

"Congratulations. And I should care because...?"

"See, Clete, he doesn't want any kids – he won't take Will to raise. He says I have to get rid of him - "

Rage rose up in Matthew and he found himself looming over Dinah, fists clenched. She drew back, eyes wide.

"Get rid of him! What kind of a way is that to treat a kid?"

"You're scaring me," Dinah whimpered.

Matthew backed off. "I'm sorry. But how can you even talk about your own kid like that?"

"The same way you can, I guess! I don't know what-all you've been doin' with your life while I've been raisin' *your kid*, but looks like you have it pretty good here. Lady in town said you got no wife or kids – I had to laugh, like you'd ever have kids if you could help it! So here's the deal. I'm going to marry Clete and travel and have fun, and Will's not part of the package. It's your turn to step up, buddy. We'll go to the court tomorrow and sign the papers, then I'm headed back to Louisville."

Matthew's heart thundered in his chest, choking him. *No, this can't be happening! I can't do this!* "No," he said. "No dice, Dinah. You know why I said I'd never have kids. You know what my dad was like. I *can't* keep the boy."

"Too bad. If you don't want him, give him to somebody who does." She uncrossed her legs, preparing to stand.

Panic deepened in Matthew's chest. "Wait a minute, Dinah! Think! That kid doesn't even know me! Does he even know who I am?"

"Yeah, he knows. I told him on the way up here. You'll get to know each other. He's not such a bad kid. Clete taught him how to be quiet and stay outta the way." She rose; Matthew stepped in to block her exit.

"Did you tell him what you were plannin'?"

"Nah. I figured I'd tell him before I left."

Matthew breathed deeply, in through his mouth, out through his nose. "This is wrong. I have a job now – I can pay child support, and I will. But I can't take a boy to raise. It wouldn't be right. It wouldn't be safe. You *know* that. If this Clete guy doesn't want your boy, then maybe he's not the right guy for you."

Dinah adjusted herself within the confines of her neon green tank top. "Are you the right guy, Matt?" she purred.

"No!" He backed away again. "I never was. You and I – it was just – we never should have -"

Her lips compressed for a moment, leaving a smear of bloody lipstick on her teeth. "I guess you're right about that. We never should have. Then I wouldn't have this problem now." Turning on her heel, she marched back to the kitchen.

"There's your mom," Carolyn said to Will as she spotted the woman leaning on the door frame.

"Tell the nice lady thank you for the cookies, Will. We gotta get goin'. Nice meetin' you, ma'am."

In moments the front door closed softly, leaving Matthew and Carolyn standing in the hall. He glanced at her sideways through his lashes, cheeks flaming.

"You never told us you had a wife and child," Carolyn said evenly.

"I don't! I never did!"

"Don't," she said. "Anyone can see that little boy is your son. He knows it, too. And not everything you said in the living room was quiet."

Matthew closed his eyes and threw back his head. "I'm sorry, but I can't talk about this." He bolted up the stairs to his room.

"Where's Matthew?" David asked as the family gathered for dinner.

"Working on something," Carolyn told him. "He'll be around in the morning."

Matthew managed to fall asleep somewhere around midnight, having wrestled his conscience to the ground. *I offered to pay child support, and I made her see why he's better off with her. Maybe Clete's not a great guy, but there's no sign he hits them. He has to be better than I'd be, or else she needs to leave him. A kid needs to be with his mother.*

§ § §

As Matthew, John and Ed were finishing breakfast the next morning, a faint sound caught John's ear. "Someone's at the front door."

"I'll get it," Carolyn offered. "I'm up." In a moment she called, "Matthew, please come here."

He pushed away from the table, exchanging quizzical looks with the men. "I don't know," he said. As he approached the open front door and peered through the screen, he saw the boy standing on the porch, a worn backpack beside him and an envelope in his hand.

Eight

"He wouldn't come in," Carolyn said. "He asked for you."

"Oh. Ah..." Matthew ran his hand across his face as if he could wipe away confusion. He looked at the boy again. The boy looked back. "Come on in," Matthew said.

The boy hoisted his backpack and stepped inside as Matthew held open the screen. He stood unnaturally still, looking at his frayed sneakers. Without looking up, he held out the envelope.

"Come sit down," Carolyn urged, trying to take the envelope with one hand and steer the child with the other. He tightened his muscles against her and pushed the envelope at Matthew.

"Okay." Matthew took it. "Let's – uh – let's go into the livin' room." He headed in and was relieved to hear the shuffle of sneakers behind him. Dropping into John's chair, he gestured to the couch. "Have a seat, kid."

The boy stood directly in front of Matthew. "My name is Will – sir."

"Yeah. Will. So sit down, *Will.*"

Will sat down on the couch, on the edge, so that his feet could touch the floor. He stared at Matthew.

"Where's your mom?" Matthew asked.

"I don't know," Will answered, trying to hide the tremor in his voice. "She said to tell you to open the envelope."

"Right." Matthew looked at the long rectangle, logo of a cheap motel in the upper left corner, his own name written in cheap ball-point ink across the middle in large, unformed round script. He ran a finger under the flap, which released its cheap glue easily. Will watched carefully as Matthew drew out several pieces of paper and studied them.

"Do you know what this is?" Matthew asked.

"Yes, sir. That little one's my birth certificate."

"Right." He fought the urge to crush the papers and fling them into the fireplace.

"D-does my mom's letter say where she's going or when she's coming back?" The little voice was higher now, the tremor too much to hide.

Matthew was horrified to see tears rising in Will's eyes. "Uh – don't cry, kid. She's just – she'll be - "

Will crumpled sideways onto the couch and began to cry, hard, but almost silently. Matthew thought a series of words he tried not to say any more and spun on his heel to leave the room as fast as he could.

I'm not fallin' for this! He can cry all he wants, but I'm not doin' it. A piece of paper doesn't make me a daddy, even if it does make me a father.

He found Carolyn alone in the kitchen and slammed the papers down on the kitchen table. "She's gone! That - She dropped the kid off like a bag of trash and took off for Louisville. Look at this!" He gestured at the papers.

Carolyn picked up the three sheets and read them quickly. "Your name on the birth certificate – but you knew that. He's older than I thought... Immunization record, so you can enroll him in school – and this letter! She makes it sound like you agreed to take custody. I didn't think you had said that... And doesn't it have to be done in court?"

"I didn't agree to anything. I don't know the rules, but I can tell you: I'm not takin' that kid."

"What are you going to do with him?"

"Me? Nothin'. He's not my problem."

Carolyn frowned. "But he is your problem, Matthew, because she's gone and Will is here."

"I don't care! She can't force me by takin' off. I'll just take him to the welfare office and they can do whatever they do with abandoned kids. A good foster home, or whatever."

Carolyn twisted her hands together. "Let me get John and we can talk about this."

"No." Matthew took the papers and snagged the truck keys from their hook. "We're on our way. Don't interfere, Carolyn."

In the living room he found Will still muffling his sobs in the couch cushions, leaving splotches of tears and slimy trails from his running nose all over the upholstery. Sternly suppressing a memory and a pang of sympathy, Matthew lifted the boy to his feet by one skinny arm and thrust a blue bandana at him. "Clean up your face. We're going."

Will ineffectually mopped his face. "G-going where?"

Matthew applied the bandana to better effect. "To town to talk to some people." He gave Will a small shove to get him started. "Let's go."

The child grabbed his backpack and went obediently to the truck, his worn sneakers slipping a little on the slick walk. He buckled himself in without being told and sat silent for the full half-hour trip, paying no attention to the scenery. When Matthew parallel-parked in front of the county courthouse, Will sat there until told to get out. He brought his backpack with him up the thirty granite steps to the huge, bronze-hinged double doors, down a block-long expanse of black-veined white marble floor, onto a jarring contrast of stainless steel elevator.

Matthew jangled the truck keys nervously as the elevator jerked its way to the third floor. *Dinah shouldn't have done this to the kid. He's scared to death.* He shook his head sharply. *No. Too bad, but not my problem.*

The elevator decanted them onto another marble floor, where a sign directed them to a solid oak door midway down the hall. The sign riveted to the wall beside the door said, "Job and Family Services. Please ring bell." Matthew rang the bell.

A glass panel next to the door slid open and a young woman with a sleek brown bob asked how she might help him.

"I need to talk to someone about this kid."

"And the nature of the problem is..."

"He's – uh – his mother – look, can I come in and talk to someone, please? I don't want to say this stuff in front of him."

A buzzing sound signaled the unlocking of the door. Matthew

41

shepherded Will into a large white waiting-room full of metal-rimmed brown plastic chairs and fiberboard tables. A few battered toys clustered dispiritedly in one corner. The young woman gestured to them to sit down and began making phone calls. The two sat side by side, not looking at each other, until the woman beckoned.

"A caseworker will see you after you fill out this intake form, sir." She handed him a paper on a clipboard with a pen firmly attached by a curly plastic cord. "Don't forget the other side, and just bring it back to me when you're finished."

Matthew filled in his name, address and such but found himself short-circuited by "Service(s) Requested," even though there were nearly two dozen little boxes to check. He turned the form in unfinished.

"Mr. Ryersen? I'm Cathy Horvath, a caseworker here. How can I help you?"

Matthew and Will both looked up at the short, stocky woman planted squarely before them on sensible shoes. Her coppery polyester pantsuit lent a pleasant glow to her light brown skin and its dusting of copper freckles. She held a clipboard.

"Uh – I need – I need to talk about – please, ma'am, could we just – I don't want to talk in front of the kid."

"I see." She squatted in front of Will. "Honey, I need to talk to your dad for a few minutes. Why don't you go over there and play with the trucks or color, okay?"

Will nodded, picked up his backpack and moved off to the toy corner. The other two moved through a maze of corridors to a small cubicle, where Cathy sat behind the desk and waved Matthew into the single chair in front of her.

"Now, Mr. Ryersen, what's the problem with your son?"

"Why are you calling him my son?"

"I beg your pardon?" she asked, obviously confused. "You mean he's not your son? I'm sorry. It's just that he looks so much like you, and he has your mannerisms -"

Matthew bit back a vile word. "Look, I guess he is my son – I mean, I probably am his biological father – but I've never even seen him until yesterday. His mother and I, we never married, never lived together – he was an accident. I didn't want a kid. I didn't want anything to do with either one of them. I still don't. Dinah showed up yesterday and I told her I wouldn't take him. Then he turned up on the porch this morning with that ratty backpack and an envelope with my name on it." He paused for breath, jangling the truck keys with one hand, scrubbing across his face with the other.

"Look, here's what was in the envelope." He handed over the papers.

Cathy read through the documents carefully. "According to her letter, Ms. Boone seems to think you've agreed to take custody of the child – Will – and to raise him – permanently."

Matthew jumped up. "No! She made it up! I can't take a kid!"

"Please sit down," Cathy soothed. "I understand that you don't want custody. It's not that easy, anyway, with the custodial parent gone. Do you know where she is?"

"Not exactly. Louisville. But I don't know where she lives or who she lives with. The kid might know."

"Under the circumstances, Family Services will have to take temporary custody of Will. We'll place him in foster care until all the legal issues are resolved. Unless – you are his natural father, is that right?"

Matthew nodded hopelessly.

"Then you could have temporary custody, and he could stay with you, provided your home –"

"No! I told you – I can't. I'm sorry for the kid, but I *can't*."

"Would you like to talk about this?" she offered. "Maybe if you explain, we can figure something out."

Matthew stood again. "No, ma'am; no, thank you. I – I have to get to work. You just tell Will I'm sorry, but this is better for him."

"Mr. Ryersen, you can't just – "

"Yes, ma'am, I can. You know where I live – let me know if I owe child support. That's all. Take good care of him." Matthew strode back down the ugly industrial carpet, Cathy's short legs rushing to keep up with him. In the waiting room he passed by Will without a glance, slamming through the door out into the hall.

As the door slowly swung shut behind him, Matthew heard the boy call, "Daddy?" The keys fell from his hand, ringing on the marble floor, but he snatched them up and fled down three flights of marble stairs rather than wait for the elevator.

Nine

Carolyn was waiting for him when Matthew came into the kitchen. "Where is he?"

Matthew moved past her to hang up the keys and took a coffee mug out of the adjacent cupboard. Back turned to her, he replied, "With that caseworker, I guess." The coffee flowed into his mug as dark as ink, but much thicker. "Coffee's been sittin' a while; I'll make fresh."

Carolyn's hand closed on his wrist and forced the coffeepot back onto its burner. "Look at me."

Matthew turned to meet her eyes and was amazed at how glacial their warm blue could become.

"How could you leave that poor little boy alone with strangers? Shame on you!"

Her glare threatened to freeze him where he stood. "I told you before – I can't take on a kid. I'm as much of a stranger to him as those people are, and I'm a bad risk." He broke eye-contact and buried his face in his mug. The coffee slid down his esophagus with a hydrochloric burn.

The ice in Carolyn's eyes melted and she put her arms around him. "Oh, Matthew, you have no idea what a good man you are."

He twitched away. "You're right; I don't. I'd better get to work." He left her standing there, tears in her eyes, his coffee mug in her hand.

§ § §

"Heard you got yourself a boy," Ed remarked as he assisted Matthew with the afternoon milking. "Where is he? Missus says he's the spit 'n' image of you. I'd sure like to see that for myself!"

Matthew ground his teeth to keep from saying something hateful. He checked gauges and connectors in silence, grimacing as John came into the barn.

"There's a call for you up at the house," John said. "I'll take over here."

"Who is it?"

"Uh – a Mrs. Horvath, I think she said."

"Never mind; I'll stay here. I don't want to talk to her."

John sighed. "If you don't want to talk to her, that's your business; but it's your job to tell her that, not mine."

Matthew threw down the towel he had been using to wipe down the tank and stamped out of the barn, muttering under his breath. In the kitchen he snatched up the wall-phone's dangling receiver as if it were hot. "This is Matthew Ryersen."

"Oh, Mr. Ryersen," Cathy Horvath's smooth voice oozed into his ear.

"What?" His palm was suddenly sweating, the receiver slipping.

"I thought you would want to know that we have Will in a temporary foster home. They're a nice couple with half a dozen children, theirs and ours, and if you want to visit Will there - "

"I don't." He wiped one palm on his jeans, then switched the receiver and wiped the other one.

"Oh. Well... You do need to know that Will's court date is set for a week from tomorrow. At that time, if you sign a waiver, he will officially become a ward of the court. They'll place him in a permanent foster home as soon after that as possible. Oh, and they'll also do a paternity test. If it's positive, which will take at least several weeks to find out, then they'll set up your child support payments."

"Fine." A bead of sweat ran down the side of Matthew's face, another trickled into his eyebrow, as he heard that she would send an official letter telling him where and when to appear.

Hanging up the phone, he sank into his chair at the kitchen table and buried his face in his hands. *God, why are You doing this to me? And why make that kid pay because his – parents – are fools? Huh. Why should I be surprised, considering the way they say You made Your son pay for other people's mistakes.*

45

He heard John and Ed coming in and knew by the heavy onion-beef-garlic odor of chili from the large pot on the stove that Carolyn would appear any minute to serve dinner. His sweat turned clammy as his stomach began to lurch.

John came over to put a hand on Matthew's shoulder. "You doing okay?"

Matthew forced himself to look up. "Yeah, fine."

He made it through dinner on sheer grit, hardly able to look at David, then excused himself to lie on his bed staring at the ceiling. *Dinah, come back and get your kid. What if those foster parents are secret child abusers or perverts or something? Mothers aren't supposed to abandon their sons.*

§ § §

As the week passed, Matthew began to understand what people meant when they talked about "the elephant in the living room." No one was asking about it, but they gave him sideways glances. And the thing seemed to have taken up residence in his stomach. Finally, the night before his court date, he felt he had no choice but to tell John and Carolyn. They gathered in the living room.

"I need to tell you about some stuff."

"Go ahead," John responded, leaning back against the couch cushions.

"Y'all think I come from Kentucky, right? And I did grow up there after I was twelve. But I was born in Baltimore." He took a deep breath and let it out slowly. "My father was a cop from Baltimore. My mama's people came from Grayson County, Kentucky, on the ridge near Rough River. My dad met my mama the summer she was sixteen, found her clerkin' in the bait shop at Rough River Dam. He and some other cops had come to the state park there for some fishin' and beer-drinkin'.

"He was almost twenty years older than she was, good-lookin', she told me, could sing like an Irish tenor when he was drunk. I guess he sorta swept her off her feet. Three weeks later he married her and took her back to Baltimore.

"My father's family were all gone. Mama and I used to spend summers in Kentucky with my grandparents. Then when my father - died - we moved back down home. My gramma was the local 'yarb woman,' knew every plant in the hills and hollers, and what it was good for. She taught me a lot about that...

"We were really poor there - no electricity 'til I was twelve. We had a big garden every year, a peach tree or two, and Gramma canned. We kept chickens and sold the eggs. Granddaddy's cash crop was tobacco, but he only had a little bitty acreage up there on the ridge. I learned to plow it with a mule named Bess and a singletree plow, and more harness on me than on the mule." He laughed at the memory, and John smiled with him.

"The year I turned twelve, my father died - 'in the line of duty.' He fell off a fire escape chasing some two-bit thief who was dumb enough to rob a liquor store while my father was in it. He lost his balance and fell because he was half-lit, as usual, and he fractured his skull."

"Oh, I'm so sorry!" Carolyn said, reaching toward him.

Matthew backed away. "Yeah? Well, I'm not. I was glad! He was a mean drunk. Used to beat my mama, and me, too, for no reason. Just a mean, rotten, nasty drunk!"

Matthew drew a couple of deep breaths and shoved his hair out of his eyes. He began to examine the carpet carefully, avoiding John and Carolyn as he continued. "That's what I know about bein' a daddy, and that's why I'm never gonna have kids. I don't know I wouldn't turn on 'em and hurt somebody. Dinah and me, we were just kids—bored and drinkin' – I didn't even like her much, just wanted what she'd put out, you know? She was like that, guys said. When she told me she was pregnant, I never believed the kid was mine. Could have been a dozen guys'. She knew about my dad, knew I can't raise a kid." He raised his eyes to theirs again abruptly. "I can't imagine I'd ever turn on David, but how can I be sure? I'd rather cut off my hand than raise it to your boy – but – I - maybe I've taken too many chances already, and I ought to go before I lose it. I'm feelin' real close..."

The moment hung suspended as Carolyn gripped John's hand and looked at him and Matthew watched them both.

"Well," John finally said, "I can see why you'd be concerned, if you think the sins of the fathers always repeat in the sons. But I don't see it that way, Matthew. You may not know how to be a good father, but you already know how not to be a bad one. And our personal faith is that with God all things are possible. He changes people all the time, and I think He's been changing you. I've always trusted David to you, and this doesn't change that. Caro?"

Carolyn looked from John to Matthew. She rose and enfolded Matthew in a hug. He was shocked and overcome by the scents of rosewater and vanilla, the feeling of her small hands patting his back. "You poor thing!" she said, holding on. "What a terrible way to grow up! Of course you'd never do anything like that to David!" She leaned back to look Matthew in the eye again. "I hope you won't leave, Matthew. We would all miss you so much."

"There's more," he said miserably. "About the kid. He's in a foster home now, and I have to go to court tomorrow to sign a paper to – to give up any claim on him."

"Oh, no!" Carolyn said. "Matthew, bring him here to us!"

"No."

John looked at him sternly. "You really don't want to be responsible for this, do you?"

"You're right. I don't want any part of it. If I had, I would have married Dinah and found a factory job or somethin.'"

"What did you plan to do with your life instead?" John asked.

"I don't know. I guess I figured I'd farm with Granddaddy and inherit the place when he passed." He coughed against a sudden tightness in his chest.

"You never wanted anything different?" Carolyn asked. "Never wanted to be an astronaut or a country singer or anything?"

"I reckon I had the dreams beat out of me by the time I was seven or eight. I knew I was too stupid to do much. I liked the farm okay; it was peaceful there."

"And you never wanted a wife and children to share it with?"

"No. I can't risk it. I surely didn't mean to make a baby with Dinah."

"But you did," John said, "and now your son is stuck with strangers when he could be here with us."

That's it. Matthew stood up. "John, you're my boss, so you can fire me and kick me out. You-all have been like family, so I reckon you get to have your say. But you don't get to tell me how to live my life. If you can't respect that, I'll just be goin.'" He headed toward the door, thinking, *I could leave tomorrow. They have huge wheat harvests in Canada. Or maybe an oil rig in Texas. I've never been west. I don't have to be here. I can go anywhere. Someplace nobody knows me. Alone's as good one place as another, and nobody gets hurt.*

"No! Wait!" Carolyn cried. "Please."

"Sit down," John offered. "Don't run. We don't want you to leave, and we can respect your right to make your own choices – can't we, Caro?"

She nodded mutely, tears in her eyes. Matthew returned to his seat.

"I have to be there tomorrow at ten-fifteen," Matthew continued doggedly, "and I don't know how long it will take. Sometimes you have to wait a long time to be called up. And there's another thing..."

"Yes?" John asked.

"I'll have to take a paternity test and pay child support. But they won't let me just pay it. You'll have to take it out of my check and send it in."

"No problem," John said casually. "Good thing I started paying you by check and keeping records."

"I'm sorry you have to be involved."

"No," John said, sitting up straighter and looking Matthew directly in the eye, "you're sorry *you* have to be involved."

Ten

They swabbed the inside of his cheek with a huge Q-tip and made him sign all kinds of releases of information and statements about his relationships with Dinah Boone and Will Boone. They vaguely threatened him about jail, which made no impression, as he didn't understand why he might have to go there. A fat sausage of a woman dressed all in black introduced herself as The Child Advocate and glared at him, warning that she was there to represent The Best Interests of his child. Matthew sat at the worn oak table in the incredibly small, crowded conference room full of official people and accepted the battering. He figured he deserved it for having been so stupid in the first place.

"Mr. Ryersen," Cathy Horvath said, in the only gentle voice in the room, "don't you want to think about taking custody of Will? If the paternity test is positive - and I'm sure it will be, aren't you? - then you're the logical person to care for your son."

He shook his head over and over, trying to make them understand. "I don't want him, and I can't have him. I'm just not a fit parent, can't you get it? I'll pay the child support, but the kid needs to be someplace else – anyplace!"

Finally, they let him go, warning him to stay available. He drove home on autopilot, trying to put it all out of his mind. By the time he was parking the truck in the driveway, he was feeling successful. He could deal with this. He could go on with his life.

Until David came running across the slush to grab his hand, grinning and looking at him as if he were the most wonderful present in the world. Then he thought of the skinny little boy with his eyes, shivering in his Spiderman sweatshirt, the reedy little voice calling, "Daddy?"

"I've got to get to work," he told David. "I'll see you for supper."

"Can't we play in the snow before it's all gone?" David asked, his voice dripping with manufactured sadness. "You make good snowballs. We could make a snowman."

"Not this time," Matthew said. "You go on now. I've got to do some grown-up stuff." He walked away without looking back, afraid he might see tears on the boy's rosy cheeks.

Eleven

Night after night Matthew tossed on the narrow bed while his weary mind raced on beyond his exhausted body. He replayed his last sight of Will, sitting in the waiting room, all alone. He replayed the impersonal posturing of advocates and lawyers and social workers in the claustrophobic conference room at the courthouse. Some nights he would jolt himself awake from a dream he couldn't remember to lie there trembling and sweating despite the chill air, waiting for dawn.

By day he waited for someone to say something about Will, but no one even hinted at any problem; although Carolyn seemed distant, she was unfailingly kind.

One evening after dinner, the men and the boy gathered in the living room while Carolyn and Pearl did the dishes. Matthew sat on the carpet in front of the fire helping David with a puzzle.

"What will it be?" he asked the boy.

David glanced up at him, perplexed. "*You* know!"

He looked again. "No, I don't. It's a story..."

The boy snorted impatiently. "Everybody knows 'bout Jonah and the whale!" His little hand awkwardly tried to fit in a piece which almost matched.

Embarrassed, Matthew gently replaced the boy's puzzle piece with another, guiding the little hand to fit it in. He felt his cheeks burning and kept his eyes on the puzzle as David triumphantly set the last piece.

Over his head, farmer and farmhand locked gazes for a moment.

"Good job, boy!" Ed enthused. "Let's go see if your mama'll give us a cookie to celebrate."

David was completely susceptible to bribery. He jumped up immediately and headed for the door. But almost at once he ran back to tug on Matthew's hand. "Come too! You helpeded."

"No," John said, "you go on. We have something to talk about for a minute." The boy checked his father's expression and followed Ed without further hesitation.

Matthew kept his head down, still embarrassed.

"I heard you moving around last night," John said. "It wasn't the first time."

He looked up quickly. "I'm sorry! I try to be quiet."

"Relax," John said gently. "It's okay. I'm just concerned that you're not sleeping well. Is the bed uncomfortable? Are you warm enough?"

"The bed is great! The room is great! I slept in fields and barns for a year, so anything with a mattress is a big improvement. And no bugs or rats." Matthew shuddered visibly. "I hate rats!"

"Me, too," John nodded. "So, is anything bothering you that I can help with?"

Matthew looked down at his hands, embarrassed again. "No. I'm tired, but my mind keeps going." *And I can't tell you where it goes.*

John waited, saying nothing. A log in the fireplace burned through, dropping onto the coals and sending up a shower of sparks. David's laughter drifted in from the kitchen.

"I thought you were going to fire me," Matthew finally said, staring into the fire.

"Why would I do that?"

"Harvest's over. It doesn't take three men to do the work now, and you were so angry with me a while back...And this – this other thing - "

"No! No. We're hoping you'll choose to stay a long time. There's plenty of work, even in winter, and we've sort of gotten used to having you around. Carolyn is knitting you a sweater for Christmas - but don't tell her I told you, or she'll kill me! And I thought you were going to make a boat for David."

John rose and walked over to the built-in bookshelves flanking the fireplace, briefly touching Matthew's hunched shoulder in passing. He took a book from the shelf and sat down beside Matthew on the carpet.

"When I have trouble sleeping," John said, "it helps if I read for a while. I know you like to read, because I've seen you at that book of poetry Pearl gave you. So I'd like to give you this book. My dad gave it to me when I was twelve, when I accepted Christ; now I'd like you to have it." He held out the book, a worn, cardboard-covered Bible.

"I can't take the Bible your father gave you!"

John smiled, continuing to hold out the Bible. "Sure you can. I think my dad would like very much for me to give this to someone who doesn't have one. I'm using a different Bible now, so this one has just been gathering dust on the shelf."

He backed away from the outstretched book. "Listen, I, ah - I'm not - I don't - "

"That's okay. Even if you're not a believer, it's a pretty good book: love stories, war stories, famines, floods and other natural disasters - also a lot of real practical advice for living a successful life. Plenty of poetry, too."

"Poetry?" Matthew was intrigued in spite of himself.

"Absolutely. Psalms, Proverbs, most of Job, lots of Isaiah... Please take it. And when you can't sleep, just read it for a while. If you're having a tough time, feel free to come down here. My chair is really comfortable for reading or watching TV."

"*Your* chair?"

"Sure. I'd feel good to know you were tucked up in that chair with the Good Book. Please let me give you that, the book and the chair."

Slowly, tentatively, Matthew reached out and closed his fingers over the Bible. As John let go, the weight of the book became a satisfying pull on his hand. "Thank you," he murmured. "I don't understand, but thank you anyway." He stroked the worn black cover with his other hand. "I'll take good care of it."

"I know you will," John replied, rising and stretching. "Let me know if you have any questions as you read. We can kick 'em around."

"I will," Matthew said, thinking at the same time, *I'm not going to read this. No way. If I get tired of Robert Frost, I'll go into town and get a library card.*

Matthew put the Bible under the volume of Frost on his bedside table. John knocked on his closed door and poked his head in to say, "The story of Jonah and the whale is in the book of Jonah. There's an index in the front of the Bible." Then he was gone.

"Yeah, Jonah," Matthew muttered. He turned out the light and lay back on the pillow, drifting slowly toward sleep. *If there were a God,* he thought drowsily, *I'd thank him for letting me end up here. If there were...*

Twelve

Although Matthew had contented himself with little information about Pearl, since Ed was so reluctant to say much about her, he continued to learn more from their day-to-day contact. He observed that she often read her Bible when she wasn't cooking, mending or knitting and quoted it freely to encourage or to reprimand anyone she thought needed it. Several times he tried to pass casually behind her chair to see what she was reading, but age had not dulled her hearing. If he tried to hover, she turned that beady stare on him and asked, "Do you need something?" Each time he blushed, muttered something and sped away, his rapid retreat preventing him from seeing the twinkle in her eye and the smile she sent after him.

He liked to watch her knit or sew: her gnarled, spotted hands reminded him of his grandmother's hands, the only gentle touch he had known after his mother died. He noticed that when she sewed or knitted she often hummed quietly, in a cracked little voice, gentle tunes he didn't quite recognize but very vaguely remembered from somewhere. He noticed that her posture was fiercely erect, even when sitting. Pearl was formidable; Matthew would have avoided her but for the little pats she sometimes gave him in passing.

One late afternoon, chores finished, Matthew wandered into the living room, where Pearl sat on the couch knitting. "Oh, I'm sorry to disturb you!" he said, backing out.

"Just you wait a minute," Pearl countered, freezing him in his tracks.

"Yes, ma'am?"

"Do you have time to help me for a minute?"

"Uh, sure." He moved closer. "What do you need?"

Pearl held up a messy bundle of yarn. "I need help rewinding this. I think David and the cat had some fun with it." She was smiling, he noticed.

"Yes, ma'am, I can help with that. I used to hold the yarn for my gramma." He took the yarn and searched it for the center. Finding it, he slipped his hands through the hole and stretched them about a foot apart. One long end hung down, and Pearl took it.

"Here we go, then," she said. "Won't take too long. Your grandmother liked to knit?" She began to wind the end of the yarn into a tiny ball.

"I don't know whether she liked it or not," Matthew said. "She did it a lot, but it could have been because we needed the things she made. She made socks. Lots of socks. We were hard on socks."

"Did you live with them, your grandparents?"

Matthew ducked his head and closely examined the wool, following the shades of blue, from sky to blueberry. Finally he said, "Yes. Sometimes." His tone did not invite further questions, and Pearl nodded assent.

"I used to knit socks for Mr. Gunderman, too," she offered. "And gloves, and sweaters, and caps and mufflers... He didn't mention for so many years that wool made him itch." She chuckled a little as she remembered.

"He didn't – he didn't make you do something different?" He kept his eyes on the yarn.

"Why, no! He didn't want to hurt my feelings. He was such a good man." Her face softened briefly with nostalgia, and Matthew marveled at the change. He secretly marveled even more that the man would have endured discomfort for years without demanding a change. Pearl fixed him with her dark eyes and said gently, "You know, Matthew, good men really do exist."

He nodded shortly, thinking, *so do bad ones. And we never know who they are until it's too late to stop them. One of them is probably me. At least the kid won't ever have to find out. That woman said it was a good foster home.*

Thirteen

Having boycotted church on his first Christmas at the farm, Matthew assumed he would do so again. It was easy to say no to Ed and John, who each backed off immediately. He handled the disappointment in Carolyn's eyes by never looking up from his shoes and left the room quickly whenever he thought Pearl might mention church. So he thought he was armored and safe from further attack.

"MatthewRye," four-year-old David said, hanging on the arm of Matthew's chair watching his hero whittle at a small piece of pine.

"Hm?" Matthew's attention was on the knife.

"Did you see my costume?"

"What costume? I thought Halloween was over." He carefully shaved just a paper-thin sliver from one end, letting it fall to the newspaper between his feet.

"My angel costume!" David bounced with excitement, jigging the chair and very nearly costing Matthew a finger.

"Whoa! Don't bounce, buddy! Gotta be very careful around a knife. Okay?" He smiled at David to be sure there was no sting in his words.

"I'm sorry." David stepped back and folded his hands carefully in front of him. "I'm a angel in the Christmas pageant. I get to have a costume. It has wings!"

"Congratulations! That sounds like fun." Matthew decided the boy was too excited to remain still; it would be prudent to put away the carving tools.

"We get to sing! A big boy gets to say angel stuff to some shepherds! Maybe we can fly!"

"That sounds like fun, too." Matthew gathered up everything and stood to leave, but David stopped him.

"You're gonna be so proud of me!" he boasted.

Uh-oh. "I'm always proud of you."

"Yeah, but when you see me singing in my angel costume -"

"Uh – David – I'm not going."

David froze, his smile disappearing. "But – but everyone goes!"

"Sorry. Not me. I don't go to church. You know that."

"But you can. You can ride with us. You can sit with us. You can be with us!"

Oh, brother! Now what? The big blue eyes were wide with hurt, tears just beginning to dampen the long eyelashes. "Hey, don't cry. It's no big deal, honest. Your mom and dad will be there, and Ed and Pearl, and Aunt Livvie's family..."

David was not consoled. "I thought you would want to see me be a angel. I thought you would want to be with us for Christmas."

"I do want to be with you. And I will be, here at the house. Just not in church."

"Even Pearl is coming, and she's old! I thought you were my friend, MatthewRye. If you were my friend you would come with me." One tear broke loose and raced away down the soft little cheek. He knuckled it as he turned away and left the living room.

A variety of words ran through Matthew's mind, none of them useful in polite conversation. It hurt to see David disappointed in him. *But how much am I supposed to do? He's not my kid. He'll get over it; lots more important people than me are going.*

David did not get over it. He shunned Matthew ruthlessly – and Matthew was surprised at how much it hurt. He heard David telling his mother, "MatthewRye is not my friend any more. He doesn't love me." To Matthew's horror, the boy burst into noisy tears and was gathered onto Carolyn's lap. When she asked what had happened, the child sobbed, "He won't come to the Christmas pageant. He doesn't care if I'm a angel."

Matthew slithered away, hoping against hope to avoid the confrontation he feared would follow. She didn't catch him until four a.m. the next day, as he pulled on his coat and gloves to go milking.

"David's upset with you," Carolyn said.

"Yeah, I know."

"Do you know why?"

"Yes." He focused on the zipper of his coat.

"I know you don't go to church," she said, "but the Christmas program is different. There's no big sermon; it's just singing and the children's pageant this year. Could you think about making an exception this time? For David? It means so much to him."

Matthew met her soft eyes with a hard glare. "You cheat," he told her. "I have my reasons, and they're good enough for me. David isn't old enough to understand."

"But I am," she told him, giving no ground. "So is John. Not that you owe us an explanation, but it might make you feel better to tell someone who cares about you." She smiled.

He winced and looked away again. "No. Please just drop it." He plunged out the back door and left Carolyn standing in the entryway.

I am not going to listen to all that "gentle Jesus" stuff! The kid needs to learn that in real life we don't always get what we want. Life's not fair. Learn to live with it. He stormed into the barn, to find Ed already prepping the cows for milking. "Sorry I'm late."

"'S'all right." Ed looked up, grinned and went back to work.

They kept companionable silence until the job was done and the cows had ambled back into the lot. Machinery cleaned and ready for the next round, Ed and Matthew headed in for breakfast.

Ed's breath made little white puffs in the cold air as he said, "Anything you'd like to talk about?"

"No. Should there be?"

"I dunno. You're just real quiet. Quieter than usual. I don't mean to pry, just to let you know you got a friend if you need one."

Maybe... But they were approaching the back door. "Nah, I'm fine. Thanks anyway."

Matthew dreaded facing Carolyn again, but she was her usual cheerful self and gave him no dirty looks or reproachful glances. Breakfast passed safely.

Then late in the day, lying on his bed reading from Frost's poetry, Matthew heard a sweet, clear little voice singing Christmas carols. He remembered suddenly the Christmas figures in the window of a department store in downtown Baltimore. A soft hand holding his tiny one. A soft voice humming Christmas carols as they watched the animated figures bend and turn. One had been a laughing Santa. One had been a spinning ballerina in a short fluffy pink thing. A red-and-gold train had looped around and around the whole scene, puffing smoke. He had wanted that train. Mama had said, "Maybe someday."

Confounded by the sudden lump in his throat, Matthew sat up on the edge of the bed, leaned his elbows on his knees, and ground the heels of his hands against his closed eyelids. He might have been David's age that day, so full of hope and delight. But there had never been a train, or a pageant, or anyone but his mother to see it if there had been. Memories of disappointment scalded his eyes and the pit of his stomach.

I don't have to do to David what my father did to me. I can live through an hour of church to make him happy. I guess...

On Christmas Eve, Matthew did the best he could. He showered and shaved and slicked back his shaggy hair with water. He put on his best jeans and his only white dress shirt, purchased for the occasion.

"You clean up good!" Ed teased as they entered the old El Camino for the short ride to church.

All too soon they were parking among many cars and hiking up to the door. It felt like the infamous last mile on death row to Matthew, even though he had never been in prison. Ed nudged him to follow a family ahead of them and he managed to step inside without anything happening.

"There's the rest of the family," Ed gestured. "Come on!" He led Matthew across the wide space in which perhaps a hundred other people milled around, laughing and talking. Matthew tried not to look at everything and everyone around him. *One hour*, he told himself. *One hour. I can do it.*

"Livvie saved us a seat up front," Carolyn said, heading down the burgundy-carpeted center aisle. They followed obediently, pausing to shake hands and exchange pleasantries as they went. Matthew kept his head down and his hands in his pockets. After an eternity, Ed shoved him into the relative safety of the third pew. He planted himself at the end of the row, ready for a quick escape.

"Oh, Matthew, please change with us," Carolyn asked. "I need the center aisle seat to take pictures." She flourished her camera.

"Sure." Despairing, he moved down and was trapped between John and Ed. He tried to concentrate on the religious elevator music someone was piping into the sanctuary. Why did all church music have to sound like funerals?

Giggles and rustlings came from behind a plush navy curtain, followed by shushing noises and more giggling. The music suddenly cut off mid-note.

From the front pew, Miles Corrigan mounted the center steps to the platform. Flipping too-long dark brown hair back from his eyes, he smiled out at the people as if they were the most wonderful people in the whole world. "Welcome!" he said, with a warmth that threatened to melt the ice around Matthew's heart.

Matthew crossed his arms and scowled. By the end of the hour he twitched and quivered and could barely restrain himself from running back down the aisle to the door. He did admit to himself that David, in his white nightgown, bare feet and downy wings, had been a fetching angel. And the man in the black suit mercifully hadn't said much. Settling into the cold seat of the El Camino, he focused on the sharp ache in his left knee.

"So – What'd you think?" Ed asked, turning the key. Like a faithful horse to a tongue-click, the engine turned over smoothly and began pumping out great blasts of cold air from the heater. "Aah! Invigorating!" Ed laughed.

Matthew rubbed his knee, where the pain intensified in the cold air. "David was cute."

"Yeah. All those kids was cute. Sang like little angels, too, except maybe the one with his finger up his nose the whole time. What'd you think of Pastor Miles?"

"Looks too young to be the head of a church. Looked like he was wearing his father's suit."

Ed laughed, then sighed with pleasure as the cold air began to warm. "Good ole girl, she always warms up to a guy pretty quick if he treats her right." He patted the dash.

Matthew took a chance. "What was all that stuff about Christmas not being a big deal, that it's all about Easter?"

"I think what he said," Ed answered slowly, "was that *without* Easter, Christmas wouldn't mean anything."

"Which means - ?"

"Uh – well – if Jesus was just born and had a nice life and helped some people and then died, He wouldn't be any different from a lotta guys. But because God gave us His Son, and He died on purpose to pay for our sins, and then He rose again – well, see, that's what makes Him a big deal. That's what proves that He's God and He loves us."

"Oh." *Right. What a line! How can anyone believe that? I can believe a father wouldn't care if his son died, but for the son to volunteer to die? Never.*

"If you got any deeper questions than that, go to John. Boss knows just about everything in the Book. Or call Pastor Miles. Lotta folks go in and talk to him."

"Thanks. Got it." *And I'll do it when hell freezes over. I know all I need to know about God.* He rubbed his knee again, biting back a curse as the pain stabbed through it.

Fourteen

Matthew was grateful to escape going to church for Easter. Apparently those people didn't dress up their kids as Easter bunnies, so David wasn't after him. He also escaped something that summer called "Vacation Bible-School," which, as far as he could see, fed David all kinds of sugar and taught him loud, repetitive songs. He managed to listen politely most of the time; but the words made no sense, and the music was irritating.

Fortunately, as October approached, David's enthusiasm for Bible-School was replaced by excitement about his approaching birthday. "Mama says October is the very best time to have a birthday," he informed Matthew. "When is your birthday?"

"Don't you remember? Mine was in June, at the beginning of the summer."

"Oh, yeah. But that's not as good as October."

"Hey, buddy! I didn't get to choose!" Matthew laughed.

"You can share my birthday," David promised. "Five is big enough to share. I'm going to get a puppy and a baby brother and a red bike – with no training wheels."

"Gonna share your presents, too?" Matthew teased.

"Well," David deliberated, "well... You can pet my puppy. And I suppose you can hold the baby..."

When apprised of the gift list, John swallowed down his feelings and told David, "I don't think you will be getting either a puppy or a baby brother, son."

David knew how to cut his losses. "Then a bike, Daddy, a red one – with no training wheels?"

John and Matthew spent the rest of October running along behind the red bike, holding on to the seat as David wobbled from side to side. Finally the day came; he soloed!

"Life's a lot like that," John said to Matthew, wiping sweat from his brow.

"How so?"

"Well, it starts out like a new, red bike, all shiny and full of possibilities. But learning to ride is hard, and some people take a lot more spills than others. Some people's bikes get pretty scuffed up. Once in a while a person decides learning to ride just isn't worth it and they walk through the rest of their lives, feeling mad and sorry for themselves. Other folks, though, they finally get the hang of it and away they go. Almost everyone who gets it had, at some point, somebody running along behind holding on to the seat."

"That's a pretty picture," Matthew said. "But some of us never had anyone holding on to the seat."

"Oh," John said slowly, "I think you did. I think when people can't do it, that's when God comes along and holds on to us."

Yeah, sure. This again. Everything's a God-lesson. "I'll go get started on the chores," he said, leaving John there on the driveway watching David fly with the wind in his hair.

Fifteen

Matthew came upon Pearl one afternoon playing the piano in the living room, pounding out a majestic, stormy piece, her fingers flashing, her whole body throbbing into it. She didn't even know he was there until the last note had died away and she sat there breathing heavily.

"I didn't mean to intrude," he said.

"Nonsense!" the old woman said briskly. "Rachmaninoff. Do you know it?"

"No, ma'am. It was - it was powerful."

She smiled. "I think so. When I was a girl I wanted to be a concert pianist and play such things all over the world."

Matthew was intrigued enough to forget shyness. "And did you?"

"No, it seemed the Lord's plan for my life was different from mine." Pearl smiled again. "While I was a student at the Cincinnati Conservatory of Music, I met Mr. Gunderman. And then it seemed after graduation that 'all over the world' was too far away."

"You never got to use all that talent and training?"

"Of course I did. I taught music in the schools and gave private lessons and played the piano for the church wherever we lived." The dark eyes misted a little with memory. "I truly never regretted any of it. Mr. Gunderman was a fine man, a fine husband, and the Lord gave us a good life together."

Matthew nodded, trying to imagine a young, vibrant Pearl giving up her dream for the man she loved.

"You like music," she said suddenly. "Do you play?"

"No, ma'am." Matthew's hand unconsciously caressed the shiny wood of the piano.

"You could," Pearl said. "If you wanted. It's hard work, but you're no stranger to that. Think on it," Pearl ordered.

"Yes, ma'am, if you say so," Matthew agreed, more from fear of disagreeing than from faith in his ability to learn. Still, a tickle of hope made him twitch restlessly. *Maybe? Someday?*

§ § §

David practiced on his mother the soulful look which would steal the hearts of pretty girls and their mothers in another ten or twelve years. "But I want to sail my boat in the bathtub, Mama! Why can't I? Please!"

Trying not to laugh at her son's machinations, Carolyn pulled the stopper from the tub drain. As the water level dropped from overflowing to just over-full, she dried her arm and hands and passed the large towel to the boy.

"Mop!" she said, indicating the puddles around them. "Pretend you're a sailor swabbing the deck or something, but get this cleaned up before it comes through the kitchen ceiling."

From his hands and knees, David looked up at her, towel poised above the largest puddle. "Is Daddy down there in the kitchen?" he asked, mischief in his bright blue eyes.

"No," came John's voice from the hallway. "Daddy's right here." He appeared in the doorway. "Let's get this mess cleaned up, son, and find you some dry clothes before you freeze"

Carolyn stepped to the door and put her arms around her husband's waist. He automatically rested his chin on top of her head as he watched the boy sop up water with more enthusiasm than accuracy.

"I think our little sailor needs more to do until spring gets here," John told his wife. "What do you think about starting him on piano lessons?"

"He's only five. Is that old enough?"

"Oh, I think it is. He likes to bang on the keys anyway. Might as well start getting music out of the thing instead of noise."

Carolyn tilted back her head to meet her husband's eyes. "And will you be the one who makes him practice when he'd rather go out and play?"

"Actually," John said slowly, drawing out the suspense as he raised one hand to cup her face, "I think we'll get his best buddy across the hall to practice with him."

She spluttered a laugh. "You're kidding!"

"Not at all. Pearl mentioned she thought Matthew might like to learn to play. He pets that spinet every time he walks past it." He bent to give her a quick kiss, tightening his embrace.

Carolyn returned the kiss with interest, then drew back, a faint blush staining her cheekbones. Smiling at John, she observed, "Petting doesn't necessarily signify a commitment."

John laughed and hugged her close again. "In my case, it does."

The boy looked up from his pile of wet towels. "If anyone asked me," he said, "I would say yes."

§ § §

So the first week of November Matthew found himself sitting beside David on the piano bench as Pearl began to explain the basics. He was chagrined to find that not only he would not be playing music by the end of the first lesson but also the boy was catching on much faster than he was.

"I have a uncluttered mind," David explained quite seriously.

"Yeah, well, I guess I don't," Matthew grumbled, shifting uncomfortably on the hard bench. His hands, turned amazingly clumsy, hit another clinker and he winced, half-expecting Pearl to smack his knuckles with a ruler.

By the time the ice on the pond had thawed and willow leaves were going gold to green in March, they could both play a decent scale and a few simple pieces. They practiced in the late afternoons, when homework and chores were finished, and - if they felt like it - right after breakfast, before the school bus came. They encouraged one another, competed some, and laughed a lot at their own and each other's mistakes.

John often listened from the other room or watched from the doorway with a knowing smile. Lying spooned under their warm quilts at night, he smugly teased Carolyn, "I told you so. Anything they can do together is fine with both of them."

She smiled in the darkness. "Mmm."

"You could show a little more admiration for my brilliant idea."

"Mmmm."

He pinched her gently in reproof, and she rolled over to hug him extravagantly. "Oh, please forgive me, dear, sweet, wise, brilliant, wonderful husband. You were right, as usual!"

"That's more like it," the farmer told her before making sure she understood how much he liked her apology.

Sixteen

A long spring and short, hot summer had suddenly given over to winter, with no fall to prepare them. Harvest yields were poor as icy rains make it almost impossible to get into the fields and mildewed corn and soybeans in the ear and pod. They battled sleet every weekend into December.

Even inside the felt-lined boots and gray wool socks, Matthew's feet were numb with cold. His left knee ached, throbbing worse each time he bent it or put weight on it. His face was chapped raw and red by the stinging little ice particles blasting him on the north wind. Half-way through December and it already felt like January. At six o'clock it was so dark he made his way from the barn to the house more by intuition and memory than by sight.

Tonight no warm light beckoned from the kitchen, and no promising smells or friendly voices reached out to him as he opened the back door. His cold, stiff, gloved hand swept the wall searching for the light switch, fumbled it on by chance. The kitchen snapped into focus: pine cupboards, pale blue walls, shiny white appliances, the nesting hen cookie jar, the goose salt and pepper shakers Matthew privately detested but never mocked because Carolyn loved them.

The furnace grumbled, then sprung to life with the roar of an old bear roused early from hibernation. Matthew stuffed his gloves into his coat pockets and pried off his boots with awkward fingers so he could stand on the floor register in his socks. Circulation returned to his feet with a vengeance, bringing tears to his eyes and an involuntary cry to his lips. Even standing on the hot grid, hot air pouring over his feet and legs, he was cold. He left his coat on and stayed in the heat for many minutes before he figured it out.

"I'm lonely," he said out loud. "I don't like being here by myself."

It had seemed like a good idea at the time, Matthew recalled, staying at the farm alone while the Abbotts went to spend the weekend with relatives in Indiana. He hadn't been comfortable with their invitation to go along. He hadn't wanted to intrude, hadn't wanted to deal with all those children and their loving parents. Even David's half-tearful pleading had not convinced him. Besides, with Christmas so near he could use the time to finish the presents he was making.

The day had begun promisingly enough. A pale, watery sun had blessed the departing family and had kept the chill from Matthew's knee and his heart as he did the necessary chores. Then he had gone to the storage barn and spent the whole day there, forgetting lunch, ignoring the impending storm, as he exercised the woodworking skills John and Ed had taught him. Matthew had turned out to have a gift for woodworking. He could look at a piece of wood and see what it was to be. He was proficient now with power tools, but he really preferred to do most of the work by hand.

He had spent most of the day finishing the long shelf he was making for Carolyn. Over several weeks he had carved the back into a line of gossiping geese bobbing their heads at one another, a painstaking struggle to call them out of the rock-hard maple whose close grain held them fast. Today he had sanded until every surface was so fine that silk wouldn't snag on it, then hand-rubbed warm oil into the raw wood. Then he had wrapped it again in a soft old blanket and laid it next to the new boat he had made for David, the small inlaid box for Pearl, the carved sheepdog for Ed. John's present wasn't finished yet. Matthew felt unsure about it - would work on it a while, then put it back.

When stiffness and cold had finally caught Matthew's attention, it had been time for chores again in the heavy gray light of the approaching storm. Trying to outpace the ice had kept his mind away from the emptiness waiting in the house. Now he stood in the silent kitchen, in the silent house, where even the furnace had fallen still, wishing he had had the courage to go with the family.

"They've never left me all alone before," he muttered. "I don't like it. Why did they do this to me?" The sudden sound of his own rusty laugh startled him as he realized how ridiculous the last thought had been. "So whose choice was it?" he asked himself, and he laughed again.

Nevertheless, it was a long evening. He turned on the lights in every room, then radios, then the television. Still the house seemed resoundingly empty. He drifted from room to room in search of - something - but couldn't find it. He imagined them all gathered with their relatives in some big, warm living room with a lighted Christmas tree, laughing, talking, maybe singing carols. He pictured David's pale blond hair drifting into his eyes as he leaned into his father's shoulder and fell asleep. He imagined John gathering the boy's small, limp body into his arms and carrying him off to bed, Carolyn tucking a bright quilt around his little frame and kissing his soft cheek.

"I wonder if Mama ever tucked me in when I was little," Matthew mused. "I wonder if anyone ever will again." He ruthlessly put away an intruding image of Will alone in a narrow bed in a dingy room, afraid of the dark...

In the end, he tucked himself in, as usual, and slept uneasily in the echoing house, dreaming of the year he had slept in barns and on the verges of wheatfields.

The next day was no better. He did the farm chores. He cooked and ate and cleaned up his messes. He mopped the part of the kitchen floor where dirty snow had melted from his boots. By four o'clock he had finished all the chores he had to do and all the ones he had manufactured. He had re-oiled the shelf twice. Leaving lights, radios and television on behind him, he reluctantly trudged up the stairs to his room.

In the spare, white room, Matthew felt for a moment like a small boat finally moored in a safe harbor after many long days at sea. Sitting on the edge of his neatly made bed, he reached one hand under the trailing edge of the spread to pull out a bundle wrapped in an old yellowed pillowcase. He placed the bundle on the bed beside him, reached out his hand to open it, drew back his hand again. The calm deserted him. His heart began the old, familiar thump of anxiety.

He noticed the Bible lying on the bedside table, and as he stretched over to pick it up, a card fell out from between the pages. It was a birthday card David had made from bright red construction paper. The front featured a big, yellow sun, an equally large, white daisy, and a same-sized boy - with yellow hair, round blue eyes with eyelashes all the way around, a grinning red mouth with dozens of sharp teeth, no neck, an impressively blue-and-red-striped shirt. The inside said, in block letters of various sizes and slants, "HAPY BIRTDAY! I LOVE YOU JESUS DOS TO."

Matthew returned the card to its usual place at the third chapter of John. He read the verses again, since he was passing by, not even registering that they were now part of his routine or that he had come to believe in the God whose existence he had denied a year ago. "How could You love anybody that much?" he asked. He didn't expect an answer. He suspected God spent a lot of time talking with John and Carolyn, but he didn't believe he and God were on those terms. Still, he felt compelled to ask, as he had asked before - and would probably ask again. He could vaguely imagine dying for the Abbott family, who had been so kind and had given him so much. He could not imagine dying for strangers, for the children who had jeered at his ragged clothes, for the farmers who had turned him away with no work without even offering him a meal, for the farmwives who had let him drink from their tin cups but had never offered him ice or a bath or a clean shirt. Why would anyone volunteer to die for people who hated him or mocked him or wounded him or ignored him? Why would anyone volunteer to kill his own son to save a bunch of hateful, ungrateful strangers? It made no sense.

With a sigh, Matthew closed the book and returned it to the table. As if they were not attached to him, his reluctant hands folded back the pillowcase beside him and lifted out the block of wood concealed there. He was afraid to look, but those traitorous hands raised the wood squarely before his eyes. He looked into a face carved into agony, into fathomless eyes brimming with compassion. The long grain of the wood shaped lank hair falling around the tortured face. It was ugly. How could he have ruined the wood like that?

Even as he grieved the ruin of his creation, Matthew's hands were fumbling for the carving knives and chisels, feverishly attacking the wood, paring away every extraneous sliver to expose the corded neck straining to hold that suffering head erect, to hint of bony shoulder and collarbone.

When his hand cramped fast to the knife, he knew he couldn't do any more. He saw with surprise the hands of his wind-up alarm-clock meeting one another at midnight. He noticed spasms in his tensed back muscles, a screaming pain in his hand, another in his knee. Then all those distractions fell away as Matthew saw his finished work whole for the first time.

Oh, my God, what have I done? The suffering his hands had called out of the wood washed over him like lye, burning all the way to his heart. "Oh, God, I'm sorry!" he cried. "I didn't know what I was doing!" He dropped the figure onto the bed and buried his face in his hands. The caustic images of his past rushed in to form a huge acid puddle in his mind and in his gut, trying to burn through his soul until he was eaten away. Over and over he repeated, "I'm sorry, I'm sorry, I'm sorry," until it became a mindless, agonized litany he no longer heard or understood.

Caught between the silent scream of his carving and the clamoring accusations of his conscience, Matthew heard neither his own voice nor the sounds of the family returning.

§ § §

John parked by the front porch and unloaded the suitcases while Carolyn unbuckled the sleeping boy and lifted him in her arms. She smiled as John reached for the child and shook her head. They started up the steps but stopped to really notice the lights blazing all over the house. As they entered, they saw the television broadcasting the snow of an off-air channel and heard several radios, each on a different station. Carolyn turned to her husband with a worried frown.

"Relax," John smiled. "The truck is here, so he's home."

"Then what in the world...?"

John smiled again. "I imagine this big old place feels pretty lonely when we're not home."

"Oh. Oh, I knew he should have come with us! There was plenty of room, and -"

"Honey, take David up to bed before you drop him. I'll check on our hermit for you."

They climbed the stairs together, bumping companionably, and separated at the top. John rubbed a weary hand across his face and stepped to Matthew's open doorway. His tired eyes quickly took in the mess of tools and wood shavings, the carved block he couldn't quite make out, the man rocking back and forth on the edge of the bed with his head in his hands. John stepped inside and moved to kneel before the distraught figure.

Matthew vaguely felt John's hand on his shoulder, more clearly felt the fingers biting in, shaking him gently. He raised his head, met the eyes full of loving concern, wondered where he had seen that look before. Remembered. Jerked away and tried to stuff his carving back into the pillowcase.

"Wait," John said. "What is it?"

"It's nothing. Never mind. I ruined it. I never should have -!" Matthew's voice rose and trembled. John's hand closed over his, stilling his trembling.

"It's all right. Let's see; maybe it's salvageable."

Before Matthew could hide the figure deeper, John drew it out into the light. He studied it for a long time, tracing the strong lines, the delicate lines, with one finger, then closed both hands around it and bowed his head for several minutes. Then he looked up.

"Tell me," John urged.

"It's Philippine mahogany. I found the wood at the lumberyard while I was getting maple for another project. It-it had a face in it, I thought. The wood is - was - beautiful. I wanted to give it to you for Christmas. I saw such a beautiful face in there - but when I carved it - " Matthew swallowed convulsively, shuddered and took a long breath. "When I carved it, this thing came out - this other face."

"Is it a different person, or just a different expression?" John asked.

Matthew thought for a moment. "Same face. But not beautiful any more, because I tortured Him!"

"You carved this tortured expression..."

"No! I mean what I said! I know you know who He is! You have to understand: I sat here and every bad, wrong, hateful, cruel, evil thing I've ever done went through my mind - all my *sins* - " He spat out the word as if it were unspeakably bitter. "He feels all that pain because of me. If anyone did that to my son - or to your son - I would kill him!" Matthew continued to shudder with revulsion, drawing away from the wooden figure. John caressed the suffering face, studying it intently.

"You certainly captured His pain, almost as if it were your own. And you're right: He did die for our sins. But look again at what you carved." John again held the figure before Matthew's face. "Look. Do you see any anger there?"

He reluctantly raised his blurred eyes to his work. The muscles were strained, the mouth twisted, the hair sweat-soaked, the skin tight over the bones. Drops of what might be blood or sweat beaded the forehead and tears lay on the cheeks. The pain was horrible. He began to turn away, but John said urgently, "No! Not yet! Look into His eyes."

Matthew forced himself to obey the sharp imperative, blinking rapidly to clear his vision. The eyes were huge, deep-set and shadowed. Somehow, in the midst of that twisted, tortured face, they were deep and still, tinged with sadness, radiating compassion and love. The artist in Matthew recognized a remarkable piece of workmanship, while the rest of him slid off the bed onto his knees, bent almost double by the weight of his grief.

"I need to do it," he told John, his voice breaking but resolute. "I need to pray that prayer you told me about. Can I do it right now?"

John's heart leaped in his chest. He permitted a faint smile to show and managed to keep hands and voice steady. "Here and now is just right. Do you need any help?"

Matthew thought for a moment, then shook his head. The words were already forming themselves in his heart. He bowed his head, closed his eyes, groped for and hung on to John's warm, hard hand. "Jesus," he said quietly, "I know You're the Son of God and You suffered and died for me. I don't know why - it doesn't make sense to me - but thank You for doing it. I'm sorry for everything I've done that hurt You so much. Please forgive me for my sins - I don't want to hurt You anymore, ever. Please fill up the empty place inside me and teach me to be like You. Amen."

Stillness fell over the room, over his mind, over his heart. The light in the room seemed both softer and clearer as Matthew opened his eyes. John seemed to be praying, his smiling lips moving silently while one tear slid from under his closed eyelids. Matthew waited quietly, knee to knee and hand in hand with this man who had become so many things to him: rescuer, employer, teacher, mentor, friend. A new idea crept into his resting mind: *John is my brother. The Bible says when we believe in Christ we become sons of God, so he's my brother! Carolyn is my sister-in-law! David is my nephew!*

"Now I do have a family!" he blurted, leaping to his feet.

John laughed then, rising more slowly. "That's what we've been trying to tell you," he chuckled. "Wait 'til you get to know our Father better! Now we need to see if there's any cake among all those Christmas cookies downstairs."

"Cake?" Matthew asked as they headed down to the kitchen.

"Of course. It *is* your birthday!" As they entered the kitchen, John slowed and became serious again. "I want you to know this is the best Christmas gift I've ever received. I'll never forget it."

Matthew frowned at the carving still balanced in John's hand. "No. I'll make you something better."

John smiled again. "I didn't mean the figure. I meant your decision to accept Christ. We've been praying for you to receive the gift of salvation since the first night you came to us. Now you have real life, and I got to be there. That's the gift!"

"Oh." He reached for the carving. "Still, I'll make you something better."

John held on. "Please let me keep it. God showed himself to you in a special way here. Maybe other people will find Him the same way you did when they see this work. Maybe you and I will need to be reminded sometimes."

Matthew took a step back, shaking his head. "Oh, no! I'm never going to hurt God or anyone else like that ever again."

John's smile was bittersweet as he found and cut into chocolate cake. Suddenly he was bone-tired. He thought longingly of his wife and son sleeping upstairs, of his soft pillow and warm quilts and dawn coming all too soon. Matthew didn't understand what his decision would mean over time. *God, give us both strength*, he prayed silently as he drew himself up straight and handed over the huge slice of cake with a genuine grin.

"Happy birthday, brother!"

After a cursory pursuit of crumbs, which they knew was doomed to fail Carolyn's inspection in the morning, they turned out the lights and went upstairs. They parted with whispered good-nights, though it was nearly morning. So much dawn and starlight reflected from the white walls of his room that Matthew didn't need lamplight to guide him as he hung up his clothes and climbed into the narrow white bed.

Swaying gently in the cradle between awake and asleep, he replayed the evening. He imagined he carved the face he had first seen in the wood, the beautiful face, and it smiled at him. It might have been saying, "I love you" as he fell asleep.

Had he come awake to check, John would have seen Matthew's face glowing in the starlight, resembling David's in its innocence and peace. In that moment he was as beautiful as anything he would ever carve. He was born again, and anything was possible.

PART TWO

THE REFINER'S FIRE

1994 – 1995

Behold, I have refined you,
> but not with silver:
>> I have chosen you
>>> in the furnace of affliction.
>>>> *Isaiah 48:10*

Seventeen

I t was his own fault, Matthew conceded to himself. If he had kept his mouth shut, maybe he could have gone on riding on the high of his new relationship with Jesus without having to do anything different except be nicer to people. But he had asked John the next morning, "What am I supposed to do now?"

John had been swift and clear. "Start reading the Gospel of John – not just 3:16, the whole thing from beginning to end – and start praying when you wake up and when you go to bed and any time in between when you need guidance or want to give thanks. And come to church with us on Sunday."

Matthew had thought he had made himself clear: "I don't do church."

John had laughed. "You do now, brother. It's in the Book. It's how we learn about our faith and encourage one another. Try it; you might like it."

So now he sat between Carolyn and Ed in the third pew, listening to Pastor Corrigan preaching about Moses. The sanctuary was cold. His knee ached. *Yeah, yeah. Baby in the bulrushes, whatever those are. Grew up to be a bigshot then got himself into trouble through his anger. Got that part! Ran away to hide in the hills herding sheep so the Egyptians wouldn't kill him and heard from God. Sure he did. Burning bush – right.* Matthew rubbed his left knee and tried to pay attention. For all he knew, John might throw a pop quiz over dinner. His mind drifted, thinking of dinner and the warm house and some piano practice with David...

"...over and over," Pastor Corrigan said. "But Moses kept making excuses. 'I can't speak well,' 'send Aaron, he's good at it...' Now before we get too high and mighty, thinking what a jerk Moses was to refuse God, let's consider for a minute: Have I ever said no to God? Have I ever known He wanted me to do a thing, but I made excuses? 'Lord, you know I'm not good at that, but Tom is. So send Tom, okay?' 'I don't want to go on the missions trip, but I'll make a donation for the other guys to go.' 'I can't; I'm too tired/busy/overworked...' You fill in the blanks. Moses is such a clear example of the stubborn heart refusing, saying no to God and causing grief to God, to himself and to the people he was supposed to help. All through his time in the wilderness..."

Matthew had heard enough. He was caught in the coils of one phrase: "the stubborn heart refusing." *Is that me? Lord, am I refusing something You want me to do? Couldn't You just give me more time to figure this all out?* He groaned silently, hearing the refusal even in the prayer – if you could call it a prayer.

As they left the pew and headed back up the aisle to the main door, where the Corrigans were greeting people as they left, Ed leaned in and said to Matthew in a soft voice, "You okay?"

"Sure. Why?"

"Well, son, you look like a man under conviction."

Matthew jolted. "What do you mean? I haven't done anything."

Ed laughed. "I'll explain it to you in the car, okay?"

"Whatever," Matthew muttered, bracing himself for the hand-shakes and friendly comments. He had learned that keeping his hands in his pockets would earn him a hug instead of a shake, so he didn't do that any more.

Riding home with Ed in the El Camino, Matthew asked again, "So what's this thing about conviction? Do I look like a convict?"

"Nah, not lately," Ed teased, focusing on the road ahead of him, where powdery snow eddied back and forth. "We say a person is 'convicted' or 'under conviction' when the Holy Spirit has ahold of his conscience. God's telling him he needs to do something or he's doing something wrong and he knows he's going to have to change."

"Oh."

"So you looked like something from the sermon got ahold of you."

"Yeah, maybe." Matthew examined the road also, as if his scrutiny would keep the old truck between the lines.

Ed didn't pry. Ed never pried much. Sometimes Matthew wished he would, either to give him a reason to talk or to give him a reason to be angry. Today he wouldn't offer up any more, but he knew he would wrestle with the notion of his "stubborn heart refusing" and what it had refused.

Eighteen

Spring wandered by casually, dripping gold-green willow leaves and rosy magnolia petals. The chicks ran around the yard in a frenzy, little puffs of bright yellow pecking at bugs and chasing shadows. The air held the fecund scents of freshly turned earth, worms after rain and new birth. Under Carolyn's instruction, Ed and Matthew planted the garden, sixty feet by forty, filling it with peas and spinach and early lettuce, then later with beans and cucumbers and tomatoes and cabbage and radishes and carrots.... "Why no potatoes this year?" Matthew asked, standing up to stretch his back.

"Oh, Ted and Livvie put in the potatoes this year," Carolyn said. We'll do the melons and cukes; they'll do the potatoes and corn. Then we'll share the harvest."

That made sense. Family, they were showing him, was about sharing. Looking over the rows of young seedlings, Matthew felt a proprietary pride. His sweat helped to water this field nearly every day, and his aching muscles testified to triumph over weeds.

"You won't feel so good about it come August," Ed warned, "when the temperature hits a hundred and the missus starts to canning. You're low man on the totem pole, so you'll sure get drafted to help some way or another." He grinned, wiping his face with his blue bandana. "Me, I'll be sitting in the shade drinking lemonade."

"Sure you will." Matthew knocked dirt off his boots with the edge of the hoe.

"Well, probably not, but it's a nice picture in my head, me sitting there and you sweating."

Matthew swung the hoe over his shoulder and Ed picked up a thing that looked like the rowel of a spur on a long handle. They headed for the equipment barn. "Do you remember that sermon Pastor Corrigan preached about Moses a while back?" Matthew asked.

"Nope."

"How can you not?"

"Heard a lot of sermons," Ed replied easily. "Can't remember them all. Mostly I remember the ones where it seems like God is talking right to me. Guess Moses wasn't one of them."

They hung their tools on the pegboard. "Coffee break?" Ed suggested. Together they moved from the barn into the kitchen, pausing just briefly to wash up at the sink on the back porch. Carolyn didn't appreciate major dirt in the kitchen sink.

Over coffee, seated at the kitchen table, Matthew persisted, "Well, I keep thinking about Moses, about what the pastor said. 'The stubborn heart refusing.' How do you do it?"

"Do what?"

"Just know what God wants and then do it. It seems so easy for you."

"You think?" Ed laughed. "Takes time, takes effort, takes making a choice."

"What kind of choice?"

"Choice to let God be the one in charge of your life. Any cookies in that jar over there?"

Matthew rose and walked over to the nesting hen cookie jar. He uncovered a treasure in fresh chocolate chip cookies and piled half a dozen on a napkin. "Here." Placing the napkin in front of Ed, he resumed his seat and his train of thought. "I have made that choice. Isn't that what we do when we accept Jesus?"

"Yep. But I reckon if you have to ask about it, you maybe aren't as sure as you thought you were. I think Pastor'd tell you for Jesus it's a done deal, but for us it's not just a one-time choice. Gotta recommit as needed." Ed dunked a cookie in his coffee and slurped it up.

"Well, it's a great idea, but – you know – on a daily basis – I just can't see God paying that much attention to everybody all the time. And he sure isn't sending me any telegrams or billboards. So I just – do whatever seems good."

"Bible has a line about that," Ed said, working on his third cookie. "Says something about 'everyone did what was right in his own eyes.'

Thing was, the people was full of sins and God let their enemies have them. Bad, bad scene. Also says in another place, 'This is the way; walk in it.'"

"Great. How do you know the way? How do you know it's God? How do you know it's not your own imagination or the devil or something?"

"Here comes John; let's ask him," Ed suggested. Matthew had a mental image of Ed wiping sweat from his forehead, although the man didn't move.

John sat down with them, sipping gingerly at a full cup of coffee, and reviewed the questions. "Okay," he said. "If you're down at the barn and I need you up here at the house and I call you, what happens?"

Matthew laughed. "I come running."

"Why?"

"Well – because – because you called me."

"How do you know I called you, not somebody else?"

Matthew tilted his head to look at John, perplexed. "I know you called because it's my name and your voice."

"Exactly! You come running because you know my voice, and you know I wouldn't call you if I didn't have something to say to you or something for you to do, right?"

"Yeah."

John took a cautious swallow of the coffee, then a larger one. "Jesus tells us in John 10 that sheep know their master's voice and follow him and that He – Jesus – is our shepherd, Who is willing to die for us. He says, 'I am the good shepherd; I know my sheep and my sheep know Me...'"

"It's in the Book, huh?"

"Yes. John, chapter 10."

"But how do you know the Book is right?"

Ed rolled his eyes and shoved back his chair. "I gotta get back to work. See you guys later."

Matthew fiddled with his mug, twisting it back and forth, not drinking the coffee. He looked sideways at John to see whether he had gone too far.

"I can't prove the Bible is the Word of God," John said. "It's a faith thing, bottom line. Either you believe it or you don't. If you think it's just another good book, instead of *the* Good Book, then none of this will make much of an impression. But I believe it *is* the Word of God, all of it, and I believe God speaks to us through what we read there. It's meant to show us what He values and what He wants from us."

"Like I said to Ed, I need telegrams or billboards. So, okay, even if you do believe the Bible is the Word of God, how do you know it's accurate? My Bible says it was translated in 1970-something. There must have been a lot of translations between Jesus and now."

John laughed and bit into a cookie. "True enough. Pastor Miles said once that even though so much time has gone by, the translations we've had, Protestant and Catholic, old and new, all are so close to the original texts, and to each other. So if you compare Bibles, you'll find some differences in the wording but not much in the meaning. That's almost a miracle in itself, after nearly 2000 years, don't you think?"

"I don't know about miracles," Matthew insisted. "I just wish I'd be driving along and see a huge billboard that said, 'Matthew, do this' – whatever 'this' is."

§ § §

Two weeks later John asked Matthew to take the truck to the lumber yard for some plywood. An early morning drizzle had blown off and the sky was bright blue above him, temperature rising enough to make having the windows down in the truck a need as well as a pleasure. Matthew enjoyed the ride, crops rising in the fields, black and white Holsteins grazing in the pastures, a red-tailed hawk gracefully circling overhead. The noise in the back of his mind receded a little as he took in the peace around him.

Heading home again, sheets of plywood jouncing in the back of the truck, Matthew continued his appreciation of the countryside. It was harder to push the thoughts back now, though, and he felt a growing compulsion. Finally, giving in to it, he yelled out loud, "*Okay*, what do You want me to do? Why don't You quit playing games and just tell me!"

Of course he heard nothing. *Right. He doesn't speak to me. Why would He?*

Almost to the edge of town, Matthew looked to his right and saw it. *No, it can't be!* he thought wildly, grabbing the wheel to keep from driving into the ditch. *I must be hallucinating.* He pulled abruptly onto the shoulder and threw the truck into park, noticing that his hands were shaking. A huge billboard, white on black, said, "Confused? Tired of trying? Try prayer." It was signed "God."

"It's a billboard," Matthew laughed out loud. "I asked for a billboard – I got a billboard." Shaking his head, still laughing, he put the truck into drive and went on his way. *Lord, I guess I owe You an apology. The message is pretty clear. But I don't know how to pray very well, and I don't know what to pray for. Please help me. Amen.*

As it happened, there were a number of white-on-black "God messages" dotting the highways at that time, but Matthew took it personally. If John hadn't needed plywood, if Ed hadn't been in the middle of something else, if he had taken a different route home, if he had been fiddling with the radio dials as he came to that spot... No, it was a message from God. He began to pay more attention to the way other people prayed. He began reading the Bible every day, some days more than others, and asking questions. Most of it either seemed too simple or made no sense. "I need a first-grade version," he grumbled to John one evening as they sat together on the porch in the twilight.

"Yes," John agreed, "we all do. I always pray before I read – ask the Holy Spirit to show me what He wants me to know."

"Does that work?"

John shrugged. "Fairly often. If I can be still and listen."

"Do you remember Miles's sermon on Moses?"

"The one about 'the stubborn heart refusing?' I do."

"I'm trying to forget it. But it won't go away." Matthew stared at his feet, bare against the wooden floorboards. "You didn't tell me it would be so hard to be a Christian."

John shrugged again. "It seems to be harder for some than for others, and no one knows in advance who will have the most struggles. I do know nobody gets through without any struggles."

"Nobody?"

"Nobody. So don't beat yourself up about it, just ask forgiveness and try again."

Matthew scuffed one foot back and forth, risking splinters rather than eye contact. "I – I asked for a billboard, and I actually got one."

John chuckled. "I heard about that!"

"But all it said was 'pray.' I've been doing that – nothing."

John struggled to suppress another chuckle. "You're expecting to hear a Voice?"

"Well, yeah! Isn't that what you mean when you say you heard from God? The Bible says 'My sheep know my voice,' not 'My sheep get telegrams.'"

"Some people actually do hear voices, like Moses did. Some people see something like a TV movie inside their heads... But for most of us, most of the time, it's more like reading something in the Bible that strikes us, or hearing a phrase in a sermon like you did, or just having a – well, a strong impression that we should or shouldn't do something."

"Then how do you know you're right?"

"Good question. Sometimes – at least for me – it's about seeing how what I think I'm supposed to do lines up with what God says in His Word – because He would never ask me to do anything that contradicts His Word – then I do it and see what happens."

Matthew stopped scuffling and looked at John, now an indistinct blur in the falling dark.

"And if it turns out right, then I know I heard right. Other times, I also check with other people. And once in a while somebody says something out of the blue that confirms it to me."

"That's spooky!"

"No, that's reassuring. Anyhow, that's the way I do it." John stretched and stood. "Time to go to bed, brother. Morning comes early." He went into the house, closing the screen door gently. Matthew continued to sit there, watching the stars turn on like runway lights across the sky.

I can believe You talk to John, but I don't think You're talking to me. I wouldn't mind a made-for-TV movie. He waited for a few moments. *That's what I figured. Lord, it's hard to trust You and impossible to love You like this. I sort of know You're out there somewhere, but –*

Oh, nuts. Never mind. He turned his back on the skies and the prayer and trudged his way to bed.

Nineteen

"**Y**ou have mail," Carolyn said over her shoulder as she added canned fruit cocktail to some soupy red Jell-O. "I put it in your room since I was on my way upstairs anyway."

Matthew shuddered, looking at the Jell-O and almost feeling the squeak of canned peach and cherry bits on his teeth. "Thanks. I'll go up and shower and check it out before dinner." He took the stairs two at a time, curious. Other than one brief note from Miss Evvie of the Rough River Post Office, the only other letter he had ever received had come from the court, about Will.

On his taut, white bedspread Matthew found a long, white envelope imprinted with some legal-looking design and many words. His name was imprinted on the envelope, too, as if it came from a computer list. Above the legalese in the return address corner was hand-printed, "C. Horvath, MSW."

"Now what?" he said aloud, picking up the letter and looking at it warily. "Oh, well, what the heck - " He tore it open.

It seemed the second set of foster parents wanted to adopt Will, but Ms. Horvath wanted to be sure Matthew hadn't changed his mind...

He dropped onto the bed with a thump, staring at the letter. *Lord, what are you doing? Nothing has changed. I feel bad for the kid, but this thing is good, right? Adoption is good ... right?*

In the morning, after breakfast, Matthew made an excuse to go into town. He hadn't told anyone about the letter, but it wouldn't leave him alone. Parking in the side lot, Matthew entered the courthouse and climbed the three flights of marble steps to the agency's offices. Gulping a huge breath and blowing it out, he rang the bell.

"How may I help you?" asked a young woman with clouds of curly black hair from the other side of the sliding window.

"I'd like to see Ms. Horvath."

"Do you have an appointment?"

"No."

The woman's brow wrinkled delicately. "Well, you're supposed to make an appointment."

"Ma'am, I got a letter from her yesterday, and I need to see her."

"Then I'll make an appointment for you. She has an opening at ten-thirty next Wednesday morning - "

"No, ma'am, that's too late. Please just call her desk now and tell her Matthew Ryersen is here."

Apparently convinced by Matthew's determination, the young woman placed the call and explained the situation. When she hung up the phone, she buzzed him in through the heavy oak door.

"Please have a seat," she told Matthew. "Ms. Horvath will need about fifteen minutes more with her client."

Matthew sat, remembering the feel of the brown plastic chairs. Some old magazines sprawled untidily across the plastic table in the center of the room, but he was too nervous to read. His eyes caught the toy corner, which seemed exactly the same as the last time he had seen it. He changed his seat so his back was toward the battered trucks and dog-eared coloring books.

Just as Matthew was making up his mind that he was a fool to be there and should leave, he saw that same pair of sensible shoes striding toward him. Today a bright yellow blouse enlivened Cathy Horvath's light brown skin and copper freckles.

"Thank you for waiting," she said, smiling broadly. "Come on back to my office."

"Uh – no, ma'am, I don't figure to stay. I just had a question."

Cathy sat down one chair over. "All right." She waited, her smile not fading.

"About the kid – about Will – I just wondered – Those people who want to adopt him, do you like them? Do you trust them?"

"I see. They seem like nice people. They've been studied and approved by the State of Ohio. And Will seems to like them."

"That's good – that's good." Matthew stood abruptly. "Thank you, ma'am, that's all I wanted." He turned toward the door.

Cathy stood also, blocking his way. She had stopped smiling. "Obviously you're concerned about Will's well-being. Are you thinking about asking for your parental rights back? Because if you are, I want to help you. I've always felt – oh, I know it's not professional or scientific, but I've always felt you and Will belong together."

"Ms. Horvath, you-you're a nice lady, but you couldn't be more wrong. I do *not* want to be the kid's daddy. I just wondered, is all. Thanks for your time."

Driving home, Matthew tried to feel relief. *This could be the end of it. I never have to think of Will again. He'll be safe with his new parents. It's almost like it wasn't real – it never happened. And now that I know it's a sin to make love if you're not married, I won't ever have to worry again about makin' a kid. Because marriage is sure not in the works for me!*

Twenty

Summer came again, the fourth since Matthew had come to the farm, another marathon of copper sun that sucked the moisture out of the corn and cracked open the earth like Easter-egg shells. At just past noon he stood in the middle of an endless harvested wheatfield holding a baling hook, hands covered by sweat-soaked leather gloves, lower lip cracked like the ground before him, and flexed shoulders aching from baling the straw. The skin across his shoulder-blades, burned once too often, crinkled like carbon paper. Sweat prickled down his scalp with ants' feet to sting his eyes and tickle his ribs; he imagined it puddling in his shoes.

Through itchy eyes he watched the two teenaged boys John had hired to help with the baling. They laughed and teased one another as they swung the bales with an apparently endless supply of energy. He looked down the field at the work remaining and wondered if he had ever been that young and energetic and hopeful. He wondered if he would ever get out of this field. Maybe the heat would continue to suck the moisture from him as it did from the corn until he dropped and mummified there in the brassy stubble. *What difference would it make anyway?* he wondered. After this field came another, and another and another. If he lived to finish all these fields on time, they would go to neighboring farms to help with the harvests there.

His head ached from the relentless sun. His lungs, clogged with dust, labored to strain oxygen out of the soupy air. *It's no use,* he thought. *I can't do this job well enough or fast enough to make any difference.*

And then suddenly he thought, *I don't have to be here!*

Sinking his iron hook into the nearest bale, he stripped the wet gloves from his claustrophobic fingers and threw them into the wagon. Just short of a run, he headed across the field, his eyes fixed on the farmhouse, ignoring several voices calling his name, asking where he was going, whether he was all right. He ignored the chaff-dust that clogged his lungs and the trickle of blood from his split lip and the sunburn flaming across his back. *I don't have to be here.*

He plunged across the road without looking for traffic, ignoring the heat of the blacktop searing his feet through the heavy soles of his work shoes and rising in hallucinogenic waves around his face. He ignored the dust his rapid passage raised from the stone driveway, wiping it out of his eyes automatically. He took the porch steps in two giant bounds and slammed through the screen door into the living room. *I don't have to be here.*

This time he didn't appreciate, as he usually did, how cool and quiet the house was, set back from the road, shaded by oaks and maples, blinds drawn against the heat of the day. He didn't see this time, because his focus was so inward, all the things he had come to love about this living room: the old fireplace, with its moss-green ceramic tile facing and ornate Victorian mantelpiece; the farmer's huge worn leather chair, where he was free to sit; the family photos in mismatched frames crowding tables and bookshelves; the spinet piano he and David were learning to play. He didn't see any of it this time, just barged through and stormed the stairs to his room.

He closed the door behind him quickly, leaned against it as if keeping someone out - and as quickly straightened when his back screamed a protest. He heard, then, his own gasping breaths, felt his legs shaking, and forced himself to stand still for a minute. *Relax*, he told himself. *It's okay. You don't have to be here.*

He sank down on the edge of his bed and clenched his hands in the white candlewick spread he had neatly drawn over clean white sheets at four o'clock that morning. He looked around. After three years, it remained a spartan room: white walls, white linens, white cotton curtains at a white-shaded window. The dresser, chair and bedside table were plain, square varnished oak. The dresser top was bare; the chair had no cushion. The tabletop held an old-fashioned wind-up alarm clock, a white-shaded lamp, a Bic pen and a worn Bible. The only personal touch in the room was a beautifully-finished scrolled cherry-wood shelf. He had positioned it on the wall opposite the bed so he could see it as he lay there. It held a deep green pothos whose exuberant vines trailed down the wall and sideways across the tops of his books, a small collection which filled the rest of the shelf.

Now the peace he had created for himself in this room was not forthcoming. It seemed as small and barren and confining as the rest of his life. Cursing under his breath, he grabbed clean underwear and jeans from the dresser drawers and crossed the sunny hall to the bathroom.

Dropping filthy clothes on top of dusty shoes, he turned on the shower and stood beneath the cool spray for a long time, not washing, not thinking, just letting the water run over his upturned face and down his aching, itching body like tears. At last he soaped away dust and dirt and sweat until his hair squeaked and his skin was pink again. As he dried himself on a huge white towel smelling of sunshine and Clorox, he glimpsed himself in the mirror over the sink. The blue-gray eyes looking back at him were flat, eyes he had seen in the faces of hopeless men so many times, in so many towns, on his travels. He turned away.

In clean briefs and jeans, shirtless and barefoot, he dropped the wet towel on top of his dirty clothes and stepped back into the hall. Before he could reach the sanctuary of his room, David was there.

"You should wear a shirt today. Your sunburn is bad. Let's get Mama to put some of that plant stuff on it."

"It's fine. I don't need your mother's stuff. Go out and play." He turned away, but not before he saw David's eyes widen in surprise, his lively little face go still and sad. As he retreated into his room, he heard the boy's light footsteps fading away down the uncarpeted stairs.

I don't need this. I don't need to be here.

He threw open the closet door, dragged out an old duffel bag from the back and began to stuff his clothes into it hanger by hanger, then drawer by drawer. It overflowed; sweat popped out on his back and chest as he tried to stuff the last of his things back into it. With an oath of exasperation, he dumped out the whole bag in a mess in the middle of the bed. As his hands randomly selected some of this, some of that, and fitted it into the bag, his mind remembered arriving there in his only shirt and jeans, with nothing to carry but a cheap jean jacket. He looked around the room at the things he called "his" - the clothes, the plant, the shelf, the books - he even called it "his" room. An ache rose in his chest as he thought of leaving these things behind. For so long he had had nothing...

He ran his fingers over the glossy pothos leaves, over the satiny finish of the shelf. Carolyn had given him the plant, just a tiny start from one of her own, and it had flourished under his care. John had helped him find the right piece of wood for the shelf, helped him design the scrolling. Ed had taught him how to use the tools to make the shelf, and David had helped him sand it. Pearl had given him the first book on the shelf, the volume of collected poetry of Robert Frost. Matthew had been surprised how much he loved poetry.

With a sigh of regret, he took the Frost and left the other volumes. No room for all of them. As he turned to the bed, his glance fell on the table. He touched the worn cardboard cover of John's Bible with one finger. Sometimes he and John talked about it while they worked; sometimes he read it late at night, downstairs in John's chair, when he couldn't sleep and couldn't be quiet inside his head. He teased John about its being a "trade journal" because it had so many farming stories in it. But it was too big to fit into his bag unless he left the Frost. He zipped the bag with a loud, final sound.

As he turned toward the door, bag in hand, he heard quick, steady footsteps on the stairs. For the first time in three years, John entered Matthew's room without knocking. "Going?"

"What if I am? I don't have to be here."

"Of course you don't," John agreed. He crossed the room to sit on the straight chair. "But you might want your shoes and a shirt, and maybe something to eat."

Embarrassed and angry, Matthew stomped across the hall to retrieve his work shoes from the bathroom. He deliberately left the rest of his dirty clothes in a heap on the bathroom floor. Back in the bedroom, he fished a pair of socks from the tangle of clothes on the bed, pulled them on, stuffed his feet into the hot shoes under John's watchful gaze. Without a word, he took the bag again, put it down to pull on a wrinkled blue chambray work shirt, grabbed it a third time and headed down the stairs. John followed.

"Want to talk about it first?"

"No." Matthew turned toward the door.

Carolyn rushed in from the kitchen. Her small hands fluttered. "Are you leaving? What's wrong? Where are you going?"

"Nothing's wrong. I'm just going."

She turned to her husband, alarm sharpening her soft voice. "Can't you stop him? He can't just go!"

John put an arm around her shoulders as he shook his head. "I can't make a man stay if he's bound to go."

"But why?" she persisted. "What have we done? You're part of the family now!"

"You haven't done anything. I just don't want to be here or to do this – this - " he gestured wildly, taking in the house, the family, the unfinished fields - " - any of this - any more! I'm hot! I'm tired! I can't breathe! This isn't my farm, it isn't my crop, it isn't my responsibility!"

In the muted light of the shaded room, Matthew saw tears begin to well in Carolyn's eyes. He realized how much David looked like her, and how much it hurt to see either of them cry. Before he could say anything, though, John took one step toward him and said, through lips compressed to whiteness, "Go on then. You can run. You've been running from one thing or another all your life. You're good at it." John took out his wallet and held out a handful of bills. "I owe you for most of this week; this should help until you decide what to do. If you decide to stop running, give me a call."

Matthew shoved the money deep into his pocket, stepped through the door and down the porch steps. He listened for John's footsteps behind him, but all he heard was a katydid near the porch and what might have been Carolyn weeping inside the house. He headed down the driveway.

He was glad he had put on a shirt, because, in spite of the late afternoon sun glaring down on him, he was cold to the bone, the blood freezing in his veins and his heart turning to a lump of ice in his chest. The anger that had driven him out of the house didn't make it to the end of the driveway, but pride carried him on down the road and pride kept him from turning around to see whether anyone was following him, or even watching.

He hitched a ride into town with a neighbor, who asked no questions. He bought a bus-ticket as far west as his money would go and sat over hot coffee which never thawed him until the bus pulled in.

97

I'm sick of wheatfields. I'm sick of getting up at four a.m. to milk some-body else's cows. I'm going to go as far from Northwest Ohio as I can get, where nobody knows me and nobody tries to make me into something I'm not. I'll work in a gas station or stack cans in a supermarket - or drive a truck; I've had a lot of practice at that.

He boarded with half a dozen blank-faced strangers, found an empty seat and mostly slept his way across the country. In his waking moments he recited poetry to himself and watched telephone poles whiz by the bus window. He refused to wonder how the boys were doing in the wheatfield or whether Carolyn had stopped crying. *I'm sorry they're hurt - if they even are - but it's not my problem. I did my job. Now I want something else. I want - I want - Whatever it is, it isn't being tied to a farm and a bunch of farmers. I did enough of that before Granddaddy died. Look what it got me.* When his ticket ran out two days later, he found himself in another little town, Bucklin, Kansas, surrounded by ripe wheatfields.

After an hour or so of walking down the road west out of town, Matthew sat down on his bag at the side of the road, with silver-gold wheat behind and ahead as far as he could see, and laughed bitterly, alone again in a stranger's field, empty again of love or hope or any-thing but ice. *I don't want to be here, either! Oh, God, where am I supposed to go? What am I supposed to be?* Of course, there was no answer. Then he did hear a voice, and he recognized it. *You're noth-ing, and you're never gonna be anything but nothing. We'd have been better off if you'd never been born. Who needs a wimp like you? Nobody!* Finally he picked up his bag and kept on walking, because he didn't know what else to do.

Then Matthew heard a vehicle approaching from behind. He mentally catalogued it as a pick-up truck and turned, thumb out, to hitch a ride. Facing into the sun, he couldn't clearly see until the truck stopped beside him.

"Hop in," the farmer said.

Matthew stood very still. "What are you doing here? I didn't call."

"Funny - I thought you did," John replied. "And you forgot your Bible. I thought you might want it, even if you aren't ready to come home."

"How did you find me?"

"Oh, I asked around. They told me what your ticket read, so I headed for Bucklin. Thought I'd catch up with you sooner, but I missed a turn. I got to Bucklin maybe an hour behind the bus. Then there were only so many roads you could have taken." John smiled and opened the passenger door. "C'mon. Since I'm here, you might as well let me give you a lift."

Matthew continued to stand still. "I don't know where I'm going."

John's voice became very gentle. "Where would you like to go?"

He laughed a bit hysterically. "It doesn't matter! Everywhere I go, it's all wheatfields!"

The farmer nodded. "One harvest is pretty much like another. In a good wheat year like this, almost every farmer needs help. You can probably panhandle pretty well right now, too. That way, you never have to commit to anyone, or get close to anyone, or help anyone if you don't feel like it.

"So you can keep on running, 'til your shoes wear out or your knee acts up or you reach the ocean. And you'll still find wheatfields. Now, some people like to work in those faraway, out-of-the-way places. And some are really suited to going from place to place to help with other people's crops. The thing is, they're not running *from* something, they're going *to* something. So their bodies are on the move like yours, but their minds and hearts are resting."

"Did you drive all the way out here to give me a lecture?"

"No," came the gentle voice, "I drove all the way out here to offer you a ride home."

"Home."

"You know - how did Robert Frost say it? - 'that place where when you have to go there, they have to take you in'? Home. Your job, your room, your family. We miss you. We love you. We want you to come back."

Matthew met John's eyes for the first time, searching for truth. "You told me to go."

"I did. I was angry at you for just taking off like that, and for making Carolyn cry, and maybe my feelings were hurt, too. I'm sorry, Matthew, and I'm asking you to come back. Will you come?"

Matthew tossed his bag into the truck bed and crawled into the passenger seat. He fell asleep almost immediately. Later he would remember most of the long trip home as a vague blur of sleep and brief, dazed awakenings in truck-stops.

"You would have taken me somewhere else if I'd asked, wouldn't you?" he asked as they crossed from Indiana into Ohio.

"Yep. I've always told you there are no strings." John grinned, and his eyes sparkled. "But I was counting on you to decide to come home."

Matthew glanced sideways and returned a faint smile to John's grin. "How could you know that when I didn't?" Then even that faint smile faded. "We'll be there pretty soon. Are you sure they - I mean - " Anxiety clouded his face and shortened his breath. *What if they don't want me?*

John's expression became serious and determined. His hands gripped the wheel firmly, but he turned his head to make direct eye contact. "We all miss you; we all want you back. No matter how many times someone gets angry, no matter how many times you leave, once you're part of the family you'll always be wanted at home. Even if you leave over and over, every time you do, someone will come after you - to be sure you're all right and have everything you need, and to ask you to come home."

Matthew frowned, the words pouring into his head like a code he couldn't quite decipher. "Why would you do that? Why bother? You can always find another farmhand."

John smiled again. "You're right. We can find another hand. But he won't be you. So we'll still need you, and we'll still want you. Because, no matter what, we'll still love you."

Before Matthew could even begin to decode that last remark, the truck was coming to a stop by the front porch of the farmhouse. David was sitting on the second step. He saw them pull in but remained seated there, still and watchful.

Matthew climbed stiffly out of the truck. He walked over to the porch and squatted down carefully in front of David. "I'm home."

The boy met his gaze but remained silent and unsmiling.

"I thought I had to go - but I had to come back."

The boy nodded but said nothing.

"I'm sorry I yelled at you. I was wrong. I know you were trying to help me. And - and I'm sorry I left without saying good-bye."

David nodded again, his face still solemn. Just before the silence grew too painful to bear, he leaned forward and wrapped his arms around Matthew's neck.

Matthew took the boy into his arms, close enough to feel the light, rapid heartbeat and to smell the tang of little-boy sweat. "I went hundreds of miles away," he murmured into the downy blond hair, "and all I saw was wheatfields. I learned some things in all those days, and then we pulled up and there you were, sitting on the steps."

David leaned back to look into his face. "What did you learn?"

"I learned how cold and lonely alone is, and something about how much people care, and what matters to me the most." He drew the boy close again and said in a roughened whisper, "I love you." He cleared his tight throat and repeated more strongly, "I love you."

He sat on the second step and took David onto his lap. The boy nestled against his chest and they sat quietly for a few moments as the afternoon sun waned. Matthew thought about the apology he owed Carolyn for the mess he had left in the bathroom. She would accept his apology, hug him, and tease him a lot. *Because she loves me*, he thought, *and that's the way families act.*

David stirred in his arms. "You can put me down now. I gotta help set the table." The boy hurried up the steps, but he paused at the door. "Aren't you coming?" A tiny worry line creased the little forehead.

"Yeah," Matthew said, rising and stretching. "I'm coming." He turned for a brief look at the fields, all harvested now, waiting for the plows to turn under the dark stubble to begin the cycle all over again. *At least*, he said to himself, *it'll be corn next spring. I can use a break from wheatfields.* With another laugh at himself, he hoisted the boy onto his shoulders and entered the house. "I'm home," he hollered, and it sounded sweet in his ears.

Twenty-One

Matthew followed Ed a bit stiffly up the back steps into the kitchen to clean up for lunch. With a wry grin, he gave thanks to the God of tractors that his vertebrae were not permanently frozen into a C-curve from spending the morning bent over the John Deere. He doubted he would ever walk fully upright again and wondered how Ed, who was at least fifteen years older than he, could be moving with such a quick, springy step after having been bent over beside him all morning, patiently instructing.

Carolyn, removing a pan of biscuits from the oven, glanced up with a smile at their arrival. Her cheeks were red from the heat, almost matching her apron; the color deepened the blue of her eyes to resemble the pansies she grew on the sunny side of the house. Those eyes narrowed at the smudged faces and grease-blackened hands of the two men.

"Oh, no, you don't!" she laughed. "Out! Use the porch sink!"

Exchanging an exaggerated look about the unreasonableness of women, they followed her instructions. By the time they returned, as pink, damp and shiny as five-year-olds, the table was filled with stew and biscuits and salad and corn. With a pang, Matthew remembered days on end of being so hungry his belly hurt. From the corner of his eye he saw David filch a piece of biscuit and pop it into his rosy mouth. Remembering hunger so vividly, Matthew was hard-pressed not to do the same. His "amen" to John's blessing was unusually fervid, drawing an amused look. He didn't care. He finished the first biscuit without waiting for butter or jam and had made headway on the second before the stew came around to him.

The chatted a little as they ate - the pleasant Indian-summer warmth of mid-October, the parts Ed had needed for the tractor. David made a wall of potato chunks across his plate to keep the gravy from touching the salad. Then he picked the tomatoes out of his salad and drove them like lemmings over the edge of his plate. When his mother quietly suggested this was not appropriate to civilized dining, the boy burst into tears and ran from the room.

The grown-ups looked at one another in mild surprise. David wasn't given to tantrums.

Before they could remark it, the boy was back, tears still damp on his cheeks, blue eyes huge with wonder. "You gotta see!" he cried. "Celeste is having kittens!" He grabbed Matthew's hand and pulled. "C'mon! She's having them on your bed!"

Ed roared with laughter. "Solomon and Sheba! You're a daddy!"

At David's urging, Matthew rose and followed, up the stairs. Sure enough, the dusty-brown tabby had delivered a large litter in the middle of his clean white bedspread. "Oh, Celeste," he groaned, "how could you? You're a barn cat. You never come into the house." Celeste gave him a smug feline wink and began to tidy up the kittens.

David was enthralled. "Look! There's seven! Seven: four like Celeste, one calico and two black. The calico's gotta be a girl. Mama says only girl cats are calicos. Mama says they don't open their eyes til later. Mama says... Oo, they squeak!"

"You live on a farm. Haven't you ever seen kittens before?"

"Well, sure. But never just borned. They always have 'em in the barn and hide 'em. Celeste must really like you a lot to have 'em in your room."

"Yeah. Thanks a lot, Celeste." As he ruefully surveyed his once-clean bed and wondered how to move the little family without getting shredded, Matthew noticed one of the tabby kittens wasn't moving. Celeste had nosed it aside as she tended the others.

"I'm afraid there will only be six," he said. "That one's dead."

Horror crossed the little face. "No!" David cried. "You fix it! Make it not dead!"

"I can't do that. I'm sorry, David, honest I am. But dead things can't come back to life." He reached toward David to offer comfort, but the boy struck his hand away. The little face turned red with anger and tears welled up.

"Liar! You're a liar! My daddy can fix it!" David grabbed the limp kitten with both hands and ran back down the stairs screaming for his father.

"Oh, Celeste," Matthew sighed, slumping down on the foot of the bed, "why did you have to go and do that?" Celeste, as usual, ignored him. She continued to ignore him as he cleared everything out of the bottom drawer of the dresser and padded it with a worn-out towel. She ignored him as he filled the saucer from under his pothos with water and placed it on the floor by the dresser. And fortunately she ignored him as he ever so gently transferred her and the kittens to the drawer. He changed the sheets. By the time he returned from putting the soiled linens into the washer, cat and kittens were ensconced again in the middle of his bed.

"So," Matthew asked her, "am I supposed to sleep in the drawer?"

As Celeste chirruped what seemed a decided affirmative, he wandered over to the window overlooking the back yard and the fields beyond. There by the lilac bush he saw John digging a hole. David watched, holding a Velveeta Cheese box reverently in both hands. There was no doubt the box coffined the kitten. As Matthew looked, the boy saw him and gestured for him to come down. He nodded and went at once.

As he approached, David smiled at him. "My daddy says for now only Jesus came alive again. For now, dead is dead - except for the part of people that goes straight to Jesus. Someday, though, my daddy says, we'll all come alive again with Jesus. But now we have to have funerls to - um, to show - respect. That's it, respect! Because God made us."

"I see," Matthew responded gravely, taking his cue from John's serious expression. "Thank you for inviting me to the funeral."

They laid the kitten to rest with a brief prayer thanking God for all things great and small and commending them to his care. Matthew offered to return the shovel to the tool shed and invited David to go with him. They went in silence, a contrast to the boy's usual chatter. Matthew figured the child must be pondering life and death. It was a topic he himself avoided as much as possible, so he was glad not to have to answer any of David's usual flow of questions. They parted company at the shed, Matthew to return to the tractor, the boy to wander listlessly back toward the house.

As Matthew entered the barn, he heard the farmhand say, "Oh, Psalms and Proverbs!" in an exasperated voice.

"What's that about?" he asked with amusement as he approached the tractor.

Ed rose slowly from beneath the green monster, wrapping a blue bandana around his knuckles. "Wrench slipped."

"You okay?"

"Yeah, fine. Bloody but unbowed, I think the saying goes."

Laughing companionably, they went back to work on the tractor. Matthew considered the last few hours: he had never heard the boy say less, rarely heard Ed say more. It felt good to be working alongside this strong, quiet man who had first literally led him into the family. He knew he could learn much more than farm machinery from Ed. In his own way, the farmhand had as much to teach as the farmer.

Shortly before supper, they congratulated each other at the smooth sound of the John Deere engine, only to be shot down by Pearl, who remarked, "Took you all afternoon? You should have been done by lunch."

Dessert was apple dumplings with fresh cream and well worth a fervent request for seconds, but Pearl had made only one apiece. As Matthew stifled a childish pout, David came to his rescue.

"Here. You can have mine. I don't want it."

He looked sharply at David, then at Carolyn. She was studying the child intently. "Are you sure?" Matthew asked.

"I *said* I didn't want it!" the boy snapped. He shoved the dish toward Matthew so hard the thick, opalescent cream sloshed over the edge and slowly soaked into the tablecloth.

John frowned. "Now, that's enough," he began, but was stopped by his wife's small hand on his forearm.

"He doesn't feel well today," Carolyn said quietly. She rose and went to the boy, placed a hand on the side of his face and led him from the table. He went unprotesting up the stairs.

The untouched dumpling sat like a fat obscenity in its pool of curdling cream. Matthew looked away from it, feeling queasy, and gestured toward it to Ed.

"Naw, I don't think so. Guess I'm full." They excused themselves quickly and went outside. Something about the house felt unsettled to both of them, though neither could define it.

§ § §

David ran a fever for several days and stayed home from school. Matthew spent his spare time lying next to David on the bed in the boy's room telling stories about the constellations glued onto the ceiling, teaching him a poem by Stevenson about sailing boats down the river. David slept a lot, but he didn't complain much when Matthew was there. Matthew was surprised, then, when he bumped David's leg and the boy yelped.

"I'm sorry! I didn't mean to hurt you."

"Well, you did," the boy sniffed, rubbing his calf.

"Let me see," Matthew said, reaching for the leg of David's pajamas. He was horrified to find a huge, dark blue mark. "Aw, David, did I do that?"

Mollified by Matthew's concern, the child dismissed his injury. "I don't know. It's okay. Read me the rabbit-in-the-moon book again, please."

Matthew continued to feel guilty and was careful of how he approached David. The next day he noticed a bruise on the back of the boy's hand, and another on his knee. "I didn't do that, did I?"

"No," David said, "they're just there. They only hurt if you press 'em."

By Sunday David was jumping around like a flea and demanding to be released from bed. His mother was too weary of his demands to argue any more, and David went back to school on Monday.

As the week progressed, Matthew and David enjoyed resuming their piano lessons. They sailed David's new boat on the pond and stargazed one warm night on a blanket on the lawn.

"You kept David up too late last night," Carolyn teased over lunch. "He didn't want to get up for school this morning."

Matthew smothered a yawn. "More like he kept me up. Four o'clock came way too early today."

On Saturday the family went to the Seibeneks' for the afternoon so the boys could all play together. Mid-afternoon David came into the kitchen, where the wives were preparing dinner, and plunked down on a chair.

"What's the matter, David?" Livvie asked. "You look kinda sad."

"No," he sighed dramatically, "I'm just tired."

"Would a cookie make you feel better?" Livvie offered.

David shook his head. "No, thanks. I'll just go sit with Daddy for a while."

"That's odd," Livvie observed. "He's usually bouncing around until you get him in a headlock."

Carolyn frowned. "I think – I hope – he's just not completely over that bug he had."

By the middle of the next week it was clear to Carolyn that something was wrong with David. "I've made an appointment with Nate for tomorrow afternoon," she told John as he helped her with the dishes. "He had a fever again this afternoon, and he hardly ate any supper."

"I noticed he's a little quiet. Well, if anyone can figure it out, Nate Hanna can."

Ed and Matthew had noticed David's disinterest in dinner. As they walked out together, Ed remarked, "Huh. Boy ain't right."

"Yeah."

They worked off their uneasiness checking the stock, the barns and the near fences. It was a long, clear twilight, quietly musical as flocks of blackbirds and sparrows settled in for the night. Everything was as it should be, so Matthew didn't understand the constant prickle at the back of his neck, the ping! of adrenaline in the pit of his stomach. As they strolled off toward Ed's little house across the road, he admitted: "I feel funny. Something isn't right."

"Yep."

"Well, what is it?"

"Don't know."

"But you do feel it?"

"Yep." Ed leaned against the porch, hands in his pockets. He seemed as calm as always.

"So what do you do when you know something isn't right, but you don't know what?" Matthew was pacing in a tight circle of frustration at the farmhand's nonchalance.

"Gotta get up at four, so I'm going to bed."

"That's it? You're going to bed?"

"Well, while I'm showering and brushing my teeth, I'll mention it to the Lord. And when I hit my knees, I'll put us all together under His hand like I do every evening and morning."

Matthew was suddenly aghast. "You pray in the shower? While

you're naked?"

"Don't usually shower with my clothes on," Ed laughed. "You think God don't see you naked, son?" He laughed again, then sobered. "Look here. Something's wrong, but God's in control. So it all comes right, in the end. Jesus said not to worry about anything, and - mostly - I don't. I trust Him. You might try that." He grinned and waved as he took both steps at once and disappeared into the house.

Left alone in the small yard, Matthew looked back across the road at the farmhouse, still visible in the navy blue light of early evening. Lights were warm beacons from many of its windows, which stood open to the mild air. He thought he heard music from an upstairs window. For miles across the open fields everything was quiet, everything was peaceful. He headed home, shaking his head as if to clear it of unpleasant thoughts. Maybe he would try praying on his knees one of these nights. He knew John and his wife prayed on their knees. But he would *not* pray in the shower. *No, sir!* he thought, *I shower alone!*

§ § §

In the long dark of three a.m., Matthew woke with such a start he sat straight up on the narrow strip of bed Celeste and the kittens allowed him. His hands were sweaty; his heart thumped audibly, shaking his chest. His ears strained to hear while his dilated pupils sieved the thick silt of darkness for stray particles of light. Nothing.

Had it been a dream? Celeste gave him a token growl for disturbing her rest. One kitten squeaked, then another. Tiny suckling sounds began, followed by the nursing mother's contented purr. Still he could not relax.

"Okay," he muttered. "Here goes." Stealthily he moved to his knees beside the bed, furtively folded his hands and bowed his head. Inside his mind, where no one could overhear him, he began to pray.

Remembering his first time on his knees, just before Christmas the year before, Matthew gave thanks for his salvation, for Christ's death on his behalf. He renewed his vow never to hurt God or anyone else again. He gave a passing thought to how he was doing in that regard and decided he was doing very well. Smug satisfaction filled him and he slipped from prayer into a daydream, where those who loved him praised his growth and his goodness. He smiled to himself and started to climb back into bed.

To his surprise, he found himself back on his knees, bent forward so far his forehead rested on his outstretched palms on the floor. The smug pleasure had been routed by horrible anxiety, as the family whose praise he had been imagining began to tumble through his mind in turmoil. Waves of feelings swamped him, held him flat on the floor. He couldn't tell whether it was his pain or someone else's. He was terrified, cowering, needing to cry out but unable to make a sound. *God help me!* he screamed inside his head.

Then he heard his own anguished voice praying out loud, "God, help them! Help them! Please help them!"

And then he heard David crying, Carolyn calling, John speaking quickly.

Freed to stand, Matthew headed for the door to break his own rule against intruding on the family's privacy. As he reached for the handle, John was already there, feet shoved into shoes without socks, shirt unbuttoned, speaking urgently: "His fever is high - we're taking him to the emergency room - " and turning toward David's room before the last words were even out of his mouth.

Matthew watched from his doorway as John scooped up the white-faced, trembling boy quilts and all and ran down the stairs. Carolyn ran behind him, barefoot, her shoes in her hand, wearing only her cotton nightgown and robe. The truck roared to life immediately and reeled away into the night, scattering gravel in its wake. They had left the front door open. As Matthew closed it, through the little window he saw a light come on in the farmhand's house across the road. Four a.m. Another day beginning. He went back upstairs to dress.

Twenty-Two

As Matthew came back downstairs, he heard the back door open, the light switch snick! as the farmhand came in for coffee. He heard a sigh, then the sounds of the coffee-maker being filled and turned on. Ed looked up from his seat at the kitchen table. "Where's everybody?"

"They took David to the hospital just a little bit ago." Matthew sat down opposite the farmhand. "He had a high fever. They just grabbed him up and ran down the stairs. She - she went in her night-gown, in her bare feet, with her shoes in her hand. They left the front door wide open."

"Coffee'll be ready in a minute," Ed said. "Maybe you'd like to join me in a prayer while we're waiting." His usually cheerful face was serious.

"Well -uh- sure... But I don't know how to..."

"Just kinda hum along, then, until we get to the chorus," Ed offered, a ghost of his grin returning.

They bowed their heads and the farmhand began to praise the Lord for being faithful. As he listened to the simple words and calm voice, Matthew wondered how the man could be so comfortable with the process, so patient about getting to the point. His own mind was racing ahead, shouting an incoherent plea into the darkness.

As Ed's prayer droned on, Matthew's mind became quieter, and he mentally whispered, *Please. Please. Just as he says. Please.* He echoed Ed's firm "amen."

"Now," said the farmhand, "coffee and then chores."

Around seven, after chores, as Matthew was washing their few breakfast dishes, John called. "They're admitting him. I don't know when we'll be home."

Matthew carefully replaced the receiver and banged his fist on the wall beside it. He wanted to slam the mugs into the sink just to hear them crack apart against the porcelain. Instead, he washed and dried everything with fast, hard strokes and put it all away as roughly as he dared, relishing the clatter of heavy china pieces against each other.

Ed came in with Pearl as Matthew was sweeping the floor. "How long does it *take* to do up a few dishes?"

Pearl marched up to him and took the broom. "This floor is clean enough. Go change your clothes. I'm going to get some things together for you to take to the hospital. Go on!" Matthew went.

He drove John's car with exaggerated care and parked far back in the visitors' lot, where no one would be likely to hit it. Brown paper grocery bag on his arm, he went to the information desk and gave David's name.

The middle-aged, middle-brown, middle-bored volunteer in her middle-green smock looked at him over her glasses. "No visitors. No gifts."

Matthew's first impulse, born of those years of rejection, was to turn silently and go. But he thought of David's white face, Carolyn's small bare feet.

"I'm not a visitor," he claimed. "I'm family. Where is he?"

"PICU. Third floor."

"What is that?" Matthew asked, "and where?"

"Pediatric Intensive Care Unit, north end of the third floor. Elevator's right over there."

The elevator opened into the middle of a long yellow hallway. A stencil of red and blue balloons ran down the center of each wall. A sign opposite the elevator directed Matthew to turn to his right. He followed tiny yellow shoeprints down a navy blue stripe of tile along the hallway. The stillness was eerie to him, nothing to see but closed doors with strange labels, nothing at all to hear.

At the end of the hall a closed double door stopped him. "Pediatric Intensive Care Unit," the sign read, followed by a long list of rules, on which Matthew wasted no time. Like a knight-errant, he adjusted his mental armor, drew his mental sword and charged through the door.

The dragon wore white from toe to cap and stood just a fraction over five feet tall. Her nametag read "Allison West, R.N." She was so pretty and so fierce that Matthew dropped his sword before she even opened her mouth. He softly spoke the boy's name. "I just - uh - I brought some clothes for his mother."

The dragon turned into a princess as Allison smiled. "Oh, that's good of you! We gave her some scrubs, but I know she'll be glad to have her own things."

"David. How is he?"

The smile disappeared, replaced by Allison's professional face. "His parents are in the waiting room, just over there," she said. Then she left Matthew so abruptly a cold breeze seemed to sweep away behind her.

He silently approached the waiting room. Several small groups of people huddled in the corners of the room as if they were trying to keep as much distance as possible between them. Carolyn, in faded blue cotton drawstring pants and baggy shirt, sat on a short orange couch with her feet tucked under her, her hands pleating the hem of the shirt. John stood at the east window, facing into the early morning light. His hands gripped the marble sill. He didn't move.

Carolyn saw Matthew first. She held out one hand to him while the other remained busy with her shirt. He went to her, took her hand, sat beside her. "I brought you some clothes."

Carolyn smiled just a little as she took the bag. "Thank you. I'll go put them on. John can tell you..." She fled to the restroom.

John had been listening. He came to sit beside Matthew on the orange plastic seat. "Thank you for coming," John said formally. Then he looked down at his hands and said no more.

Strange, cold prickles crawled on Matthew's scalp. "Do they know what's wrong?"

John nodded. He didn't look up.

Icy sweat beaded on Matthew's hairline and upper lip. "Please!"

"He has some kind of leukemia."

"Just like that? With no warning? He was fine the day before yesterday!"

"I know." John continued to stare at his hands.

"So what are they going to do? How do they cure it?"

"They don't." The farmer's voice was flat.

"No!" He leaped to his feet. "No! That can't be right! Another, bigger hospital, another doctor..."

"Dr. Hanna called St. Jude's in Memphis. They prescribed a course of chemotherapy. We'll try it. He's too sick to be moved." John finally met Matthew's eyes. "But most of all, we'll pray. Medicine doesn't offer much hope, but God - God works miracles all the time."

Matthew saw the farmer's intense gaze from a far distance, as if John were one of those red balloons from the hallway floating away on a long, long string. He sat down on the floor. John dropped down beside him.

"Oh, no, you don't!" Allison snapped. "Come back here!" She slapped him, just hard enough to sting. He looked at her obediently. "That's better," she smiled.

As quickly as she had come, she was gone.

"While we're down here..." John suggested.

Matthew looked at John in surprise, then at the dozen or so other people clustered around the room pretending not to look. *Oh, no, not now. Not in front of all these people. Not on our* knees *in front of all these people!*

"Please," John said.

Matthew had no idea how long they had knelt there, praying, sometimes silently, sometimes out loud. He knew Carolyn had joined them, and Pastor Corrigan and his wife, and several other men and women from the church. He remembered a man's voice raised in objection, the princess-dragon's fire-breathing response driving off the objection. Matthew never opened his eyes, never ceased to batter the gates of heaven with his single petition.

At last Carolyn gently touched his shoulder. Matthew looked into her pale, worried face. "He wants to see you," she said.

Matthew leaped to his feet, rushing after her to the small glass cubicle opposite the nurses' station where the boy lay as motionless as a human sacrifice, bound by tubes and wires. All around him machines hummed and clicked and beeped. His feathery, pale hair was darkened by sweat and stuck to his forehead, angling out stiffly at the sides where he had fretfully tossed his head. Huge purple shadows ringed his closed eyes and ugly bruises mottled his bony bare chest and arms.

Beside Matthew, Carolyn took and released a long, trembly

breath. He watched her square her shoulders and smooth her face into a calm smile before she stepped up to the bed. He knew he must do the same.

As he gently stroked the damp hair, David opened his eyes. The clear sky-blue was clouded by pain and fever; the boy seemed to take a long moment to come back from wherever he had been, to focus and to recognize his friend. Then he smiled, showing his pearly little teeth.

"I need my boat," he said.

His mother intervened, "Sweetheart, you can't have your boat in here. In a few days, when you go to another room, if you still want it..."

David ignored her completely, focusing all his will and attention on Matthew. His voice was barely a whisper, but his determination was powerful. "I need my boat."

Matthew understood that something powerful was happening, although he couldn't grasp the nature of it. "Okay," he promised, "I'll get it."

David smiled again, relaxed, and closed his eyes.

Back in the waiting room, Matthew traded keys with John, telling him where the car was parked. He pulled on his coat and headed for the door. On his way down the hall, Allison West stopped him.

"Do you really believe in that prayer stuff?" she asked.

Matthew searched her face for mockery or sarcasm but could find only honest curiosity and some deeper feeling. "Well, yeah," he said slowly, learning as he spoke, "I really do."

"You think God's going to heal that little boy?"

"Yes. I do."

Her hand seemed to burn through the sleeve of Matthew's coat. "Then he'd better hurry!" she cried fiercely. Before he could respond, Allison was gone again, leaving behind on his sleeve a single tear.

§ § §

As Matthew parked the truck by the front porch, Ed approached from the barn and Pearl came to the door, wiping her hands on her apron. They gathered at the foot of the stairs inside and he told them what John had said.

"Matthew, Mark, Luke, John, Acts, Romans!" Ed expostulated,

turning away to wipe his eyes surreptitiously on his blue bandanna.

The old woman seemed to sag and grow smaller for just a moment. Then she straightened again. "I'll call the church to be sure it's on the prayer chain," she said, "and have some of the women's group make casseroles. And you," she said to the farmhand, "quit that swearing and call the neighbors to get some help over here for the farm."

"Yes, ma'am," Ed agreed meekly. He left at once.

"And *you*, take that child his boat."

"Yes, ma'am," Matthew echoed and took the steps to David's room in great bounds. The room had been cleaned since that morning. The untidy mess of sheets and pillows was neatly made and covered with a blue/beige/green dinosaur-printed spread which matched the curtains. The little cars and big trucks and Legos and Lincoln Logs and storybooks and crayons were regimented in orderly display on the bright blue shelves. The carpet had been vacuumed.

Matthew stood there a moment, feeling uneasy prickles along the back of his neck. The room was so neat and clean he couldn't feel David's presence. The boy was a busy, messy child, always into several things at once. He hated to waste time picking up his toys and always left things where they lay until his mother threatened to throw them out. He bounced on his bed and made indoor tents with his blankets. When he made his own bed, the result was lumpy and crooked, nothing like this sterile, military precision.

Matthew gave himself a small shake and crossed to the desk to gather up the three-masted schooner he had made for David last Christmas. It held the place of honor on a special platform. But the boat was not just for show; they had sailed it in the pond all summer. It was beautifully crafted, carefully detailed, completely seaworthy - a big improvement over Matthew's first crude attempt three years before. He carefully carried it down to the truck and placed it on the passenger seat for the drive back to the hospital.

On the return trip he parked much closer to the visitors' entrance. Any farm truck worthy of its tires had nicks and dings galore anyway. A few more wouldn't make any difference. He tucked the boat under his arm and headed straight to the elevator, bypassing the volunteer at the information desk.

On the third floor, going through the PICU double doors, Matthew was again accosted by the tiny dragon-princess. Although not quite breathing fire, she made it clear he could *not* take the boat into David's cubicle. Matthew listened politely, nodding his understanding. Then he stepped around her and went on down the hall.

"Now just wait a minute!" Allison snapped. "Did you hear me?"

He turned back. "Yes, ma'am, of course I did," he replied with mild surprise. "He needs this boat, though. He asked for it."

Allison's face softened. "I know he wants it. But no toys or flowers are allowed in ICU. It's because of germs."

"Germs aren't what this is about, miss. He could be dying - you said so - and he needs this boat. I am going to give him this boat."

She moved back and allowed him to continue without saying anything more. His quiet but absolute determination had quite vanquished her.

In David's glass cage, his parents flanked the bed, mother sitting on the near edge, father standing at the far. They looked up to acknowledge Matthew's entrance. Carolyn called the boy's name in a low voice and added, "Look who's here to see you!"

David frowned and winced several times before he opened his eyes. The effort of lifting his eyelids seemed almost too much for him. Then he saw Matthew and smiled.

That pallid little smile directed only at him almost broke Matthew's heart. Swallowing a lump of grief the size of Texas, he smiled back and held out the boat. "Hi, buddy. See what I brought you?"

David took in the man, the boat, and then, to everyone's horror, began to cry. First the tears just filled his eyes, but then he began to weep great, choking sobs, gasping almost unintelligibly, "I need my boat! I *need* my boat!"

Matthew was genuinely confused and tried to reassure the boy, putting the boat right next to him on the bed. But David became even more agitated, trying with his weak, pinioned little hand to push the boat onto the floor. "No, no, no, no! I need my boat!"

Carolyn was crying, too, trying to keep the child from hurting himself or pulling out the i.v. lines. John stood very still, his jaw locked against any show of emotion. "Get that thing out of here!" he demanded harshly.

Matthew snatched up the boat and nearly ran from the room, David's weakening cry chasing him down the hall: "I need my boat! I need my boat!"

116

Twenty-Three

Brushing past the dragon-princess without seeing her, Matthew slammed through the double doors into the cheery yellow hallway. He aimed for the elevator, fell against the down button and hung there, panting, until the door opened into an empty car. He stumbled inside, pressed "lobby" and clung to the rail. When the machine spat him out, he fled to the truck, bumping into people, striking his shoulder on the doorframe as he left the building, finally collapsing behind the wheel.

Only then, sealed in the silent capsule of the truck, did he allow his mind to be engaged again. He permitted himself to see David's boat there in his hand, the boy's face contorted with grief and his weak voice wailing, "I need my boat." He drove home automatically, constantly replaying those painful moments where he had failed the boy, wounded Carolyn, angered John - and he didn't know why.

Reentering the silent farmhouse, Matthew carried the schooner back upstairs to David's room and replaced it carefully on its display platform. Although the Mickey Mouse clock said barely noon, he was exhausted. He lay down on top of David's dinosaur spread, feet hanging over the edge of the bed, and stared at the glow-in-the-dark stars and planets John had glued to the ceiling. At night, they gave off a greenish glow, teaching David the constellations and taking away his fear of the dark.

Matthew had spent several nights lying here beside David until the boy fell asleep, holding off the dark with star-stories. They had laid outside on summer nights, watching real stars and finding the rabbit in the moon from the Japanese folk-tale. David loved that sad story of lost love, had made him tell it over and over. The first song they had learned together on the piano was "Twinkle, Twinkle, Little Star."

Matthew smiled, remembering, acknowledging David was much better at the piano than he but refused to continue lessons without him. "Oh, God, please," he begged aloud. "Please don't take him. He's so little - and he's still afraid of the dark."

No one acknowledged Matthew's prayer; no one ever did. Sometimes, like these, he envied those around him who remarked with such certainty, "The Lord says..." *All I know is what I read in the Book,* he grumbled to himself, swinging up into a sitting position. *And I don't know what it says about sick kids. Maybe there's a clue in the index.*

As he headed for the door to fetch his Bible, something made Matthew stop, almost as if someone had called his name. "The *old* boat!" he said aloud. "He wants the *old* boat."

The old boat was nowhere in sight, although the shelves around the room held enough other toys and books for several little boys. Fatigue banished by a sense of mission, Matthew plowed through the dresser drawers, crawled half-way under the bed, burrowed into the closet. Nothing. Had they thrown it out?

Frustrated, he turned in a slow circle, looking for any place he might have missed. *I need to go downstairs,* he thought then, *to the piano. It's on the piano.*

"You know, you're nuts," Matthew told himself aloud as he clattered down the stairs. The clatter of the wood quieted to muffled thumps as he hurried across the deep green carpet in the living room. The piano sat primly against the far wall, keys covered. Half a dozen primary music books crowded the music stand. "Really nuts," he added, reaching behind the music stand.

The boat lay on its side there, hidden by the clutter of songbooks.

"How the hell did I know that?"

"Better try 'Hosea, Ezekiel, Leviticus, Lamentations," laughed Ed from behind him.

Matthew spun around, embarrassed, boat in hand.

"Haven't seen that one in a while," Ed remarked. "What's up?"

"I took the boat, the triple-masted one, and it - it upset him. He cried real hard and kept saying, 'I need my boat.' He tried to push the other one onto the floor, so I brought it back. Then I - uh - I thought maybe he wants this one."

"Let's rustle up some lunch, then you can take it to him."

"I'm not hungry. I'll just go - "

"Hungry or not, you gotta keep up your strength. I can't work this whole place by myself."

Ed bullied him into the kitchen and put him to work setting the table and microwaving a spaghetti casserole. The farmhand deftly sliced carrots, celery, a turnip into even sticks, remarking amiably, "Don't quite trust you with sharp objects right now. But maybe you could pour us some milk, if you use plastic glasses."

"Sure will," Matthew teased, "but I might drop the carton while I'm walking past you. Wanna take the chance?"

They sat down together at one end of the large table. As he bent his head to ask a silent blessing, scents of garlic, tomato and turnip turned Matthew's stomach. He slid his chair back abruptly.

"No," Ed admonished. "Get a grip. You don't help nobody by getting sick or moping around. The worse it is, the more this family needs you. It's time to think about somebody besides yourself."

Matthew was dumbstruck by his friend's acerbic, unexpected dressing-down. Silently he spooned the red-drenched pasta onto his plate, but he couldn't put it into his mouth. Still unspeaking, he went to the breadbox, fetched out a loaf of Pearl's homemade bread. Ignoring the serrated bread knife, he tore a chunk from the loaf and carried it back to his place. By chewing each bite for a long time and washing it down with milk, he was able to eat all of it.

Ed nodded his approval. "That's the idea. Now go on back to the hospital while I clean up here."

For the second time that day, Matthew placed a boat on the passenger seat and piloted the truck to a safe berth in the hospital parking lot. He sat there looking at his very first wood-carving effort, remembering how difficult it had been to draw the image from his mind out of the wood, how awkward his hands had been with the tools, how many times he had slipped, cutting himself or marring the wood. Although it was recognizable as a sail-boat, it was clumsy and ponderous. It had never sailed very well, but David had loved it. They had forged their friendship while painting the little boat and sailing it on the pond for three summers. When Matthew had given the boy the new schooner for Christmas, though, this boat had been put aside at once. Why had David been playing with it again? Why did he want it now?

Only one way to find out, Matthew thought. *Here goes.*

The nurse on duty glanced briefly over him and waved him on. He stood on the threshold of David's cubicle like a wary deer testing the wind at the edge of a meadow. Something had changed in that small space, and he needed to understand it.

David still lay tiny and motionless in the huge white expanse of hospital bed. The machines continued their mechanical background conversation. John was still on the far side of the bed, kneeling now on the cold, stone floor, hands folded on the edge of the bed, forehead resting on his knuckles. Carolyn still sat on the near edge of the bed, her eyes intent on the boy's still face, one hand holding his hand, the other endlessly stroking his hair and the side of his face.

"Come closer," she said without looking up. "It's all right. He's asked for you several times, and for his boat. Then he just - drifts away..." Her soft voice quivered, but her gentle hand never faltered.

Matthew came to stand beside her, reviewing the scene. Blood and some other fluids were being transfused into David's arm at a rapid rate. David's breathing seemed faster and shallower. His soft little mouth and small fingertips were a strange dusky color Matthew could not name but did not like. It was a wrong color, a bad thing. A fine thread of blood trickled from the boy's nostril.

"He's bleeding!" Matthew whispered urgently.

"Yes," Carolyn said. "His blood isn't clotting, and he's bleeding inside, too. They tried to put an oxygen mask on him to ease his breathing, but it terrified him. So they tried the little tube that fits into the nose. That's when his nose started bleeding. We told them to leave it off. They're transfusing him with whole blood, and with platelets to help him clot. But he's bleeding at the i.v. site, too.

"You know," she continued, her soft voice conversational, "I've been remembering so many things. Did I ever tell you that after 'dada' his first word was 'boat'?"

"No, I don't think so."

"Oh, yes. He loved pictures of boats and stories about boats and plastic boats in the bathtub. I've probably read *Scuffy the Tugboat* a thousand times over the years. We've joked - but seriously, you know - that he'd never stay here to take over the farm. The day he was born we opened a college savings account for him. By the time he was two, we were calling it the Annapolis fund."

"I didn't know that, either. The night I came, he and his cousins were playing, 'Row, Row, Row Your Boat.'"

"All those constellations on his bedroom ceiling - they were just pretty nightlights until his father gave him that book about Magellan and he learned ancient sailors navigated by the stars. Those nights you laid with him until he fell asleep, didn't he ever talk about learning to steer by the stars?"

"Yeah, he did. I told him someday we'd find some old charts and a sextant and build ourselves a tall ship and run before the wind to mysterious islands..."

"I'm glad he had his dreams. I'm so glad you gave him such wonderful boats and such wonderful dreams."

"Maybe they're my dreams, too," Matthew mused. "Or were, one time... I won't ever build a tall ship, but he can go to Annapolis."

John's head snapped up. His voice was low but vibrated with ruthlessly suppressed emotion. "No, he can't go to Annapolis. He isn't going to be here. He's going a lot farther away from us than Maryland."

The boy opened his eyes just then and smiled a dreamy smile. "I need - my boat-" he gasped out.

"I have it right here." Matthew held it close, where the boy could see the scratched hull, the poorly mended sail. "I'm sorry I didn't understand right away that this was the one you wanted."

David tried to reach for the boat but couldn't raise the weak hand taped to the i.v. board. "Please," he whispered. Matthew carefully placed his offering on the bed beside David's unpinned left hand. He gently lifted the flaccid arm and draped the limp fingers over the hull. David smiled at him again.

"Thank you," the boy managed with strange dignity. He gathered his strength. "I know - all - the stars – now-" he gasped. "I'm going to - sail away - to Jesus." The boy's eyes fell shut again, but his hand remained firmly on the boat. They waited in still tableau for several hours, as nurses and doctors came and went with quiet, brisk efficiency, but the boy never moved or opened his eyes again.

The second-shift nurses went home into the clear, chilly night, and the third shift came by less frequently. Dr. Hanna came in, read the chart, looked at John and shook his head. He reached out one large hand toward Carolyn but drew it back. "I'm sorry," he rasped. "I wish I could - " John turned his back and the doctor left the room, still shaking his head.

Pastor Miles and Penny returned. They reminded Matthew again of a pair of storks with their long, gangly legs and beaky, narrow faces. They were younger than John and Carolyn; Penny Corrigan still wore her light brown hair around her shoulders and giggled when she laughed. But they were filled with ageless compassion as they embraced all three adults and prayed with them in one weeping circle around the bed.

The boy's breathing began to change to an ugly, guttural sound with long pauses in between. Allison returned. She had traded her crisp uniform for a soft pink velour jogging suit and remarkably tiny pink running shoes.

"That breathing - it's called Cheyne-Stokes breathing," she explained. "It means the end is coming, although we really don't know how soon. It's time to say good-bye now. I believe he can still hear you." She stood quietly for a moment, then took the pastor and his wife, leaving the three alone with the dying child.

Carolyn laid her head on the pillow beside her son's and spoke to him softly for a long time. Tears were flowing over her cheeks unnoticed and unchecked. She kissed his hair, his forehead, his half-open mouth, then stepped away from the bed.

Matthew stepped into Carolyn's place and stared down at the still child, at John still on his knees. He placed his mouth close to the boy's ear. "I love you so much," he said. "I don't want you to go." He breathed the scent of the boy deep into his lungs, deep into his memory, sorting it out from the sharper stench of illness. He kissed the boy's sweet little mouth one last time, tasting death on his lips.

"Remember the Stevenson poem I told you?" Matthew asked. "'Dark brown is the river, golden is the sand. It flows along forever, with trees on either hand... Away down the river, a hundred miles or more, other little children will bring my boats to shore.' I'm going to think of you going like that, all the way to the sea. And when you get there, fix your eyes on a star, set sail, and run before the wind."

John cradled David's head in one hand, laid his face in the curve of the little shoulder. He told the boy of his love, of his hopes and dreams that now could never happen, of the joy he had felt in being his father. In a strong, clear voice he gave his only son to the Lord's care and gave the boy permission to set sail.

Twenty minutes or so later, the boy's breathing stopped on a gentle exhale and did not resume.

Twenty-Four

Allison led them to Pastor Corrigan and his wife in the waiting room. The young couple had obviously been weeping and rose quickly to embrace the boy's parents. John moved away to stand again looking out the window. After a few awkward minutes, the Corrigans left. The three remained, apart from one another, as passive as cattle, until Allison returned to take them back to David.

The machines had been stilled, the tubes and tape and patches removed, the linens changed. A basin of warm, soapy water, washcloths and towels and a comb lined the table. "I thought you might like to wash him yourselves," Allison said. "You can do as much or as little as you want for the next hour or so." Her voice was so soft it was hard to remember she was a fire-breather.

The three of them stood dumbly for several moments, each locked into a pain which locked the others out. Finally Carolyn sat on the bed and gathered her son to her breast for the last time. She rocked back and forth and began to wail, a wordless sound so primitive it made the hair stand up on the back of Matthew's neck. She could have been a cavewoman keening for a child eaten by wolves or an Israelite mother mourning her baby slain by Herod. At last she became silent, although tears continued to etch her face. She met Matthew's eyes and held out the child like an offering. "Wouldn't you like to hold him?"

He moved forward and took the boy from her, supporting his head like an infant's. He sat on the bed and looked down into the pale, still face, charting the downy eyebrows and long, feathery lashes, the tiny nose and sweet little mouth. He held one small hand and traced each finger and nail. He saw they had diapered the boy and thought, *I hope he didn't know that. It would have humiliated him.* He thought, *He's so light! He doesn't weigh anything. It was easier to put him on my shoulders than a bale of hay. His legs have gotten so long this year, but he has little bird-bones. His skin's so soft, and his hair's like dandelion fuzz. That scar on his knee from falling off his bike in the driveway is the only part of him that isn't perfect.*

"I love you so much," Matthew told the silent form. "What am I going to do without you?" He kissed the cooling forehead, the chilled eyelids, the cold mouth. He gently placed the boy on the bed, composed his limbs, then walked out of the room, closing the door behind him. He couldn't bear to see John's grief.

For the last time, Matthew followed tiny yellow shoeprints backwards along the navy tile in the bright yellow hallway, escaping the building with a gusty sigh of relief. There on a wooden bench near the door, face raised to the clear, predawn sky, arms locked around her raised knees, sat the dragon-princess.

Matthew walked over to her, feeling awkward. "Hey," he said. "Thanks for coming back tonight. I know you weren't on duty."

"You're welcome. He was a - sometimes a kid just seems - you know, special. You all are. His parents, all those people who came, you - Are you - I mean, were you his uncle?"

"Yeah... something like that. I live with them. David and I take - took - piano lessons together. I made him some boats." Matthew felt the heavy weight of unshed tears mounting in his throat and behind his eyes and turned toward the truck.

Allison stood quickly and took his arm to turn him back to her. "I know it's hard. Would you like to go somewhere - get a drink and talk for a while?"

"No, thanks. I gotta go home and - and let people know. The church will want to help."

"Oh. Sure. I understand." Her small frame seemed even smaller as she stepped back and manufactured a smile. Her eyes seemed large and lost, which he told himself must be some trick of the light. He nodded to her, left her standing there alone as he drove off.

He drove slowly home, postponing the time he must say the words aloud. The farmhouse was dark, but lights shone from Ed's little white house across the road. Matthew turned in and parked the truck beside the farmhand's old brown El Camino, then sat there unsure of what he was supposed to do next. He felt numb and stupid.

Ed came out to the truck and led Matthew into the house and placed a thick, white mug full of coffee in his hand.

Matthew's empty stomach rebelled at the smell of coffee and he saw his hand shaking so hard the steaming liquid sloshed over the rim of the mug. He didn't feel the heat on his hand or through his pants-leg, but he vaguely heard Ed mention something about Ecclesiastes while taking back the mug.

"I'm sorry," Matthew said. "I didn't mean to spill it."

"Shoot, it's my fault. Shoulda known better than to give you a full mug. Want a half?"

"No. No, thanks."

"You want to tell me how the boy's doing?"

Matthew looked up into Ed's anxious face and struggled for the words. "He's - dead. He just - died - a little while ago. Died."

"Awwww," the farmhand moaned, sinking down next to Matthew on the couch. "Aw, the poor little guy." He fished the blue bandana from his back pocket, applied it to eyes and nose. "So how's his folks?"

"Like you'd expect, I guess. They never left him, all day and all night. She sat there holding his hand and talked about when he was a baby - a lot of that kind of stuff. John knelt on the floor on the other side of the bed for hours and hours. Just knelt there, hardly saying anything."

"Praying, I'd guess."

"Yeah, some of the time. But it was more like he'd been turned to stone. When David - stopped breathing - they sent us to the waiting room. John jerked away from the pastor and just stood there like a statue looking out the window until they called us back, didn't touch anyone, didn't say anything. Then this nurse took us back to - him - and said we could wash him or hold him. Carolyn held him real close, and she started to rock and cry - No, it was more like wailing or moaning - It was the worst sound I ever heard in my life! And John never moved. He never tried to comfort her. He never even said one word! It was awful!" Matthew shook his head violently, unconsciously trying to negate the memory. He looked at Ed, who was openly teary now.

"He must be hurting so bad. It's gotta be even worse this time." Ed blew his nose resoundingly. "They're gonna need a lot of prayer and love and support. Guess I'll start by doing the chores, if you're okay to be alone. Can't call folks for a couple of hours yet."

"Can I just stay here for a while?" Matthew asked, unwilling to face the farmhouse alone again.

"Sure. Sack out on the couch or take a shower or whatever."

Matthew felt beyond tired but unable to relax. A subliminal hum reverberated through him as he half-lay sprawled in the corner of the couch and watched daylight crawl by inches up the sky. A bird called. The sun began to shine. A maple tree in the front yard of the farmhouse blazed with orange and red.

How can it be such a beautiful day, when David is dead? How can the sun dare to shine? At least it should be raining.

At seven Matthew made himself go home to make phone calls. Just as he picked up the receiver, John and Carolyn returned.

"I took care of it," John said without preliminaries.

"Okay." Matthew replaced the receiver. "What can I do?"

"We're too tired," John replied. "We have to sleep first. Then, this afternoon, we'll go to the funeral home. You can take any calls, if you would. Maybe heat up something from the freezer so Carolyn doesn't have to cook."

"Sure." Matthew looked helplessly at the grim-faced farmer and his pale, silent wife. They headed up the stairs, but John turned back.

"One more thing - " John hesitated.

"Anything."

"On the back seat of the car, there's... a sack..."

Matthew understood. "I'll take care of it."

John's grim expression lightened just a little with relief. He turned again and followed his wife upstairs.

The phone rang three times before Matthew could go to the car, but at last he was able to retrieve a small plastic drawstring bag from the back seat. He carried it into the living room and sat down with it in John's chair. By its size and weight he had already guessed its contents; he took them out and laid them on his lap. There were little pale blue flannel pajamas, a tiny pair of superhero briefs - and the old boat. He bent over these sad little remnants and buried the sound of his sobs in pale blue flannel until the phone rang again.

"What should I do with his things?" Matthew asked Pearl when she called.

"Put the boat in his room where it belongs. Wash all his clothes that are in the laundry room and fold them and put them away, so Carolyn doesn't have to. She'll decide later what to keep and what to throw away. And put something in the oven. I'll be there directly."

"Yes, ma'am," he agreed gratefully. Pearl would take charge. That thought gave Matthew courage.

He set about his assigned tasks, noticing in a detached way how numb and clumsy his hands were, dropping the casserole dish the last few inches onto the oven rack. He banged his hip on the kitchen door, his left knee on the oven door, but felt no pain. *I'm in shock*, Matthew told himself. *My knee should hurt like the devil.*

As David's clothes came out of the dryer, Matthew folded each little shirt and pair of pants with exquisite precision. With the stealth of a cat-burglar, he crept upstairs and put each thing away in its own proper drawer. He placed the boat on the pillow and slipped quietly into his own room.

Taking off his work shoes, he lay down on top of the bed and waited for the pain.

Twenty-Five

When he wasn't doing chores, Matthew busied himself chopping wood and checking fence-wire. Not feeling the little splinters and barbed-wire bites as he slammed his anger and grief into wood and iron, welcoming the sweat dripping into his eyes as an excuse for tears, he ran ahead of feelings that would have pinned him to the earth. He refused to go to the funeral home for the visitation, saying he would take care of everything on the farm instead so that Ed could go. *I remember how it was when Mama died, oily music and stinking flowers and people pretending to be sorry. And Daddy – all those bagpipes and uniforms and lies from the pulpit – no. Never again. I want to remember David alive, running across the lawn or sailing his boat – Oh, God, why?*

The night before the funeral Matthew went to bed early, seeking refuge in sleep from the images of David playing over and over in his mind, chased off sometimes by darker, angrier images of his father's and mother's and grandparents' deaths and funerals. He was safely under when a knock on the door jarred him. "What?" he called, groggy and disoriented.

John entered the room. "Did I wake you? I'm sorry."

"What time is it?"

"Oh – ten or so. I wanted to ask – Matthew, tomorrow is the funeral, and it would mean a lot to Carolyn to have you there." He cleared his throat. "To me, too. Please?"

Matthew drew his concentration tighter to study the farmer. He saw new lines of pain and exhaustion etched in John's face, deep shadows beneath his eyes, a tightening and thinning of his lips. *Have I been asleep ten years?* Matthew wondered. *Even his hair seems grayer!*

"Will you try?" John asked. His tone might have been pleading.

"Yeah. Sure. What time?" Matthew rasped.

"We'll leave for the funeral home at nine. The funeral is at ten. We want you and Ed to ride with us." John stood slowly, stiffly.

"I'll be ready."

John nodded and left the room, moving as if his joints ached. Matthew heard their bedroom door close, the faint murmur of voices, then quiet.

He became aware of throbbing in his left knee and a dull ache in his hip. Examining his naked body, he found deep purple bruises at both locations, remembered bumping into the washer and the oven door. It could not, by the color of the bruises, have been more than a day or two since -

Now comes the real pain, Matthew thought, bracing both his body and his mind. Although the ache in his knee escalated sharply in the cold room, his mind continued to resist. *Okay*, he told himself. *Later. After I do what I have to do.*

Pulling on a red and gray plaid flannel bathrobe, one of John's "cast-offs" which had come to him with the price tags still on it several years before, Matthew limped across the hall to the bathroom. As he washed down three aspirin tablets with tepid water, he heard Carolyn crying, John's voice comforting. Since it couldn't wake them, Matthew indulged his aching body in a long, hot shower. If he wept under the noisy barrage of hot water, no one heard him; the water served as some comfort in place of a hug.

In the morning Matthew shaved, brushed his teeth and combed his hair without really seeing his own face. He dressed carefully in the formal navy blue suit he had bought to wear to church, added black socks and plain black shoes, which felt absurdly light after his steel-toed work boots. His fingers fumbled the laces, fumbled the buttons on his white shirt. He reached for his dull blue-on-blue striped tie, which hung like a noose from a hook in the closet. As he popped it over his head and fumbled the knot up to his throat, he was glad he never untied the thing between wearings. Today he couldn't have mastered the intricate loops.

The kitchen looked like Sunday morning, John at the table in his dark gray suit, Carolyn turning eggs in a big iron skillet, a flowered bib-apron over her cornflower blue dress. Ed hurried in, wearing his Sunday suit, rusty black over a muted green plaid shirt. His dark hair was carefully slicked back from his freshly scrubbed face and his fingernails were almost completely clean.

They all drank coffee and pretended to eat eggs and toast until Carolyn couldn't stand the tension stretching taut across the room. She jumped up and began to clear the table with sharp, jerky movements. Ed rose to remove a plate from her hand just before she tilted its contents onto the floor.

"I got this," he soothed. "You go get ready."

At last the four of them climbed into the car. From the back seat, Matthew heard a slap-slap noise and realized the windshield wipers were fighting off an army of wind-driven raindrops. Flying leaves clung to the blades for a few strokes before rushing on. The sky was the uniform gray of a dull aluminum pot.

In the parking lot, a grave man in a serious black suit assisted Carolyn out of the car under a serious black umbrella. He escorted her into the funeral home, John and Ed trailing along behind, oblivious to the slanting rain.

Matthew sat in the back seat, grateful to be ignored, taking in his surroundings. Obviously he had never been here before; he didn't recognize the gracious, green-trimmed white building. In earlier times, it must have housed a large, wealthy family in its many floors and rooms. Its Victorian turrets, gables and gingerbread were echoed in the huge carriage-house behind it, from which another grave man in a serious black suit drove a long, shiny, dove-gray hearse up to the back door.

Unable to consider the implications of that sinister vehicle, Matthew bolted from the car into the building.

He found himself in a long, narrow lobby populated by beige-brocaded chairs and settees and low cherry side-tables. The walls were papered with pinkish-beige silk paper. Rose-beige- and-blue-flowered drapes softened a series of tall windows on his left. Underfoot, thick blue carpet eliminated any sound of walking. The air itself seemed thick and still. Sweat broke out on his upper lip and he felt a sudden sensation of choking.

A tall, heavy, grave man in a serious black suit appeared beside Matthew. In a hushed voice, the man said, "This way, sir, to Parlor A."

He gestured to an open doorway in the middle of the long wall on Matthew's right.

Obediently, Matthew went through the doorway into the back of a huge room whose decor matched the lobby. He stood in an absolutely straight aisle between two long ranks of beige-padded folding chairs. A slow walk to the end of the aisle brought him just over halfway into the room. To either side were more of the chairs and settees and low tables, interspersed with dozens of vases, baskets, planters, wreaths of flowers - green, flowering, artificial, tall, wide, beribboned, plain. Matthew had never seen such profusion. His attention was wholly captivated by the floral abundance, cataloging each piece, naming each flower he knew - a surprising number, thanks to his grandmother. Then he noticed the cabbage-rose floral wallpaper border near the ceiling, the subtle pink indirect lighting, the tissue boxes placed discreetly on each table and the innocuous organ music oozing from discreet speakers in the ceiling.

A short, grave man in dark-rimmed glasses and yet another serious black suit interrupted Matthew's observations by taking his elbow. "Please, sir," he said in a hushed tone, "won't you join the family and the deceased?"

Matthew jerked his arm away; the little man dropped Matthew's elbow, backing up quickly and pushing his glasses back up his nose with a trembling finger.

Matthew knew his anger was misdirected, even as he used it to move him the rest of the way across those long miles of carpet to the last place on earth he wanted to be. Time had begun to stretch out like a bead of molasses falling from a wooden spoon. He had plenty of time to see the cluster of chairs to his left, shielded from the rest of the room by a folding wall, where the family was gathered with the pastor and his wife. He noted Penny's shiny hair scraped back into a tight, ugly knot; the row of little blond cousins, fidgety in their dress-up clothes; Pearl's chalky white face contrasting with her black dress and coat. He smelled the heavy, sick odor peculiar to funeral flowers and tried to shake the viscous organ music out of his ears, off the sleeves of his jacket. He saw Ed, John and Carolyn all watching him as he approached.

Then all he could see was the little white casket, its white-satin-tufted lid propped open to reveal the precious contents. Drawn, horrified, he came as close as he could and stared down.

They had dressed the boy in a soft blue, long-sleeved polo shirt with narrow bands of red on the woven collar and cuffs. His lower body was covered by a puffy white comforter. His pale, silky hair had been washed and combed straight back from his forehead instead of being allowed to flop into his eyebrows as it naturally did. His long lashes lay gently on his cheeks and his tender little mouth shaped an almost-smile, as if he harbored a wonderful secret. Tucked between his quiet little hands lay the old boat.

Matthew was unprepared as the first wave of pain slammed into him, knocking him to his knees, forcing a hoarse cry from deep in his chest. More waves battered him, scraped him along the bottom, flaying the skin from his bones, as he wept until he was drowning in sorrow salt and fathomless, praying the next wave would kill him. The surf roared in his ears until soft hands touched him and strong arms grabbed him and dragged him onto the beach. He burrowed against a broad chest and a rough, wool-covered shoulder, gasping for breath.

The familiar blue bandana appeared in Matthew's hand. Like a dutiful child, he blew his nose and mopped his eyes. At Ed's stiff gesture, he stuffed the bandana into his pants pocket. "Up we go," said the farmhand, dragging Matthew to his feet. Everyone returned to the outpost of folding chairs, drawing him with them.

In the peculiar way of shock, Matthew's eyes seemed to focus on things with unnatural clarity, though everything around the edges of his vision turned blank. He could hear sound, as if it were filtered through heavy cloth, but could make no sense of it. His body was numb, moved with great difficulty, seemed to register no feeling but the cold, damp clutch of Carolyn's hand.

The pastor must have prayed, because all the heads were bowed. Then a grave man in a serious black suit began to lower the lid of the casket.

"No! No!" Carolyn screamed, straining toward the casket. "No, please! It's too soon!"

"Shhh, we have to do this," John said. He held her in a steely embrace against which her struggle was useless. "We have to do this," he said again, his voice as hard as his grip. Carolyn subsided into helpless weeping.

The sound of the latches closing was as loud and final as a suicide's gunshot. Matthew flinched as his hearing returned and flinched again as Carolyn's fingernails dug into his hand.

At the church, they were taken into the pastor's office to wait. Matthew turned to watch battalions of raindrops hurl themselves against the window as he listened to the monotonous weeping behind him. *This isn't really happening*, he thought. *I'm going to wake up pretty soon with the sun in my face and David bouncing on the end of my bed. We'll eat pancakes. We'll practice our piano lesson.*

The rain and the weeping continued. Matthew did not wake up.

Pastor Corrigan entered, his young face pale, eyes dark with compassion. Matthew could not help noticing that Pastor Corrigan wore a serious black suit. "The church is full," the pastor said. "So many people want to come alongside and love you and help you through this. We're ready for the service now, if you are."

John rose and lifted his wife to her feet. "Do it," he said.

They entered the front pew from an adjacent door, so that Matthew had only a brief, confused glimpse of all the faces behind them. He and John flanked Carolyn, who clung to both of them as if her life depended upon it. John put his arm around her shoulders, freeing her hand to mop at the unending streams of tears with a succession of tissues. Matthew wondered if she would eventually dry out and blow away like a tumbleweed from shedding all those tears.

Organ music happened, and a soprano, and the pastor's voice. Matthew heard some quavery little voices - David's schoolmates – Pearl's papery tones, a little more hesitant than usual - Miles again - only sound, no meaning. Then they were filing into a long, sleek, dove-gray limousine, sinking into soft leather seats, watching the rain's reserve battalions, fewer in number but no less determined, slashing at the vehicle, battering the trees, driving leaves ahead of them like frantic refugees.

Carolyn sat tightly sandwiched between John and Matthew, quivering with the force of a spent bowstring. Her cold, damp hand kept its death-grip on Matthew; her eyes dripped their tears without blinking as she watched the cemetery appear and spread out before them. John held her steady but did not look at her, did not speak. His profile was granite; from time to time a muscle twitched along his jaw.

The limousine parked behind the hearse. They followed six pall-bearers and the tiny white casket slowly, solemnly, under an arch of serious black umbrellas.

Matthew saw that a backhoe had lumbered across the lush wet grass, leaving muddy tracks and then ripping a huge bite out of the soft earth. The dark green canvas canopy and beige folding chairs on bright green artificial turf did nothing to soften the ugliness of the pile of raw dirt and the open grave.

As they sat on the cold chairs waiting for the rest of the mourners to pick their way across the sodden ground under serious black umbrellas, Matthew tried to keep his attention away from that hole. This section of the cemetery was relatively new, he saw, for there were no mature trees, only a few young plum and apple trees and one weeping cherry. Here and there white marble benches encouraged visitors to linger awhile. In the center of the area knelt a huge white marble Christ with his arms around three small pink marble children. A brass plaque at the bottom of the statue reminded, "OF SUCH IS THE KINGDOM OF HEAVEN."

All the markers in this section were on-ground bronze plates. The ones Matthew could see gave names and nicknames and dates of births and deaths. The oldest child he could find had been ten years old, but most of them were infants. The little graves had mementos lying on them: pinwheels, photographs, storybooks wrapped in plastic, cars and trucks, a teddy bear safely sealed in a canning jar.

Matthew thought, *We're burying David with his boat. We'll bring him flowers. Maybe I'll carve him a dog, or a cat like Celeste, and leave it here. And he won't care. Will it make us feel better to do it?*

He ignored the pastor's graveside service. He stood when others stood, moved as they moved, left when they left, without ever allowing himself to see that little white box poised over the deep black hole.

As they lock-stepped back to the limousine under the arch of umbrellas, Matthew's attention was caught by an old bronze plate very near the new grave. It bore the name "John D. Abbott, Jr. Johnny."

Matthew stopped abruptly and they went on without him, John carefully angling his body between his wife and the open grave. Matthew stared at the worn bronze numbers. This child had been born - had lived five months - had died - four years before David was born.

Oh, Lord, Matthew thought, *do they bring flowers and birthday presents to this little grave? Now they'll have two to visit, two to grieve. Both of their sons. All of their sons! How could You?*

"C'mon," Ed urged from behind him, taking his arm.

"You knew about this." Matthew gestured.

"Yeah. I was here. Gotta go now, do the church supper thing."

"I don't want to."

"Look," Ed said sternly, "this ain't about you. I know you loved the boy. But he's their son, and the second one they lost. We gotta think about them, about what they need and want and how we can help. It's time for you to grow up and think about somebody else first."

Matthew felt the sting of embarrassment in his face, along the tops of his ears. "You're right," he agreed.

Near the long line of cars, a flash of color amidst all the black and gray drew Matthew's eye. There, alone, rain beading in her hair and on her bright blue coat, stood Allison West. She saw Matthew, stretched out one hand and drew it back, disappeared quickly into the crowd, leaving only the afterimage of her bright blue coat lingering behind his eyes.

Twenty-Six

November plodded on toward Thanksgiving through a sea of mud. Matthew thought the sun had not shone one day since the day David died. The cold damp penetrated the house, seeped into their bones, could not be routed by furnace, fireplace, hot coffee or hot showers. Carolyn continued to weep and John continued to be silent.

Matthew's own grief overtook him at odd moments, never the same way twice. He wept in the driveway when the school bus didn't stop, in the supermarket when he walked the cereal aisle, at the piano as he tried to practice a lesson he and David had worked on together. He couldn't go to sleep without David's good-night kisses. He woke with a start in the reaches of the night, imagining he heard David calling him.

He hated to sit in church, hated to hear Miles's earnest young voice, hated to see the pastor's stork-like frame in its serious black suit. But Matthew went to church, as he went to the store, because he had promised Ed. And he never, never spoke of his grief or shared his tears with David's parents.

He did share with Ed when John was not around, which happened more and more frequently. They slogged along together in their high rubber boots, reminiscing about David, until one day near the end of November Matthew found himself laughing over one of the boy's escapades.

"That's the ticket!" Ed grinned. "First you cry, then you talk, then you laugh. You're gonna be okay now; God never lets us down."

Standing there nearly knee-deep in cold mud, rain drizzling over his face and into his ears and running its icy fingers down the back of his neck, physically as miserable as he had been in a long while, Matthew felt a small glow begin inside him at the truth of the farmhand's words.

That night he watched John and Carolyn during supper. Carolyn's tears were somewhat less frequent now, but the sadness never left her face. She moved as if her feet were cased in mud, rarely made eye contact or spontaneous conversation, pushed her food around the edges of her plate but rarely put a bite into her mouth. She had lost weight, Matthew saw. Her clothes hung; her apron nearly wrapped around her twice. John was gentle with his wife, helping her set the table and do the dishes, touching her often, speaking to her softly. He said nothing when she flinched or pulled away from his hand, said nothing when she refused his help, said nothing when she ignored his comments. If the look in his eyes was hurt, he quickly masked it. His hands at their tasks were steady, his movements deliberate. He ate mechanically, fueling the machine for the hard labor with which he was exhausting himself enough to sleep.

Matthew thought that no one who hadn't known John before would ever suspect he had sustained so great a loss. One would have had to know that the clenched jaw and grim mouth had once been an easy smile, that those deep-set eyes had once held light and peace instead of this dull pain.

But Matthew said nothing to John because it was not his place.

Thanksgiving arrived in pale, watery sunlight. Taking off their boots at the back door, the three men shared a smile and a half-joking word of gratitude that just maybe they wouldn't have to build an ark after all.

They sat down to bacon and eggs amidst odors of sage and cinnamon and roasting turkey. Carolyn, liberally dusted with flour, had interrupted her baking frenzy long enough to plunk full plates in front of them.

"But that's it!" she warned. "Nothing more from this kitchen until two o'clock."

Matthew thought she sounded almost like her old self in that moment. "You're so busy," he said, "how 'bout I spend the morning in here helping you with the pies?"

"Oh, no, you don't!" Ed laughed. "I got seniority here!"

"Well..." drawled John, "I am the head of the family, not to mention: the boss..."

"Thank you so much!" Carolyn teased in a syrupy voice. "I guess you could peel enough potatoes for twelve people. And there will be plenty of pots and pans to wash in a couple of hours."

Ed began rapidly, unsubtly, backing toward the door. The other two held their ground.

"And you'll really enjoy it," Carolyn continued, "working with the women. There should be three of us in here in about an hour."

John and Matthew grinned at each other, then looked back at Carolyn.

"But what we'll really need," she said, half laughing, "is someone to mind the children -"

Like a shark, memory hit her from behind, bleeding the color from her face and the smile from her eyes. John let out all of his breath at once, sucker-punched. He moved quickly to embrace his wife, but she shoved his arms away and ran from the room. John stood hunched over the sink, head down, eyes closed, gripping the edge, cursing fluently in a quiet, despairing voice.

It wasn't that Matthew had never heard the words before, but he had never imagined John using them. Matthew felt embarrassed, and perhaps a bit afraid. Silently he let himself out the back door, unwilling to intrude further upon John's pain.

The rest of the day was no better for Matthew nor, he thought, for John and Carolyn. They limped through it somehow. Food which had smelled so good that morning nauseated Matthew in the afternoon and tasted like ashes in his mouth. He hid in corners to avoid the giggling, chattering little cousins, whose laughter and pale hair reminded him so painfully of David. He watched Carolyn carefully avoid any contact with her husband, listened to a note he couldn't identify in John's voice.

The hazy sunlight gave over that night to a hard, clear sky full of stars. Matthew lay under crisp, white sheets and heavy woolen blankets, watching starlight cover his room like frost, remembering Thanksgiving the year before, when he had been truly thankful for the blessings of home and family. His heart ached where David's death had torn away a piece of it.

"I miss you," he whispered into the cold silence. "I miss you so much."

Twenty-Seven

Water froze standing in the fields, and on some farms children could be seen ice-skating where the wheat should have been sleeping. Unusual cold gripped the land with iron fingers. Inside the farmhouse, nothing thawed.

At night, as Matthew lay in his narrow bed trying to find a position in which his knee didn't hurt quite so much, he heard Carolyn crying. In the beginning he heard John's soothing tones, although he couldn't quite make out the words. As the weeks went on, he heard only the weeping. In the daylight they all carried out an elaborate ritual called "normal," in which each person played the part for which he or she had been cast long before, using lines from earlier productions. They were experienced in the gestures and intonations and could give fairly convincing performances, at least to themselves, if not to one another.

But at night the scripts were put aside with the debris of the day and they lived an ad lib existence.

On the longest, coldest of those nights, when Carolyn's weeping cut through him like the north wind, Matthew prayed in a whisper for mercy for them all. When he woke the next morning, it seemed his prayers had been unable to penetrate the ice.

Pearl came, bringing bread, dispensing brisk encouragement; but she, too, admitted to being cold and tired. Her skin had a pallor Matthew didn't remember from the year before, and her step was slow and heavy. He stared at her across the dinner table and suddenly could see her lying in a coffin. Panicked, he wondered if there were prayers to ward off premonitions. *Please don't!* Matthew prayed. *We can't take another death! We're not doing well at handling this one.*

"—gathering!" Pearl said.

"What?" Matthew realized the old woman had been speaking to him, but he had been speaking to God and had missed her remark.

"I said it's time for you to stop wool-gathering over there and give us some ideas about Christmas."

"Christmas?" Matthew was baffled. He rubbed his knee with one hand and pushed peas into his mashed potatoes with the other.

"Do you have any idea what the date is?" Pearl asked sharply. Her peas were gone, and she was eating potatoes and meat in tidy little bites. She reminded Matthew of a beady-eyed bird pecking up seeds.

"Uh - no, ma'am, I don't."

"It's December thirteenth, and less than two weeks to Christmas."

Carolyn sat up straight and looked directly at Pearl with her sad blue eyes. "How can you expect us to celebrate Christmas this year?" Her soft voice was angry and accusing. "How can we ever celebrate Christmas again?"

"Just think," Pearl said. "We celebrate Christmas this year and every year because no matter what has happened in our personal lives, Christ came to save us and He did, and Christmas honors His Incarnation." She laid down her fork and leaned forward, ready for battle.

Carolyn's pale face registered a line of color along the cheekbones; her eyes glittered with anger instead of tears. "My child is dead!" she shouted. "I don't feel like celebrating anything!" She shoved her chair back from the table so forcefully it fell over with a noisy thud. Slamming her napkin down into the middle of her untouched plate, she stormed out of the room and pounded up the stairs. In a moment they heard the bedroom door slam with the force of a felled tree.

Pearl smiled. Ed nodded in what seemed to be satisfaction. John, as he usually did these days, said nothing.

Matthew was deeply uncomfortable with the displays of temper and of satisfaction. The ways people were acting made no sense to him. His chancy appetite had deserted him completely, so he rose to take his plate to the kitchen.

"Not so fast," Pearl said. "I asked you for some ideas about Christmas."

Her comment arrested Matthew in mid-flight. He stood there, plate in hand, poised to take off again at the least provocation. "But - you heard - "

"And I'm not taking any mind. Of course she doesn't want to celebrate. But the plain truth is, life goes on and we have to make the best of it. I've waited for her to get hold of herself and take charge. But if she can't, why, then, we'll do it for her."

Ed was nodding in agreement. He looked like one of those silly dogs some people put in the back windows of their cars. "I agree," he said, nodding some more. "If we get started, maybe she'll come around. Can't avoid people and laughter and kids forever."

"I just feel funny," Matthew said, sitting down again. He broke through the wall of mashed potatoes and drowned his offending peas in beef gravy. A survivor bobbed to the top and he mashed it viciously.

Ed turned to John. "What do you want us to do?"

"I don't know," John grated in a voice like iron filings. "Whatever you want. I don't want to hurt Carolyn, but this has to stop. The boy is dead." He brushed past Matthew and went through the kitchen and out the back door.

"Now," Pearl directed, "we'll get this all arranged and get busy." She paused for a moment and the starch wilted out of her. "The Scriptures tell us the joy of the Lord is our strength. Now's a good time to be finding that joy." Her snapping, dark eyes suddenly seemed vague and misted, and her spine sagged just a fraction of an inch. Again Matthew saw her lying dead in a coffin in that huge beige room.

"A tree," he blurted. "We always have a real tree."

Ed nodded again. "Right! And that garland stuff, and holly..."

"You two go tomorrow and pick a tree," Pearl ordered. "I'll make a list so you can take me shopping. I guess I have one more Christmas dinner in me." The color was returning to her face as she saw a practical way to create order in the universe again.

Matthew tried to puzzle out everything that needed to be done. "I'll have to get the ornaments and lights from the attic. Maybe - maybe we'd better skip the stockings."

"Right," Pearl agreed. "But we mustn't skip presents. Did you make things this year?"

"Not for everyone. Only for Carolyn. John and I made her a big

quilting frame out of ash. I'd planned to do other things, and then - "
Sorrow choked off the rest of his words.

"So you'll need to go shopping, both of you," Pearl noted, looking
pointedly at Ed.

"Yes, ma'am," he agreed meekly.

"I'll call the family and invite them," Pearl decided.

Matthew thought of the four little cousins, blond and laughing,
so like David. "Do you have to?" he asked.

"Absolutely!" Pearl said vigorously. Her dark eyes softened with
compassion as she met Matthew's pained gaze. "I know it will be
painful. But we need to face it and move on. And those children need
as normal a holiday as we can give them. They've had a loss, too."

"But it's too soon! Next year it will be easier, when she's had more
time to forget."

"Think what you're saying, boy!" Pearl exclaimed sharply. "She
won't forget. She won't ever forget." She looked away and sighed.
"And next year, or the year after that, it won't be any easier if she
hasn't started facing it."

An awareness rose in Matthew. "Did you lose a child?"

The old woman nodded. "Fifty years ago. Her name was Rose. She
was as dark as David was fair. All snap and sparkle - her father used
to call her his little gypsy girl. She was only five when she died. For a
while, I wished it had been me instead. I still miss her."

"But you got over it."

"No. I learned to go on. The old pastor - oh, six or seven pastors
before this one - told me 'a time to mourn' means a *period* of time,
with a definite ending. He said any less would dishonor the dead, but
any more would dishonor the Lord."

Although he didn't quite understand, Matthew could see it had
brought the old woman to a place of peace and acceptance he could
envy. *Show me, too*, he prayed.

The next day was mild and sunny, melting the ice in the fields and
at the edges of the pond. As soon as he could, Matthew joined Ed in
the El Camino for a short drive to the Christmas tree farm in the next
county, where the family always cut their own tree.

He left his coat unzipped as he shouldered the chain saw and began the trek from the stone parking area into the man-made forest of
white and scotch pines. Ed marched alongside, whistling what might

pass for a tune. Their boots grew heavy with mud and pine needles as they climbed the hill, headed for the older, taller trees.

"Reckon this is far enough," Ed said, surveying the hundreds of rows of trees beyond the crest of the hill.

"Y'know," Matthew rejoined, "the best one is bound to be over the next hill."

"Then we're gonna settle for second-best," warned Ed, "because one hill's my limit. Especially when they won't let us bring the vehicle in."

"Too muddy," Matthew said wisely, beginning to inspect the nearest trees. Rapidly, almost subconsciously, he rejected this one for sparseness, that one for its twisted trunk, the next for being lop-sided. The farmhand indicated another, but he shook his head. "Too short."

"Well, Paul and Silas!" Ed snapped. "That one's too tall, that one's too skinny, and you're gonna find something wrong with every one of them!"

Matthew was considering a medium-sized white pine from several angles. "Is Silas one of the books of the Bible?" he asked absently.

"No," the farmhand said shortly. "He was a buddy of Paul's. A friend. Somebody who *listened* to his friend."

Matthew looked over his shoulder. "What's the matter?"

Ed turned his back. Matthew was about to ask where the farmhand got off being so rude when he saw the broad shoulders shaking.

"This one is fine," he said quickly, turning back to the white pine. Swiftly engaging the saw, he checked carefully for the clearest fall path and applied the roaring blade to the slender trunk. In moments the tree lay helpless at his feet. He shut off the saw, blessing the sudden silence.

"I got it," Ed volunteered, shoving his blue bandana into his back pocket with one hand while pulling a length of rough twine from his coat pocket with the other.

Together they trussed the branches close to the trunk and carried the tree to the El Camino. Matthew paid the tree farmer and patted the gray-muzzled black lab who had devoted his life to loving the customers and watering the trees. He remembered David the year before, rolling around in the snow shrieking with laughter as the old dog washed his face with a huge, wet tongue.

The tree farmer remembered, too. "Boy not with you this year?" he asked.

Matthew froze clear through. "No," he said. "He... died in October."

"Oh, jeeze," the tree farmer whispered. His wind-reddened face was suddenly pale and twisted with guilt. "I'm sorry! I didn't know."

"No. No, it's okay. I can see you didn't know." He pocketed the change and backed away quickly.

As Matthew climbed into the passenger seat, Ed looked at him, said nothing, cranked up the heat. Although the sun continued to pour in through the windshield, they were both cold again.

Once home, they unloaded the tree and carried it into the living room, where Matthew had stacked boxes of lights and ornaments and the red-and-green tree stand the night before. However, the tree didn't fit into the stand.

"Gotta take about three inches off the trunk," Ed stated.

They hauled the tree back out to the front porch and Matthew retrieved the chain saw from the bed of the El Camino. Its grip was cold in his hand, but he knew he wouldn't be out long enough to bother putting on his coat and gloves again. Ed indicated the place to cut and stabilized the tree with one booted foot placed carefully far above the site. Matthew started the saw and bent to the trunk.

It happened so fast. The saw was bouncing away across the porch by itself. The farmhand was swearing - the real words. And someone had overturned at least a quart of red paint all over Matthew's shoes and the tree and the porch...

He heard someone screaming and his own voice saying, "I think we have a problem here."

"Lie down, you durn fool!" Ed yelled, shoving him backward. He went down obediently. Pain had begun to tear through his left thigh, gripping and shaking him with alligator jaws. Ed was improvising a tourniquet with his worn leather belt and a small pine-branch. Carolyn, white and weeping noisily, was pressing a dishtowel into Matthew's leg with all her weight, making the pain worse. He recognized his own voice crying out.

Suddenly he felt John's hard hand grasping his and clenched it until the bones shifted in his desperate grip. He was so cold! His teeth clacked together and he shivered convulsively. The pain increased. And then everything went away.

Matthew regained consciousness suddenly, painfully, in what was clearly a hospital room. His leg throbbed and screamed. When he raised his head, dizziness and nausea overwhelmed him. He laid there, eyes closed, gulping, cold sweat drizzling down his face.

As he lost the battle, a warm hand turned his head to the side and held him as he vomited into a basin. He thought the violent paroxysms would never end, but the hand stayed and a soft voice murmured encouragement until his body eased and lay still, gasping.

"There now. That should be the worst of it," the voice reassured him.

Oh, no, Matthew thought. *Oh, no. Maybe I can just lie here and die now. Maybe she'll just go away.* He was humiliated. It was the dragon-princess.

With either a delicacy Matthew didn't believe she possessed, or a summons back to her regular floor, Allison did leave and didn't reappear before his discharge the next afternoon.

Still faint despite a transfusion, slightly drunk on codeine tablets, which blunted the alligator's fangs but didn't pull them, Matthew awkwardly levered himself from crutches to the back seat of John's car and stretched his legs out along the seat. Carolyn tucked a pillow behind his back and draped a red and blue quilt over his legs. He was both moved and embarrassed by her solicitude, smiled his thanks hoping to easy the worry from her face.

"I'm sorry to be so much trouble."

"It's no trouble," John reassured him. "We're just grateful you're all right."

"I must have been careless. I don't know what happened." He winced as John put the car in gear, an expression the farmer noted in his mirror.

"I'll take it as easy as I can," John promised. "As far as what happened, as near as we can tell, the saw blade must have hit the wood at the wrong angle and bounced back. If it had bounced low, it would have chewed up your boot, maybe not cut so bad. Jeans just aren't saw-proof, are they?"

"You make it sound - " Matthew broke off to grit his teeth as the car hit a bump, then continued, "- sound like no big deal. I didn't have my gloves on. The handle was cold. Maybe if I'd had my gloves on, I could have held it."

"The big deal is you being hurt, nothing else."

The farmer's voice was final. Matthew had to believe the tone as much as the words. He closed his eyes and savored coming home.

Twenty-Eight

Forty-eight hours later, Matthew sat in John's chair, injured leg cushioned by pillows across a straight chair, staring disconsolately out the front window. His leg throbbed, his knee ached from being so long in one position, the rest of him ached from sitting. His mind ached from boredom and his heart ached from grief. His Bible lay open to Ecclesiastes under the collection of Frost, but he was tired of reading. He had found more consolation in imagining himself "a swinger of birches" than in "a time for every purpose under heaven."

As he gradually urged his self-pity to a crescendo, a small, bright blue car charged up the driveway and stopped in a shower of gravel. Out popped Allison West in her bright blue coat.

Matthew would not have called himself a vain man, but one hand rose to his unshaven chin while the other tried to smooth out his hair. Looking at his worn gray sweatpants, the left leg slit to accommodate the bulky bandages, he considered a quick retreat to his room - and abandoned the idea. He was too slow on the crutches to outrun her. And he had no doubt Allison would follow him right into his room anyway.

He heard the bell, Carolyn's slow steps, the low exchange of women's voices. He braced himself.

"Hi!" she said. "I just thought I'd see how you're doing."

"Fine."

"That's good! Have you changed the dressing? Any pain or fever or redness?"

"It's fine."

Allison cocked her head. "Maybe we could try this again." She backed up to the doorway. "Let's see... I come in and say, 'How are you?' Then you say, 'Fine, thank you.' Then you say, 'Please come in. It's nice of you to visit. Won't you sit down?'" She waited.

Matthew wanted to make her smile again. "Fine, thank you, please come in, it's nice of you to visit, won't you please sit down."

Allison rewarded his effort with a brilliant grin. "That wasn't too awful, was it?" Removing her coat to reveal jeans and a bright blue sweater, she plunked herself down in Carolyn's chair opposite him.

Matthew had no idea what to do next. Who was this woman in her bright blue sweater, the efficient nurse who had held his head while he vomited his guts out or a pretty girl visiting a man she found attractive?

Fool, he told himself, *that one's pretty obvious.*

Allison seemed oblivious to his inner turmoil. She was admiring the tree, now fully decorated, drawing from him the story of his accident, remarking the sunny weather.

Carolyn brought in a tray with coffee and undecorated Christmas cookies. She set it on a nearby table and left, never saying a word.

"She's still pretty broken up, isn't she?" Allison asked, busying herself with the tray. "How do you take your coffee?"

"Black." Matthew took the mug from a hand which seemed almost too small to hold it. "Yeah, she's really sad. She cries a lot. She - cries in the night." He cupped the mug with both cold hands.

"And how's the rest of the family? How are you?"

Matthew watched, fascinated, as Allison's competent little hands stirred four spoonfuls of sugar into her coffee and added a generous glug of real cream. She looked up at his prolonged silence, saw him watching and burst into an unselfconscious laugh.

"I know - how can such a little person take in so many calories and not be the size of the Goodyear blimp, right?"

"Well?"

"Easy. I burn it all off handling big lugs like you every day."

"Wrong answer! Your regular job is with kids."

"Oooo! Okay: truth. I inherited my metabolism, my size and my curly hair from my mom. Just lucky on two out of three."

"You don't like curly hair?"

"I don't like being smaller than some of my patients!" She offered the cookies. When Matthew refused, she began to demolish them by herself. "You haven't answered my question," she reminded him.

"Oh. I guess we're okay." He added slowly, "It hurts."

Allison leaned forward to place her hand on Matthew's sock-covered left foot, the only part of him she could reach from her chair. For a minute she said nothing. The humor in her pretty face was replaced by compassion, then by curiosity. Matthew was aware his left foot had unfrozen where her hand rested on it. He twitched.

Curiosity replaced by confusion, Allison withdrew her hand and returned her attention to the cookies. "Sometimes," she said, "when a child dies, the parents end up divorced. Lots of times. Because they don't communicate, they don't grieve the same way, at the same time..."

"Nothing like that is going to happen here!"

"I'm sorry. I know you're church-people and you probably don't believe in divorce, do you?"

"No, we don't." Matthew noticed she had suddenly become fidgety, reducing the last cookie to crumbs. "Do you?"

"Do I what?" She looked up at him.

"Do you believe in divorce?"

"No, not really. As long as people get along. But if they get fed up with each other, or they find somebody else - "

"What about the vows? 'Until death do us part'?"

"That doesn't mean much any more. Oh, it sounds nice for the wedding, but nobody takes it seriously."

Matthew held her gaze and replied, "I do. And God does."

Allison's eyes were suddenly bleak. "I don't believe in God. If He existed He wouldn't let bad things happen, like babies dying." She came to her feet, scattering crumbs, and put on her coat. "I have to go. I'm glad you're okay. Merry Christmas."

Before he could respond, she was gone.

Matthew would have liked to ask John about their troubling conversation; but these days he never asked John anything but farm questions, and those only if he couldn't find Ed. John's kindness the day of the accident had been only an interlude. He had quickly returned to hard silence. When he did speak, his voice grated like metal on metal, his words like short, sharp rows of staples.

That night, after a silent dinner, Matthew hauled himself awkwardly up the stairs to his room. Exhausted, he struggled to get ready for bed, then lay there in the cold dark unable to sleep. He replayed his visit from the dragon-princess, recalled with painful clarity the heat of her hand on his foot, decided that was not a prudent line of thought.

Don't be a jerk, Matthew warned himself. *She doesn't like you that way. How could she? A woman that pretty, smart enough to be a nurse, she's probably engaged to a doctor. A guy with a future.*

He sighed and squirmed restlessly, trying to find a comfortable position. He considered the pain pills but decided against the effort required to get them. He heard the front door close, the El Camino come to life. Ed was taking Pearl home. Soon he heard John and Carolyn coming up the stairs, heard water running, an occasional faint voice. Gradually he drifted down into sleep.

Some time later he was awakened by rising voices across the hall. Trapped by his injured leg, he lay there, helplessly eavesdropping.

"I can't!" Carolyn was saying.

"The hell you can't!" John yelled.

"I can't! How can you even ask?"

"Because I'm your husband!"

"How can you even think of - that - when my son is – is - "

"Dead. Say it! He's *our* son, and he's dead! But I'm not! I need you. It's been months, since before the funeral - "

"You disgust me! Don't touch me. Don't you dare!"

Matthew heard the farmer slam the bedroom door and pound down the stairs. Then he heard Carolyn begin to cry. The words of the dragon-princess filled his mind: "...the parents end up divorced..."

A few days later, Matthew realized Carolyn was sleeping in David's room.

John told Pearl to forget about Christmas and ordered Ed to get rid of the tree.

Carolyn fed five dozen Christmas cookies to the garbage disposal.

On Sunday John did not go to church.

On Christmas Eve day, when Dr. Hanna removed his stitches and told him he could phase out the crutches, no one at home remarked Matthew's recovery.

"I dunno," Ed said. They sat side by side on a bale of hay in the barn, watching the recently weaned kittens pretending to be tigers. "The Lord sure hasn't showed me what else to do." He shook a kitten gently off his shoe. "And this divorce stuff - well, I can't imagine that!

"Of course, I couldn't have imagined him refusing to go to church, neither. What makes you think they'll get a divorce?"

Matthew couldn't bring himself to reveal what had happened. He felt shame for all of them, that he had been party to such private matters. Instead, he repeated what the dragon-princess had said.

"Well, now, she must be a smart one, being a nurse and all, but it's different for Christians."

"Is it?" The bitterness in his voice surprised him.

It surprised Ed, also. "Why, sure it is! We got the Lord's strength and His Word to fall back on. We got prayer."

"So why isn't it working? How come, if God answers prayer? We prayed so hard, and David died anyway!"

"Whew!" Ed exclaimed. "Get right down to it, don't you?"

"Well?" Matthew pushed.

"First, Second, Third John, boy, if I knew that - !" Ed took a deep calming breath, let it out slowly. "The boss told me a long time ago, when I was a new Christian like you are now, the answer to 'why' is 'because.' God's Word says His ways are not our ways and His thoughts are above our thoughts. All we need to know is that He knows."

"Are you going to lecture me about faith now?"

"Naw, not me. I leave that to Pastor Corrigan. He's a smart man."

"Shoot. He isn't any older than I am."

"So? Look at me, son. Age don't make smarts."

"Don't let this go to your head," Matthew said fondly, "but looking at you - I kinda think it does. Besides," he continued, to avert Ed's embarrassment, "where is the pastor with all his wisdom? Lots of other people have come by."

"Came the day after the funeral. Boss run him off."

"You're kidding!"

"Nope. Told him he'd call when he's ready to forgive God. Guess he ain't ready yet. Or he figures God ain't ready to forgive him."

Matthew turned to stare at the farmhand, who was teasing a kitten with a long piece of twine as if he had not just delivered several sledgehammer blows to his friend's foundations.

Ed met his eyes. "The first time, they woke up late and the baby was dead. She thought, if she'd woke up to nurse him - He thought, if he hadn't overslept - "

"But it was crib death. That just happens."

"Yep. And parents just naturally think, 'if only.' I think maybe they was up later than usual - you know - because it was their anniversary - " Ed paused delicately.

"Oh." The dialogue from John's bedroom suddenly took on new meaning.

"Then the second time," Ed continued, "he figures he should have seen it coming. If he'd paid more attention, noticed something sooner, maybe he could have got help for the boy in time."

"But they said - they said it happens like that sometimes, so fast. He can't possibly - He *loved* David! He paid attention to him *all* the time!"

"Now, I didn't say it makes sense, did I? They had a hard time getting pregnant. Took a lot of years the first time, a long time the next time. They both wanted a lot of kids, too. I heard the boss praying one time, thanking the Lord for David, for the second chance. Never had no more after him, neither. So maybe he figures he had the second chance, just one, and he blew it."

Twenty-Nine

Pastor Corrigan had not seemed surprised when Matthew called for an appointment, even though he never had before. Washing up after morning chores, Matthew put on a clean blue chambray shirt and made sure his fingernails were Sunday clean.

"I'm going into town for some supplies," he told Carolyn.

She nodded without looking up from the load of towels she was folding.

"Do you need anything while I'm there?"

Her hands methodically snapped towels and matched corners. "Nothing you can bring me." She gave a short, bitter laugh. "Have a good time."

"Yeah. Well, uh, I might be gone a while." Receiving no response, Matthew grabbed the keys to the truck from their hook by the back door and made his escape, feeling incredibly guilty, as if he had lied to her.

On the short drive to the church, he tried to rehearse what he would say, but he couldn't even be sure why he was going.

I must be crazier than I thought, Matthew told himself. *I don't even like this guy, with his funeral home black suit.*

I'll just leave, he told himself as he parked the truck in the church parking lot.

I'm out of here, he told himself as he roamed the halls in search of the pastor's office. Although he knew he had been in that office, he couldn't remember where it was. The church sprawled in several directions and felt like a maze.

Matthew passed the sanctuary, one place he did recognize, and paused in the rear doorway. He liked the narrow golden oak strips horizontally paneling the walls and vertically rising up and across the high ceiling like the ribs of a sailing vessel. He liked the soft rose, pale blue and amber windows. It was a peaceful place. He glimpsed a man sitting, head bowed, near the front and decided to ask directions. The man wore a bulky blue and cream wool sweater. His dark hair straggled a bit over the neck of the sweater as he lifted his head.

"Excuse me," Matthew began in a hushed voice.

The man turned. "Hi! I wasn't expecting you for a few minutes yet."

"Pastor?"

The pastor grinned. "I was the last time I checked. But why don't you just call me Miles? I guess you've never seen me in civvies before."

"No. Never."

"Would you be more comfortable if I ran home and changed?" Miles asked, rising and turning toward the door.

"No, that's okay. I mean, uh, I just was surprised. I guess I thought - I don't know what I thought."

Miles grinned again, a sweetly crooked grin which exposed a slight gap between his front teeth and made him look even younger.

I can't talk to this kid! Matthew thought.

"Let's go into the office," Miles suggested, moving into the aisle.

Head for the truck now, he told himself, following the pastor. The office was just across the hall from the front door of the sanctuary.

"I remember," Matthew whispered.

Miles turned back from the office door. "Maybe you'd rather come over to the house. The kids are in school and my wife's at work."

"Yes, please, I would."

Miles did something with the answering machine on his desk, then led the way across the lawn to a little white Cape Cod house.

They entered directly into the living room, a cheerfully untidy mix of worn plaid slipcovers and vibrant needlepoint pillows. Books lined one wall and were stacked on every table. A huge, healthy fern hung in the window.

"Make yourself comfortable," Miles urged, moving several books from a big recliner and stacking them on top of the books already on the table beside it.

Matthew sat instead in a huge armchair which promised to keep his feet on the floor. *I'll just stay a minute,* he told himself.

"Nobody knows I'm here!" he blurted.

"And they won't find out from me," Miles rejoined, sitting in the recliner. "Anything you want to talk about is confidential among the three of us."

"Three!" Matthew looked around nervously.

Miles laughed. "Sorry," he said. "The three of us is you, me and my Boss. And I trust Him with all my secrets."

"Oh." Matthew felt stupid, resented the man for making an in-joke.

Miles stretched out his long, jeans-clad legs and crossed them at the ankles. His arms were relaxed along the arms of the recliner and he waited as if he had forever.

"I'm not sure why I'm here," Matthew began. "But ever since David died..."

The pastor waited.

"We're all going crazy! Carolyn cries all the time and John won't talk; I hear David's voice in my dreams - sometimes not in my dreams, even. They - fought; I had an accident with the chain saw - "

"You feel crazy."

"Yeah."

"Like things are out of control."

"Yeah!"

"And you want to know..."

"*Why?*" His voice came out so loud, so pained it shocked him. "What kind of God kills little kids, and twice in the same family?"

Miles nodded and looked as if he truly understood. "What do you think?"

"Don't give me psychology," Matthew said. "If you don't know, just say so!"

The pastor smiled gently. "I don't know why. I wish I did. I do know God doesn't kill children. Illness and death are consequences of human choices way back when."

"You mean He couldn't have prevented it?"

"Oh, of course, He could have. But for His own reasons, which He doesn't have to explain to us, He didn't."

"So He let it happen."

"Basically, yes. And He didn't tell us why. But all through the Bible, from the Old Testament to the New, God's Word teaches us He is in control. Paul tells us in Romans that 'all things work together for good for those who love the Lord and are called according to His purpose.' And God says He will never leave us nor forsake us. That means when things are bad, He's right there with us, carrying us over the rough parts."

"Then where is He?" Matthew whispered, tears suddenly clouding his vision and clogging his throat. "I can't find Him. I don't think they can, either."

Miles sat up straight, folding his skinny legs like a marionette and leaning forward. His youthful face grew serious. "When you decided Jesus Christ is Lord and Savior and you asked Him to forgive your sins, He answered you *immediately*, He came to you *immediately* and took up residence in you. Jesus said, 'I am with you *always*.' He's still right there, loving you, carrying you. As He is David's parents.

"The problem is," Miles continued, "when we suffer a real body blow, like a death, something seems to go numb so we can't *feel* His presence. And so we think He's gone."

Matthew was skeptical. "Did that ever happen to you?"

The pastor smiled. "Yes, it did. My dad died while I was in seminary. We were pretty close; I loved him a lot."

"So what happened?"

"I wish I could tell you I realized all this stuff I'm telling you right now. But, in fact, I was so mad and hurt - God seemed so far away I thought for a while maybe He didn't exist."

"But you're a pastor!"

"I'm a man, too. I couldn't feel that love and peace I had always had and had always taken for granted. I tried to pray and either nothing came out of my mouth but curses, or my prayers seemed to be bouncing off the ceiling. I got drunk – once - " He paused to laugh at the memory. "That *sure* wasn't worth it! I decided to drop out of seminary."

"What changed your mind?" Matthew asked, fascinated in spite of himself.

"A couple of things happened. Time, for one. A couple of friends who hung in there without preaching even after I got drunk and they had to clean up our dorm room. A professor who told me feelings aren't facts."

"Feelings - ?"

"Aren't facts. He reminded me that truth is the Word of God, not how something feels. God keeps His promises, and it's documented in His Word."

"So then - ?"

"I reread the Book. Oh, I started with Job, because he suffered so much, but pretty soon I went to the Gospels, for Jesus' own words. And the Psalms. They seemed comforting. And I kept praying, even though it still felt like my prayers were going nowhere."

"And you got over it."

"Not exactly. I still miss my dad. He was wise; lots of times - like today - I wish I could talk something over with him. But I know he's happier than I can begin to imagine, with the Lord. And as I look back, I can see how God's grace took me every step of the way. It was like the weather: my dad died in August, but my heart felt the way it looks and feels outside right now. It was a bad winter. And then, little by little, the ground thawed and the trees budded, and one day I realized it was spring."

Matthew nodded, understanding the metaphor, rubbing his knee unconsciously. Smiling shyly, he admitted, "I kept telling myself it was crazy to come here - you wouldn't understand."

"Too young, right?" Miles grinned.

Matthew blushed deeply and looked down at his hands.

"Hey, I'm used to it. My wife loves it!"

"I was wrong," Matthew admitted. "Thanks for explaining. I'll just - keep trying. But what about them?"

Chagrin swamped Miles's face and hunched his bony shoulders. "We need to be like my friends from seminary - just hang in there. Pray for them, be there as much as they let us. I'm afraid you have a lot more opportunities than I do, right now."

"I can't intrude," Matthew protested. "John doesn't want to be bothered."

"Sometimes that's just exactly what we have to do."

"No, I really couldn't!"

The pastor fixed him with a steady gaze. "Last summer when you took that little unscheduled vacation, John didn't wait for you to invite him to help. As I recall, he came after you."

"How did you know about that?"

"He called me before you reached the end of the driveway. We prayed for you together, and I put it on the prayer chain. You had a hundred people praying for you before you even left town."

Matthew sat there stunned, mouth hanging open, as a tidal wave of embarrassment surged over him at the thought of everyone in town knowing. Then he felt something warmer. He looked at Miles with wonder. "For me! They prayed for me!"

"Sure," Miles acknowledged matter-of-factly. "You're part of the Body of Christ, Matthew, part of the church family. Of course we prayed when you needed us. Just as we're praying for all of you now."

"I understood the Abbotts were my family. I never thought about the rest of you."

"Takes some getting used to," the pastor sympathized. "The best thing about the love that prompts a hundred people to pray for one is the little hint it gives us of Christ's love for us. Now you have a chance to give some of it back, in a way maybe nobody else can. This is the 'doing unto others' part."

Matthew sat in stubborn silence, wrestling with new ideas and old fears. The pastor waited. *He does that really well!* Matthew thought. *I bet he could outwait anybody. Well, he's nicer than I thought, and smarter, too; but he can't make me confront John. I won't do it.*

"I better go," Matthew said.

"Would you like to pray together before you leave?" Miles offered.

No way, he thought. "Sure," his treacherous mouth said without his permission.

Thirty

Through the snows of January and part-way through the bleak ice of February, Matthew watched the people he loved best grow colder and colder, more and more separate. Carolyn began to speak again of ordinary things, but her soft voice held an eerie, unfamiliar lack of inflection. The warm blue of her eyes now had a perpetual gray overcast, and her hands, if they brushed his in passing, were always cold.

Pearl had taken to wearing a heavy black cardigan sweater over everything. One day she came for supper with a loaf of store-bought bread in a plastic wrapper, and from then on she didn't bake again. She and Carolyn talked together in hushed voices in the kitchen, day after day, but laughter never once punctuated the rhythm of their words.

John held his anger under iron control. A muscle twitched along his jaw line much of the time; his words remained sparse, infrequent, his voice the grating of a rusty hinge. It was the slack time before planting, when he could have relaxed before the fire in the evening or taken a nap on Sunday afternoon. Instead, he drove himself to keep busy every minute at any labor which would keep him away from the house. He pitted his strength against the farm machinery, expending his energy steel against cold steel.

Ed flowed through this world of ice like a southeasterly breeze, warming them briefly wherever he passed, a faint promise of spring. Matthew knew Ed's blessing on them had a cost. Now instead of whistling under his breath, the farmhand prayed. Matthew felt better, somehow, knowing those prayers were rising like a thermal current, melting tiny holes in the ice. They were a blanket of protection thrown over the family, the only thing which kept them all from freezing to death.

Perversely, as the ice around them deepened, Matthew's own grief heated and melted and percolated through him, scalding his eyes with tears and his stomach with acid. He would wander out of doors without his coat, unable to feel the cold any more, fall asleep at night on top of the covers. Ed patiently fetched Matthew's coat and handed him his gloves day after day. One morning when he awoke on top of his covers, Matthew found himself wrapped in the red and blue quilt from John's bed.

Already too hot, he wiped his eyes on a corner of the quilt, folded it neatly and replaced it carefully in John's room. Of course, they didn't speak of it.

On Sundays, Miles Corrigan looked at Matthew with unspoken questions. Ashamed, he would turn away from the steady gaze. *I told him I can't*, Matthew said to himself. *He doesn't know how it is.*

On Sundays, too, when only John broke their custom of no unnecessary work on the Sabbath, Matthew thought about Allison and her bleak pronouncement. He remembered the warmth of her little hand on his foot and the way she had reached out to him at the cemetery. He found her name in the phone book and memorized her number, but every time his hand reached for the phone, he forced it back and put it in his pocket.

On Valentine's Day, Matthew leaned into a pitchfork in the dairy barn, sweating in his shirtsleeves, mildly cursing cows for their unending digestive process. A sudden, loud meow caught him mid-swing and he dropped the pitchfork, whirling around to see what was going on. "Joshua and Samuel, Chronicles and Kings!" Matthew yelled, stumbling backward and nearly falling over the pitchfork. Celeste sat there in her Egyptian cat-goddess pose, looking extremely proud of herself. At his feet she had placed a huge, bloody, dead rat.

Ed ambled up from the other end of the barn, grinning. "Some *fine* scripture memory, I do declare!" he teased. "And looky here! Celeste always *did* favor you, son. Here, she's brought you a valentine."

Celeste regally inclined her head just a fraction at the mention of her name, obviously waiting for her subject to demonstrate appropriate gratitude. Recovering his breath, Matthew bent to pet her, running his hand from the top of her head to the tip of her arrogant tail in one hard stroke. Having accepted this homage as her due, Celeste walked away without a backward glance.

"What am I supposed to do with that?" he asked the farmhand, gesturing at the rat.

"Why, son, that's fresh meat she brought you! You're supposed to eat it." Ed shook with laughter.

Matthew shook, too, with a shudder of disgust he couldn't suppress.

"Them things carry vermin and disease," Ed said. "Anything in the burn barrel?"

"Enough." Matthew delicately insinuated the tines of the pitchfork under the carcass and carried it at arm's length across the barnyard. As soon as the fire was blazing, he heated the metal tines enough to burn away all traces of the rat and jabbed them into the snow. The image of the creature's long, sharp, yellow teeth, bared fiercely even in death, rode him.

"I hate those things!" he told Ed. "When I had to sleep in barns, I was afraid they'd bite me while I was sleeping."

They headed for the house for a coffee break. "Rats is just a natural part of farm life," Ed said. "I don't know why God made them, but He don't make mistakes. So they must have their part in the cycle of things."

They entered the empty kitchen. The coffee-maker murmured, keeping the pot warm, and the washer grumbled from the utility room. A plateful of donuts sat on the kitchen table.

"Car's gone," Ed remarked, pouring coffee into two large mugs adorned with blue geese. "Guess the missus went to the store." He brought the mugs to the table, set one in front of each of them.

"Or the cemetery."

"Cemetery?" Ed helped himself to a donut.

"Yeah. She told me yesterday she's been going there every day the last couple of weeks."

Ed nodded, his mouth full, powdered sugar dusting his lips and chin and drifting down onto his shirt.

"Is that a good thing, going there every day?"

"What do you think?" Ed mumbled around another bite of the donut.

"I don't know. On the one hand, she's getting out again. And she told me about it. So I guess that's good. On the other hand, how good can it be for her to sit there in the cold day after day, surrounded by all those little graves and all those sad little tokens?"

"Well - " Ed paused to wash down the last of the donut with a generous swig of coffee. "It seems to me she's facing up to it some by going. Like having a splinter, y'know, and you keep pressing on it to see if it's still there, if it still hurts. Until finally you get tired of it hurting and decide to get rid of it, even if it pains you real bad for a minute or two."

Matthew considered that as he watched the farmhand devour another donut and drain the last of his coffee in a lusty slurp. He rose to fetch the coffee pot.

"Do you really think," he asked, carefully refilling Ed's mug, "that David's death is just a little thing like a splinter?"

"Now, you know better than that," chided the farmhand. "All I'm saying is, that's the process, the way she's testing the pain. Says to me she wants to come out of it. On the other hand, think what happens to a splinter when you pretend it ain't there. It goes in deeper and deeper, hurting more all the time, until it gets infected and festers and poisons your whole system. That's how the boss is."

"Yeah. He must feel like life's given him one big, ugly, dead rat."

"He feels," came John's voice like the rasp of a file from behind them, "like you get paid to work, not to gossip like a couple of old women." The back door slammed.

"Aw, Nehemiah!" spluttered the farmhand. "We better get back to the barn. Doggone it, I wouldn't hurt him for the world."

"He knows that. You go on. I have to do something here first."

"You gonna eat that last donut?" Ed asked.

Matthew's stomach was churning, the coffee eating at him like battery acid. "No, go ahead."

Ed headed out the door, donut in his teeth, zipping his coverall to the neck. Quiet settled over the house again.

Matthew wandered away from the kitchen, leaving the mugs by the sink and crumbs all over the table. In the living room, he allowed his hands to play "Twinkle, Twinkle, Little Star" and "Row, Row, Row Your Boat" while his mind roamed. He had avoided the piano for weeks because the memory of David pressed up against him so strongly there. Now he could almost feel the heat of the boy's little body beside him on the bench, could smell him -

"No!" Matthew slammed the lid over the keys, laid his head on his hands on top of the lid. This grief was no splinter; it was an arrow clear through him, a mortal rip in his heart from which he continued to bleed but somehow could not die.

Matthew turned away from the piano and sat in John's chair. It was a safe place, a sorting place, even now, when its owner could provide no stability.

"Lord," he prayed out loud, "You had a spear in Your side. You know how this feels. You must know how it feels for them, too, losing a child. Lord, something terrible is happening here, and I don't know how to stop it. Please, just this once, tell me what to do! Show me how to help them. Please, God, have mercy on them - please!"

It wasn't much of a prayer, Matthew knew, compared with the ones he heard in church, or with John's in other times. He worried about leaving something out, some formula, some ritual required to make the prayer count. He waited for an answer without much expectation, and none came.

"God," he tried again, against his better judgment, "I don't mean to be rude. I understand that I don't understand and that You don't have to tell me anything. But, Lord, Your children are hurting so bad! John is locked away where no one but You can reach him, so mad at You and himself and everyone, so sad he's chained up and can't get free. Oh, Lord, if You don't want to give me a key for him, then please at least let me carry some of the pain for him!"

He found himself kneeling in front of John's chair, beating his fists on the leather seat. Tears were coursing down his face and his nose was running. Over and over, he repeated, "Please let me help them, please let me help!" and "God have mercy on them!"

Exhausted, he finally slumped over and rested his messy face on his hands, breathing like a winded sprinter. He didn't hear footfalls on the soft carpet and was startled upright by John's voice: "Are you all right?"

"I think so," Matthew replied, fishing out a handkerchief to mop his eyes and nose. "I was just, uh, praying. I'm sorry. I'll be right out."

John sighed. "I'm sorry about what I said in the kitchen. If you can pray, more power to you."

Matthew stood and met the farmer's eyes. "You were the one who taught me how to pray, and how important it is. Can't you do it any more?"

"So!" John laughed, sounding almost like his old self. "The worm turns!" His smile deserted him almost as fast as it had come. "No. I can't pray much now. I can't cry, either. I envy you for that, sometimes. Maybe most of the time. And I want you to know I'm grateful: for your tears, for your prayers, for sticking around and making Carolyn's life a little easier..."

Matthew was embarrassed and distressed for John, who seemed so humble and so vulnerable all of a sudden. He couldn't imagine why John should be grateful when all he was doing was loving the people who had loved him first.

"I wish I could do something," Matthew said.

The steel returned to John's voice. "There isn't anything to do but go on as best we can. David won't be back and we aren't allowed to join him." He turned and left the room as quickly and quietly as he had entered.

"Lord," Matthew said, "was that a start? It's the first time John's ever said anything about his feelings since the day David got sick. Please let it be a start!" He headed for the door, then paused. "Oh. Thank You. Amen."

Thirty-One

Three times more in the next week, Matthew found himself on the floor in front of John's chair, sobbing until he choked, begging God's mercy for the farmer. The ferocity of his feelings, the way they blindsided him, terrified him.

Exhausted and frightened, he manufactured another errand and drove again to the church. This time he had no problem finding Pastor Corrigan's office and banging on the door.

"Come in!" called the pastor.

Matthew flung open the door, rushed in and slammed it behind him. Miles looked up from his paper-strewn desk and smiled as if he were delighted to be interrupted.

Matthew was nearly gasping for breath. "You were wrong," he said without preamble, "I *am* crazy."

"Okay," Miles said amiably. "Should I be alarmed?"

"What?"

"Should I be worrying about being murdered before I finish my sermon, or would you like to sit down?"

"Oh." Matthew began to laugh in spite of himself and dropped into a singularly ugly, uncomfortable armchair near the desk. Its frayed orange nylon upholstery prickled through the back and sleeves of his work shirt while its springs poked the seat of his jeans with unwarranted familiarity. He squirmed.

Miles grinned. "At least certain parts of you are in contact with reality, aren't they? Why don't you try the couch instead?"

He moved across to the couch and Miles rolled his desk-chair over to close the distance. "I'm sorry about the sermon," Matthew said. "I should have called. Should I come back another time?"

"Nah. I was kind of stuck anyway, taking a breather. Somewhere between a prayer and a daydream. Besides, if you're crazy you probably need immediate psychiatric attention. I'd be pretty irresponsible to let you go." His engaging grin flashed again, then dimmed. "But maybe you'd rather go over to the house again. I know being in here is painful for you."

Matthew looked around the small, messy room, its overflowing bookshelves and mismatched castoff furniture. More bright needlepoint pillows punctuated the couch and chairs, while needlepoint pictures and photographs of the three Corrigan children graced the wall space not given over to bookshelves or windows. He realized he liked the room; there was no pain in being there.

"It's okay. Actually, it's fine. It doesn't - hurt - anymore."

"Great! So tell me about being crazy."

He observed Miles assuming his waiting posture, long legs outstretched and crossed at the ankles, long arms at rest along the arms of the chair. The man seemed completely at ease, as if he had all the time in the world, even though it was Friday and his sermon lay scattered about the desk unfinished.

"I can't sleep any more," Matthew began. The pastor nodded.

"Look, just don't say, 'Um-hm, I see, go on,' okay?" The pastor smiled and nodded.

"Anyway," Matthew tried again, "three times this week I woke up at three o'clock in the morning, like some giant hand just reached down and jerked me out of bed and - and- shoved me down the stairs!"

"You fell down the stairs?"

"No, no, it just felt like I *had* to go downstairs, like a - a mental push."

"So you *went* downstairs..."

Suddenly Matthew wished he were able to outwait Miles. He squirmed on the couch, rearranged half a dozen needlepoint pillows, looked everywhere but the pastor's patient eyes. He took a deep breath and continued.

"I went into the living room and sat in John's chair. I always do if I can't sleep and want to think or read the Bible. It's like a safe place, you know? Like part of him is there even when he isn't."

"Um-hm," Miles nodded. Then he grinned sheepishly. "Sorry. I know what you mean about a special place."

"Well, I go down and sit in that chair in the dark and the next thing I know I'm on my knees or flat on my face on the carpet in front of the chair, bawling like a baby, nose running all over my face..."

"It's not crazy to be grieving."

"I know that now, but that's not it. I'm not crying about David, or for myself. It isn't about me. All the while I'm bawling, I'm praying, too - crazy prayers - about chains and keys and begging God to have mercy on John – and - " He stopped abruptly, quivering.

"And?" the pastor repeated softly.

"I heard myself asking God to let me carry some of his pain, to let me suffer for him."

Miles was perfectly still and quiet. The silence began to stretch out awkwardly. Matthew's agitation grew until it threatened to explode.

"So I must be crazy! Nobody volunteers to suffer!"

Now Miles moved, sat up and leaned forward as he always did when making a point. "Jesus Christ volunteered to suffer for the people He loves. He even agreed to die for us, and He did it."

"Yeah, I know, but I'm not crazy enough to think I'm Jesus!"

"Of course not. I just meant there's precedent. Do you know much about intercession?"

"Never heard of it."

"Well, my friend, you seem to have the gift for it." Miles dragged one long, bony hand across his face and took a deep breath. "Let me see if I can make sense of it for you." He swiveled back to the desk to sort his Bible out from the papers. Rolling back again, he opened the Book.

"Here's First Corinthians, Chapter 12. It begins, 'Now about spiritual gifts, brothers, I do not want you to be ignorant...' Then it says the Holy Spirit gives every believer spiritual gifts, different ones to different people, all for the good of the whole group of believers, the Body of Christ. All the way to the end of Chapter 14, Paul talks about these gifts, what they're for, how no one gift or person is better than another - well, you can read all of it later, or take the class at church. The point is: everyone who accepts Christ and receives the Holy Spirit also receives one or more spiritual gifts, and you seem to have received the gift of intercession."

Matthew felt no more edified than he had before. "Well, that's nice, I guess, to get a present. But what is it, and what does it have to do with what's happening to me?"

Miles laughed ruefully. "I'm not doing a very good job of this, am I? Let me try again." He closed the Bible and leaned forward once more. "Spiritual gifts aren't just presents. They're God-given supernatural abilities we're supposed to use to help the Body of Christ and to reach those who don't believe yet. Okay?"

"Yeah, I guess so." Matthew frowned, concentrating hard.

"Okay! One of the gifts is intercession. That means the gift of being able to feel someone else's pain or need and to bring it to the Lord in intense prayer - and to stick with it until the prayer is answered or the Lord says to stop. So you're not crazy. The Lord is letting you intercede for the people you love." Miles smiled gently and leaned back in his chair again.

Matthew did *not* like the understanding he was reaching. He frowned harder. "So God throws me down on the living room rug to cry for John because he can't cry and to ask to be allowed to carry his pain for him."

"Basically, yes."

"Well, basically, no. I can't go on doing this. How do I trade this thing in for something else?"

Miles tried unsuccessfully to smother a chuckle. "I'm sorry, friend, but it doesn't work that way. You get what the Spirit gives you; and with at least some of the gifts, like intercession, you feel awful if you don't use them."

"I feel awful when I do!"

"Well, yeah, but you get the satisfaction of knowing you're doing God's will and you're helping people, too. And it feels great when the crisis is over, and you're closer to God."

"No! I'm gonna quit." He stood abruptly and paced the three or four steps the room allowed.

The pastor waited. Matthew spun and paced back.

"I *can't* quit, can I?"

"Nope. Oh, you can refuse. But the Lord will keep asking you anyway. And it grieves Him when we refuse to obey. It hurts Him when there's someone in need and no one willing to help."

Matthew sank back into the couch and closed his eyes, remembering the tortured face he had found in the woodcarving his third

Christmas on the farm and his vow never to cause such pain for Christ or anyone else ever again. *I'm doomed*, he thought. *I promised.*

Matthew opened his eyes to the pastor's scrutiny. "If I'm not crazy, then I'm a real jerk, huh? I don't know anything. The kids in children's church know more than I do."

"The kids in children's church have been around longer than you have," Miles countered. "You aren't crazy, and you aren't a jerk. You're a son of God by adoption and as precious to Him as His own Son. You just need education, not criticism, and you've taken a while to be ready for it. Try to be gentle with yourself."

"I'll tell you the truth," Matthew said earnestly, "I'm scared. I think this is more born-again than I signed on for. I don't want to be so close to God that He's talking in my sleep!"

"I know. All of a sudden things are happening too fast. I can promise you two things: one, you're going to catch up to yourself and find it all making some kind of sense; two, God loves you so much He'll never hurt you no matter how close you get, just like your own dad."

The words stunned Matthew for a moment. Images of the tall, dark figure in uniform looming over the pale woman and the cowering boy slammed into his mind. *God's like my father?*

"Miles," Matthew said in an acid voice, as he abruptly headed for the door, "you never knew my dad."

Miles suddenly found himself alone in the small room, staring at the empty doorway. "Speaking of feeling like a jerk..." he muttered aloud.

Without conscious decision, Miles took off through the church at a dead run, long legs eating up the distance. He burst into the parking lot just as Matthew slammed the truck door. "Wait!" he yelled, running up to the truck and grabbing the door handle.

Matthew started the engine, ignoring the tall man outside the window. *I was right in the first place,* he told himself, shaking with anger. *He doesn't know anything!* With a jerk, he put the truck into reverse.

Miles opened the door. "Please, listen for just a minute."

Matthew eased the gear shift back into park and waited.

"That was really stupid of me. I'm sorry. You're right; I don't know anything about your past or your family, and I had no right to make assumptions. Please forgive me."

Matthew turned his head to look at the young face and begging eyes. "You don't let any grass grow under your feet, do you?" he asked wryly.

"I can't seem to help causing people pain sometimes," Miles said, "or making them mad. But I can take responsibility for my behavior. It would be bad to let someone hurt for even one extra minute once I know I'm wrong. And it seems I was really wrong this time!"

"Forget it," Matthew said, engaging the gears again. "You couldn't have known."

"I'd like to know. Why don't you come back in and tell me?"

"No." He shook his head violently. "I don't talk about it. Let's just say you were lucky, Pastor. Not everyone's father is like yours." He gently closed the door and backed out. As he drove away, he saw in his rearview mirror Miles still standing there in his shirtsleeves in the cold parking lot.

Thirty-Two

The past continued to collide with the present as Matthew drove through town, exploding in shell-fragments of memory, slicing him with ragged, razor-sharp edges, the pain reminding him of the chain saw accident.

I need medical attention, he told himself.

As he circled to find a parking space, he scanned the hospital lot. There seemed to be at least a dozen small, bright blue cars. Bullying the truck into a space beside one of them, he headed into the building. *I'll just see. Not even say hello.*

He knew the way, three floors up, down the long row of tiny yellow shoeprints, through the double doors. At the nurses' station he froze, swamped by memories and embarrassment. The large, plain nurse standing behind the counter looked at him curiously.

"May I help you?" she asked.

The color and heat rose in his face. "Ah - no - thank you, I - don't - "

Light dawned in the nurse's eyes, followed by a sly smile. "Honey, you just wait right here one minute," she ordered in a voice which expected to be obeyed. She took off down the hall with a brisk, shoe-squeaking stride. Obedient by nature, he waited.

In no more than a minute, she reappeared. "Keep waiting," she ordered, returning to her post.

He waited.

Then, suddenly, there was Allison, appearing in front of him from nowhere in that amazing way she had, tiny frame covered by crisp whites, pretty little face shining with a smile. His heart rolled over in his chest and fell into her outstretched hand.

"Hi!" she bubbled, and Matthew could feel his lost heart beating between their hands. A long moment drifted by.

"Oh, I forgot," she said. "It's my job to write the dialogue. Okay: you say, 'Hi.'"

"Hi."

"Good! Now I'll say, 'I'm glad to see you. I hoped you'd call, but I'd just about given up.' Now you say: 'I meant to call or come by sooner...'"

"I meant to call or come by sooner - I really did!" Matthew blurted. "But I didn't think you'd want to see me..."

The other nurse gave a huge, unladylike snort of laughter. Allison quelled her with a sulfuric glare. "This rude person is my supervisor, Alice Campbell," she said.

He retrieved his hand and offered it to Alice. "I'm Matthew Ryersen, ma'am."

"Oh, I know who you are!" Alice laughed. "I've heard all about you."

Allison pointed one finger at her boss. "You're dead," she said succinctly.

Unperturbed, Alice said, "Go to lunch. Take your half-hour and mine, too."

Allison put her little hand in his again, and Matthew noticed that his fingers automatically curled around hers as tightly and naturally as the honeysuckle growing up his grandmother's back fence. "Would you like to take me to lunch?" she asked, drawing him toward the double doors.

His emphatic "Yes!" drew another laugh from Alice. The pleasant, raucous sound lingered in the stillness around them all the way to the elevator.

"You don't have a coat," he suddenly noticed.

"I thought we'd just go to the cafeteria here, if that's okay with you. Then we'll have more time." Her free hand was pushing a button on the elevator panel. "Besides," she added, "I'll get the employee discount. I want you to see I'm a cheap date."

Matthew told himself it was rude to keep holding Allison's hand, but his fingers clearly had a mind of their own. He hoped she wouldn't suddenly try to pull away, because he didn't think he would be able to let go.

They walked down several long, underground corridors, guided to the cafeteria by the strong food odors. The swinging door funneled them into a noisy confusion of bright lights, loud voices, rapid movement, garish colors and a steamy blend of smells. Matthew followed Allison's lead, taking a plastic tray, packaged plastic utensils, a plastic glass, and putting a large, red apple on his tray.

In a moment, Allison turned around and noticed the solitary apple. "Oh, no, that won't do! I'll show you the good stuff."

Hands roving constantly between Matthew's tray and her own, Allison moved them rapidly to the end of the line, where a bored young woman in a peach-colored smock and matching one-inch-long fingernails quickly relieved Matthew of ten dollars and seventeen cents.

Allison led the way to a small table in relative seclusion near the windows. As he sat down before the tray, Matthew stared at meatloaf and mashed potatoes and gravy and broccoli and salad and milk and chocolate chiffon pie. He looked at her tray, which held broccoli and salad and coffee and six chocolate chip cookies.

"Okay," Allison grimaced, "so I'm not a nutritionist. I've got two from the veggie group and six from the chocolate group. I'll put cream in my coffee and that'll be one from dairy."

"How about taking half the meatloaf?"

"Oh, no! Too much fat."

"Thanks a lot!"

"It's okay for you," Allison explained. "You're too thin anyway, and you do physical labor."

"You don't?"

"It's not the same. Let's eat!" She plucked her fork out of the plastic wrapper and attacked the broccoli.

Matthew bowed his head and folded his hands to give thanks for the food he didn't want and the company he did. When he looked up again, Allison was staring at him.

"Do you always say grace before meals?" she asked.

"Sure."

"Even in public. You always pray in public."

"Yeah. Well, not out loud."

Her eyes grew absolutely round. "When you're alone, you pray out loud?"

"Yeah, sometimes."

Allison shook her head and returned to the broccoli. He wrestled the flimsy plastic cutlery out of its wrapper and attempted the meatloaf. They ate silently, she from hunger, he because he had no idea how to make conversation with her. Partway through the cookies, she found time to talk again.

"Why'd you show up today?"

A bite of potato suddenly clotted in Matthew's throat; he washed it down with milk. "I just wanted to see you."

"No. It's been weeks. You've never called me, even after I gave you all those unsubtle hints that I'd like to go out with you, even after I visited. Why now?"

"Boy, you just don't quit, do you!"

"Not usually. So you might as well confess. I'm just going to be bamboo under your fingernails until you do."

"I thought about you lots of times. I just didn't think you would be interested. But today - I had a bad experience this morning, and it brought back all kinds of lousy memories. It felt like seeing you would make it feel better. I wasn't even going to say hello..."

She placed her warm little hand on Matthew's bare wrist where it extended beyond the cuff of his shirt. "Tell me about it," she urged. "Talking usually does make things feel better."

She doesn't want to hear this, Matthew thought. *It's boring. It's pathetic. She'll know what a jerk I am. I can't think of anything clever to say. I should get out of here.*

But the light weight of Allison's fingers on his wrist held him captive as surely as a handcuff.

"I haven't told many folks up here," he began.

"I promise I won't repeat it," Allison said, no trace of her usual smile visible.

He took a deep breath and let it out slowly. "My father was a cop from Baltimore. My mama's people came from Grayson County, Kentucky, on the ridge near Rough River..."

As he filled in the details, Allison's eyes filled with tears. "I'm so sorry your dad died," she breathed, full of compassion.

"Yeah? Well, I'm not. I was glad! He was a brutal drunk and he beat my mama and me somethin' fierce."

She felt Matthew's hand quivering under hers and saw the anger and pain on his face. He was breathing rapidly, shallowly, striving for control. Allison stroked the back of his hand and his skin twitched involuntarily, like a nervous thoroughbred's.

"So," he continued after a moment, "we moved back to Kentucky. I liked it there, bein' able to walk to school, bein' out of doors workin' that sorry piece of land with Granddaddy. The police pension made it easier, let us bring in electricity. Gramma never would give up her wringer washin' machine, but at least we had hot water and good light to study by.

"Then when I was fifteen, my mama died. They said she had cancer, but I think she really had a broken heart. I don't know why, but she always did love him. When she died, the money stopped. Granddaddy made me finish high school, then I got a job at the feed store in town and helped him as much as I could after work. I gave him 'most all my paycheck, too. But when they died a couple years later, the farm was auctioned off for back taxes. There was nothin' left.

"That's when I hit the road."

They sat there quietly for a few minutes as Matthew pondered the enormity of his foolishness in sharing so much of himself and Allison grieved for the boy who had lost so much of himself.

"Well," she finally said, "you really are a survivor!"

He looked at her blankly.

"I mean," she persisted, "you've had so much hard stuff happen to you so young, and here you are, living and working and having a life... Some people drink themselves to death, or blow their brains out, or find someone they can beat up to prove they aren't little wimps any more... But you - you're responsible, and gentle, and - and - good."

Matthew was too embarrassed to meet her eyes any more. "Thanks for listenin'," he said. "But don't judge how 'good' I am until you get to know me better."

"Does that mean I'm going to get the chance?"

"Do you still want to, knowin' where I come from? You could be goin' out with a doctor or a lawyer, somebody from a good family, without all that baggage."

"You're right; I could. I did." She took her hand from Matthew's arm and tilted his chin until he was again looking into her bright eyes. "I know what I want and who I want to be with. I'm off on

Friday and Saturday this week. That's tonight. My number is - "

"I know it," he admitted sheepishly. The smile she gave him in return warmed every corner of his being and carried him all the way home.

Thirty-Three

When Matthew arrived home, John was waiting for him. They went into the living room, not their usual pattern in the middle of the day, and John sat in his big chair. Matthew remained standing before him like a child in the principal's office.

"You're not in trouble," John smiled. "C'mon; sit down."

Matthew sat in Carolyn's chair and waited.

"Miles called," John said in his metallic voice. "He was worried about you. Seems he said something to upset you and feels he didn't get a chance to put it right." The farmer looked at him squarely. "When you didn't come home after that, I was worried. Are you all right?"

Matthew squirmed in the chair but met John's eyes. "I'm fine. Honest. I really didn't think anyone would miss me. I *sure* didn't think Miles would call."

After a considering pause, John continued, "I didn't know you were seeing Miles."

Matthew squirmed some more, a motion not lost on John. "Just a couple of times. I'm sorry."

"Why would you be sorry about seeing the pastor?"

"Well, I know you're - I mean, you and he - I mean, you haven't gone - but I just had some questions..."

John's face softened and grew sad. He sighed deeply. "I haven't been helping you much lately, have I? Did you think I wouldn't know the answers, or were you afraid to ask?"

Matthew sat silent, staring at his shoes. How could he answer?

"Just give me a little more time," John asked. "Don't leave us, please."

A tiny catch in the farmer's voice horrified Matthew. He started to protest, but John stopped him with a sharp hand gesture and a negative shake of his head. "Miles is a good man," John grated. "I'm glad you trusted him. But I won't bite if there's something you want to ask me." He left the room abruptly, as if he had said too much.

Oh, Lord, Matthew prayed, staring at John's chair, *he feels as lonely as I do sometimes. Please let him know You're there. Let him know we love him, no matter how he feels or acts. Please. Please!*

Gradually he prayed his way upstairs to change into his work clothes, then out to the barn to do the afternoon chores. Ed came in to help with the milking, rubbing his chapped, ungloved hands together.

"Oh, man, I don't think it's ever gonna warm up!" Ed complained. "Colder'n yesterday's coffee out there!"

Deep in internal conversation, Matthew failed to respond to the farmhand. His hands mechanically coupled the machinery, patted the beige Jersey cows. His lips moved a little from time to time, and Ed respected his distraction.

Later, at the supper table, Matthew continued the prayer inside his head without really being aware of it. Somewhere the nature of his prayer had changed from begging to thanksgiving. Ragged attempts at conversation passed over and around him and occasionally he heard a few words, enough to nod or to mumble something. Mostly, seeing the expression on his face, they smiled a little at one another and left him alone.

After dinner, Matthew went directly to his room, where he knelt beside the bed to continue his prayers.

Downstairs, the phone rang. John jumped up to catch it in the middle of the second ring. They heard him say, "Yes. Yes, it is. No, I'm sorry, he can't come to the phone right now. Yes, I'll give him the message..."

As John returned to his seat, the two of them looked at him expectantly.

"Who was it?" Carolyn burst out. "Matthew's never had a phone call before Miles called today."

John smiled a lazy smile at his wife and peeked at her through slitted eyes. "It was a woman."

"No way! He doesn't know any women."

"Apparently he knows one." John closed his eyes again, remembering the summer he had coaxed a deer to take grain from his hand. He could practically hear curiosity fermenting inside his wife.

"Well? What did she want?"

John opened his eyes and smiled again. "I might trade information for pie," he teased. "Then again - I might not."

"Hmm..." Carolyn considered.

Come on! John coached silently. "I know who she is."

"Well... we'll deal," Carolyn countered. "If both of you come out to the kitchen with me and you," she said, pointing at John, "talk while I serve." She rose.

Ed lumbered to his feet, yawning. "I gotta go home and get some sleep. Four a.m. seems even earlier these cold, dark mornings. Thanks for supper." He headed for his coat, on a rack by the front door.

"Wait!" Carolyn said urgently. "Don't you want some more pie? It's apple, your favorite."

"No, thanks," Ed answered, zipping up his coat, "not tonight. See you tomorrow." Then he was gone, leaving the two of them alone together, unbuffered.

John held his breath. *Please*, he thought. *Just the pie. Please.*

"You can deliver his message," Carolyn said, moving away from him.

"What about our pie-for-information deal?" he asked, standing very still.

She hesitated briefly, then headed up the stairs. "He'll tell me tomorrow for free," she tossed back over her shoulder.

John locked the front door and leaned his forehead against the glass. Something black and ugly rose up in him. Muscles straining, teeth grating, he wrestled it down again before climbing the stairs to his cold, empty bed. Lying there wide-eyed in the dark he heard the door across the hall open, Matthew's bare feet slapping softly down the stairs, the faint murmur of his voice.

I hope he's calling her, John thought. *I forgot to tell him. I hope I forgot. God forgive me if I didn't.*

§ § §

Matthew stood by the wall phone in the dark kitchen, shifting from foot to foot on the cold linoleum, trying to think of something to say to Allison if she ever stopped chattering. Her brisk, light voice pleasantly tickled his ear as she thanked him for lunch and told him about her afternoon.

Then she asked, "Did you mind that I called you?"

Matthew was confused. "I thought I called you."

"Yes, but I meant before. The man who answered said you couldn't come to the phone, but he'd give you the message. He didn't?"

"No. I mean, it's probably written down here somewhere, but nobody told me. I was in my room all evening, didn't hear the phone."

"What was so important you couldn't take a call?"

Oh, brother. "I was - uh - talking to somebody."

"Oh, really? In your room?" Allison's voice was becoming dangerous. "Were you with some other woman in your room?"

Matthew laughed. Knowing she might be insulted by his laughter, even knowing the truth could be worse than her supposition, he laughed anyway. It was just too ridiculous. He imagined he could feel the wires melting inside the phone as she began to breathe fire.

"No, wait," he choked out. "I'm not laughing at you! Let me explain!"

Hot silence enveloped him.

"Please," he said. "It wasn't a woman. I'd never do that here! Besides, there isn't any woman except you. Honestly!"

"Oh, come on! A good-looking single guy like you - "

He blushed in the darkness. "Honestly. None. Not one."

"Well, then," she relented, mollified by his obvious sincerity, "who was it you were talking to that kept you from talking to me?"

Nuts. "It was - God."

He could tell exactly when the fire went out of Allison and the ashes turned cold. He had expected it. "Oh," she said.

That one little word dropped into his ear like an ice cube. His whole body shivered and froze over.

"Maybe this isn't a good idea," Matthew said. "I like you, Allison, and I'd like to get to know you better. I was going to ask you to go to a movie tomorrow night, but maybe - "

"No, no, no, no!" she cried. "I'm sorry! I'd love to go to a movie with you. We just won't talk about - that. I can talk about lots of other things, you know I can."

He felt the ice melting rapidly as they made plans and she chattered a little longer. Heading back to his room, he thought about this tiny, incandescent bundle of energy. He could imagine loving her, making love with her, sitting across the table from her, turning gray with her. He could almost imagine a baby in his awkward arms, a little girl with Allison's curly hair and long eyelashes.

I'm an idiot, he laughed as he crawled into bed. *Oh, but I wish -*

Thirty-Four

At breakfast, John said, "By the way, you had a phone call last night."

"Yeah, thanks. I called her after you went to bed."

Carolyn could hardly stand it. "Who is she?"

Matthew flushed and looked down at his plate. "She's just someone I met - well, a nurse from the hospital. Allison West."

"And?" Carolyn persisted.

"Don't push!" John interjected sharply.

"I'm sorry." She subsided, shrinking back in her chair. John's face reflected the ache of sorrow and guilt and loneliness. He quietly left the room.

Carolyn sighed. "I didn't mean to push."

"I know. It's okay," Matthew reassured her. "I'm just embarrassed, I guess. I haven't - dated - for a long time."

"Are you dating her?"

"I guess so. I bought her lunch yesterday and I'm taking her to the movies tonight."

Carolyn suddenly smiled, her old heart-warming smile. "That's wonderful! Do you like her a lot?"

"Yeah, I do." He smiled shyly in return.

§ § §

Later, in the barn, he asked John hesitantly whether he might borrow the car. "I know I can use the truck any time, but - "

"But this is special. Sure you can borrow the car. Have a good time. But before your hot date, I want to see if we can get the east field plowed."

They found the earth still frozen, but John insisted on tearing at it anyway, despite the protests of men and plow. The tractor cab was almost warm enough, but the hard ground jolted them until their teeth rattled. By late afternoon Matthew was sure he was too tired to go anywhere but his own bed.

"You go get cleaned up," Ed urged. "I'll do the chores, no problem."

"Thanks." Matthew plodded to the house, left his boots and coverall in the enclosed back porch and plodded upstairs to shower.

As hot water cleansed away sweat and grime and eased the aches from his muscles and his left knee, he gave thanks for every blessing he could think of, until John pounded on the door and begged him to save just a little hot water. Quickly complying, Matthew shaved in cold water and combed his hair through the steamy haze on the mirror. He paired his best jeans with a pale green, long-sleeved cotton sweater and found a decent pair of sneakers at the back of his closet.

Allison was ready when he rang the bell at her modern townhouse apartment on the far side of town. Her bright blue coat was buttoned to the neck, but her hands were bare. She joined one with Matthew's as they walked the short distance to the car.

"Oh!" she exclaimed. "I thought you had a truck."

"I drive the truck most of the time, but this is a special occasion." He handed her into the passenger seat and carefully closed the door. "But I need to tell you," he continued, sliding into the driver's seat, "they both belong to my boss." He busied himself with seatbelt and ignition, afraid to see disdain in her face for a man who owned nothing.

"It's nice of him to lend them to you," Allison remarked. "And it saves you the hassle of car payments until you decide you really want something."

He risked a sideways glance, saw nothing but her usual good-natured smile. Could she mean it?

The movie was wonderful for Matthew, though he remembered little of it. Allison ate two-thirds of their huge tub of buttered popcorn with one hand while hanging onto his arm or hand with the other. She huddled against him during the scary parts and warmed him with her laughter during the funny parts. During the obligatory romantic interludes, she stopped chewing and put her head on his shoulder. He couldn't be sure, but under the sound track he thought he heard her purring, rather like Celeste. Did small dragons purr?

Hunger apparently unappeased by a mountain of popcorn, Allison urged him afterward to the local fast-food hangout, where Matthew sipped very hot black coffee and watched her demolish one of almost everything.

"I eat when I'm happy," she told him.

"When *don't* you eat?" he teased.

"When I'm asleep," she mumbled around a mouthful of french fries, "and when I'm making love. Usually." She laughed. Matthew did not, struggling to reject the image. "I'm ready to go whenever you are," she said.

As he drove back to Allison's apartment, she sat close, holding Matthew's hand when he wasn't shifting gears. The apartments were mostly dark, the cars in the lot huddled down in the cold for the night like sled dogs. He pulled into an empty space and killed the engine. Allison moved away slightly, drawing him toward her.

They kissed several times, tentatively, gently, before she opened her mouth to him and unbuttoned her coat. Matthew surged toward her almost violently, then backed away even faster.

"What's wrong?" she asked, her eyes drowsy and her voice furred with passion.

"I can't!" he panted from the relative safety of the driver's-side door.

"Oh, I think you *can*," she said pointedly, reaching for him.

"Don't!" he ordered sharply, grasping her wrist to push her hand away.

"What *is* your problem?" The softness of her voice was now all sharp edges.

Humiliated, he met her eyes in the faint light from someone's porch. "I can't - I don't - "

"Don't bother saying you don't want me!" Allison snapped.

"Of course I want you," he groaned miserably. "But I can't - we're not married - "

"Married? How old are you?"

"Thirty-two."

"And you expect me to believe you're some kind of thirty-two-year-old virgin who's never had sex before?"

Matthew was stung. "I didn't say that!"

"Are you gay or something?"

"No! And I'm not a virgin!"

"Well, then," Allison's voice softened again, "you want me, and you know how to, and I want you - so why don't we go inside and get you back into practice?"

Matthew was sweating. *Oh, Lord, help me!*

"Please," he begged, "try to understand. Back – before - I'd take what I could get and think it was okay as long as I gave, too, and didn't make any promises."

"Sure. I understand. That's what I'm suggesting now. I'm a nurse; I can guarantee I don't have anything catching. Oh, gosh! Do you? Is that what you're telling me?"

"No, nothing like that. It was a long time ago, and not many girls..."

"Well, I have protection if you don't, so let's go!" She took his hand and tugged impatiently.

"Please," Matthew tried again. "What I'm trying to say is that's how I used to be. I'm not proud of it, but it's true. But everything's different now. I can't do things I used to, because now I know they're wrong."

"It's the God-thing again, isn't it?"

Matthew nodded helplessly. He saw his dreams under his feet like the crumpled candy wrappers and empty popcorn boxes on the sticky theater floor.

"I think," Allison challenged, "that you've got the wrong take on this. This God of yours is supposed to have made everything, right?"

"Yeah," he replied cautiously, scenting a trap.

"So he made sex, too."

"Yeah."

"And if He made it, and He's all-good, then sex is good."

"Yeah..."

"Then when two people like each other and respect each other and - and desire each other, having sex together is good."

He drew his hand away from hers just before the trap clanged shut. "No. The Bible says it's a sin unless the two people are married to each other. And sin hurts God."

Under her breath Allison muttered something Matthew was sure he did not want to hear. Then she lunged at him and kissed him long and hard.

"Just so you'll know what you're missing," she snapped, shoving her way out of the car. "Thanks for the movie." Swiping away a tear, she ran up the walk and into the building.

Thirty-Five

The next morning Matthew straggled out to the car at the last possible moment. To his surprise, John sat behind the wheel. "We're almost late," John said as casually as if he had never missed a Sunday, "but there's time for you to grab a donut and a glass of milk if you want to."

"No, thanks." Matthew crawled into the back seat. John smoothly backed out of the long driveway. Carolyn turned around to inspect Matthew, taking in his pallor, the dark circles under his eyes. She had heard him come in before eleven; she faced front and asked no questions.

Matthew heard little of the sermon, didn't even try the songs. He acknowledged to himself that he felt sorry for himself and more than a little angry. He was angry with Allison for not understanding, with himself for being such a coward and with God for making the rules too hard. He watched with languid interest as John greeted people after the service, nodding to the pastor's delighted grin while avoiding his outstretched hand.

A light snow sifted down on them as they traversed the church parking lot, and Carolyn took Matthew's arm to keep from slipping. Matthew saw something happen behind John's eyes, something dangerous and alien, rapidly squelched. Once he had the engine going, the defroster blowing noisily, John sat there for a long moment staring straight ahead, both hands tightly gripping the wheel. Then he flicked the wipers, and it was as if they removed his dark mood along with the light covering of snow.

"What's for dinner?" John asked, his voice close to normal, his hands deftly maneuvering the car into the flow of traffic.

"Chicken," Carolyn replied. "With stuffing. If the oven turned on."

"Having a problem with it?"

"Well, yes, I have been. Just a couple of times."

"You should have told me. I'll take a look at it for you."

"Thank you." Her voice was cool enough to drop the temperature inside the car by ten degrees.

In the back seat, caught between his own misery over Allison and the pain emanating from the estranged pair in the front, Matthew wished he could just have a tantrum, to release some of the accumulating pain by hitting and kicking and screaming. He had no idea what to do to help them. *Shoot, I can't even help myself!*

§ § §

The week went downhill with the weather.

On Monday evening, just as Matthew was coming in from a last check of the barns, the phone rang. "I'll get it!" he yelled as he picked up the receiver.

"Matthew, is that you?"

"Yeah, who's – Allison?"

"It's me. Can you talk?"

"Sure." He made sure the door from the kitchen into the dining room was closed. "What's up?"

"I'm sorry."

He waited a moment, but she didn't say anything more. He could hear her breathing unevenly. "Allie, are you okay?"

"I'm sorry. I'm sorry I was so mean to you. I'm sorry I made fun of you. I wish – I wish you – Oh, I'm sorry!" She was clearly crying now.

Matthew rubbed his hand across his face and tried to figure out what was happening. "Allie, listen to me. I know you were upset, and I understand. It's okay, really. We're still friends."

"You mean it?"

"Well, sure." He continued to try to understand, and a suspicion formed, unwelcomed. "Allison, what are you drinkin'?"

"Me? Just a beer. What are you drinking?"

"Nothin' right now. How many have you had?"

"Oh, maybe three...maybe... Listen, since we're still friends, do you want to come over and have a beer with me? We don't have to do anything, just have a drink together. Please, Matthew, I'd really like to see you again. I can respect you, I promise!"

"I'm sorry, but I – uh – I can't do that right now."

"Oh." She paused for a long time. "Oh. Maybe some other time, huh?"

"Yeah, maybe. Thanks for calling. Take care now."

He gently replaced the receiver and considerably less gently punched the refrigerator. *Why does it have to be like this? Why did she have to take a drink to call me, and why can't it be safe and easy for us – for me – just this once? She isn't going to change any time soon, and I can't – I don't dare – Oh, God, I want to!*

§ § §

By Tuesday all of them had miserable colds, sneezing, coughing, wincing every time they swallowed. Snow kept coming on raw, damp winds. There was mildew in the hay. They kept each other awake at night with their coughing.

"It's gonna be a biracle if sprig eber comes," snuffled Ed, blowing his nose loudly into yet another blue bandana.

"I'd argue with you," Matthew said in a husky half-whisper, "but it hurts too much to talk."

When they went in to supper through the ugly gray twilight, Pearl was presiding over the table. She placed before them huge bowls of hot chicken soup and slices of her own whole-wheat bread, still warm enough to melt the butter completely.

Although unable to smell the food, and not at all hungry, Matthew picked up his spoon. If he refused, Pearl would bully him. Besides, he was relieved to see she had felt like baking - and that she was wearing a coral-colored sweater instead of the ugly black one she had worn all winter.

So he filled the spoon, blew on the hot liquid a little and swallowed the first mouthful. Immediately he began to choke and cough uncontrollably as heat and acid tore at his raw throat. His eyes and nose streamed, his face turned bright red, he coughed until he gagged. Every now and then he managed a wheezy little breath which kept him from passing out or throwing up. As he struggled and the family

clustered around in alarm, he thought wildly, *I'm going to die of soup!*
That's what they'll put on my tombstone: Died of Soup! And then he
nearly did asphyxiate himself by laughing.

Finally he subsided into wheezing gasps and chuckles. "I thought
you liked me," Matthew accused the old woman in the whisper that
was all that was left of his voice.

"Before *I* try this soup," John said, "I want to know what's in it."

"Gonna stick with the bread, myself," Ed added.

Pearl pretended indignation. "That's homemade chicken noodle
soup, with homemade noodles, I'll have you know!"

"And what did you season it with," Matthew whispered, "turpen-
tine?"

That remark drew a raspy guffaw from the farmhand and a frown
from the cook. "Don't be smart with me, young man!" she snapped.
"It has plenty of onion and garlic and crushed red pepper and ginger
- all good for colds and chest congestion. They'll open everything
right up."

"Yes, ma'am," he whispered meekly, "but my throat's so sore I
can't - "

"You just give it another try. All of you!"

Four heads nodded, four spoons began cautious forays from bowls
to mouths. All four noses ran, all eight eyes watered, but no one refused. Pearl smiled, satisfied.

"Actually," John rasped, "it's pretty good. I think."

"Ma'am," Ed said respectfully, "it sure does seem to be doing like
you say, and I thank you for taking care of us. But I notice you ain't
eating any."

"Mercy, no!" the old woman exclaimed. "I'm not sick!"

Matthew would have laughed again, but it made his head ache.
As soon as he was able, he dragged himself up the stairs and crawled
into bed. He was freezing, shaking with cold, and piled all the quilts
and blankets on top of him. Then he was hot, so hot! that he kicked
them all onto the floor. He dozed, dreaming he was awake, and woke,
thinking it was a dream. *I must have a fever*, he thought, but he didn't
have the energy to get up to find out.

Around two in the morning, Matthew heard John coughing,
heard the door to John's room open, heard Carolyn's voice drift across
the hall. "You sound awful. Can I get you anything?" she asked.

"No. I'm okay. Get some sleep." John coughed again.

"Please let me help. There's some cough syrup in the bathroom..."

Come on! Matthew coached silently from his eavesdropper's post. *Come on -*

"All right," John conceded.

Matthew heard the sounds of water running, cupboards opening and closing, then the clink of spoon and bottle, a sound of disgust from John.

"I'm sorry it's so nasty," Carolyn soothed. "But it should help. No, don't drink any more water just yet; it's supposed to coat your throat."

Matthew heard the farmer grumble something, his wife murmur gently. Then he heard their bed creak and settle. Was she staying?

Oh, Lord, please. Please let her stay with him. She went to him, Lord, and he needs that more than anything. He'll find his way home to You if she'll just love him again. I know he will.

By Friday they were recovering, the snow had stopped and Carolyn had spent three nights in John's bed.

By Sunday they were well, the ice on the pond was thawing, Carolyn had returned to David's room. The phone was silent. The whole house was silent. The ride to and from church was silent. Matthew decided he couldn't stand it any more.

After dinner, he stopped John with a hand on his arm. "Can we go somewhere and talk?"

Surprise showed on John's face. "Sure. Where would you like to go?"

"Oh. Uh - how about my room?"

"Fine with me. Lead on!"

They climbed the stairs and settled themselves in the spartan room, Matthew on the bed, John tilting the straight chair comfortably back on two legs. Matthew jumped up and closed the door, then sat again on the edge of the bed. The farmer waited.

After several long minutes, Matthew blurted out, "Did you and Miles go to school together?"

John raised one eyebrow. "What?"

"There has to be some school where they teach you to wait like that!"

"Oh, I get it," John laughed. "No, he's a lot younger than I am. He learned it in seminary; I learned it from milking cows."

"Cows."

"Cows. Think about it. Now why did you need to sneak off to talk to me? Woman trouble?"

"Partly." Matthew flushed and fiddled with the bedspread. "How'd you know?"

John smiled gently. "It wasn't too tough. You borrowed the car, got all slicked up, left here eager as a pup. Then you came slinking home early with your tail between your legs and haven't made a phone call since."

"Can I tell you?"

"Of course."

"We went to the movie, like we planned, then out to eat, and it was nice. We talked, we laughed, I held her hand..."

"And then?"

"I drove her home. We – we - " He twisted a handful of the bedspread and avoided John's eyes.

"You made love." The farmer's voice was gentle.

"No! We didn't! I wanted to, but I stopped."

"Why?"

He looked at John then, shocked. "Because it was wrong! You know that!"

John nodded. "Just so. But I don't quite see the problem yet, aside from frustration. You like the woman, you respected her and yourself, you acted like a gentleman."

"She didn't want me to 'act like a gentleman.' She wanted to - 'have sex,' she called it. She was really mad when I kept refusing."

"Oh."

"She asked if I was gay!"

"Mm-hm."

"Well, I'm not! And I'm not a virgin, either, I told her. So when I still said no, she figured it was 'a God-thing,' and that made her even madder! She stormed off. What am I supposed to do?"

"She's not a Christian, then?"

"No. She told me one time she doesn't believe in God."

John brought the chair gently down onto all four legs and leaned forward, resting his arms on his knees. "That's the bottom line of the problem," he said softly. "You have two really different views of life."

Matthew nodded miserably. "So what'll I do? I really like her. I could love her without much trouble. But I can't keep - I mean, she was real persuasive! And then she was so angry - " He shook his head in confusion.

"What do you think would happen if you went out with her again?"

"I think pretty soon we'd end up in the same mess again."

"Why?"

"Well, because! Because she's a warm, affectionate woman who touches, and she - well, she makes me - want - and for some reason she seems to want me, a lot. I don't think I could go through that too many times without giving in. I wanted to!"

"I know. I remember." John chuckled at Matthew's expression. "Don't look so shocked. We were young and in love once, a lot younger than you. The thing was, we were both believers, so we dealt with it together, by prayer and by planning."

"Planning?"

"When we saw where our feelings for each other were headed, we talked about it, about what we wanted right then and what we wanted for the long haul. We were agreed about what was right and wrong - well, maybe not quite agreed about where some of the boundaries were, but close enough - so we arranged our social life to 'lead us not into temptation.'"

"Like not spending a lot of time alone?"

"Exactly right. But also, as we saw the attraction was becoming real love, we talked a lot about what each of us wanted out of life, what we believed was most important, how we wanted to worship and serve the Lord, about children - "

John stood abruptly and faced the window. His pain beat itself against the walls and ceiling of the small room like a wounded hawk.

"The best thing to do," John continued, in a voice so metallic Matthew could suddenly taste the fillings in his own teeth, "the best thing to do is to forget her. If you let yourself love her, she'll only break your heart."

As John fled his room and clattered away down the stairs, Matthew knew absolutely that it was not his love and not his heart John had been talking about. He heard the back door slam, the truck rattle off down the driveway. "Oh, God, I tried," he exclaimed aloud. "I meant to bring it up. But I never got a chance."

Bending down, he pulled the old pillowcase out from under the bed. For reasons unbeknownst to himself, in the last few weeks Matthew had been carving a family of tiny mice from scraps of white pine. The soft wood gave up the little figures easily; eight of them already lined his dresser-top and one, wearing glasses, peeked whimsically from under a pothos leaf over the edge of the pot. Today, however, as he fingered a larger piece of wood, he thought perhaps he saw a dragon there, maybe three or four inches long from head to tail-tip, wearing a pointy little crown.

An hour or so into the work, he was disturbed by a knock on his door. At his invitation, Carolyn entered.

"I'm sorry to bother you, but did John say where he was going? He looked so upset when he came flying down the stairs - he didn't say anything, just grabbed his coat and keys and slammed out the door."

A strange feeling tightened Matthew's hands on the knife and the wood. He laid everything carefully on the bed. "No. He didn't say."

"Did you and he - have words?"

Matthew's throat was tight. "In a manner of speaking, yes." He looked Carolyn in the eye. "Could I have some words with you?"

"I suppose so. May I sit down?" She gestured to the chair.

"Yes, please do." He forced the politeness. Carolyn seated herself primly on the edge of the chair and looked at him expectantly.

"I know this is probably none of my business," Matthew began, "but sometimes it's like I'm right in the middle of things."

"You're right," she said coldly. "It's none of your business." She rose to leave.

"Don't you want to know what we were talking about?"

"Not particularly." She moved to the door.

"Well, you need to hear!" Matthew insisted, arresting her flight with a boldness not his own. She came back to the chair with obvious reluctance.

"I asked him how to deal with my 'woman-trouble,' the falling-out we had."

"I'll bet he had great advice about that!" Her voice dripped sarcasm.

He realized he was furious with Carolyn, wanted to shake her. He sat on his hands and prayed for peace. "As a matter of fact, at first he did. He told me how he developed his relationship with you, praying and planning together, figuring out what mattered, where God fit into your lives, about knowing it was real love - "

Carolyn continued to look at him coldly.

"But the last thing he said - He said, 'If you let yourself love her, she'll only break your heart.'"

Carolyn was silent.

"Don't you see?" he forged on desperately. "John wasn't talking about me, he was talking about himself. He loves you so much - you're almost all he has left now that he thinks God's mad at him. Why did you go back when he was sick and then move out again? Can't you see - "

In one beautiful, fluid, Olympic-quality move, Carolyn rose from the chair to the edge of the bed and slapped his face. "How dare you?" she hissed. "Who do you think you are?"

Except for the small handprint flaming on his cheek, Matthew was frozen solid again. Alone, on his knees, he considered Carolyn's parting questions. How did he dare? Who did he think he was? He looked at the closet, where the duffle-bag still hid.

Oh, Jesus, why did You let me do that? All I wanted to do was help, like Miles said, and instead I've hurt both of them. Was it like this for You with Your disciples when things got rough? Was it like this for Your family when You died? Maybe I should just pack that bag and go. I'm sure no help around here!

John 15:12, Matthew thought. "What?" he asked out loud. *John 15:12*, he heard again. "Here we go again," he muttered, taking his Bible from the night stand and turning quickly to the gospel of John. "I should know this chapter by heart," he groused, leafing through the pages.

There it was: "My command is this: love one another as I have loved you."

Okay, Matthew thought, *I get it*. Then he read the next verse. *Terrific!* "Greater love has no one than this, that he lay down his life for his friends."

Okay, Lord. I got it. But couldn't You please make me more like Ed?

As long as he was down on his knees, Sunday afternoon and all, Matthew figured he might as well pray for wisdom. Then wisdom seemed to suggest he confess his sins and seek forgiveness. Then he lay on his face and prayed again for this sad family, for their deliverance from pain and from estrangement. His tears were bitter and lasted a long time. Exhausted, he finally fell asleep where he lay.

Waking, stiff and chilly, in the middle of the night, he found that once again someone had slipped in and covered him with quilts.

Thirty-Six

Easter came and went that year, with its resurrection message bittersweet for those who loved David. Finally, mid-April, everything bloomed at once. The woods became fairy-tale landscapes of lacy trees, fuchsia of redbuds, pink and white of dogwood, pale, pale green of oak, maple, cottonwood, sycamore, walnut and dozens of others. Lilacs, forsythia, pussy willows and all the spring flowers turned farmyards into technicolor postcards. Ducklings played follow-the-leader down the middle of the pond and new chicks chasing bugs on the lawn matched the dandelions.

They had plowed the muddy fields at last, and now they were planting corn. Hour after hour, day after day, they seeded the long furrows and prayed for decent weather. They had three new calves and were debating whether to take a pair of black lambs as soon as they were weaned.

Matthew remarked to Ed, "We'll need a dog for all this live-stock."

"Usta have Killer. Mean old shepherd – got hit on the road about a year before you came, and John was going to get a new one when David was older. But..."

"Then you got me instead."

"Yep. And you notice we never got no dog after that. Reckon you been that hard to train."

Matthew quickly baptized the farmhand with the contents of the bucket he had been using to bail out the watering trough, then sprinted for the house.

Safe in the kitchen, he took advantage of Carolyn's absence to raid the refrigerator. He took pity on a lonely pork chop and saved several peach halves from drowning in their own syrup. He drank the peach-juice straight from the jar and was just wiping his mouth on his sleeve when Carolyn returned. He stood silhouetted in the light from the open refrigerator, jar in one hand, pork chop bone in the other, like a deer in her headlights.

"Caught in the act!" she chortled, obviously contemplating some fiendish revenge.

Matthew knelt dramatically before her, arms stretched wide, still holding the evidence. "It's not what you think," he said passionately. "I was performing an act of mercy on these poor, suffering foodstuffs."

Carolyn snorted. "You were poaching, you robber! You'll have to pay. I could have your hand cut off - or have you hanged - but then you wouldn't be good for much..."

"Please, your majesty, pardon me instead."

"Oh, no. Get up, you ninny! Your sentence is to help me unload and put away the groceries. The whole back of the truck is full."

Matthew rose, grumbling about a fate worse than death, and served out his sentence promptly. It took quite a long time, even for the two of them.

"You'd think," Carolyn said, handing him canned goods to place on the highest pantry shelf, "a farm as big as this would support itself without having to buy so much."

"I don't think we can grow sugar or coffee," Matthew mused. "'Course, it'd be all right with me if you skipped stuff like canned lima beans." He hid three cans of them behind some soup.

"I saw that," Carolyn warned.

"Well, you can't blame a guy for trying," he said lightly, closing the cupboard doors.

"That's right," she answered, and something in her voice made Matthew turn around to look at her.

"I've been wanting to say something to you for a long time," Carolyn continued. "It's taken me all these weeks to work up to it - every day I've felt so bad. That Sunday I slapped you, I knew even then you were sad and scared for us and just trying to help. Every time I look at you, I see my handprint on your face. Can you please forgive me? I never in my life hit anyone before!" Her voice was trembling, her eyes full of tears.

"Hey," Matthew said gently, taking her into his arms. "It's okay. That handprint's been gone a long time." He patted her awkwardly as she clung to his shirt. "I'm sorry, too, because good intentions don't make up for butting in."

Carolyn's body began to shake in his arms and Matthew felt hot wetness through his shirt. "Aw, hey, don't cry! Please!" But she did, making very little noise, though her whole body heaved with sobs. He didn't know what to do but to stand there and hold her, bracing his back against the cupboard. His own eyes filled up and a huge lump filled his throat. He buried his face in her hair and tried to absorb some of her pain.

When finally his teeth and bones were aching for her, she began to calm. Matthew gave her his mostly clean handkerchief and patted her some more. She gave him in return a watery smile and said, "That girl was a fool to let you get away." Wordlessly she left him standing there and returned with a clean shirt and handkerchief for him.

"I could have done that," Matthew protested as he changed.

"I figured I owe you that much, even though I did have my eye on those peaches."

"I have to get out there for milking. I'm sorry about the peaches. I must not have eaten enough dinner, because I was really hungry."

"Don't be a dope," she fondly told his departing back. "You're welcome to raid the refrigerator any time - and you know it."

Matthew waved acknowledgment and hurried to the dairy barn. There, the cows were milling about but Ed just stood there, an odd look on his face.

"What's up?"

"I come up to the house a while ago to see if you'd like to try that bucket trick again against an armed man."

He grinned cheekily at the farmhand. "Decided you were too old to take me, huh?"

"Saw you. Saw you and the missus was busy in the pantry."

"Yeah. She caught me raiding the fridge and made me help her put away the groceries."

"I didn't see no groceries. I saw the missus plastered to your front and your hands all over her." Ed's voice was flat and accusatory.

"Yeah?"

"What was you thinking of, boy? That's his wife!"

"I know that. What - ?" Suddenly Matthew felt as if the cartoon lightbulb had come on over his head. "Oh - you thought - No, no, listen! I really was putting away groceries. And she said she wanted to tell me something. Then she apologized for that day she slapped me, and she got all teary, so I kinda put my arms around her and patted her - you know - and then the dam busted and she cried all over me. That's all."

Ed inspected him closely, gauging his honesty. "Sorry I jumped to conclusions," he finally said. "But you got to be careful! The way things are right now, if John'd come in instead of me..."

"He'd never think - how could *anyone* think I'd betray the best friend I ever had! How could *you* think that?" Matthew felt indignation rising rapidly in him.

"Easy, boy. Easy! You're right. Except this family ain't exactly on an even keel these days. So we're more than likely to misread things."

"Yeah, you're right. Will we ever be normal again? Miles talked about grief being winter and finally spring comes. I guess I hoped when the weather changed..."

"Help me get these cows going."

They worked in well-coordinated silence, each pondering, until the tasks were done, the peaceable Jerseys ambling back out into the gentle sunset.

"I heard a line on TV one time," Ed said. "Something about 'the seasons of the heart.'"

"And?"

"I don't know. Maybe this is the long winter season. You still worried they'll get a divorce?"

"More than ever," Matthew confessed.

"I thought it was a good sign, him going back to church. And old Pearl getting rid of that - that - Job-Joel-Jeremiah black sweater."

Matthew laughed. "Yeah, for sure, the sweater!" He did not mention, as he never had, the sleeping arrangements in the house, nor the near-total absence of conversation after Ed went home at night.

"Funny," the farmhand said, "how much faith we put in the way things look. A few flowers bloom, sky looks real pretty like now, I feel better. I read them as God's promise to give me 'hope and a future'! Me and every other believer."

"What about people who don't believe?"

"You know by now what the Book says. Jesus was pretty clear in his own words, don't you think? 'No one comes to the father except by me.'"

"So they're all going to hell?"

"Thinking about that pretty little nurse, ain't you?"

"Yeah, I guess I am. But what about babies and Down Syndrome people and crazy people and – and - "

"Whoa, son! Them's pastor-questions. Tell you what – come on in to supper and ask the boss. That'll keep the ball rolling for a while!"

"You go on in. Tell 'em to start without me, okay? I want to watch the sunset a while longer."

As the farmhand headed for the back door, Matthew walked away toward the pond. The ducklings were tucked up with their mothers among the cattails on the bank, and the calm surface of the water reflected rose-and-gold cirrus clouds. The water was unusually high this year, after all the rain and snow. He had to sit in the grass on earth still cold and damp.

We would have had the boat out by now, Matthew thought. *We'd have chased those ducklings and picked the flowers and hunted Easter eggs. David would be riding his bike and pestering for skates and tossing a baseball with his dad and deviling me to skip piano lessons and run outside...*

He plucked and idly chewed a sweet, tender, new blade of grass. *Oh, Lord, if I miss him this much, how much worse must it be for them? Are You ever going to deliver us from this pain? I'm so lonely...*

Lying back on the grass, Matthew saw the first star twinkling faintly just where the twilight blue began. *I wish -* he thought, *I wish - Oh, I wish you were here with me to wish on this star and to run in and hug your mom and dad and to hitch a ride on my shoe one more time.*

He turned onto his face and wept into the grass.

Before too long, someone sat down beside him, and he felt a familiar hard hand on his shoulder. John gathered him up and held him as he wept.

"He'd have jumped off that bus today and come flying up the drive," John said. "He would have thrown his book-bag down on the floor and grabbed his boat and run out here as fast as he could, hollering for you and evading his mother and getting grass-stains all over his school pants."

Matthew nodded wordlessly against John's warm flannel-clad shoulder, amazed by John's speech.

"And you'd have begged off whatever you were doing," John continued, "just to sail that silly boat with him. And I'd have let you, just like I always did, because it made him so happy... And I'd give my whole life to make him happy that way just one more time - "

Matthew felt the steel walls shattering inside the farmer's heart before he heard the horrible, tearing sobs begin. Now he held John, as tightly as he could, absorbing the violence of his grief, trying to be an anchor. The harsh, wracking anguish went on and on, interspersed with wordless outcries jagged with pain.

Half a year, Matthew thought. *Half a year of all this agony trapped inside. No wonder he was so quiet! It took all his energy to keep it in. Jesus, please let him keep on 'til he's finished!*

The sky turned navy blue and a small breeze ruffled the surface of the pond. A bat flickered by. Celeste, gravid again, stalked through the grass after foolish mice or unattended ducklings.

John's grief finally exhausted itself. Matthew continued to hold on, to pray, to murmur what he hoped were comforting sounds. Ed ghosted up and immediately slipped silently away. A few minutes later, Carolyn appeared.

She knelt beside them, her face pale in the starlight, her hands fluttering a little as if she didn't know quite what to do with them. She watched and listened to her husband's pain dispassionately. *Jesus, let her see!* Matthew prayed. *Let her understand what she needs to do!* And then, watching her watching John, Matthew saw the exact moment when her own heart broke for her husband's.

She barely touched John's shoulder. It was enough to raise his eyes to her face, where he also saw the forgiveness he had needed all those months. He reached out to her and she came to him.

Matthew eased quietly back to the house, his supper and his prayers.

PART THREE

DARK NIGHT OF THE SOUL

June – November, 1996

In the dark night of the soul,

    it is always three o'clock in the morning.

St. John of the Cross

Thirty-Seven

Spring finally inched its way into summer, rain giving over to saturating humidity, relentless chill to brutal heat and white sunlight.

"It's only June," Matthew mumbled around a mouthful of nails. Sweat beaded in his eyebrows and pooled in the hollow between his collarbones. Inside the leather gloves, his fingers swelled and sweated. He drove the small nails into a growing lattice of furring strips at Pastor Corrigan's direction, creating wooden skeletons he didn't recognize, until finally he couldn't go on without a drink. He spat the remaining nails into his palm, dropped them into the pocket of his nail apron, hooked the hammer into its loop and pocketed the gloves.

"Don't you ever sweat?" he growled at the pastor, wiping his face on the damp sleeve of his white tee-shirt.

Miles laughed. "Not usually when someone else is doing the work. You could let me hammer for a while, and you hold the wood."

"We tried that." Matthew grimaced and walked over to a blue plastic cooler just outside the church's back door. Selecting bottled iced tea, he downed the whole thing without stopping and reached for another. "You want one?" he called.

"Sure!" Miles replied, moving toward Matthew with long, ungainly strides. They leaned against the warm brick wall side by side, drinking the cold tea in companionable silence, looking at the long framework standing in the parking lot.

"What're we making?" Matthew finally asked.

"Jerusalem."

"You could have fooled me!"

"When the painted cardboard is tacked onto the framework, you'll see. And the Bible-School kids will see. This year we're doing a pilgrimage to the Holy Land."

"Why?"

"Why Jerusalem?"

"Why Bible-School, I guess. It's an awful lot of work, isn't it? I've seen a dozen women running around every day I've been over here, doing all kinds of stuff. The kids have Sunday School every week. Why this 'big event'?"

"A couple of reasons, I guess," Miles explained. "The 'big event' gets 'em all excited and proves church can be fun. They learn lots of Bible verses they'll remember all their lives. They learn about Jesus and how much He loves them, and some of them - lots of them, we hope - will ask Him to be their Lord and Savior for the first time."

Miles leaned toward Matthew, eyes intense, speaking faster as his enthusiasm grew. "Some of the parents of these kids will see Christ through their children's eyes and renew their own commitment to Him. And the kids will bring their friends from the neighborhood - kids who never get to go to Sunday School - kids who may be hearing about the Lord for the very first time!"

"But other than that, it's no big deal, right?" Matthew teased.

The pastor laughed again as he collected the empty bottles and deposited them in the dumpster. "Not that I get excited or anything."

"Yeah, right," Matthew grumbled, going back to hammering. "At least when Solomon built the temple, he had help."

"I never claimed to be a carpenter," Miles said with exaggerated dignity, drawing himself up to his full and rather impressive height. "I am merely a genius of design - and delegating."

They laughed together as Penny rushed up, long hair bouncing from a high pony-tail, face, hands, cut-off shorts and long, skinny legs spattered with red paint. She hugged her husband hard, planted a quick kiss square on his mouth, inspected the framework and bounced away.

"I do love that woman," Miles said softly, his usually sharp eyes dreamy for a moment.

Matthew struck the nail so hard he split the lath with one blow.

The frame shuddered.

"Whoa!" Miles cried, refocusing his attention.

"Sorry."

"What just happened here, friend?"

Matthew turned so his back was to Miles. "Nothing."

Behind him, Miles waited. Faint music drifted from the church; a wasp buzzed noisily around the dumpster. *Oh, Jeremiah*, Matthew thought. *He outwaits me every time. He won't give up, he won't go away, he'll just stand there like Ichabod Crane until I tell him.*

He turned around, holstering the hammer again. "I thought we'd gotten to the part where everyone lives happily ever after, that's all. But we haven't. You and Penny - that's how it used to be for John and Carolyn. And I thought I might have found someone - you know that story - "

"You're saying the family isn't completely healed."

"Yeah." Matthew met the pastor's eyes, frowning. "Oh, it's better than a couple of months ago. But it's like one of those old-fashioned dances where they move together and then move apart, and hardly ever touch - They're awkward with each other. And John still clams up or gets mad over nothing - " He looked away again.

"And?" Miles prompted softly.

"And *nothing*!" Matthew exploded, clenching his fists.

The pastor stood still, waiting.

Heat unrelated to the sun suffused Matthew's face, neck, even his chest. He struck his clenched fists against his thighs. "The worst part is, when they *do* move toward each other, when they talk or laugh or touch the way it used to be - I'm jealous!"

"Mm-hm."

"I said, I'm jealous! That's sick! I love them! I prayed for them to get back together! But all those months, when John was so angry and Carolyn was shutting him out, I was the one she talked to, I was the one she cried with. Now they sort of have each other, and I don't have anyone."

"Mm-hm."

"Well, aren't you going to quote something at me, like the sixth commandment or the part about lusting in the heart or something?"

"Are you lusting after your boss's wife?"

"No! No, I swear that's not it. It's just wishing I had someone, too."

"That's what I figured," Miles said. "Let's carry this frame into the fellowship hall so all the women can cover it." He took one end.

"Wait a minute! Is that all you're going to say?"

"Lift!" Miles ordered. They muscled the long, awkward frame through the door, down the hall and into the big open room where a dozen or so young women were painting scenery, making up packets of papers and lettering signs. By the time they had the frame in place, Miles was sweating, too. Someone handed them each a glass of lemonade with lots of ice cubes.

"Let's take these to my very quiet air-conditioned office," Miles invited, heading in that direction.

They sank gratefully into chairs in the cool, still room. Matthew now felt so at home in this office he could barely remember the pain he had first associated with it. Sipping the lemonade, he relaxed into the cushions, then straightened and grimaced at the bitter aftertaste of artificial sweetener. "Diet!" he spat. "Not a grain of real sugar in it."

"Ever hear the one about the gift-horse?" Miles teased, mirroring Matthew's grimace. "Some dear, calorie-conscious churchwoman is making sure neither one of us starts bulging over the tops of our jeans."

Both thin enough to count every rib, they laughed together.

"Back to our conversation: It takes over a year for couples to mend after losing a child. That is, if they don't end up divorced. And this couple's gone through it twice. John's had - and survived - a real crisis of faith. So don't be discouraged. Just keep on praying. Have you asked God to forgive you for being jealous?"

"Sure. Every time."

"Here's your quote: First John 1:9 says, 'If we confess our sins, he is faithful and just and will forgive us our sins and purify us from all unrighteousness.'"

"Every time?"

"Every single time."

They sat quietly for a while, sipping the lemonade, clinking the rapidly melting ice cubes. "What became of your girl?" Miles asked.

Deep sadness took him hard and fast, like swimmer's cramp. "After she called me that one time, I never heard from her again."

"And you didn't call her?"

"I couldn't. What she wanted - I couldn't do. And she didn't like 'the God-thing.' She told me she doesn't believe in God." Matthew swirled the remaining ice around and around. "I don't guess she ever went to Bible-School."

"Mm-hm." Miles gulped the last of his drink. "Did you ever explain it to her, or tell her how you came to know about the Lord and to turn your life over to Him?"

"She'd never have listened. Anything about God ticked her off."

"And did you try?"

"No. She always got mad. Except," Matthew closed his eyes and swallowed hard, remembering, "the day David - went to the hospital - a bunch of us were praying in the waiting room and - and some guy complained. She made him shut up and go away."

"So she has some knowledge and respect."

"Not much, I don't think."

Miles glanced at his watch. "Oops! I have to get cleaned up for a meeting." He stood quickly. "Thanks a lot for taking your afternoon again to help out. Diet lemonade isn't much pay, but the reward in heaven will be outstanding." He headed for the door, then turned back. "One last quote for you: read Acts 8, starting at verse - uh - oh - about 26, to the end of the chapter."

"What's it about?"

Miles grinned. "It's about the apostle Philip and an Ethiopian eunuch. You can borrow my Bible," he gestured to the book precariously balanced atop a stack of papers on his messy desk, "if you want to read it before you leave."

"Thanks," Matthew told Miles's rapidly departing back. Ignoring the last swallow of lemonade, he sidled over to the desk, feeling strange, almost guilty, even to be in the office without Miles. The pastor's Bible seemed much too personal and too powerful a thing for him to use. He prodded the badly scuffed black leather cover with one finger, ready to withdraw quickly if it exuded heat or current. *I'd better go*, he thought, even as he picked up the Bible.

Instead, he sank into the couch and opened the book. He knew to find Acts after his familiar friend John and found chapter 8, verse 26, easily.

Huh. An angel told Philip to hang out with this Ethiopian eunuch guy, and the guy was reading Isaiah out loud. Isaiah's one of those prophets in the Old Testament, isn't he? Yeah, the one John the Baptist quoted. So - ?

He read the passage through, then read it again. Parts of it hummed in his head:

> *"Do you understand what you are reading?" Philip asked.*
> *"How can I," he said, "unless someone explains it to me?"*
> *...Then Philip began with that very passage of Scripture and told him the good news about Jesus.*
> *"Look, here is water. Why shouldn't I be baptized?" ...and Philip baptized him.*
> *...He went on his way rejoicing.*

Careful of the tissue-thin pages, Matthew closed the Bible and returned it to the desk. He headed back to the truck, working his way through the beehive of Bible-School preparation, stepping over and around parts of the holy city from one end of the building to the other.

"Do you understand what you are reading?"
"How can I, unless someone explains it to me?"

Matthew heaved the cooler easily into the truck-bed and climbed into the driver's seat. The key ring dangled from the ignition and the key burned his fingers as he turned it to start the pick-up. The vinyl seat burned his back through the thin tee-shirt, which was rapidly becoming wet again in the humid heat.

A shower, he thought, easing the truck out of the parking lot. *I want a long, cool shower and a clean shirt and a cold beer. Oh, well. Two out of three...*

"Do you understand what you are reading?"
"How can I, unless someone explains it to me?"

Matthew reached the farm just in time for milking. The barn was muggy, the cows radiated heat and the flies bit. Ed's attempts at humor annoyed Matthew. *They ought to sell these stupid cows and buy their milk at the store like normal people*, he thought. *John says he likes these dumb cows, but he almost never milks 'em. And he never mucks out this barn!*

"Do you understand what you are reading?"

"How can I, unless someone explains it to me?"

"Shut up!" Matthew snapped.

"What?" Ed asked in surprise. "I didn't say a word!"

Oh, man, I'm losing it. "I'm sorry; I wasn't talking to you."

Ed wandered over, looking around. "Who was you talking to?"

Matthew flushed. "Just the thoughts yammering in my head."

"Weeell," Ed drawled, "they say it ain't so bad talking to yourself unless you start answering yourself. Keep me posted!" He swatted Matthew's damp shoulder and sauntered away again, chuckling to himself.

Joshua! Matthew swore inside his head. *I should have asked Ed what it means when a verse keeps rerunning itself like this. What am I supposed to do?*

He managed to find time before supper for the long, cool shower and the clean shirt. As he combed back his damp hair and did up his buttons, he thought of the cardboard Jerusalem and the dozens of little pilgrims in Bible-School tee-shirts pretending they were walking where Jesus had walked.

With a pang of sadness, Matthew imagined how much David would have enjoyed the make-believe journey, especially if it included the Sea of Galilee. *I never asked how he knew about Jesus,* Matthew mused, *or who helped him ask Jesus into his heart. He was only three when I came here; did he know then? Maybe it happened for him in Bible-School. And then he died. What if he had died before it happened? Would God have refused to let him in? They say adults go to hell if they don't accept Christ as Lord and Savior. Does that apply to kids, too?*

"Do you understand...?"

"How can I, unless someone explains...?"

He wandered barefoot down to supper, too hot to be really hungry. Carolyn had set the table in the dining room, which was cooler than the kitchen, so Matthew helped her to carry in salad and relishes and cold roast beef, then poured iced tea into four tall glasses.

"Thank you!" Carolyn said, giving him a warm smile. "I hope nobody minds a cold supper. It was just so hot..."

"Nah, it's too hot to eat much anyway."

"Speak for yourself," Ed countered as he moved to his chair. "I could eat a horse!"

John joined them. "I couldn't eat more than a large pony, myself." He politely seated his wife before taking his own place at the head of the table. At his signal, they bowed their heads as he asked a blessing and gave thanks for the meal.

"Are we ready for Bible-School?" John asked Matthew.

"I don't know. There was stuff all over the church when I left, and women were scurrying around like beetles." He took a single slice of beef, one slice of bread, half a dozen cherry tomato wedges from the salad.

"Is that all you're going to eat?" Carolyn chided. "Do you want me to fix you something else instead?"

"No, thank you. This is fine." He made a show of putting one tomato piece into his mouth, although he couldn't bring himself to bite down and release its juices.

"Last year," Carolyn continued, "we were finishing the scenery on the stage at eight-thirty Monday morning, and the opening was scheduled for nine. I think they're actually ahead this year. I didn't offer to help this year because I - I thought it would be too - painful. Too many memories. But I miss it."

"They'll durn sure have another one next year," Ed mumbled around a huge bite of roast beef sandwich.

"Next year should be easier," offered John.

Matthew washed the unchewed tomato down with a long, cold gulp of tea and took a deep breath. "I heard a Bible verse while I was at the church today," he ventured, "and I keep on hearing it. What does that mean? Am I supposed to do something with it?"

"That what you was chewing on in the barn?" Ed asked. "Like to bit my head off," he explained to the others.

Matthew drew a geometric design in the condensation on his glass, avoiding everyone's eyes. "Yeah, it was."

"What was the verse?" asked Carolyn.

"Does it matter?"

"Well, of course it does! How can we tell you what to do if we don't know?"

"I think," John intervened smoothly, "we could start with a few general principles."

"Like what?"

"First, we know the Bible is the Word of God. So He's always speaking to us through Scripture. Next, we know we're not supposed to take God's Word out of context. If we did, it would be too easy to misinterpret or manipulate the meaning. So you need to know the story surrounding the verse."

"I do."

"Okay. In my own experience, when one Scripture or one idea that lines up with Scripture keeps coming back in my head, the Lord is trying to teach me something - or to get me to do something. Usually something I didn't think of myself or don't want to do."

Matthew arranged the bread to cover the rare meat so he wouldn't have to look at it. Nausea was beginning to build in his belly like a line of thunderheads on the far horizon. He finally looked at John. "Thanks. I get it."

"Thought you would," John rejoined, reaching for the relish tray. He crunched through a crisp radish.

Matthew could suddenly taste that radish in the back of his throat. "Please excuse me." He left the table as fast as he could and made it upstairs just in time to vomit up the single bite of tomato. Unconvinced, his stomach continued in painful dry spasms for a long time. Finally he sank down onto the cool tile floor, shaking, sweat dripping from his face and the ends of his hair, eyes and nose running, gasping for breath.

John came and handed him a damp washcloth. He said gently, "I think it was the whale vomiting up Jonah, not the other way around. But Jonah got into trouble because he said no when God told him to go to Nineveh to warn them to change." He crossed the hall with Matthew to Matthew's room.

Matthew lay on his back, eyes closed and muscles aching. "I'm dying here," he accused, "and you're making fun of me with Bible stories."

John laid a warm, dry hand on Matthew's shoulder. Matthew could feel the calluses through his tee-shirt. "You've been part of our family for what, almost five years, now? Don't you think we know each other pretty well? You've never had the flu, but you get sick to your stomach every time you're worried or upset about something. Obviously, the Lord has laid something on your heart with whatever verse this is, and you wouldn't be throwing up unless you didn't want to do it."

"You're right," Matthew conceded. "But I can't! I just - can't."

"I don't think God ever asks us to do something without giving us what we need to do the job. May I pray with you about it?"

"No!" He sat up quickly, alarmed.

"Okay, okay," John laughed, raising both hands in surrender. "I'll just ask the Lord to give you a good night's sleep and a peaceful tomorrow. How's that?"

"Thanks." Matthew yawned hugely. John gently pushed him back down onto the pillow and turned out the light.

"Call if you need me," John said, leaving the door ajar as he went.

Wrapping his arms around his aching middle, Matthew curled into a ball to ease the pain. *I remember Jonah,* he thought. *He finally did say yes to God, and then he sat on a hill and sulked because God didn't handle Nineveh the way he thought He should. I don't think I appreciate the comparison! Besides, it was Jonah's job to tell those people. He was a prophet. I'm not. I can't do this. So I'm off the hook. Yeah...*

He fell asleep quickly, then gradually uncurled as he slept and kicked the covers onto the floor. A faint breeze dried his sweaty hair and cooled his body. He dreamed of a small boy, a tall black man, a beautiful little blue-eyed woman, each one asking:

"How can I understand, unless someone explains it to me?"

Thirty-Eight

On Sunday, forty mildly hyperactive children and ten or twelve of their exhausted parents, all wearing slightly grubby Bible-School tee-shirts, stood before the congregation in ever-shifting rows. Pastor Corrigan introduced fifteen of the children, who had asked Christ to be their Lord and Savior for the first time - and two parents who had rededicated themselves to the Lord.

Matthew joined in the wild applause, grinning at John as he removed John's elbow from his ribs.

The piano began a soft introduction, and the children began to sing. Their sweetly off-key little voices piped the simple words, and Matthew heard them again for the first time:

Oh, how I love Jesus...
Because he first loved me.

The pastor spoke briefly and simply, tying the Bible-School pilgrimage theme to his text. "We go to Jerusalem looking for the Messiah," he said. "We walk where He walked and remember what He said. Everywhere we go, He has already been there - but He has moved on. And finally, hot and tired and thirsty and heartbroken, we end up at the tomb - only to be told yet again: *He is not here*. But this time we are told, *He is risen as he said, and gone before you into Gallilee.*

"So now we must keep on walking, faster and faster, hoping, praying, trying to catch up. We have blisters and sunburn and we're hungry and scared and we know we can't go on much farther. And just at that moment, when the sun makes us faint, or the strap on our sandal breaks, when our hearts ache from seeking Him and our doubts begin to bury us - there He is!

"He comes to us, wherever we are. He embraces us. He says, 'I love you more than My own life.' He says, 'I am with you always!' He says, 'Follow Me!' He says, 'You shall be witnesses for Me to the very ends of the earth.'

"Do you believe Christ loved you enough to die for you? Do you accept His love? If you do, have you shared that love lately with someone who needs a Savior as much as you did when Christ came to you?

"Let's pray..."

Thirty-Nine

When Matthew came in for lunch the first day of harvest, Carolyn had left a message beside his plate: "Please call Cathy Horvath." It listed a number with extension. Matthew dropped into his chair with a thud.

"What's the matter?" Ed asked, sandwich halfway to his mouth.

"I got a phone call from that woman at the welfare. The one I left Will with that day."

"Been five years, right? Wonder what she wants now? Better call and find out!" Ed bit into the sandwich with gusto.

Matthew walked over to the phone and dialed the number, to learn that Mrs. Horvath was out to lunch. No, the woman on the other end of the line said, she had no idea what the call was about – but Mrs. Horvath had asked her to make an appointment if Matthew called back.

"Yeah, three will be fine. I'll be there." He hung up the receiver and dropped back into his chair.

"Trouble?" Ed asked.

"Has to be. But I won't find out until this afternoon." Appetite ruined, he drank watery, tepid iced tea and tried to imagine what could have happened to Will.

§ § §

According to Cathy Horvath, it couldn't have been much worse. "You see," she said after escorting him to that same single chair in front of her desk, "the adoption didn't work out very well. And then the mother came to town looking for her son – wanting him back –

and, well, the court made it happen."

"You mean Dinah took him?"

"Yes, she did, about two and half years ago. She moved to Detroit for a while, and then to Toledo. She had developed a cocaine habit, it seems, and she made the money for her habit by prostitution. She and Will lived in a lot of really bad places, and he was exposed to all sorts of things he should never have had to experience. He got arrested a number of times, too. The last time was bad – he was in DYS and he attempted suicide three times."

Matthew stared at her. "He tried to kill himself?"

"Three times. The prison psychiatrist said he'd undoubtedly succeed if they kept him there, so the court decided to try what they call a therapeutic foster home. It's supposed to offer counseling and structure and – well – he didn't do well there at all. He's so angry, Mr. Ryersen, and so – scarred by his experiences... Now we have him in another foster home, here in Fulton County, with an older couple who don't have any other foster children. He has a new probation officer here, and we hope to find him some kind of work for the summer."

Matthew didn't know what to feel – what he felt – how to respond. *Lord, what are You doing? What do you expect me to do?* "And you're telling me this because..."

"Because, Mr. Ryersen, you are the only living relative this boy has now, and I still believe the two of you are meant to be together."

"Dinah - "

"Two weeks ago she died of a cocaine overdose. I'm sorry, Mr. Ryersen. I know she meant something to you once."

He shook his head. "That's the worst part of it," he said. "She never did mean anything to me. But the kid – does he know his mother died?"

"Yes, we told him and we took him to her funeral. He cried, Mr. Ryersen. He loved her in spite of everything. And now he has no one."

"What do you expect me to do?"

Cathy smiled faintly and shook her head. "I don't *expect* anything. But I hope maybe you'll take this child into your life. You are his father, and he needs a father desperately. I know you think you can't do it; you made that clear before. But time has passed, and people change, and I'm hoping you're in a position to reconsider."

Mouth too dry to speak, Matthew sat rigid in the hard chair, staring at his nemesis across the desk. He realized he was shaking his head and told himself to stop it. Finally he managed, "I told you I don't want – I can't have a kid. Don't you people ever listen?"

"Of course we do. I just never give up on things when the people are still breathing." She smiled more broadly. "Could you consider letting him work on the farm this summer? He has to have something to do, and hard work outdoors might be good for him. He doesn't have to live with you, because he has the foster home, but you'd have a chance to get to know him – and he to know you."

Matthew again stopped himself from shaking his head. "I can't – Well, John might – well, John might take him on for the harvest. I'll ask. I'll let you know."

Cathy grinned and shook his hand before leading him out to the main door. "This is a good thing you're doing," she told him.

"I'm not promising anything!" Matthew snarled, bulling his way through the door and down the stairs to freedom.

I'm not promising anything! I'm crazy even to let her talk me into asking! God, what are You going to do about this mess! Dinah, you poor, stupid girl, why'd you go and mess up like that? Will needed you. He didn't need me. I remember how it feels to lose your mama when you're fifteen. And I had Gramma and Granddaddy to hang on to. This kid only had you, and now he has nobody.

Driving home, Matthew continued to chase his thoughts in circles. He parked the truck and sat there with his head on his folded arms on the steering wheel. Ed came up and knocked on the window.

"You okay in there?"

Matthew opened the door and got out. "Yeah, fine."

"Look like somebody died."

"As a matter of fact, Ed, somebody did."

Ed wiped a hand over his face in embarrassment. "Oh, Ezra! I'm sorry, boy. Want to tell me about it?"

Matthew gave him a tired smile and turned toward the house. "I'll get changed and help with the milking. Ask John to join us, okay?"

§ § §

The three men leaned in a row against the outside wall as the cows gave up their milk in the quiet hum of machinery and soft classical radio music. Matthew gave them the short version of Will's story, avoiding their eyes. "So she asked me if he can work here on the farm this summer."

"No way!" Ed said immediately. "Kid's a walking problem, sounds like."

"No, wait," John returned. "He could help with baling hay and things like that. How much trouble could he get into? Matthew can supervise him and they can get to know each other."

Ed snorted and walked off.

"He's pretty much against it," Matthew noted with a wry laugh. "You think it's a good idea? I mean, he's a bad kid, from the sound of it."

"He's your son, Matthew, bad or not. You thought you could get away from the whole thing by giving him up for adoption, and here he is again. Think God might have something to do with that?" John straightened and looked directly at Matthew. "You might pray about it. I'm willing to take him on for summer work, and I'll pay him, just like the other boys." He headed back into the barn.

Talk to me! Matthew begged. *Tell me what You want me to do! Oh, what's the use*, he growled. *You won't tell me anything. But You're supposed to care about kids, so You ought to start looking out for this one. You haven't done much of a job so far!*

Forty

Matthew looked across the harvested wheatfield at the long, even rows of straw-bales and back at the three teenaged boys teasing one another in the wagon he was towing behind the tractor. *We'll never get it all in before the rain*, he worried, stopping the tractor. *No matter how we hustle. Solomon and Sheba – and Ezra and Nehemiah!*

"Let's go!" he called back to his laughing passengers. "Rain's coming!"

Two of the boys, nut-brown from hours in the hot, sunny fields of their father's farm down the road, jumped quickly to the ground and began pulling on leather gloves. Just a year apart, with equal size and nearly identical faces, they were often mistaken for twins. In the fall they were tackles for the high school football team; in the summer they built their muscles and financed their car insurance by hiring out to local farmers. Well-experienced, they grabbed their hooks and bent quickly to the task.

Will, much thinner and paler, pushed long, dirty-blond hair out of his narrowed slate-blue eyes and sauntered to the edge of the wagon-bed. He had no gloves, and his white skin attested to an indoor lifestyle. "So?" he asked.

Punk, Matthew thought. "So," he said, "you sink your hook into a bale and heave it up here so I can stack it."

"I'd rather stack," the boy said flatly.

"No."

The boy climbed down very slowly, scowling, swinging the wicked hook in a vicious arc.

"Listen, kid," Matthew said quietly through his clenched teeth, "that hook can kill a man. It's not a toy. Farm work is dangerous work, and we look out for each other. So be careful. Watch what you're doing."

The boy's unprintable response, mumbled as he headed to the nearest bale, sent a flare of anger through Matthew's chest. *Jerk. Idiot! Why'd I get stuck with him? I never wanted this! It's bad enough being responsible for the Hardy Boys, but at least they're nice Christian kids. This one's a weasel.*

And, he thought he heard, *he's your weasel.*

As the bales began thudding onto the wagon, Matthew hauled them to the back and began the careful stacking which would allow him to overload the wagon. Suddenly a heavy bale caught him behind the knees, sending him sprawling face-first into the stack.

His involuntary shout of pain and surprise brought the brothers running. The elder climbed up to help him to his feet. "You okay? What happened?"

Matthew spat out a mouthful of chaff. "I must have tripped. It's okay, nothing hurt but my pride," he grinned. The boy returned his smile and headed back to work.

Will stood quietly beside the wagon, watching. Something ugly gleamed in his half-shuttered eyes. As Matthew moved toward him across the wagon-bed, one of the boy's thin shoulders flinched just a little.

Seeing that one tiny movement, Matthew checked his stride. "Save your energy," he remarked neutrally. "Don't throw 'em quite so hard." He deliberately turned his back and began to stack again.

As they always did at wheat-harvest, one day and one field blurred into the next. They started early, worked late, coughed up dust and itched from sweat, chaff and sunburn. The brothers grew browner and their eyebrows and lashes had already begun to bleach blond. They worked at a brisk, steady pace, with ceaseless good humor, finding energy to tease one another on breaks. After the first day, they didn't include Will again. They seemed confused by his blue language and the personal viciousness of his remarks.

By the end of the second day, Will was badly sunburned. His gloveless hands, unused to physical labor, blistered, cracked and bled until he could scarcely hold his hook. At dinner break on the third day, Matthew ordered the boy into the truck.

"Where we going?" Will snarled.

"Up to the house. Those hands need attention."

"What's it to you?"

Matthew exhaled a long slow breath. *God, help me not to hit the little weasel.* "Kid, I'm the crew-boss, and I'm responsible for you. Besides, if I send you home in this shape, your foster mother will come after me with an iron skillet." He shifted into first and bumped out of the field. The boy winced and said nothing.

Parking by the back door, Matthew led Will into the kitchen. The boy took it all in avidly, obviously cataloguing the room's details.

"Sit," Matthew ordered, gesturing to a chair at the table. After trying him with a long stare, Will sat.

As he bumbled around looking for the supplies he would need, banging cupboard doors, sloshing warm water into the dishpan, the noise drew Carolyn from some other part of the house, as Matthew had hoped it would. She was barefoot, wearing pale blue shorts and a matching tee-shirt with a picture of a lion and a lamb lying down together. She stopped as she saw the boy slouching by the table.

"Hi," she said, smiling. "What's up?"

Will gave her tee-shirt an insolent and thorough inspection.

"The kid's been baling without gloves," Matthew said. "His hands look like hamburger. Gotta fix 'em."

Carolyn moved immediately to take Will's hands in hers, to inspect them. Matthew didn't miss the way the boy's face changed from lust to fear, the way he ducked his head involuntarily as she approached, the brief softening of the hard eyes when she touched him.

"Oh, you poor thing!" she cried. "We have to make that feel better fast!" She began her ministrations at once, keeping up a steady flow of commiseration and consolation which required no response. Will set his lean jaw against the stinging pain and kept his eyes glued to her unsuspecting face.

"There!" Carolyn exclaimed, patting the back of the boy's hand. "You'll be fine in a day or two. Just give me a minute to put some aloe on that sunburn, then Matthew can drive you home." She went over to the sink to break several fleshy leaves from the plant flourishing on the windowsill.

"Whaddaya mean, home?" Will asked.

"She means you can't work, so you get to go home." *Jerk*.

Will turned that dark gaze against Matthew. "No. I'm not goin' home. I can work." He sat straight now, tensed, poised for action.

Carolyn gently touched his bony shoulder. Take your shirt off, please, so I can see how badly your back is burned."

"No! I'm not takin' my shirt off! What are you, lady, some kind of pervert?"

Now I will kill him. "Shut up, kid! This is your employer's wife, a good woman, and you will treat her with absolute respect. Get it?"

"I'm not taking off my shirt."

"All right," Carolyn agreed. "May I do the back of your neck and your arms and your nose?"

"I c'n do it." He looked again at Matthew. "Oh, all right." He shrugged and submitted to her application of the aloe sap. Carolyn threw the used leaves into the trash and left the room.

"Let's go," Matthew said. "Gotta get you home and get back to work. Those guys won't get enough done with just two."

"I told you I can work. I don't want to go home."

Matthew pushed a chair close to the boy and straddled it backwards, boring into those rebellious eyes over the ladder-back. "We both know you like working wheatfields just about as much as you like root-canal surgery. You sure haven't set any records for speed or cooperation or teamwork."

"So?" the boy challenged.

"So here's your chance to leave gracefully. Take it."

"No! I need the money."

"So go flip burgers at Burger King."

The boy dropped his gaze to the floor. "I can't."

Looking at the chin-length curtain of slightly greasy hair behind which Will shielded his features, Matthew saw in his mind the boy's bony wrists in tight silver handcuffs. "What did you steal?" he asked.

Will jerked upright, alarm whitening his face beneath the sunburn. "I didn't steal anything! I'm just sitting here!"

"You're thinking about it here. I saw you casing this room. And let me tell you, don't even think about it. First, they don't own one thing that's worth the risk. Second, if anything goes missing, I will personally make you very sorry you took it. Third, you stupid kid, if you just ask, they'll give you whatever you need. No, I'm asking what you stole before, what got you to jail."

"So who do you think you are to ask about that?"

"I'm your crew-boss, kid, the guy who says whether you work or not."

"Oh, yeah? You didn't hire me."

"You got that right. I *wouldn't* have, either. And you're right, I can't fire you. But I *do* say whether or not you work and get paid, and what jobs you get."

Matthew was tired of the smart-alecky kid, the greasy hair, the sly face, the sullen mouth, the battle of wills. He wanted to shake the boy, to slap him, to kick him out and make him walk home. As he silently glared and enumerated the boy's faults to himself, his hands quite independently made several thick sandwiches and slapped them down in front of the boy along with a tall glass of milk.

Will sniggered. "You discipline all your crew this way, *boss*?"

He sat opposite the boy with his own glass of milk. "This is the third day in a row you 'forgot' your lunch. You can't do a man's work on an empty stomach."

Will swallowed but made no move toward the food. "What's the catch?" he asked. "What do I hafta do for you to pay for that?"

As images flashed through his mind Matthew closed his eyes and breathed deeply through his mouth for a moment. When he opened his eyes, the boy was standing behind the chair staring at him, shaking and wild-eyed.

"No, kid," Matthew said quietly, in the gentling voice he used with animals. "It's not like that here. No special favors for a cheese and baloney sandwich. You don't ever owe me anything but a little respect."

"How'd you know – about the men?"

"I was a lot of places before I ended up here. Spent a few nights in jail for vagrancy, one for public drunkenness. Stole a few things, too, mostly food or clean shirts, but I never got caught for that. Hitched a few rides, too, and had to get out of the car fast a couple of times."

The boy wilted back into the chair. "You're not gonna touch me."

"Nope." *For God's sake, I'm your father! Not even my father ever -*

"And I get both of these sandwiches."

"Yep. If you're fast enough. I might get hungry."

Will attacked his food like a starving wolf, eating hunched over it as if Matthew might change his mind. He drank the milk in several long gulps; Matthew pushed his own untouched glass across the table. Will reached for it but paused and looked up. "You're not eating?"

"Not today. Big breakfast," he lied.

Ed stood on the other side of the screen door. "Hey, slackers! Boss wants to know what's going on. You left them football heroes all alone in the east field almost an hour ago."

"Are they all right?"

"Well, sure. Just going a lot slower with only two. You need me to take over there?"

"Yeah, I think so. Maybe for a couple of days. We'll take the barns and the garden instead, if that's okay with you."

"Sure. What'll I tell the boss?"

"Tell him I got sick in the sun. Tell him I'm keeping the kid with me so he doesn't hurt himself again."

"Got it!" The farmhand loped away.

"What'd you do that for?" Will asked suspiciously, wiping his mouth on his sleeve.

"Darned if I know!" Matthew exclaimed in exasperation. "You don't want to go home, but you can't bale with those hands, so I figured I'd find something easier for you to do 'til you're mended."

"You didn't get sick from the sun. You were fine until a little while ago, in here."

"If I tell 'em you can't work, then you have to go home."

"Oh. Well. Uh - thanks."

"Go get in the truck."

"Now what?"

"I'll grab the errand list and we'll run into town. Gotta get you a pair of gloves." Matthew quickly rinsed the glasses, palmed the crumbs from the table and dropped them into the trash. He took the list from its blue goose magnet on the refrigerator and ushered Will to the truck. They rode in silence, the boy bracing with his elbows to save his palms.

A twangy gospel song from the Christian radio station filled the silence. Contempt showed clearly on the boy's face. "Do we hafta listen to that crap?"

"No," Matthew replied with careful patience, "we can change the station. Second button is country, third is elevator music, fourth is NPR."

"NPR? Is that like NRA?"

Matthew laughed in spite of himself. "No, it's National Public Radio - classical music, opera, high-brow talk shows - "

"Who listens to that stuff?"

"Well – "

The boy sniggered again. "Man, you're blushing! You like opera 'n' stuff?"

"Sometimes," he said defensively. "I like all kinds of music."

"Yeah? Then let's find the good stuff!" Will twisted the dial until a harsh, driving rock beat filled the truck.

I can survive this for a few miles, Matthew told himself. *At least we can't talk over the noise.*

At the farm-supply store they loaded huge bags of cat food and grain, a salt block for the cows, a nasty bale of barbed wire. Then Matthew took Will to the glove display and fitted him with a good leather pair. The boy winced and bit his lip as he pulled them on over the bandages. "They're too tight, man! They hurt!"

"No, they're just right. They'll give a little because they're leather, and there'll be more room when the bandages come off. Then they'll get wet when you sweat and dry to the shape of your hands. You need to make sure you keep 'em wrinkle-free across your palms and fingers until they're broken in. A good pair of gloves will fit your hands like a second skin and last a long time. If they're too big, they slide and rub and give you more blisters."

"Yeah, well, that's great. But I can't afford these anyway." He stripped them off and put them back on the rack. He picked up a cheap canvas pair.

Matthew gently put the canvas gloves down and took up the leather pair again. "Canvas doesn't fit well and wears through too fast. These are for you. Part of the job equipment, like the baling hook."

They rode back toward the farm under the continuing assault of rock music. Half-way home, head beginning to throb, Matthew switched back to the Christian station. Will sat through two songs in sullen silence before asking, "You like that crap?"

"Let's make a deal, kid. You don't talk like that about my music, and I won't badmouth yours. And to answer your question, I used to think Christian music was pretty stupid, but now I *do* like it."

The boy slumped down in the seat. "You're one of those, aren't you? Like your boss. Jesus freaks."

Matthew abruptly pulled the truck over at the edge of someone's unharvested wheatfield. Clenching the steering wheel to contain his temper, he turned to the boy. "Kid, what is your problem?"

The boy would try to give as good as he got. "First off, my name isn't 'kid'! It's Will, and you know it. And I know all about you people! Think you're so much better than everybody else, claiming to believe in some fairy-tale god, looking down your noses at the rest of us, all the while you do stuff - " He subsided into mumbled obscenities.

Matthew rested his forehead on his clenched hands. *Lord, forgive me, I sure haven't been a very good advertisement for Christianity! I'm sorry I added to the kid's hurt. Please help me to make it right with him.*

"I'm sorry," Matthew said. "You're right; I was rude. Will is a good, strong name and I'll use it from now on." He set the truck in motion again.

For the rest of the week, Will followed Matthew around from chore to chore, complaining or sulking most of the time but learning quickly and 'putting his back into it,' as Ed said, when he thought no one was looking. In an unguarded moment, he bragged about his gloves to Carolyn. Every day he ate lunch at the kitchen table, learning to say thank you after only one sharp kick in the shins.

Ed teased Matthew Friday night at supper, "Seems you took that stray pup to raise after all."

"Somebody dumped that pup off on my doorstep. What else could I do? God knows his foster home isn't much of a place for a kid. He won't hurt a woman, but he's been - abused - by men. And he -he stole- something...He held up a convenience store with an adult and another boy. Used a cap-gun. He did six months in the youth prison for that."

"Well," Pearl said decisively, "he couldn't be in a better place to learn about hard work and honesty and charity - and the Lord. And family." She looked pointedly at Matthew.

"Better lock up the silver," Ed muttered darkly.

Carolyn laughed. "What silver? I'd *thank* him for stealing the tableware we're using!"

"Nah," Matthew teased her, "he'd probably go for all the geese."

The temperature dropped that night, waking Matthew somewhat after midnight to pull up the quilt. *I wonder if Will is warm enough?* he thought as he slid back into sleep. Later he dreamed the dream again: the small boy, the tall black man, the beautiful blue-eyed woman - and now the sullen, blue-eyed Will - asking:

"How can I understand, unless someone explains it to me?"

Forty-One

Tuesday evening of the second week of harvest, as Matthew lay across his bed listening to frogs in the pond, a car with a rough engine came up the driveway. A few minutes later, John called him downstairs.

Since John's voice was calm, Matthew took a moment to pull on a clean tee-shirt with his jeans and to run a comb through his shower-damp hair. Barefoot, as usual, he descended to the living room. A man about Matthew's own age and height, but easily twice his weight in muscle, wearing rumpled khakis and a navy polo shirt which strained across his chest and biceps, was planted like an oak in front of the cold fireplace.

"I'm Will's probation officer, Dan Winsler," the oak rumbled in an amazingly deep voice, extending a huge hand.

All senses on alert, Matthew stayed by the door and nodded.

"I just need to ask you a few questions," the p.o. continued.

He nodded once, sharply, giving no ground. He had met men like this in Kentucky jails; he wouldn't give up Will to him.

"It's all right," Dan said, "Will isn't in trouble. This is just a routine visit."

"Oh, yeah? At this time of night?"

Dan smiled. "I'm sorry. I guess I should have called. I had a home visit this evening, and I know farm folks are out in the fields late this time of year, so I just figured this would be a better time for you."

"Oh." Still on alert, Matthew moved to the couch and sat down. John offered his chair to the p.o., who plunked down into it gratefully. John sat beside Matthew on the couch.

"You're Matthew Ryersen, is that correct? Will's natural father?"

"Yeah."

"I understand Will is working directly with you, is that right?"

"Yeah."

"Well, could you maybe give me some idea how he's doing?" The p.o. was patient.

"He's doing fine."

John snorted in exasperation. "*Tell* the man about Will! Tell him about lunch, about the gloves..."

"He's a good worker; he learns fast. He had a lousy attitude when he came, but he's fine now." John rolled his eyes. "Well, he is! At least, he's better. He'd be a whole lot better if he had enough to eat! He comes every day with no lunch packed, so we feed him - and he eats like it's the only meal he gets. What kind of people are those foster people, anyway?"

Dan scrubbed one heavy hand across his face and the back of his neck. "They're old. Too old and set in their ways to raise a rebellious teenager. The state doesn't pay them much to raise Will. They just took him so he wouldn't end up in another institution, because they're really big-hearted. For fifteen, Will has a long record - runaways, shoplifting, underage consumption, DUI in a stolen car, then this armed robbery."

"It was a cap-gun, for Pete's sake!"

"Yeah? And did he tell you he hit the clerk in the head with that cap-gun and gave him a hairline skull fracture? Frankly, I don't know why they didn't try him as an adult for that one. They planned to keep him in DYS until he was at least eighteen."

"If he's so bad, why did they let him out?" John asked.

"He attempted suicide three times and darn' near succeeded the third time. He didn't take to prison very well... They picked on him a lot because he was pretty, and because of the books. Called him a queer and all."

"Books?" Matthew asked.

"Well, it's a funny thing about your son. He's real smart. No matter what kind of trouble he was in, he never missed school. Got real good grades, too. He was allowed to have books in his cell when he wasn't in the hole, and he was always getting more from the prison library. Math, science, poetry - you name it. But it didn't win him any popularity contests. And I suspect - I don't know - he was – sexually abused...

"And the thing is, these foster parents just can't cope with him like they hoped. He's gonna do something stupid any minute and violate his probation. Then I'll have to send him to court, and the judge will send him back to prison and throw away the key." The p.o. clasped and unclasped his hands, looking at them as if they held the answer to a question he hadn't asked.

John looked at Matthew. "Do you really believe he's changing?"

Dan had raised his head. "Do you, really?" he asked.

"Yeah, I do. Look, he's a tough guy, but all he really wants is a safe place and someone to love him. And a chance." Matthew looked at John. "There's room in my room for another bed. You could take his expenses out of my salary. I don't spend much of it anyway."

The farmer smiled. "We'll have to talk it over. All of us will have to agree, including Will."

The p.o. looked dazed. "You want to take him in?"

"I do!" Matthew said. "I mean, I suppose I should be responsible..."

"We could use another boy around here," John agreed, only the slightest tremor in his voice.

The p.o. left, shaking his head, and they went out onto the porch, where Carolyn was swinging.

"You guys are so loud," she teased. "You forget how well sound carries on a still summer night."

"Honey, did you hear everything?"

"Just about. You want us to become foster family to Matthew's fifteen-year-old emotionally disturbed, sexually abused, suicidal, convicted felon son. Oh, who probably will steal our books. Did I leave anything out?"

John sat beside her on the swing and wrapped an arm around her shoulders. "I think that pretty well covers it. How do you feel about it?"

"I guess - I guess we could give it a try. He needs - But Ed," she gestured to the farmhand's little house across the road, "he doesn't like Will."

"Do you?" Matthew asked bluntly, an uncustomary hint of belligerence in his voice. "Do you trust him in your house? Do you think he's gonna murder you in your bed?"

"Oh, for heaven's sake, don't be silly! Of course I like Will! And no, I'm not the least bit afraid of him. On the other hand, he does have the questionable taste to like you."

"The lights are still on over there," Matthew said. "I'll go across the road - "

"After you put your shoes on," Carolyn admonished.

. Minutes later, he jogged down the driveway and across the road. Ed welcomed him, mildly surprised. "I was just fixing to lock up. Everything okay?"

"Yeah, fine. Just something I want to talk over with you."

"Well, come on in and sit down." Ed held the screen door open wide, then followed him in to the couch. "Can I get you something to drink? I got beer, if you don't tell the missus." He winked.

"No, thanks, I'm fine." Matthew relaxed into the soft, lumpy cushions.

Ed sprawled comfortably on the other end of the couch, waiting. Matthew wondered how to begin. "Did you hear a car earlier?" he finally asked.

"Did."

"It was Will's probation officer."

"Oh, yeah? What's that little snake gone and done now?"

Ouch! Matthew thought. *This isn't a great start.* "He hasn't done anything. The guy came by to check us out and to see how the kid is doing."

"Oh. Well, if he ain't in trouble yet, he will be."

"Why do you dislike Will so much?"

"You mean besides the fact he's a sneak and a slacker and a liar and a thief?"

"Hey! That's not fair."

"Truth, ain't it? I heard what he done. I don't like him looking stuff over all the time like he's figuring what he can get for it, and I don't like him sniffing around the boss's wife, even if he is your boy."

Oh, man, this is worse than I thought! "Do you remember the night I came, when you found me standing in the driveway?"

"Sure do. Some sorry specimen you was, too!"

"You took hold of my arm and steered me right into the house. Never asked my name or my record or anything. Just welcomed me like - like a brother. All these years now, and you've never really asked me any questions. So why are you so ready to judge Will all bad?"

"You was - different. That kid is mean."

"I've been in jail. I've stolen. I've been angry enough to kill someone."

The farmhand met Matthew's eyes, his own cloudy and troubled. "I know what you're saying. I know what the Lord says about treating strangers and poor people and prisoners and such as good as we'd treat Him..." He looked down at his work-worn hands, picked at a ragged cuticle.

"Can I tell you what I know about Will?" Matthew asked.

Ed sighed heavily. "Sure. Why not?" He leaned his head back against the couch and closed his eyes.

Quietly, intensely, Matthew told as much as he could, feeling the absent boy's fear, pain, rage, disgust, despair until he was no longer sure whose story he was telling. At last he leaned forward and dropped his head into his hands, breathing like a winded sprinter.

Ed left the room and returned a moment later. "Here." He nudged Matthew's quivering shoulder with a frosty, open beer bottle. "I won't tell if you won't. And if you promise not to puke on me."

With a trembling hand Matthew took the bottle and tipped it to his mouth. After several seconds' consideration, his stomach agreed with him that just this once beer was a good idea.

"Thanks," he whispered.

"Don't mention it. And I *mean* don't mention it!"

"No problem." He drank deeply.

"Some lousy story," Ed remarked, sipping his beer. "The Lord must have something pretty big in store for that kid, bringing him through all that."

"You think? The p.o. seems to think there's more jail time in his immediate future. We've helped him start some muscle working here; so maybe next time instead of just trying to kill himself, he'll kill somebody else first." He finished the beer and plunked the bottle onto the end table. "I could use a couple more of these."

"Nope," the farmhand said, shaking his head, "only one to a customer. Milwaukee, Cincinnati and St. Louis put together don't make enough beer to drown what ails you."

"I know. You're right; I tried that a few times. That's one of the times I was in jail." Matthew laughed darkly, remembering. "Oh, Lord, I was so sick! They threw buckets of water on me."

Ed grinned at the image. "So what say you stay sober tonight and tell me why you come by at the tail-end of the evening."

"I came to ask you to think about us taking Will in. John says we all have to agree to it."

"Colossians and Ephesians, boy!" Ed yelled, sitting upright. "Cleopatera took a snake to her bosom, and look what happened to her!"

"Is that in the Bible?" Matthew asked innocently, masking a smile.

"Never mind! This is the dumbest idea I ever heard!"

"Just a minute ago you were feeling sorry for the kid."

"That was before you was talking about bringing him into the family. He ain't coming under *my* roof!"

"I wasn't asking you to do that. I figured we could put another bed in my room. After all, he's my kid, so he should be my responsibility."

"Your room! That's no bigger than a shoebox. At least here he'd have some privacy and breathing room - *if* I was to take him – *which I ain't*!"

"I understand." Matthew rose, sighing, feeling old. "Thanks for the time and the beer. I'll see you in the morning." He moved to the door as stiffly and slowly as a very old man. Ed just sat there and watched him leave.

Forty-Two

The next evening, Will was the topic of discussion all through supper. Over fried chicken, biscuits and corn on the cob, they discussed his history and debated his entrance into their family.

"He's a snake!" Ed warned, piling strawberry jam onto a biscuit and cramming it into his mouth.

"He's so thin," Carolyn lamented. "And his clothes are just about worn out. He needs to be looked after. And he needs his father."

John put down his half-finished chicken breast and pushed away his plate. He wiped the grease from his fingers, then continued to wipe them, over and over, eyes on the napkin. "We can't take him as a substitute for David and Johnny. That wouldn't be fair to him or to us. If we take him at all, we have to do it for the right reasons."

"Matthew 25:35," snapped Pearl. "What other reason do you need? That's 'I was a stranger, and you took me in,'" she explained to Matthew.

"Yes, ma'am, I know. Been there."

"I tell you, it's a mistake," Ed warned. "Besides, what makes you think he wants to live here?"

"That's a point," John nodded, pleating a clean paper napkin. "Not much entertainment out here for a city boy."

"Hey! I thought you were in favor of it!" Matthew blurted.

"Part of me is. Part of me hates like - that it isn't *my* son." The rusty-metal sound was back in John's voice, the muscle-twitch along his jawline.

They sat there silently, each one remembering, each one weighing the past against the present. Carolyn finally rose, and Matthew jumped up to help her clear the table.

In the kitchen, he asked, "What do you really want to do? Honestly? If I weren't involved."

"Why, take him in, of course, He needs us even more than you did."

Matthew plopped the stack of plates into the sink and enveloped Carolyn in a hug. "A-hem," John said from the doorway. "I had a feeling you were out here politicking. If you would please unhand my wife, we have some selling to do in the other room."

Scalded with embarrassment, Matthew let go quickly and backed away. Carolyn patted his hot cheek and took up a plate of Pearl's homemade gingersnaps. John snagged a gallon milk jug from the refrigerator. "I need milk with my cookies," John said. "How about bringing a stack of glasses?"

"Sure. Uh - you know - about what just happened - "

"Yes, I know. Relax. I know she's too tall to be your type." John's eyes glinted with mischief.

Seated again, Matthew dunked a gingersnap up and down in his milk until it broke off and fell to the bottom of the glass. Bereft of appetite since the beginning of the meal, he floated the last piece of the cookie and watched it turn soggy and sink.

"You're worse than David for playing with your food," Pearl said. "We'll never fatten up Will if you don't set a better example. Don't insult my cookies: eat!"

Matthew nodded and fished out the gingery mush with a spoon. Actually, it tasted pretty good. He did it again with a second cookie, then with a third.

"Man doth not live by bread alone," Ed intoned in television-announcer tones. Then his face and voice became serious again. "I know Will's Matt's boy, and I know you all want to take in the little snake, and I expect you wonder what my problem is. I just don't know! You know I don't usually take a dislike to nobody first off." His face was a study in confusion.

"Why don't we pray about it?" John suggested.

Accustomed by now, Matthew closed his eyes and bowed his head immediately. John offered a short prayer for wisdom, and each of them began privately to seek guidance.

Lord, Matthew prayed, *please show us Your will in this. If there's really some reason why we shouldn't help Will this way, please tell us. If it isn't supposed to be us, then please, please tell me before he gets in trouble again! Am I supposed to take him and go someplace else? I believe he could grow here - I know we could love him - be his family - he could find You here, just like I did. How will he ever feel safe or loved if he doesn't know his Father? Oh, Jesus, didn't You die to save Will, too? Then You can't let him - "*

A heavy hand grasped his shoulder, and Ed's voice cut across his prayer. "Chores, fella. Come gimme a hand."

Matthew looked up in bewilderment. "We milked before supper."

Exasperation edged the farmhand's voice. "Would you just come?"

Matthew rose obediently and followed Ed through the kitchen and out the back door, hurrying a little to keep pace. About half-way across the back yard, Ed paused, veered and headed for the pond. The sun, still two hours above the horizon, glinted from the water's surface, where the ducks played follow-the-leader. A fishing pole leaned against the dock, dangling a small, shiny lure.

"Too hot earlier," Ed noted in his normal placid voice. "Maybe they're biting now." He stood on the dock, casting smoothly, reeling in steadily, for several silent minutes. "Lord say anything to you?" he finally asked.

"To tell you the truth, I was talking too much to listen." Matthew sat on the dock and pulled off his shoes and socks to dangle his feet in the water. Minnows immediately tasted his toes.

"Seemed to me I heard a verse."

"Oh, yeah? Which one?" He kicked away the minnows.

"The one goes, 'Behold, I make all things new.'" The farmhand cast out his line again and watched the red-and-white bobber for a moment. Finally he said, "Y'know, I'm more than old enough to have a son Will's age. He could have been mine as easy as yours."

"And?"

"I dunno. It's all tied up with this kid and with the Lord making all things new. But - I dunno."

Suddenly the bobber dipped and the farmhand became all business. Skillfully he played and reeled in a large bluegill. Celeste materialized immediately, followed by the latest batch of kittens. "Naw, cat, you don't get this one," Ed said, gently releasing the fish back into the pond. Celeste made what was clearly an unladylike remark and flounced away with her retinue behind. Ed put up the pole and sat cross-legged beside his friend.

"Did you ever want kids?" Matthew asked. "I know you said your wife did."

Ed ducked his head shyly. "Yeah, I did. But this ain't a bad life at all. I got a family and a house and the Lord..."

Matthew assured himself the changing angle of the sun on the water was bringing the tears to his eyes. "You have more room in your heart than you do in your house," he said. "Maybe God wants to make things new for you, not just for Will."

"Maybe pigs have wings," Ed offered, but it was a half-hearted attempt at sarcasm. They sat a while longer, checked the barns, and said good night in the driveway. Matthew watched the farmhand go home alone, waiting for the lights to go on in the little house before he turned away.

Pearl met Matthew at the bottom of the steps. "Did you talk some sense into Ed?"

"No, ma'am."

"Well, why not? We both know this is the right thing to do!"

"Yes, ma'am. But I think the Lord is working on him. I'd just as soon stick to praying on this one."

Pearl looked up at Matthew, her dark eyes full of intelligence and wisdom in her wrinkled face. "You're absolutely right! You've learned a lot in the last year, since David died." She patted his arm and went to her car. He got there in time to hold the door for her, earning himself a smile and another pat.

As Matthew stood alone in the shadows by the porch, he reflected on the last two encounters. *I don't want to be going home alone for the rest of my life*, he thought. *I don't want to be fifty and look at a kid and think, I could have had all those years with Will, if only -* Allison hovered in his mind. *It's too late*, he thought. *I already had my 'if only.'*

The next day Will was impossible, sulking, complaining, finding fault with everything. His complexion was pasty; his eyes watered; his nose ran and he wiped it on his sleeve. When he kicked at Celeste, Matthew grabbed him by the tee-shirt and flung him into the watering trough. The boy emerged from the scummy water coughing and cursing, ready to fight. Matthew pushed him under again, then dragged him up at once.

"Listen, you little jerk!" Matthew yelled, utterly frustrated with both of them. "We don't abuse the animals here, and we don't whine and snivel all the time! We thank God we have a job to do and be paid for." He let go of the soggy tee-shirt and the boy stumbled back a step.

"No, you don't abuse the animals!" Will countered. "You just abuse the slaves instead! Well, forget you! I don't have to get yelled at and half-drowned and lectured to by a stupid loser like you!" He wiped the green scum from his face and hair, shuddering with disgust, and took off toward the road.

Good riddance! Matthew thought. *Let him go. I was stupid to think we could help him here. He acts like some junky, sure as - oh, Lord!* He took off after Will at a dead run, but the boy had disappeared. Frantic, Matthew looked in every direction. The road was long and straight and uninhabited. The yard and the adjacent fields were empty.

"I believe I have something you're looking for," Carolyn called from the porch as he trudged back up the driveway.

"Huh?"

"That boy you lost. He's in the shower."

"Thank God!" He sank down on the second step, weak with relief.

"What did you do to him?" Her voice was stern.

"I dunked him in the watering trough. Twice." He couldn't meet her eyes, the censure he knew he would find there.

"How could you! We spent hours talking about how much he needs to be loved and taken care of. How could you humiliate him like that?"

"I'm an idiot, that's how. My dad was – rough. I guess I have a lot to learn about how to treat a kid."

"Teenagers are harder for everyone than little boys," Carolyn said, forgiveness replacing censure. She smoothed her hand over Matthew's hair, a gesture he had seen her bestow hundreds of times on David. "Why don't you lend him some of your clothes and bring me his to wash?"

"Okay." Matthew hurried to his room and unearthed his smallest tee-shirt and tightest jeans. He took them across the hall to the bathroom, where he could hear the shower running. Will didn't respond to his knock, so Matthew turned the knob to put the clothes inside. The door was locked. *Of course, it's locked,* he said to himself. *He may never get to the place where he can take a shower with the door unlocked.*

He waited until the water stopped to knock again. "Hey, Will! I'm leaving some dry clothes outside the door." He placed the little bundle on the floor and retreated to sit on his bed. He heard the door open and close, then open again a few minutes later.

"In here," he called.

Will came to the doorway and looked in. The tee-shirt bagged half-way down his thighs and he bunched the jeans at his waist with one hand to hold them up. He wiped his nose on his sleeve.

"How much did you do?" Matthew asked, fishing a handkerchief out of his top dresser drawer and handing it to Will.

"What?"

"The coke. How much did you do?"

"You're crazy, man!"

"No, I don't think so. Listen, Will, I didn't do a very good job of keeping my promise to treat you with respect. I apologize for manhandling you out there. I'm sorry."

"Yeah, right."

"And I didn't - see - right away why you were having such a lousy day. But now I do."

"You don't see squat!"

"Will, if the p.o. decides to pop you for a drug screen, you'll be on your way back to DYS in a heartbeat. Please don't let that happen!"

"What's it to you? I mean, if I *was* using?"

"I've been to jail, too." Matthew paused. "This is my room. C'mon in." He carefully got up and moved as far away from the bed and the door as possible, sitting on the chair. Will came one step inside. "Do you like it?"

"What's to like? It's a room." The shadowed eyes moved restlessly, evaluating everything, lingering on the bookshelf.

"I hadn't had a room of my own for a long time before I came here. I like this room a lot, because it's safe - and it's mine. Nobody comes in here unless I say so. The stuff in here is mine."

"And?"

"I feel safe here."

Will took another step. "You got books."

"Help yourself," Matthew gestured. Will warily crossed the room to peruse the contents of the shelf. "I like the Frost - the poetry - best," Matthew said.

"Yeah," Will returned. "I've read that. It's okay. I like this Roethke guy, myself. He's got one about mice - and this other one - this line: 'I wake to sleep and take my waking slow; I learn by going where I have to go.' You know that one?"

Transfixed by the change in Will's face and voice, Matthew almost failed to answer. Belatedly he said, "No, I don't know Roethke. I know Yeats."

"Yeah, he's okay. William Carlos Williams?"

"Never heard of him. How about Edward Lear?"

"Who?"

He grinned at Will. "There once was a man from Nantucket..."

Will started to laugh, but caught himself. "Yeah, I get it. So, what's with all these mice?" His finger touched one carved miniature after another. "Hey, this dude in the plant wears glasses!"

"It's just something I do in my spare time."

"You made these?" Matthew nodded, slightly embarrassed. "They're okay," Will dismissed. "So why you want to show off your room? Rubbing it in?"

"No... I just wanted you to - to feel how safe it is, to see what good people these are. If you had a chance, would you ever want to live in a place like this?"

Will leveled a baleful glare at him. "There's about as much chance of that happening as for all these mice to start break-dancing. You got a belt or something to hold up these pants?"

Matthew sighed. "Let's go downstairs. I'll cut you some clothes-line. I only have one belt, and I need it to hold up *my* pants."

Forty-Three

The end of the week came with no resolution. John paid Will on Friday and asked him to return on Monday. The wheaten head nodded once before he climbed into his foster father's battered brown Fairlane to go home.

With the look of a man on a mission, Ed left for a weekend of fishing. On Sunday evening, his dusty El Camino pulled into the driveway, truck-bed full of tent and fishing gear. His jeans were grass-stained, his face gray and lined with exhaustion.

"You look like you spent the last two days trying to catch a whale," Matthew teased.

"Waste of time. Never put a line in the water." Ed showed him the empty cooler and the dead worms. "Boss around?"

"Sure. They're watching TV."

"C'mon." Ed took the steps in two bounds. At the sight of his face, John thumbed the remote to turn off the television. The three of them waited for Ed to speak.

"I spent most of the last two days reading my Bible or flat on my face on the ground before the Lord," Ed began without preliminaries. He paced back and forth in front of his little audience, running his fingers through his hair. "I gotta tell you, I been sifted finer than cake flour." He flopped down on the couch.

"I confess," Ed continued, "I been mean and selfish about Will. I didn't want to adjust to another new person. Felt like we had enough to adjust to in the past year. I got to feeling sorry for myself, feeling like every time there's something hard everyone expects me to be the strong, steady one - and I'm tired." He met each person's eyes for a moment.

"The other thing about Will is: I know he's gonna be trouble. And I don't want to deal with it. But the Lord asked me, 'If it was your boy, who'd you want to help him?' And He asked me, 'How's Will gonna learn about Me if you don't explain it to him?' I spent a lot of time in John and Acts, reading about evangelizing - "

A hot jolt went through Matthew and John laughed out loud. "Friend," John said, "I think the Lord's trying to tell *all* of us something."

"Well, I figure He's telling me to say yes to having Will live here. Reckon we're going to find out if He still means it when He says, 'My grace is sufficient...'"

Thank You, Matthew prayed. *This really is an answer to prayer! Please make Will willing to come. Then please show us how to explain salvation to him.*

Forty-Four

The next morning over breakfast, as Matthew tried to come awake with his third cup of coffee, John said, "Today you can ask Will to stay with us."

"Me?" He looked up in surprise. "Why me? It's your house - "

"He's your son. He needs to know you want him here. You can tell him it's a unanimous decision."

Matthew sighed. "Okay, I'll do it."

He took the opportunity later in the morning, when he and Will were alone, mucking out the barn. Will was gagging periodically, and he didn't feel too well himself. "I don't like this job," Matthew confided, leaning on the handle of his pitchfork.

"Then why're we doing it?"

"Well, somebody has to."

Will gave him a longsuffering look. "Let Ed do it. He looks like he's right at home with manure on his boots."

Matthew returned to the task at hand, quickly reestablishing a loose, easy rhythm. He talked as he worked, ignoring the fact that Will was standing still.

"So far in my life, every job has had some parts I don't like. This job's the best one I ever had, and these're the best people I ever met. So I complain a little, but I really do thank God for letting me end up here."

Will made no reply. Matthew forged ahead. "Did I tell you how I got here, and what happened then?"

Will feigned indifference and yawned elaborately. "No, but I bet you will."

Briefly, keeping as much emotion as he could out of his voice, Matthew told Will about the boy's grandparents, his grandfather's death, his great-grandparents and the loss of the farm. Will seemed to drink it in. He had questions.

"Hey, how old were you when your dad died?"

A bitter taste rose in the back of Matthew's throat. "I was twelve."

"What happened to him? Was he sick?"

"No. He was a cop. He - died in the line of duty." He spat into the straw.

"Wow! A hero, huh!" Will's usually carefully impassive face lit with excitement, but the look faded to bitterness as quickly as it had come. "At least you had him for twelve years."

Matthew spat again. "Cop or not, my dad was a mean drunk who used his fists and his belt on my mother and me whenever he felt like it." He looked directly at Will. "I never heard him say, 'I love you' or 'good job' or anything nice to anyone. He never touched me except to hit me, never praised a good report card, never came to one of my ball games - He just drank and cussed and hit us. I hated him. I still hate him."

"Yeah," Will agreed quietly. "My mom had a coupla boyfriends like that." His eyes dropped back to examining his fingernails. "And some who..." A shudder crawled across his pale skin. "Did your dad ever - ?"

"No. He was just mean, that's all. Most men don't molest boys."

"We been living in different circles," Will retorted, "but at least you had a home like this with your mom and your grandparents. A nice place to grow up." There was a certain edge to Will's voice.

Matthew laughed. "It was a great place to grow up, but it was nothin' like this! We didn't get electricity and hot running water until I was fifteen."

"You're kidding!"

"Nope. House had two little bitty bedrooms and a front room with a big bed in it where my gramma and granddaddy slept and a kitchen with a woodstove. Granddaddy built on a little bathroom when we got the hot water. Before that, it was an outhouse and a washtub on the back porch."

"Man!" Will shook his head, mouth puckered with distaste. "Even the dumps my mom and I lived in had toilets."

"About your mom - "

"What about her? You want to tell me what a slut she was and how she could have gotten pregnant by a lotta guys? That's what she said you'd say." The slatey eyes were almost black in the shadowy barn.

Matthew drew in a deep breath. "When I knew Dinah, she was just a pretty girl who liked to flirt and liked to party. She was a couple of years older than me, old enough to buy beer, and one night I got to talkin' to her at the bar. Then we went for a drive in my granddaddy's truck and went down by the river to - to talk. We were drinkin' and she was pretty and I didn't use any judgment - "

"Or any protection - "

"I didn't figure to need any when the evenin' started. And the thing was, the longer we talked, the more I knew it wasn't goin' to work between us."

"Good enough to screw but not good enough to marry, right?" Will glared and clenched his fists.

"No, that's not it. We were just really different. She was all enthu-siastic and full of plans, wanted to go to Nashville and sing in a band or somethin'. I just wanted to stay home and help Granddaddy farm. City didn't appeal to me at all, and Dinah would have hated bein' stuck on the farm. She was tryin' her best to get away."

Will kept his fists clenched and raised his chin defiantly. "So even when she told you she was pregnant, you still wouldn't marry her."

"No. No, I wouldn't. I honestly didn't think the baby could be mine, only the one time and all. And - well - I just wasn't ready to get married. I was too young. And - I'm sorry, but I didn't love her. And she didn't love me, either. It was just a mess."

"So you left her to fend for herself, huh?"

"Yeah, I did. She went to stay with her aunt in Louisville, and in a month she married Jesse Boone. She was better off there. He had money, and I heard he was a nice guy."

Will turned his back. "He was a nice guy. He adopted me. But he never let me call him 'Daddy.' He made sure I never forgot I was some other guy's son."

"Oh, Will," Matthew said, "I'm so sorry."

Wheeling back around, Will snarled, "Yeah, sure you are! Well, he treated me okay, but he bored my mother so much she started having fun on the side. And after a few years of that, he divorced her. And after *that*, we lived with different guys until she met Clete. He had a big belt with a rodeo buckle, and he didn't like kids to make noise."

"That's when she brought you here."

"Yeah, after a year. She told me I was gonna live with my real daddy. How he was gonna take good care of me. Well, thanks a lot, 'Daddy!'" Will stormed out of the barn before Matthew could say another word, leaving Matthew alone with the bitter taste of long-swallowed anger still fresh in his mouth. He tried several times more but could not spit it out.

"Genesis, Exodus, Leviticus, Numbers, Deuteronomy!" he swore, stabbing the pitchfork into the wheelbarrow full of manure. He sank down onto a bale of straw, elbows on his knees, hands buried in his hair and pulling until his scalp hurt.

That really went well, didn't it? Could I have hurt him any more? Lord, doesn't this just prove I can't do it?

§ § §

At lunch, John told Will, "I expect you to finish mucking out the barn after we eat. It's not acceptable to quit in the middle of the job."

Will glared, dropped his gaze to his ham sandwich and muttered something under his breath. Ed elbowed Matthew.

"We'll get it done," Matthew said.

Trapped together in the barn again, man and boy put as much distance between them as one wheelbarrow allowed. Finally Matthew couldn't stand it any longer. Putting down his pitchfork, he walked over to Will, who refused to meet his eyes.

"Listen," Matthew said, "I don't blame you for being mad. You haven't deserved any of the things that happened to you. And I'm sorry about your mom. I know how it feels to lose your mom when you're young."

Will's eyes welled with tears he blinked away furiously. "I don't care. She was a lousy mom – I don't need her. I don't need anybody!" He grabbed the wheelbarrow handles and shoved his way out of the barn.

"I thought you might not come back," Matthew said as Will trundled the wheelbarrow back into the barn several minutes later.

"Yeah, well if I want to get paid, I have to finish this job. You gonna help?"

They worked in silence and then went in silence to wash up on the back porch. Carolyn called them in for milk and cookies.

"Have you had a chance to talk yet?" she probed delicately, setting the snack before them.

"Oh, yeah," Will said sarcastically, grabbing a snickerdoodle and cramming it into his mouth.

"I can see you aren't finished yet," Carolyn said, "so I'll leave you to it." She disappeared up the stairs.

"What's she talking about?" Will mumbled around a mouthful of cookie.

"I'm supposed to talk to you. I was trying to earlier, but we got side-tracked about your mom."

"So talk."

"Um – yeah. Okay… Your probation officer came by to see how you're doing, and he told us he's worried you're goin'to screw up and go back to DYS. So he - "

"No!" Will interrupted. "I'm never going back there!" His face was as white as it had been the day he came.

"Easy. Let me finish. We all talked it over, and we all want you to live with us here.

"We'd like to make you part of the family, just like they did for me. I'd – I'd like a chance to – act like a father to you - " Matthew held his breath as Will looked at him with absolutely no change of expression. The charged silence between them stretched out, thinned, like a rubber band about to snap.

"What's the catch?"

"Catch? There is no catch."

"Oh, yeah? There's always a catch."

"No catch, Will. No surprises. Nothing nasty up our sleeves. We'd just like to give you a better chance at life than you've had so far."

"Why should you? What's in it for you, for any of you?"

"Some of us know how it feels to be alone, to be tired or scared or hungry. All of us are grateful for what we have and want a chance to share it. I think that's what's in it for us: the satisfaction of helping somebody. And just for me – the chance to make up for what I didn't do before."

"Buncha do-gooders!" Will spat. "I made it fifteen years without any do-gooders, and without a father. I don't need your holier-than-thou charity!"

Matthew stood abruptly, jamming his hands into his pockets. "Dammit - I mean, darn it - Will, has anybody here acted 'holier-than-thou'?" He pulled his hands back out and ran them through his hair. "Honest, now - have we?"

"Yeah, *you* have! With your lectures about how lucky I am to have a job, and your God this and God that - "

"Genesis to Revelation!" Matthew whispered under his breath. "I'm not very good at how to treat a teenager. And I know," he hurried on, "I know I'm not a good father. But I'd like to be your friend. That good woman in there, she lost her little boy less than a year ago, and she needs someone to fuss over. Pearl is perfect for a gramma. Won't you please at least think about it?"

Will stalked out of the kitchen without saying another word.

Half an hour later, he was back. "Where would I sleep?"

"I told them we can put another bed in my room," Matthew offered.

Will whitened and drew back. "No way! I don't sleep with any man!"

"Wait! Don't run off! We'll - uh - we'll think of something else. Uh - there's David's room down the hall."

"The one who died?"

"Yeah. But he didn't die in there. It'd have to be - changed..."

"Dumb idea, man. If it hasn't been changed yet, it's because his mom isn't ready. No, I know where. That dude has a spare room in his house across the road."

Oh, Lord, now what? Matthew thought. "Will, I don't think Ed - I mean, we can ask about David's room - "

"No. Across the road or nothing." The boy's tone was flat and final.

"Okay," Matthew conceded. "When we're together at lunch, we'll ask."

He let Will use the mower for the rest of the morning while he attacked weeds in the garden with a hoe. He worked with his shirt off, soaking up sun and sweating freely, swinging the hoe as if he were beheading snakes. *Lord - what - are you - going - to do - about - this?*

Matthew had no opportunity to speak with Ed before they all ended up at the kitchen table together.

"So," Will said with his mouth full of hamburger, "if I decide to stay here, I'm gonna stay in the spare room across the road." His eyes narrowed as he watched for their responses like a cat at a mousehole.

"Oh, but I thought - " began Carolyn.

"I told him I'd share my room - "

"I don't think - " began John.

"Chew with your mouth closed," Pearl said to Will. "And say please when you disrupt a man's whole life." She smiled just a bit.

Will was no more immune to her command than any of the rest of them. Dutifully he closed his mouth until he had chewed and swallowed. "Yes, ma'am. I'm sorry." He looked at Ed. "Please, may I stay with you?"

Four adults prayed silently and fervently. Will affected a careless posture and stared at the farmhand as Ed gave a remarkable imitation of the sphinx. Finally he met Will's stare with one of his own. "Why not? As long as you clean up the bathroom and the kitchen after yourself."

Forty-Five

Delighted with the project, Cathy Horvath expedited the process of certifying the whole Abbott farm as a foster home. "Do you want custody?" she asked Matthew.

"No! I can't!" he told her, panic in his voice and eyes.

"Well, then, who's going to be the foster parent?"

"I don't know. I mean, all of us, maybe..."

Cathy laughed, crinkles appearing around her cocoa-colored eyes. "I'm sorry, Mr. Ryersen, but we have to designate a person or persons."

After some debate, Ed made it clear. "I got no problem being the name on the paper. He's gonna live with me. I'll be responsible for him." He frowned at Matthew. "Little weasel needs to know somebody cares enough to go out on a limb."

Once again the school bus began to stop at the end of the driveway. Matthew tried to be in range every day to see whether Will got on in the morning and then got off again in the afternoon. He noticed John seemed to manage just the opposite. After school, Will would change his clothes in his room at Ed's house, then saunter across the road and up the driveway to the kitchen. Carolyn always met him with a snack. Once in a while, as Will sat there eating, she would forget and run her hand across his hair; after a few times, he bore it without flinching.

At lunch, Ed reported, "He's settled in pretty good, I guess. Cleans up after himself like he said he would and does his own laundry. Sets at the kitchen table after chores and does his homework. Don't talk, though."

"Not a word?" asked Carolyn.

"Oh, a word here and there, sure. But no conversation. House almost feels lonelier than when I was alone."

Matthew looked up from his meatloaf sandwich. "Do you talk to him?"

The farmhand colored slightly and examined the underside of a potato chip. "Well..."

"Men!" Carolyn snorted.

"Does he talk to you, then?" asked Ed. "While you're giving him all those cookies and brownies I never seem to get any of - "

"Yes, as a matter of fact, he does," she replied smugly. "He tells me things he's learned, or maybe about a girl - And you know perfectly well you have free access to the cookie jar any time you want, so don't overplay the 'poor me' routine." Her smile softened her words as John laughed and Ed reddened a bit more.

§ § §

Matthew continued to work with Will after school and on weekends. Will refused to milk the Jerseys or gather the eggs, but he was usually willing - if not thrilled - to try his hand at anything else. He hated mucking out the barn and loved tinkering with vehicles under Ed's tutelage.

"How come you don't work on the machinery?" he asked Matthew.

"Oh, I do if I need to, but I'm not really good at it like you guys are. I'm better with wood, or at driving the big stuff, I guess."

"You really like the live stuff," Will sneered. "And the old-fashioned stuff. Like milking by hand or hoeing instead of using the tractor."

Matthew grinned. "I guess you're right. You have to remember, I learned to plow with a mule. Your great-granddaddy never owned a tractor."

Will tossed the long hair out of his eyes and stared. "You gotta be kidding!"

"Not a bit. Mule's name was Bess."

"Man, you really are a hick! Who was he, my – uh - ?"

"My mama's daddy? Your great-granddaddy. His name was Walter MacKenzie. He lived on that little bitty hardscrabble farm in Rough River. That's in Grayson County, Kentucky."

"You don't talk like those hillbillies on TV, just a little bit sometimes."

"No, I told you, I grew up in Baltimore first. Until - my dad - died."

"Oh." Will was silent for a while, examining his fingernails.

"You're right," Matthew agreed after a moment, "I am a hick. A hillbilly, too, I guess. I figured to be one all my life until I ended up on the road. Thing is, though – life can change for the better. I met these so-called 'Jesus people' and everything started to change."

"Do *not* start on that stuff!" Will demanded. "I don't want to hear about it. I may be young, but I know all about fairy tales and happy endings. When I get old enough to get out of here, I'm not gonna hang with Jesus-freaks! I'm gonna get a good job and get rich and do whatever I want."

Yeah, sure you are. Gonna end up in prison again and get shanked in the shower because you can't keep that smart mouth shut. "I hope so," he told the boy. "But that doesn't mean you can't have a relationship with Jesus."

"Why would I want to?" Will retorted. "Couldn't even save Himself from being crucified, and He sure hasn't saved me from anything! If I want a god of any kind in my life, it's gonna be one that has power."

Forty-Six

On Sundays, Will refused to go to church. They had agreed among themselves to invite but not to demand, hoping Will would come to trust them enough to try it. The pastor had been supportive of their approach, suggesting they offer him the Wednesday night youth group instead. Will had laughed.

Matthew sat next to John on the Sunday following his conversation with Will, half-listening to the pastor's sermon, one in a series of phrase-by-phrase examinations of the Lord's Prayer. He was not particularly interested in the pastor's view of "daily bread," nor of trust and living one day at a time. Sounded like a television AA meeting to him. He noted the uneven haircut of the man in front of him, the cloying perfume of the man's wife. He thought about Will, sleeping late, and wished he had done the same. He forced his attention back to the pastor just in time for the closing prayer but could not concentrate on it. Matthew realized he hadn't really prayed for several days.

Oh, well. Tomorrow for sure.

Monday, however, was no better. He flipped through his Bible as if it were a waiting-room magazine and found it just that interesting. He knelt by the bed for a minute or two in a sort of mental black cloud and then leaped up impatiently to go on about his day.

It rained. The truck had a flat tire. The lug nuts took forever to loosen as the wet tire iron slipped in Matthew's hands, barking his knuckles. He was cold, wet and angry by the time he had changed the tire, and he took it out on the clerk at the feed store. He pulled a muscle in his back unloading the truck. He thought he saw a rat in the barn.

Thinking himself alone, he loudly swore the longest, filthiest combination of words he could put together.

"Anything I can do?" came John's voice from right behind him.

Matthew whirled around, heart slamming with surprise. "I didn't hear you! You nearly scared me to death!"

"I'm sorry about that. You were being - creative - pretty loudly there. Must have covered my coming in."

"Yeah. Sorry."

"You sound like Will," John laughed. "What's going on?"

"Nothing." He turned away, rubbing his back.

"Did you hurt yourself?"

"No. I just pulled a muscle a little."

"You were gone a long time. I started to wonder if you'd had an accident in the rain."

"What I had," Matthew snapped, "was a flat tire. And you don't need to worry. I know how to drive in the rain."

"Of course you do. It's just - "

"Just lay off, will you?" Matthew snarled, pivoting to glare at the startled farmer. "You're not my father!" He charged out of the barn, across the wet yard, through the back door, upstairs to his room, leaving a trail of muddy footprints and slammed doors behind him. He flopped down onto the bed, letting out another string of curses as he realized what his work shoes were doing to the white bedspread. He removed the offending shoes and lay down again, an arm over his eyes, shifting to find a position comfortable for his back.

What's the matter with me? Matthew wondered. *Why would I yell at John like that? Why am I having so much trouble praying, and why haven't I been thinking about telling people about Jesus? God, where are You? What are You doing to me now?*

Matthew said aloud, "Time to go see the pastor." He sighed and headed downstairs in his stocking feet, lugging the bedspread.

In the kitchen he found Carolyn mopping up his trail. "Hey! Let me do that. It's my mess."

"It is a mess," she agreed, "but I'm almost finished. What do you have there?"

"I'm afraid you're not as finished as you think. That trail goes clear through the house and ends up on this bedspread."

"I've got to hand it to you," Carolyn teased. "You do it up right!

Do I take it you've tracked the carpet as well as the wood?"

"I'm afraid so. I'll clean it, honest. Just as soon as I make a phone call."

"Here. Give me the spread. I'll put it in the washer while you make your call."

"Thanks." Matthew handed her the soiled bundle. "I'm really sorry to make such a mess. I was mad, and I just didn't think." He hung his head.

"Oh, come on, now! It's just mud. I know you didn't do it on purpose. I forgive you." Carolyn smiled and moved lightly to the utility room..

She'd forgive anything, Matthew thought, dialing the church from memory. The pastor's secretary quickly set an appointment for him the next afternoon. As he hung up, the phone rang.

"It's Will. I gotta stay after school for some stuff. Can somebody pick me up later?"

"Sure. What time?"

"Uh - how about five? In front, okay?"

"Okay. One of us'll be there."

Will hung up. *Little snot!* Matthew thought. *Didn't even say thank you.*

Carolyn came back up the stairs. "Did I hear the phone?"

"It was Will. Said he has to stay late and wants a ride home at five. I told him one of us would come."

"Five! That's late. He's not in sports... Did he say why he has to stay?"

"Nope. Didn't say please or thank you, either." Matthew frowned.

"My, you're grouchy today! Can I do anything?"

John, coming through the back door in time to hear his wife's question, said with mild humor, "The last guy who asked that question nearly had his head bitten off."

Matthew felt the sure jab of conscience. "I'm sorry about that. I don't know what's going on with me, but I know it isn't you."

"It's okay," John said easily. "I forgive you. I knew you weren't really aiming at me."

"Want me to pick up Will?" Matthew asked.

"Thanks," John answered, "but I think we should ask Ed to do it.

They need some time together."

"Time together? They live together!"

"And they seem to avoid spending much time together. In the car, they can talk."

"Maybe," he said, remembering his first trip to town with Will.

John's plan gave no evidence of having worked. Will and Ed came in separately for dinner and didn't speak to one another. Will, in fact, spoke to no one except in grunts and monosyllables. He ate little and excused himself before dessert.

"What's gotten into that boy?" asked Pearl.

"He was like that when I picked him up," Ed said. "Didn't say a word, just turned on that hard-rock radio station and stared out the window." He applied himself to peach cobbler and vanilla ice cream.

"Did he say why he had to stay late?" asked Carolyn.

"Nah."

"Did you ask?" Pearl challenged.

"Nah. Figured he probably got in some trouble and had detention."

"You're so quick to judge!" Carolyn leaped to Will's defense. "Maybe he's working on a report or a special project. Or maybe he met a girl."

"Yeah, maybe. But don't bet on it." Ed held out his bowl to Pearl for another serving of cobbler. "Been too good too long. 'Bout time for him to do something stupid."

Anger flashed through Matthew again. "Y'know, you're the one who said Will could stay with you. He's under your roof instead of ours and he needs you to trust him and to treat him decently. He needs a father who - "

"I ain't his father!"

"Well, can't you fake it? A kid needs a father, a good father!"

"Easy for you to say! You don't live with him. And you don't know any more than I do about being a father, so get off my back! If anybody's supposed to be doing the job, it's you!"

Pearl's lips were pressed tightly together and Carolyn's blue eyes brimmed with tears. The muscle twitched along John's jaw. It had been almost a year, Matthew realized, since they had all been so quick to anger. He turned to Ed.

"You're right. I'm sorry. I've been losing my temper at everything and everyone all day."

"Saying he's sorry, too," John murmured, his jaw relaxing.

"Well, I am sorry."

"Shoot, I forgive you," Ed muttered. "Maybe I'll just ask him if everything's okay."

A while later, helping with the dishes, Matthew swirled his thoughts around and around in rhythm with the dishtowel. It was almost October; David had been dead for almost a year. He hadn't seen Allison since March. So many empty places. And then came Will. And a new understanding of the need to share Christ with others. And a new peace between John and Carolyn, a song in the house again.

So many things lost, he thought, *but so many things to be thankful for. Why am I so angry?*

Forty-Seven

The pastor, wearing jeans and a sweatshirt, met Matthew in the parking lot. The shirt was faded from red to dirty pink and had holes and stains all over it. Matthew suddenly felt overdressed in his blue chambray work shirt.

"C'mon over to the house," Miles said. "Our youngest has chicken pox, so I'm playing nurse. I just painted her with calamine lotion and gave her two popsicles and told her she has to let Daddy play pastor until the big hand reaches the twelve."

"I could come back. It's not an emergency."

"No, no - come on in. I'm glad to have an adult to talk with, believe me. There's just so much Candyland and Animal Lotto a man can take before he turns into an idiot."

They went into the cheerfully messy living room and moved books, children's books and board games to sit at opposite ends of the couch. Miles stretched out his long legs and propped his feet on the battle-scarred coffee-table.

"What's up?" he asked.

"I need an attitude adjustment again."

Miles smiled and waited.

"I'm angry. I mean, I'm really angry - and I'm taking it out on everyone else."

Miles met Matthew's eyes, nodded, and waited some more. Matthew felt the anger rise in him.

"Could you at least say something?"

"Sure. But it works better when you figure it out for yourself."

"If I could do that, I wouldn't need to be here!" Matthew yelled, jumping up and stamping over to the window.

Upstairs a thin little voice began to cry. Miles rose with ungainly haste and took the stairs two at a time. As his soothing tones floated back down the stairs, Matthew felt as if he were receiving comfort along with the pastor's daughter. He eased back onto the couch and closed his eyes.

Oh, Lord, please forgive me for all this anger. Please forgive me for everyone I've hurt with it. Please let me understand what's happening to me so I can let go of it. Please give me back Your peace!

Something like peace flowed over him. He closed his eyes and rested quietly until Miles cleared his throat nearby. "I almost fell asleep," he admitted sheepishly.

"Along with a lot of other problems, anger makes you really tired," Miles said. "Too much adrenaline, I suppose. Big rush - big let-down." He sat again on the far end of the couch.

"Yeah, I suppose."

"Do you have any idea what's going on, or when it started, or anything?"

"I dunno... I remember talking to Will - he was asking about my dad, his granddaddy, and I told him. He got all excited about my father the big cop hero. I told him how it *really* was..."

"You've never told me."

"No. Until you brought it up last winter, I hadn't thought about him in a while. It's old history - doesn't mean a thing now."

The pastor waited.

"Well, it doesn't!"

The pastor waited.

Matthew fiddled with a cuff-button, jiggled his left leg to ease a sudden tightness in his knee. The tightness intensified to a searing pain, matched by a pain in his chest as memory rushed in.

"When I was eleven, he shoved me down the stairs because I got in his way at the top. I landed funny - something popped in my knee - I know now the cartilage must have torn. It hurt so bad I screamed - then I cried. And he slapped me for being a sissy. He wouldn't let my mamma take me to the hospital; I just laid in bed for a week and limped for a long time. That was *one* time." He rubbed his knee unconsciously with both hands as he spoke.

"He abused you a lot."

"Yeah."

"And your mother?"

"Oh, yeah." Matthew's tone was as bitter as the taste in his mouth. "Oh, yeah."

"Can you tell the rest of it now?"

"He was a Baltimore city cop - and a drunk. An alcoholic. He drank, he beat up his family, he fell off a fire escape and died drunk when I was twelve. He was chasin' a guy who tried to rob the liquor store where he went every day to get his supply. They gave him a medal and a military funeral, told Mama what a hero he was."

"Your knee still hurts."

"Yeah, sometimes. When the weather changes."

"And your heart still hurts. You've never forgiven him."

Matthew swiveled sharply to look at the pastor. "What? Are you nuts? I won't ever forgive that - !"

Miles met Matthew's look squarely. "Your father did awful things to you and your mother. Even though he had a killer disease, the alcoholism, that doesn't excuse his behavior."

"Right!"

"But - your father is dead. His sins are between him and God now. Your anger doesn't touch him at all, but it's eating holes in you."

"Maybe you don't get it yet, what kind of a guy he was. Want me to tell you about the little brother or sister I don't have because of that hero's big fists?"

Miles paled visibly but continued in a level voice, "Most people don't understand about forgiveness. They think if they forgive it means the abuse or injustice didn't matter. But that's not it."

"No?"

"No. You forgive someone for two reasons: first, because Christ forgave you; second, because forgiving sets you free, and it frees the other guy to deal with his problem."

Matthew dropped his gaze and sat for several minutes in stubborn silence, mulling over the pastor's foolish notion. Finally he ventured, "So if I forgive poor ol' Daddy for bein' such a - jerk - I won't be angry any more, and my life will be perfect?"

"Oh, come on! I never said anything about perfect, and you know it. And I won't kid you: it's that simple, but it's not that easy. Without the grace God gives, we probably couldn't ever forgive people."

Matthew rose abruptly. "I have to go back to work. Thanks for your time."

Miles stood more slowly and walked him to the door. "You know you're always welcome. If you feel like it, you might want to read the gospel accounts of Christ's words from the cross. And maybe the death of Stephen in Acts. If you want to."

"Yeah."

"May I pray for you before you leave?"

"No." Hearing the flat nastiness in his own voice, Matthew sighed. "I'm sorry. I mean, no, thank you."

"That's all right. I'll just pray after you leave," Miles said easily. "Give me a call when you want to go another round."

Matthew nodded and left silently, the anger companioning him all the way home. Every time he worked the clutch, his left knee reminded him of the stupidity of the pastor's idea.

"Knee's bothering you a lot," John remarked that evening, as Matthew shifted continually on the couch, trying to find a comfortable position. "I don't think I've noticed it this much since the first winter you were here."

"Yeah."

"Did you hurt it? I mean, recently?"

"No. I don't know what it is. Too early for snow - that always does it."

"Maybe you ought to have Nate Hanna take a look at it," John suggested. "They have some pretty good knee-repair surgery now; he could refer you to a specialist. Y'know, you never said how you hurt it in the first place."

"After all this time, are you gonna start pryin' into my past?"

John was startled, then hurt, then angry. Matthew watched the emotions follow one another across the farmer's unguarded face. He watched John wrestle down the anger. The process fascinated Matthew even more than the query had angered him.

"I didn't mean that," Matthew said at last. "I know you're not pryin'. It was a fair question, but I'd just rather not answer it."

"Okay."

"Can I ask you one, instead?"

John took and released a deep breath. "Sure."

"Just then - when I snapped at you - I saw it made you mad. But you didn't snap back. You just - what? - made it go away. How did you do that?"

John laughed, a short, sharp bark of laughter, accompanied by a shake of his head. "Well - I don't know! I just - " He laughed again. "You sure ask the darnedest questions!"

"You always have answers," Matthew grinned.

"Okay, I didn't 'make' it go away. It's more like making a choice to let go of it and asking God to take it. I don't want to be angry with you or anybody - done too much of that the past year. And I know you're having a bad time right now about something, so it isn't personal."

"So you just say, 'Here, God,' and he makes it go away."

"Pretty much. No big secret. Just prayer."

Matthew looked down at his hands. "I don't seem to be doing too much of that these days."

"Believe it or not," John said easily, "everybody gets dry spells. Trick is to do it anyway, until your conscious contact comes back. And it will - I know."

"You never stopped praying? Last winter?"

"I can't say I prayed a lot as time went on. I spent some prayers telling God how angry I was and maybe even telling Him off, but... Felt a lot of the time like my prayers were bouncing off the ceiling. It took a long time for things between God and me to get better. But you know that."

"And now?"

"God isn't any closer to me now than He was last October. But today I can feel that in my heart as well as know it in my head. I can talk to Him and I can listen to Him again. I can feel His love for me and I can love Him back."

"Just like that, huh?"

"No," John said patiently, "not 'just like that.' I had to be willing to give up the anger, willing to choose to forgive my son for dying, my wife for - turning away, my pastor for not working a miracle, every family I saw for having living children - God... I had to forgive God for letting it happen. And then I had to repent of questioning Him, of failing to admit His right to be Lord over everything in my life, including David's death. There was a point - that night by the pond - when it started to get better, but it's been a long process."

"Thanks for talking to me about it," Matthew said uncomfortably, rubbing his knee without noticing. "I'll think about it."

John laughed again. "I know you will. You always do."

Matthew limped up the stairs to bed and lay sleepless under the covers. Moonlight -buttery harvest moonlight - filtered into the room. He heard an owl calling, a far-away dog barking. He thought about all the talk. Then he thought about his father.

I won't ever forgive you, he thought. *Never. I wish you'd died ten years earlier! I wish you had died of cancer so you'd have suffered a long, long time. I hope you're in hell right now, and I hope it hurts!*

To his own amazement, he burst into tears and buried his face in the pillow. He wept hard but silently, confused and ashamed and not sure why he was weeping.

Forty-Eight

September died in a blaze of gold and scarlet. October was born in brown and russet. Large flocks of geese flew south over the pond, their raucous honking trailing away behind them. Matthew nurtured his anger deep under a layer of protective politeness so that no one would get hurt. He let dust accumulate on the cover of his Bible.

"Gonna be an early frost and a bad winter again," Ed predicted.

"I know," he agreed, favoring his knee. "It's going to snow before November."

"Gotta get that boy some warm clothes or he'll be saying he's too cold to do his chores."

"I'll take him Saturday," Matthew volunteered.

Will was agreeable to a shopping trip, if not enthusiastic. He had definite ideas about where to shop and what was "cool," but they made it through underwear to outerwear before seriously butting heads over a pair of name-brand sneakers. Will understood the economics but sulked anyway.

"Look," Matthew finally snapped, "quit acting like a baby and be grateful for what you have."

They were in the middle of the mall parking lot, far from the truck. Will spat out a few choice words, accompanied by a rude gesture, and ran ahead to the truck. When he couldn't open the locked door, he punched it.

The new dent in the door was unremarkable, but blood trickled from Will's rapidly swelling knuckles. "Look what you made me do!" he snarled.

"That's what temper tantrums get you," Matthew snapped back.

"You should talk! Mister 'everybody-better-walk-on-eggshells-around-me'!"

Wordlessly, Matthew handed Will a clean handkerchief to wrap around his knuckles, then unlocked the truck. Will flung himself inside and slammed the door. They rode back to town in silence.

"Let me out here!" Will suddenly demanded as they passed the school.

"Let you out? What for?"

"None of your business. I'm gonna see some guys, and I'll be home later."

Matthew hesitated but could see no real reason to refuse. Besides, he felt guilty for his outburst. He had been trying so hard to contain anger. "Okay. I'll pick you up here at three-thirty."

Will hopped out. "Never mind. I'll catch a ride. Don't worry, I'll be home in time for chores." He turned quickly and sprinted off down the street.

An uneasy feeling enveloped Matthew. *I shouldn't have done that. I should have made him come home with me. He's mad, and sure as anything he's gonna get in trouble. And so am I for letting him go!*

He berated himself for his own carelessness all the way home. Parking near the back door, he lugged their purchases into the kitchen. Carolyn was making oatmeal cookies.

"Hi," she chirped. "Have a good time? It looks like you bought out the store! I didn't know you were going all the way to the mall."

"Neither did I," Matthew laughed, dumping the bags on two chairs. "But the store in town isn't cool."

"Oh. Well, of course not. Did you have enough money?" She pushed her hair back from her forehead with her wrist.

"Almost enough. We got some of everything, I think. Hey, those'd be a whole lot better if you put chocolate chips in them," he said, snitching a fingerful of dough.

"Keep your paws out of there," Carolyn warned, threatening his hand with a wooden spoon. "Do you need some lunch?"

"No, thanks. We did the fast food thing."

"Where's Will?" she asked belatedly. "Why'd you bring his things in here?"

"I dropped him off in town, over by the school. He said he was going to visit some friends." The uneasy feeling twisted in Matthew's gut.

"Oh, that's nice. I'm glad he's making some friends. A boy his age needs to spend time with other boys his age. And girls."

Matthew shuddered at the thought of Will with girls but said nothing. Instead, he went upstairs and changed clothes, then went to work checking the corn-sheller. Engrossed in the mechanics of the machine, he didn't notice the time until Ed called him to the milking.

"Will ain't with you?" Ed asked as Matthew entered the barn alone.

"No. I figured he was with you. I dropped him off in town, but he said he'd be home to do his chores."

"Not here."

The uneasy feeling returned to Matthew's belly. "I shouldn't have let him go. I should have made him stay with me."

"Kid's fifteen years old. You gotta let him have some slack. I told you he's been spoiling for some trouble. But we don't know yet as he's found any, so let's get these cows milked and worry about the rest later."

The barn seemed close and hot, steamy with the mingled odors of cow and milk and manure. Flies clung to Matthew's exposed arms and bit viciously, hard enough to draw blood. Thunder rumbled far in the distance. His stomach rolled.

"Storm coming," Ed noted, swatting a fly. "Esther 'n' Ezra flies always bites before a storm." He swatted again and gave a shout of triumph.

"Will doesn't have a jacket. It's going to get cold if it storms. Maybe I'd better go look for him."

"Nah, let him be. He'll be home in time for supper; he's just avoiding chore time."

They completed the milking in unequal silence, Ed peaceful and Matthew concerned. He listened to the thunder coming closer and prayed for Will's safety.

Suppertime came and Will did not. After a quick shower, Matthew helped Carolyn carry bowls and platters to the dining room table. Savory odors of pork chops and sage gravy wreathed him, increasing his nausea.

"You look sick," Carolyn exclaimed, taking the mashed potatoes from him. "You can't throw up every time you're worried." A small frown of concern pleated her forehead.

Matthew laughed ruefully. "Shoot, if you can tell me how to stop it, I sure will!"

"I know. I'm a worrier, too, sometimes. And knowing it's wrong doesn't make it go away."

"Wrong?"

"Of course!" She ferried a dish of peas and carrots around his lanky frame to the table. "Wrong to worry when we're supposed to be trusting God. I mean, if He's in control like we say He is, then - "

"You saying worry's a *sin*?" Matthew asked incredulously.

"Well, yes, I guess I am. But I still wish Will would call or come through the door - and you'd enjoy your supper."

Determined not to disgrace himself, Matthew took his seat next to Ed. As John asked a blessing over the meal and prayed for Will's safety, Matthew considered Carolyn's words. For a change, he also considered the prayer. *Lord, if worry really is a sin, please forgive me and take it away. And please bring Will home safely...*

"Now, you just eat," Pearl admonished, filling his plate for him. Her sharp eyes raked over him so that he was sure she was counting his bones through his shirt.

"Yes, ma'am, I will," Matthew assured her, dropping butter into a hole in his mashed potatoes.

"No gravy?" Pearl asked.

"No, thank you, this is fine. See?" He forked some of the potatoes into his mouth and swallowed. "I'm eating, honest."

The old woman snorted and slathered butter and jelly on a thick slice of whole wheat bread. "Here. Eat this, too."

"Gonna stuff him like a goose," Ed teased. "Gonna make him too fat to work."

"Not any time in the near future," John replied.

The bantering helped to keep Matthew's mind from Will and the increasing thunder and allowed him to eat most of what the old woman had put in front of him. He was actually beginning to relax and enjoy himself when the phone rang.

Carolyn answered it in the kitchen, where she was dishing up ice cream for dessert. They stopped talking to listen as she gave a bright hello and then was silent. They heard her say, "Thank you," and hang up the receiver.

Matthew looked at John, whose face had gone white, whose pupils were dilated so far Matthew couldn't see the blue. *Please, God*, Matthew prayed, *for his sake, please, not again!*

Carolyn came back from the kitchen. She seemed calm enough, but her fingers kept pleating and unpleating her apron. "Will was in an accident," she said, her voice quivering only a little. "He isn't really hurt badly, they said, but they're taking some x-rays. We need to go to the hospital to fill out papers - and probably to bring him home..."

All the air whooshed out of John's lungs. His wife moved to him and he buried his face in her bosom for a moment.

Ed jumped to his feet. "I'm gonna get a change of clothes in case his're ruined."

"Bring his coat, too," Matthew said. "He didn't have one with him, and it's cold out now." He clenched his fists to stop his hands from shaking. *Please, God. I haven't had time -*

"Better take a blanket, too," Pearl advised. "And the car, in case he needs to lie down on the back seat."

John rose, color returning to his face. "There's a blanket in the trunk of the car. Caro and I will take that, and you two take the truck. Will you stay here and set things to rights?" he asked Pearl.

"Of course I will."

Matthew drove, skillfully and fast, while Ed clutched Will's coat in his arms and carried on a frantic, grumbling dialogue with himself. "Durnfool kid! Knew he was gonna do something dumb like this! Oughta never took him in in the first place. Stupid kid! Serves him right. Oh, God, I sure hope he ain't hurt bad!"

They met the Abbotts at the entrance and the four of them went through the emergency room doors together. Three faces mirrored the memory of the last time they had come this way, and the determination not to recall it to the others.

A male nurse in blood-spattered, faded blue scrubs came up to them. "You must be Will's family. The others are already gone. We would have called you sooner, but he wouldn't give us a name to call."

Ed snorted. "Fool kid!"

"Are you his father?"

"No. That's his father," he gestured at Matthew. "He's all of ours." Ed stuck out his chin as if daring anyone to deny it. "Where's he at?"

"Will is still in x-ray," the nurse explained. "He was riding in the front passenger seat when the car hit the tree, and he banged his head pretty good. He may also have broken his right wrist. It's just lucky he was wearing his seat belt. Nobody else in the car was, and two of them were ejected."

"How badly were they hurt?" Carolyn whispered.

"I'm sorry. The driver's dead. The other boy's in pretty bad shape. They life-flighted him about an hour ago. The other three - "

"Three!"

"Yes, there were four in the back seat. The other three were banged up some and scared half to death. But they'll be fine. They've all gone home."

"Who are the other two?" John asked.

The nurse named the injured boy, a family they knew from church, and the boy who had died, a stranger to them. Tears began to flow down Carolyn's face. "You can wait in the exam room," the nurse offered, ushering them in. "He should be back soon."

Carolyn slumped into the room's only chair, and John stood behind her, hands on her shoulders, as she cried. Ed huddled in a corner, clutching Will's coat. "Hate these places," he grumbled. Matthew leaned against the wall, shaking, praying silently.

After the longest fifteen minutes in a year, the door opened and the nurse pushed Will's wheelchair into the room.

The boy was slumped in the chair, chalky white, a huge bile-green hospital gown accentuating his pallor and frailty. Four black stitches closed a cut through his right eyebrow, which was swollen and purple. He already had a huge black eye, there was dried blood all over his face and neck, disappearing down his chest under the loose neckline of the gown - and he reeked of whiskey. At the nurse's gesture, he stiffly climbed out of the chair and onto the examining table. They saw he still had on his jeans and sneakers.

"I just need to check your vitals one more time," the nurse said, suiting actions to words. Will visibly flinched every time the man touched him. He didn't meet the eyes of any of his rescuers. "Checks out pretty good," the nurse said. "Doctor says you can go home as long as your folks keep an eye on you. Get dressed now, and I'll get your papers." He left them alone in the small room.

They all looked at each other. John said gently, "We're glad you're all right." Carolyn went over to the table and gave Will a gentle hug, which he endured. She patted his cheek lovingly and smoothed his matted hair.

The whiskey smell assailed Matthew's nostrils and his memory and turned a key inside him. The anger broke out of its cell as he watched Carolyn's loving gestures. He lunged at Will, yelling at the top of his lungs, "You stupid little jerk! I told you not to do it! I told you you were gonna get in trouble!" He grabbed Will's gown by the neck and began to shake the boy violently. "You could have been killed, and how do you think that would have made people feel? But do you care about anybody but yourself? No! Drinkin' and druggin' and - what? – stealin', too? It'd serve you right if you'd been killed!"

Will screamed, terrified, and pushed ineffectually at Matthew's furious hands. "Leave me alone! I didn't do anything! I wasn't drinking! I wasn't! Gary had a bottle and it broke when we hit. It's just on my jeans!"

Ed spun Matthew out of the way and grabbed Will to his chest. The boy burrowed into him as if he never meant to leave. John grabbed Matthew's upper arm with iron fingers as the male nurse and another man rushed in. "It's under control," John said in a voice which would not be contradicted.

Will raised his head from Ed's safe shoulder and glared wildly at Matthew. "Man, you are such a liar! You know that lousy old man of yours you hate so much? Well, guess what? You're just like him! Man, you *are* your father!"

Horror froze everyone in the room - except Matthew. He broke from John's restraining hand and ran. John caught up with him at the truck.

"I'll drive," John said. "Get in."

Having no better alternative, Matthew got in. Will's words pounded in his head, over and over and over and over. *You are your father. You are your father.* The truck moved out into light evening traffic, heading for home. John drove in silence. The storm broke, pouring water in sheets across the windshield and forking lightning into the fields around them. John turned the wipers on high and slowed the truck to a crawl. Visibility was near zero outside and the defroster couldn't quite keep up with the fog on the windows inside.

Matthew's rage had faded, leaving him sick and shaken, exhausted, despairing. "I'd rather be dead than be my father," he said at last.

"There might be a third alternative," John said quietly.

"I can't do it. I can't forgive him." Matthew's voice was hollow and hopeless in the noisy cab. "And how can I ever be sure I won't act that way again?"

Forty-Nine

As they pulled into the driveway, Matthew gathered himself. "I think I'd better leave in the morning, unless you want me to go tonight." He reached for the door-handle, but John reached across and clamped his wrist.

"I don't want you to go anywhere except a warm shower and your own bed."

"You have to see I can't stay - not after what I did to Will. He's right, y'know. I am my father: dangerous and mean."

"Look at me," John commanded. His force of will made Matthew turn to meet his eyes. The security light illuminated their faces, casting grotesque shadows over them. Matthew saw weariness in John's face, and concern, and something he might have called love. He imagined how his own face must look, the twisted, depraved look he remembered of his father in a drunken rage. He turned away, ashamed.

"No! I said look at me." Matthew obeyed and held this time. He couldn't distinguish the anxious drumming of his heart from the pounding of the rain on the metal truck. John continued nearly unblinking eye contact. "Have you ever lied to me?"

Nonplused, Matthew blurted, "No! Of course not."

John smiled a little. "I didn't think so. That means I can trust your word, doesn't it?"

"Of course."

"So, before we go in, I want your solemn word on two things: one - you won't leave for at least forty-eight hours; and two - you won't do anything to hurt yourself." John's voice vibrated with intensity and his hand gripped Matthew's wrist like a shackle.

"I give you my word I won't leave for forty-eight hours and I won't hurt myself."

"Thank you," John said. "In the morning, we'll sort this out. If you need to talk before that, just come and get me. I won't care what time it is. Will you do that?"

Matthew nodded and climbed out of the truck. The rain soaked him to the skin before he could make the porch. His teeth began to chatter, his stomach muscles to clench. Pearl flung open the door and dragged him into the kitchen.

"You're wet through!" she exclaimed. "Go shuck out of those wet clothes. I'll put on some coffee." She gave him a little push in the right direction.

Shaking, he struggled to untie his bootlaces and to peel off wet jeans which clung like leeches. He found a clean towel in the dryer and wrapped it around his waist. Water dripped from his hair onto his naked back and shoulders, freezing him deeper with every drop.

"You need a hot shower," Pearl said as he emerged from the utility room. "Your lips are blue!"

Matthew headed across the kitchen, but she stopped him again. "What about Will?"

Without turning around, he said, "He has a big goose-egg with four stitches through his right eyebrow, but no fracture. The rest is just bumps and bruises. He's fine and he'll be home any minute."

Lying in bed trying to stop shaking, Matthew heard John and Carolyn burst laughing into the kitchen and exchange inaudible conversation with Pearl. Then he heard John's quick, light step on the stairs, followed by a knock on his door.

"May I come in?"

"Sure," he called. "Come."

The door swung open. John stood silhouetted in the dim light from the hall. "I guess I just needed to be sure you're all right. Can I get you anything?"

"No, thanks." *Why is he being so nice?*

"Do you want to talk?"

"Not really. Is - is Will - ?"

"He's fine. He'll probably be sore as a boil all over by tomorrow, but, praise God, he's not badly hurt. He's settled in over there like a king right now."

Relief swept over Matthew. "That's good."

John continued to hesitate in the doorway. "Will asked about you. He asked if you were all right. I told him you were safe, but he wanted to come over and see for himself. I just thought you ought to know. Get some sleep now, and we'll talk in the morning. God bless you." He left quietly, closing the door behind him.

Oh, Daddy, Matthew thought, *why couldn't you have talked to me like that just once? Maybe I could believe I was worth somethin' now if you had loved me just a little. Maybe I could have hugged Will instead of hurtin' him if I knew how to love better. Why was it so hard for you to love me? What's wrong with me?*

He fell suddenly into sleep, into the tangled web of dreams. He saw again the tall black man, the beautiful woman - and Will - all asking, "How can I understand, unless someone explains it to me?" He saw his Bible sinking in the pond, just beyond his reach. Mingled fear and sadness filled him as the book went under. Then the feelings turned to pure joy as he saw David!

Dressed in jeans and a Mickey Mouse tee-shirt, barefoot in the lush grass, David carried his old boat toward the pond. Matthew watched the child's carefree progress with delight, hearing as he came closer that David was half-singing, half humming "Row, Row, Row Your Boat." Matthew realized it had all been a terrible mistake: David wasn't dead! He could hardly bear the intensity of his love and his joy. He ran toward the boy, arms outstretched, calling his name.

But as he closed the distance, David's expression turned from happiness to terror. Throwing up one little arm in front of his face, he looked into Matthew's eyes and cried out, "No! Please don't hit me!"

Fifty

Matthew woke with a start at three a.m. and lay there still and empty until the smell of coffee called him to get up. To avoid John and Carolyn, he went straight out the front door, squelching through last night's puddles to the barn.

Celeste, ever the opportunist, rubbed around his ankles, purring rhythmically. As the machinery began, Matthew scooped up the cat and sat on a bale of straw with her. After one surprised chirrup, she allowed him this unusual familiarity for a few moments before protesting her need to get down.

"I don't blame you," Matthew said, letting Celeste jump to the floor. "You'd probably get hurt if you stayed."

As he waited, John entered, carrying Matthew's coat. He put it on and sat down again. John sat beside him and waited.

The machines hummed, the cat purred, the cows stamped occasionally and mumbled their feed, a barn-swallow chittered. Matthew felt as removed from the sound and rhythm of his life as if it were happening to someone else. He supposed he should get up to send the cows out, but it was too much effort.

Ed rushed in late to find the cows getting restless and the two men just sitting there on the straw. "Timothy, James 'n' Peter, you guys! Them cows're gonna stage a jail-break!" Ed swiftly, efficiently released the little cows and sent them on their way. John rose to help with the clean-up. "What's going on?" Ed asked.

John spoke in a low voice. "I think Matthew's really beating himself up about grabbing Will and yelling at him. He's been brooding about something for a couple of weeks, have you noticed? Hasn't been himself. Then this."

"Yeah, I noticed." Ed dropped his voice to match John's. "Figured it's just it getting to be October - you know - the boy and all - Ain't never seen him mean like that before, though. Scared me near as much as it scared Will."

"It's not his way. And I know he cares about Will." John flushed the lines again and wiped his hands on the clean but ragged towel they kept hanging from a nail.

"Sure he cares," Ed agreed, glancing back down the barn to the still figure on the straw. "Will knows it, too. He pretends he don't care, but he sets a store by him - was more upset about Matthew believing he was drinking than he was about the accident."

"How's Will this morning?"

"Might stiff and sore. Kinda up and down with pain all night. Upset some, too, about the kid dying. I told him I'd stay home from church with him today. Sorry I was late getting over here; didn't sleep much myself."

"No problem. But we do have a problem with Matthew. He said he'd rather be dead - "

Ed looked sharply at the farmer. "You sound pretty worried, boss."

"Pray for us. I'm playing this by ear."

John came back to Matthew. "Let's go to the house. Breakfast will be ready."

Matthew looked up dully, then stood and walked with John across the yard.

After breakfast he said, "I think I'll go back to bed."

"How about church?" John asked.

"No." He turned and headed for the stairs. It seemed to take hours to climb them, to gain the safety of his room. He was too tired to undress, so he just lay down on top of the unmade bed.

§ § §

In their room, getting ready for church, Carolyn asked, "What's happening to him?" Her hands twisted around each other. John drew her close and held her.

"I don't know," he said. "I'm only sure the scene with Will caused it."

Her eyes filled and the tears spilled over. "This reminds me of when David died. It'll be a year on Saturday - I wish I didn't remember anything!" She began to weep in earnest; John silently cursed when she stiffened in his embrace. "Leave me alone!" she snapped through her tears. "You always do that!"

"What?"

"You always try to-to-to s-stop me f-from crying!"

"Sweetheart," John protested in amazement, "I just can't stand to see you hurting!"

"Oooooh!" she wailed and threw herself down on the bed like a two-year-old.

John stared, bemused. *I'm going crazy,* he concluded. *This can't be our safe, quiet, peaceful home. Not with a manic-depressive on this side of me and a suicidal depressive on the other! Lord, what am I supposed to do or say now?*

Carolyn rolled onto her back, nose pink and eyes already red and swollen. She grabbed several tissues and blew her nose loudly. "If I didn't love you so much," she said waspishly, "I'd leave you for being such a fool!"

"What?"

"Oh, for heaven's sake!" She scooted to the far side of the bed. "Here, lie down with me for a minute."

Still bemused, John removed his shoes and lay beside his wife. Sniffling, she snuggled close to him, head on his shoulder and arm across his chest. His hand automatically began to sift through her hair, destroying her Sunday hairdo.

"We never talked enough," she said reflectively. "Maybe we should have gone for counseling. It seemed we were never ready at the same time."

"Uh-huh." John had no idea where she was heading.

"Sometimes, when I remember, and it hurts so bad I cry - it may seem like a bad thing, but it's not."

"It's not."

"No. It's good. It even feels good, in a strange way. Like now. I feel better, even if I look like a mess - "

"You look beautiful!" John interjected quickly.

"You're going to have to confess that," she teased, stroking his face with her small rose-scented hand. "But it does get you extra points with the cook."

"Can I use 'em here?" he asked, turning his face to kiss her palm and fingers.

"Stop that! No, *really* stop it!" she laughed. "I'm trying to make a point here."

"Then you really ought to make it from your own side of the bed. And soon, or we're going to miss church, too."

"Oops!" Carolyn crawled off the end of the bed and began to change her clothes, moving with quick efficiency between closet and dresser. John lazily watched her, enjoying the scenery.

"The point?" he asked.

"The point is that I need to cry and grieve still. And it's better for me to do it than to stuff it. And frankly, I think it's better for you, too."

They went quietly downstairs together. "By the way," John remarked, "I heard you about the grieving. I'll try to let you go."

"And I'll try to take you with me."

Fifty-One

Matthew slept. Far enough down in sleep, he couldn't see the faces or hear the voices accusing him. Far enough down, he didn't care that he was worthless and dangerous and unlovable. If he went far enough down in sleep, he might never have to come up again.

If only they would leave him alone.

But they would not.

They touched him. They called his name. A strange medicinal-smelling hand smacked his cheek so hard he had to surface to push it away.

"Quit shamming and open your eyes!" a gruff voice commanded. Matthew slowly complied. Bending over him was a stocky, sturdy man with bushy, iron-gray hair and eyebrows, wire-rimmed glasses - and a serious black suit.

An undertaker, he thought. *I'm dead.* He closed his eyes.

"Matthew!" the man roared in his ear.

Not dead yet, he decided. *Too bad for heaven and not ready for hell.* "What?" he asked without opening his eyes.

"It's Nate Hanna, and I want you to look at me. Now!"

Matthew opened his eyes again because he didn't like the doctor's roaring in his ear.

"That's better," the doctor claimed, sitting on the edge of the bed. "Now let's have a look and a listen." He applied his stethoscope and blood pressure cuff and shone his little light into Matthew's eyes. "Pain anywhere?"

"No..."

"We should all be so healthy. Do I have to worry about you killing yourself?"

Matthew considered the man and the question. "It isn't anything to worry about."

"Not too depressed to be a smart-aleck, are you? Straight answer now. Got a plan?"

"No..." Matthew's eyelids drooped. He was too tired for this.

"Stay with me here!" Dr. Hanna barked. "I purely hate to see Carolyn Abbott cry. Are you going to get up and quit scaring her, or shall I have you hauled off to the psych ward?"

"If I... get up..." Matthew took a deep breath and mustered the strength to go on - "...do you... go away?"

"I do. And I come back. So don't get any bright ideas about getting me off your back."

Pushing himself to a sitting position, Matthew waited for the room to stop tilting. The doctor waited also, the patient stillness of his bulk and the kind expression in his hazel eyes at odds with the gruff energy of his voice.

"Matthew," he finally said, "you're going to have to talk to someone about what hurts. Now, that can be me, or Pastor Corrigan, or a good mental health professional - or even John - but it has to be someone, and it has to be soon. I'm not going to give you pills so you can blunt the edges and pretend whatever's eating you has gone away."

"You don't understand..."

"Of course I don't! You haven't told me anything!" In a gentler voice than he had used so far, Nate continued, "C'mon, Matthew. Give it a try."

"What day is it? What time?" His throat felt like sandpaper and his mouth like glue.

"It's Tuesday morning, about eleven o'clock. You've been mostly sleeping since Sunday morning. Remember your pastor being here?"

"No. Probably because he didn't hit me."

"Peevish is good," Nate chuckled. "How about a drink of water?"

"Please." He accepted the small glass from the doctor's hand and drained it at a gulp. Wordlessly the doctor went back to the bathroom for a refill, which Matthew dispatched as quickly. "Thank you," he said, leaning back against the pillow.

"You understand what I said before?"

"Yeah."

"Anything else you want to tell me?"

"I want to ask..."

"What?"

Matthew closed his eyes to avoid seeing Nate's expression. "About heredity. How much do we inherit from our parents?"

"Hmmm." Nate sat down on the bed again. "Well, the obvious things: physical characteristics, certain diseases - "

"Diseases - like alcoholism?"

"Yep. I think so. Sure runs in families. You got a drinking problem John didn't mention?"

"No. I mostly don't drink. My father - I think he was an alcoholic."

"Well, statistically you got about a fifty-fifty chance. 'Course it's a zero chance if you don't drink."

"And what about behavior? Is that hereditary?"

Nate hmmm'd again. "That's sure a lot less black and white than the Seibenek blue eyes or the Hanna chin. There's been a lot of research on different behaviors, or what people think are behaviors - like homosexuality, schizophrenia - some evidence in the last few years of a gene for shyness, of all things. But it's tough to tell. Environment? Heredity? Truth probably lies somewhere in the middle."

"Thank you."

"Best I could do, and probably not good enough for what ails you. Now, Matthew, take a shower."

"I will... later."

"Now!" roared the doctor, yanking back the covers.

Defeated, Matthew found clean underwear and plodded across the hall. As he stood under the stinging spray, he heard his tormentor go down to the family.

§ § §

They were clustered around the kitchen table, hunched over untouched mugs of coffee, as Nate walked in. "Save any of that for me?" he asked.

Pearl rose briskly, filled one of the blue goose mugs and placed it at the empty place at the table. "Sit," she said. "I'll get you a spoon. You're the only one who uses sugar."

"Is that an implied criticism, Pearl?" Nate asked as he sat down.

"Didn't sound implied to me," Ed snickered. "What about Matthew?"

"John, you're going to pay me double for this house call! He's a nice kid with some kind of a big problem - and he wouldn't tell me anything, even when I used my best bedside manner."

Ed snickered again but turned it into a cough. Pearl merely snorted. "Your best bedside manner was so loud it rattled the dishes in the cupboard!"

"Look, people, you can't baby the guy. If you let him, he'll lie there and will himself to die."

Carolyn began crying quietly. As Nate noticed, he became visibly shaken, his blunt, calm competence deserting him. "Aw, Caro, don't!" he begged, handing her his crisp white handkerchief.

"I can't help it!" she sobbed. "What are we going to do? Can't you give him something?"

Flushed and miserable, Nate patted her arm. "C'mon, now, please! No, I can't give him any magic pill to fix him, Caro. You know I'd do it for you if I could."

"Why not?" John asked. "Can't you give him an antidepressant or something?"

"John, those drugs take two or three weeks to kick in. He needs to deal with his problem now. And if I give him tranquillizers or sedatives, they'll knock him out but keep him from dealing with it. Besides - "

"Besides what?" Pearl asked.

The doctor began, belatedly, to stir his coffee, following the movement of the spoon through the dark liquid to avoid eye contact. "The potential for overdose is too high - Now, durnit, Caro, quit that!"

Barefoot, wearing jeans and a white tee-shirt, Matthew wandered into the kitchen. As he stepped onto the cold linoleum, he stopped and stared for a long moment at his feet. "I forgot my shoes," he said.

At the sound of his voice, Carolyn leaped up, nearly overturning her chair, and flung herself at Matthew. He staggered back a little before bracing himself against her weight. One hand came up of its own accord to pat her back as she wept against his shoulder. In a moment, John detached his wife and gently propelled the two toward the table. They sat. Carolyn began to smile, wiping away the last of her tears with Nate's handkerchief.

"Good," Nate declared. "Now eat, do your chores, decide who you're going to talk to. I'll be back tonight." He scooped up his black bag and left by the back door.

§ § §

"You're crowding the boy," Pearl said to the rest of the family. "Go do something somewhere else." As the other three left quickly, Pearl filled a small glass with orange juice and placed it at Matthew's right hand. "Start with this. No getting sick." She began to clear away the coffee mugs.

Experimentally, Matthew picked up his glass. His hand shook a little, but not enough to spill, as he guided the glass to his mouth and took a sip. The sweet, sharp tang of the juice stabbed his salivary glands and shaved his tongue like a straight razor. The whole mouthful dropped into his stomach in one cold glob. Pearl gave him a fierce glare and he willed his body to behave. Apparently his face changed as his insides settled, because her glare gave over to a twinkle.

"Toast?"

"No, ma'am."

"White or whole wheat?"

Matthew sighed. "Whole wheat."

He finished the juice while the old woman spread a little butter and a lot of grape jam on one piece of toast, cut it into quarters and placed them in front of him on a saucer. Absently he ate one piece, then another, until the little plate was empty. His finger idly rearranged the crumbs.

Pearl sat down opposite Matthew, her well-worn Bible in her hand. "You've been a good addition to this family," Pearl said. "You need us - and we need you, too, including Will. You may not kill yourself, do you understand?"

"Yes, ma'am."

"I have a few verses for you. Pay attention now:

> *The Lord is gracious and compassionate,*
> *slow to anger and rich in love.*
> *The Lord is good to all;*
> *he has compassion on all he has made...*

> *The Lord is faithful to all his*
> *promises and loving toward all he has made.*

"That's from Psalm 145."

Matthew looked blankly at the old woman. Undaunted, she read the verses to him again. "Think of it, boy: 'gracious, compassionate, slow to anger, rich in love.'"

"Yes, ma'am. Thank you." He tried to set the words into a mind which felt like Jell-O. The only solid places said, *You are your father;* said, *Please, don't hit me.*

Fifty-Two

By going through the motions, Matthew realized, he could make them leave him alone. Will avoided him, claiming to be too sore to do more than lie on his bed after riding the bus. Matthew thought it was better that way, safer for Will and less painful for him. He pushed on through the week.

Saturday dawned blood-red. The light breeze was heavy with moisture and chilled them to the bone as they silently did the milking. Silently they shivered into the house. Silently Carolyn placed plates of biscuits and gravy in front of them, poured milk and juice and coffee and took her seat. Silently John bowed his head over his plate and then began to eat. The others did the same.

Near the end of the silent meal, John turned to Ed and Matthew. "Carolyn and I are going to the cemetery this morning. Would either of you like to go with us?"

Matthew blinked. Raising his gaze to the calendar, he took in the date. *David. Oh, David.* He shook his head.

"Ed?"

"Naw, boss. Me and Matthew and Will'll do stuff here."

Placing his dirty dishes in the sink, Matthew relished the chance to be free of the Abbotts for a while. Moving faster than he had all week, he escaped to his room and closed the door. He sat on the carelessly made bed and thought about his options.

Most tempting was to crawl back into bed and sleep for hours. He was sleeping so little at night, with painful dreams often disturbing what little sleep he found. But another option was to use this time to leave. Alone in the dark at three o'clock in the morning, Matthew frequently thought about leaving. He would have to do a better job of it than he had the last time, but now he had money in the bank and could take the truck to the city if he left a note. Then he could buy a train ticket, then a plane ticket. He could go - where?

"*Psalm 139*," Matthew heard. He looked at the door, but no one was there. *Oh, no,* he thought, *not now. Please leave me alone.*

"*Psalm 139.*"

He put his hands over his ears. It was merely a reflex; he knew the Voice was inside his head, just as he knew it wouldn't leave him alone. Slowly he reached for the dusty Bible and turned to Psalm 139. He read:

> *O Lord, you have searched me*
> *and you know me...*
> *Where can I go from your Spirit?*
> *Where can I flee from your*
> *presence?...*

I'm a rat in a trap, Matthew thought. *I can't pretend there is no God. And this says wherever I go, He's going to chase me. And He'll catch me. Every time. So much for leaving...*

Depression deepening, Matthew closed the Bible. Somehow, as he fumbled it up from his lap, the cover of the book fell open to reveal the flyleaf. Matthew didn't remember ever having seen this page before. It was imprinted in fancy gold lettering, the blanks filled in with faded black ink by a strong, unpracticed hand:

This book is given to: John Abbott
By: his father, David Abbott.

The date was filled in and a personal note had been written in the margin: "Son, I am so proud of you. Love, Dad."

Matthew slammed the cover shut and slung the Bible back onto the table. He heard the car drive away and knew Ed would have gone back to work. *I could call Miles*, he thought. *Well... Maybe later...* Instead, he went down the hall and into David's room.

The dinosaurs still marched across the curtains and the bedspread; the toys and books still filled the bright blue shelves. On the ceiling, the constellations remained constant. In exactly one year, nothing had changed. And yet the spirit of the boy wasn't there, not in the furnishings, not in the toys, not in the little clothes still hanging in the closet.

"Oh, David, where are you?" he mourned. Rising in slow motion from the bed, he moved to the desk and picked up the three-masted schooner. Slowly he carried it downstairs, out the back door, across the yard to the pond. The ducks waddled out of his way, quacking mild objections. The wind cut through his shirt and raised gooseflesh on him, but he paid no attention. Sitting in the cold, damp grass, he placed the boat in the water.

The wind caught the sails immediately, propelling the boat toward the middle of the pond. Matthew hugged his knees to his chest and watched his creation, his special gift to the person he had loved best in all the world, sail away from him. Then he laid his forehead on his knees and remembered for a long time, with a grief beyond tears.

Much later, Matthew recognized a sudden warmth as a coat and an arm went around his shoulders. "We've sat here before," came John's voice, deep with sadness. Matthew nodded, still hunched over his knees. "Ed says you've been out here for hours. Aren't you cold?"

"I... don't know."

"This damp will be hard on your knee. Why don't we go in?"

Matthew considered his knee, but he couldn't feel it. He stared out at the pond.

As John followed the turning of Matthew's head, he also looked out across the pond. The boat was becalmed in the middle of the water. "Matthew, what's David's boat doing out there?"

"I'm waiting for it to sink."

"No! David loved that boat! You don't have any right to - " John stopped himself with a deep breath and settled back, loosening his grip on Matthew's shoulders but leaving his arm in place. "Carolyn and I - took flowers to the cemetery," he said, the metallic edge creeping into his voice. "And Carolyn had a - a little ship in a bottle. I don't know where she got it. We put it all on David's grave, and flowers and a pinwheel on Johnny's grave... I don't know why we do that. It's stupid. But we've always done it for Johnny - I guess we'll always do it for David. For Carolyn, it seems to ease the pain."

"And for you?"

"I don't know. Sometimes I try to imagine my sons sitting on Jesus' lap. I can't remember Johnny any more, unless I'm looking at a picture. He was too little to do much - hadn't learned to sit up or talk or do much except coo and grin a big toothless grin... I guess it's okay, not remembering. But Carolyn remembers everything about him."

"I remember David. I see him clear as day. I dream about him sometimes."

"So do I sometimes. I hear him laughing, in my dreams. I hug him - " John's voice broke and he moved away.

Matthew finally felt the cold, that strip across his back and shoulders where John's arm had been. He shuddered as he remembered the terrified little face and pleading voice of his current dreams.

"You're freezing!" John said hoarsely. "Come on in."

"I can't."

John's tone gentled again. "I don't think the boat will sink, Matthew. You made it too well. When the wind picks up, in an hour or so, it'll just drive the boat to shore."

"Yeah. I should have put a hole in it. Stupid..."

"Why do you need to sink it?"

He shrugged helplessly.

"Okay." John stood. "Come inside with me now. I'll come back this evening and get the boat. If you really need to - to sink it, I'll help you. I promise."

Matthew nodded. With John's considerable help, he gained his feet and limped back to the house. He welcomed the new-found pain in his knee as a distraction from the pain in his heart.

"Need an ice-bag for that knee?" John asked as they entered the kitchen.

"No, thanks." As he turned, pain speared through his knee, making him grab for the counter and draw in his breath sharply between his teeth. "Well, maybe..."

John filled a glass with cold tap water and handed it to Matthew with the aspirin bottle. "Here. Dose yourself up with these while I find an ice-bag. Carolyn!" he bellowed.

"Coming!" Her voice drifted down the stairs, soon followed by the rest of her, in jeans and a fuzzy blue sweater. "Here I am. What's so urgent you had to yell for me like that?"

With the grace to look just a bit sheepish, John smiled at his wife and pointed to Matthew. "His knee's hurting - needs an ice-bag."

"And?"

"And I don't know where one is."

Smiling too sweetly, Carolyn took a couple of ice-trays from the freezer and put them by the sink. "When you thank God tonight for all your blessings," Carolyn said, pulling a large plastic freezer bag from a drawer by the sink, "you just be sure you thank him for your patient wife. Now, watch: put the ice in the bag, zip-lock it, wrap the bag in a dishtowel, and voila! Instant ice-bag." She grinned at Matthew as she handed him the bag.

"Darlin'," John said fervently, "you are wonderful!"

§ § §

Lying on his bed, a pillow under his knee and the numbing ice over it, Matthew picked up his Bible again and studied the fly-leaf. "Son, I'm so proud of you. Love, Dad." *John told me he was twelve when his father gave him this Bible. Same age I was when my father died. God, why? Why does one kid get super-dad and another kid like Will or me gets Godzilla? You aren't fair!*

As the heat of old anger melted through the ice of his depression, Matthew heard unfamiliar footsteps coming up the stairs. Pastor Corrigan appeared in the doorway.

"Hi! May I come in?"

"Sure. Have a seat."

Miles folded himself onto the straight chair and looked around the room curiously. "Nice room. I didn't pay much attention when I was here on Monday."

"Thanks." Matthew heard the sullen note in his own voice, but Miles seemed not to notice.

"You look better. I'll tell you, it was pretty scary to see you just lying here like a corpse, not responding to anything."

Matthew said nothing.

Miles squirmed a little. "I – uh – I put you on the prayer chain again. Just that you were depressed and needed prayer, that's all. God is so faithful! I can see it's working."

Matthew said nothing. Miles shuffled his feet and readjusted his position.

"Matthew," he finally said into the silence, "would you rather I leave?"

Matthew experienced a mean flash of triumph – *finally, I outwaited him!* – followed by a wave of guilt. "I'm sorry. No, don't go."

The pastor relaxed. "I'm glad to see you're reading a good book," he grinned, gesturing to the Bible on Matthew's lap.

"Did I tell you about this Bible?"

"I don't think so. What about it?"

"John gave it to me. He said he was using another one, so – well, he said his father gave it to him when he accepted Christ, when he was twelve. John, I mean."

"So it's a pretty special Bible."

"Yeah. I always knew that. But this morning I found something in here – look." He showed the flyleaf to the pastor. "I never saw that before."

"Great note, isn't it?" Miles said gently, handing back the book. "John must care a lot about you to give you such a personal treasure, especially since his father is gone."

"I was lying here thinking – " Matthew looked away and stopped.

"Yes?"

"Nothing."

Miles waited. Matthew recognized the return to their usual roles, especially when the pastor leaned back and stretched out his long legs.

"Are you praying?" he asked suspiciously.

"Well, maybe just a little one," Miles grinned. "Hate to miss the opportunity, since you haven't been around much lately."

"The last time I came to see you – "

"Yes?"

"I told you about my father."

"I remember."

"Do you remember talking about it with John and Carolyn? Do you remember the first time I came to see you, telling me everything was just between you and me and God?" The anger grew, pushing away the last of his lethargy. "You lied to me."

Miles met his eyes squarely. "Matthew, I did talk with John. We needed to understand what was going on. So did the doctor. We were afraid you would kill yourself." Miles leaned forward, his thin face troubled, his voice intense. "I'm sure that feels like betrayal to you, and I'm sorry. I prayed about it first, and it seemed the best choice. We love you. We don't want to lose you."

"Whatever." He leaned back sullenly against the headboard.

Miles sighed. "Friend, we've been meeting off and on for almost a year. Have you ever heard me break a confidence about anybody before?"

"No." Matthew mirrored the pastor's sigh. The anger cooled, allowing depression to ooze back. He closed his eyes.

Miles knelt by the bed and opened Matthew's Bible. He folded up over the open book, leaning on the bed, and began to pray aloud. Matthew had noticed before how all the awkwardness and boyishness left Miles when he prayed, how his voice took on both deep reverence and quiet authority at the same time.

Listening now to the pastor's praise of God, Matthew felt chills along his spine. The man's prayer was quiet and conversational, no theatrics, but Matthew had to open his eyes to see what presence was coming into the room at the pastor's invocation. Everything looked the same – but felt different. Then Miles began to read from the open Bible, and the hair rose on the back of Matthew's neck.

> *Where can I go from your Spirit?*
> *Where can I flee from your*
> *presence?*

"That's Psalm 139!" he blurted.

"Yes, it is."

"I heard – I was supposed to read that this morning!"

"Oh, Matthew," Miles said in a hushed voice, "the Lord wants so much to heal that hurting place in you! He's telling you Himself how much He loves you, so much He'll never let you go. This psalm says He made you and knows every part of you from before you were born, and He stays with you even if you're being less than perfect."

The presence in the room lay on Matthew like a heavy blanket. Miles seemed almost to glow in its warm light.

"What's happening?" Matthew whispered.

The pastor's voice was equally hushed. "Praise the Lord your Father, Matthew. Right now, acknowledge Him. Ask Him to heal you. He wants to do it now, Matthew. He wants to do it right now!" He laid one hand on Matthew's knee and the other on his hand. He closed his eyes and his lips moved soundlessly.

God? Matthew thought. *Is that You? Right here, right now, like Miles says?* He waited for a voice or a vision, but none came. Still, something was happening. His knee was hot.

Matthew remembered his life in Baltimore, his life in Kentucky, his terrible, lonely year on the road, his rescue and adoption into the Abbott family. He remembered the endless harvest and his efforts to escape, the love which had brought him back and the love which had brought him to his knees. He felt some part of himself lift and yearn toward that love –

And then he remembered again his father's fists, his mother's weeping, the snap! In his knee. He remembered David's death and the two little graves, Will's story and the boy dead in the accident. He remembered the rage with which he had grabbed Will and the terror in the boy's battered face.

"Take your God and get out of here," Matthew snarled. "Take Him back to church where He belongs and tell Him to leave me alone. He had his chance."

Miles slowly opened his eyes and looked not at Matthew but at the palms of his hands. "How's your knee?" he asked.

Matthew considered. The pain seemed to be gone. He moved a little, experimentally, and it didn't hurt. "The aspirin must have kicked in," he said. "It's fine. You can go now." He closed his eyes in dismissal and was asleep before he could hear the pastor's shoes on the stairs.

Fifty-Three

In the fields, the corn finally began to dry. Ed remarked it gratefully at the end of a long day. "Guess we're gonna have us a crop after all. Feared the durn' stuff was going to rot if it didn't stop raining."

Matthew nodded.

"Boss says you're gonna drive the sheller, huh?"

"Sure." Matthew nodded and walked away. He was getting good at that.

Early in the evening, he fell into a troubled sleep, haunted by dream voices, only to wake with one violent start at two o'clock in the morning. He turned on the light and waited until the panic subsided, turned off the light and waited in the dark to go back to sleep.

Waiting turned into impatient tossing as his wind-up alarm clock ticked loudly toward three. Finally he got up, pulled on jeans and a tee-shirt, and padded barefoot down the stairs. He went into the living room to sit in John's chair – only to find John sitting in it there in the dark.

Matthew gasped softly, startled. "Sorry. I didn't know you were there." He turned to leave.

"Don't go," came John's voice through the darkness. "I woke up a couple of hours ago and couldn't go back to sleep. I've been sitting here thinking and praying for you."

"For me?"

"Yes. The Lord really impressed you on my mind tonight. What brings you downstairs?"

Matthew hesitated, lurking in the shadows by the door where

John couldn't see his face. "I woke up – couldn't go back to sleep."

"I guess it's going around," John laughed quietly. "Come on in and join me."

Trapped, Matthew padded over to sit in Carolyn's chair. They gazed at each other by faint starlight as the silence between them lengthened uncomfortably. Suddenly John stood up and walked over to the bookshelves. He turned back to his chair with a dark object in his hands and sat holding it before him. Even in the near-dark, Matthew knew what it was.

"Matthew, God's love never changes." John's long, hard fingers caressed the wood. "'His love endures forever.' That's Psalm 136. And 'this is how we know what love is: that Jesus Christ laid down his life for us.' That's from First John, Chapter 3.

"I remember when you made this," John continued, his fingertips exploring the wood. "Nearly every day, some time during the day, I sit in this chair and see Christ's love carved by your hand. I believe He showed you His face like this so you could see how much He loves you. And nothing you do or have done can change Him."

"Some love," Matthew muttered.

John sighed, bent his head over the figure in his hands. "Dear Father, You are so good to us, so kind, so patient with us as we struggle to understand You and to do Your will. Even when we sin against You, even when we're angry with You, You keep on loving us and calling us to come back to You. Father, here is Matthew, so hurt and so angry, and I don't know how to help him. I know You miss him, I know You grieve for him. So I'm begging You to bring him back to You soon. Please show me how to pray for him, what to say and do to show him Your love – and mine. I thank You for hearing as I ask these things in Jesus' name. Amen."

The silence returned and thickened around them. Matthew leaned across the space between the two chairs and took the carved figure from John's hands. In the dim starlight, he couldn't make out the features; but his fingers, like John's, traced over the planes and angles he knew by heart. The satiny grain of the wood was warm to the touch, as real to him as his own skin.

"I remember. I remember thinking I'd never hurt God or anyone else ever again. That's a laugh. Maybe it's all a laugh."

"I remember hearing you pray that prayer and knowing it

was doomed to disappointment. Nobody can do that, Matthew. Nobody."

"Then what's the point? It's a set-up."

"The point's in the trying – and in trying again. We make progress toward becoming godly, even though we'll never get there in this life. God forgives us our mistakes and shows us how to do better. He practically begs us to try again."

"Yeah."

They subsided again into silence. Matthew's sullen pain and anger throbbed against John's temples and weighted his chest as he said, "I don't mean to beat you up with my point of view. Just know we love you no matter what." He sighed and rose. "I guess I may as well go ahead and shower and get an early start."

Matthew vaguely listened to John's receding footsteps, the muffled sound of running water a few minutes later. After a while he saw the lights come on in the little house across the road. The light in the sky had shifted from starlight to black and now gave over to a slow, pearly dawn. He saw Ed's lanky frame ambling across the road, heard the patter of Carolyn's slippers as she came downstairs to make coffee. His eyes were gritty, his mind stupid from lack of sleep, as he dragged himself upstairs to find his work shoes, leaving the woodcarving carelessly tossed onto the floor beside Carolyn's chair.

§ § §

Around eleven, when Ed dragged him back to the house for a long overdue coffee-break, Matthew was unpleasantly surprised to find Nate Hanna comfortably ensconced at the kitchen table watching Carolyn prepare a stew.

"What are you doing here?"

"Matthew!" Carolyn exclaimed.

Dr. Hanna returned his glare. "Among some other things that are none of your business, I came to see if you've kept your word to get some counseling."

"I'm not dead yet," Matthew snarled, "so I must be fine. It's none of *your* business."

"Get your coffee, friend," Ed intervened. "We got no call to be rude to company."

Matthew snagged a goose mug from the cupboard and filled it.

Fragrant steam rose to his nostrils and the warmth of the mug felt pleasant near his hands.

"You didn't give me a straight answer, young Matthew," Nate persisted.

"That should tell you something, Doc."

"Tells me you're still hurting, still angry, and still too scared to do anything about it."

"Scared doesn't have anything to do with it!"

"No? Then why not talk to somebody about it and get your life back on track?"

Matthew buried his face in the mug and drank deeply. The coffee rose back up his throat immediately, and he swallowed hard. Ed eyeballed him knowingly.

Nate's bushy eyebrows drew together in a deep frown. He glared at Matthew and jerked his head toward the living room. The two men rose and left the kitchen together.

"Now, Matthew, what about your problem?"

"I talked with Pastor Corrigan. I talked with John. I'm fine." His voice had gone flat, a tone not lost on Nate.

"Wish I could buy that, but I can't. I take it real personal when I lose a patient, Matthew. And I get real upset when anything bothers Caro."

"She say something to you?"

"Not recently. But she will pretty soon. You're all bones again from not eating, and you have huge purple circles under your eyes from not sleeping. I heard tell you tried to scuttle that boat you made for David, and that you're on the prayer chain."

"Hananiah, Zebediah, Obadiah," Matthew muttered. "I'm gonna move to New York, where there's so many people nobody knows anybody else's business!" He slouched lower in the chair, frowning at the floor.

"What is it?" Nate's voice was intense as he leaned toward Matthew. "What's bothering you this bad?"

"I have to get back to work now. Don't worry - I'm fine." Matthew talked his way from the chair to the front door and made his escape, leaving the doctor to punch the couch cushions in frustration.

Fifty-Four

Another Sunday came, and Matthew stayed in bed. He heard the car and the El Camino leave and burrowed back into his pillow for two or three more hours of solitude, if not of sleep. The fatigue which never left him lay like pennies on his eyelids.

But there came a tentative knock on his door.

"What?" he grumbled. Who was left to disturb him?

"It's me - Will. Can I come in?"

Matthew's heart thudded wildly as he pushed himself upright in the bed. He hadn't seen Will for two weeks, since the night at the hospital, knew the youth had been avoiding him by taking his meals at Ed's house and making up reasons to skip sharing the chores.

"Matt? Can I come in?"

Oh, Lord, please, please don't let me hurt him!

"Matt!" Will's voice took on an urgent tone.

"Come in," he called, clearing the sleep from his throat.

Will burst through the doorway, fear in his face. "Are you okay? When you didn't answer me, I thought maybe you - "

In the shaded, early morning light, Matthew could see the bright pink scar bisecting Will's right eyebrow, the faint greenish-yellow of fading bruises, the tiniest tremor of his lower lip. Pain sliced through Matthew's belly. "It's okay, Will. I promise I won't hurt you. You don't have to be scared, I promise."

Will frowned for a moment, then shook his head. "No. I'm not scared of you. I was scared you had - you know - " He stopped, flustered, and looked at his feet, the bookshelf, anywhere but Matthew.

"I had - what?"

"You know. Like - done something to yourself!" Will was quivering all over now.

"Oh. No... I guess I was asleep."

Unbidden, Will came in and sat on the chair facing Matthew. He fidgeted for a moment, then blurted out, "I'm sorry I didn't listen to you about doing stupid things! I was p- mad at you about those dumb shoes, and I thought I'd show you you're not my boss by getting high with those guys - But, honest, Matt, when we got the stuff and the other guys started using - I couldn't do it. Honest!"

Matthew stared at him dumbly and Will bumbled on, "I know it was even dumber to ride around with 'em like that - I mean, I knew Gary was drinking - heck, they all were - I thought it'd be okay if I just drank some beers, not the whiskey. Only then I thought about my mom and your dad - and about how you and Ed don't drink - so I didn't. I see why you're mad - "

The pain took Matthew's breath away and nearly doubled him over. He breathed deeply to regain control of himself. "You've been thinking for two weeks that I'm still mad at you?"

"Well - yeah. You sure were mad at the hospital. And then I said - I said some pretty awful stuff to you. I knew it'd hurt you, so I just - "

"All this time, you thought everything was your fault."

"Well, it was. 'Course, it usually is." Will stared forlornly at his feet.

"I thought you were staying away because you were afraid of me, or mad at me."

Will's head came up fast and his slatey eyes met Matthew's flat gaze sharply. "No. I figured you were so ticked you'd never want to see me again. Then Ed said you were sick, but I saw you out by the barn - and in the field - so that didn't make sense. Yesterday I asked Carolyn, and she said you might kill yourself."

Matthew took in the scene, Will planted in the chair on the far side of the room while he sat there in bed in his pajamas.

"I forgave you two weeks ago, Will. I forgave you for some poor judgment - because that's what it was to ride with a drunk driver - and I forgave you for scaring me half to death - and I forgave what you said about my dad, because you were right." Matthew sighed. "I hope someday you can forgive me for acting like him. And I hope God can. I don't think I'm ever going to forgive myself." He drew up his knees and laid his head on them, eyes closed, shutting out the sight of Will's face.

"Matt?"

He shook his head a little, too sad, too tired, to answer. The room was quiet for a moment. Then he heard Will get up, take a step, two –

"Matt, this is crazy! Come on, man, talk to me!" Will demanded, shaking Matthew's arm.

Matthew raised his head and looked at Will's hand on his arm. "You're touching me."

Will startled slightly and looked at his hand. "Yeah – so?" He removed his hand and began to edge away.

"Wait - please, Will. Just think a minute!"

"What!" An edge of panic entered Will's voice, but he stopped.

"You trusted me, Will. You came all the way into my room, you sat in the chair, away from the door, you touched me - you never gave it a thought."

"Did I make a mistake?" Will whispered, beginning to shake.

"No! You didn't make a mistake! You gave me a gift. After the way I treated you, nobody in the world deserves your trust less than I do. But you trusted me anyway." Matthew's voice was husky, his throat tight. "Thank you."

"Yeah, well..." He scuttled to the door but turned back. "Hey, Matt?"

"Yeah?"

"If I forgive you for grabbing me, and if God does, how come that isn't enough?"

"What do you mean?"

"Don't you Christian guys believe God's like the ultimate Supreme Court Justice or something?"

"I suppose we do, sort of."

"Well, then, if He forgives you for something, isn't that the end of it?"

Matthew leaned back against his pillow and began to laugh, a laugh somewhat rusty and strained from disuse, but a laugh nonetheless. Will licked his index finger and drew an imaginary point in the air, then another beside it.

"I'll give you one," Matthew said, still laughing, "but what's the other one for?"

"Made ya laugh."

With that, Will made a speedy exit and Matthew drifted back to sleep.

He was wakened from dreamlessness by a soft voice at his door announcing, "Dinner in twenty minutes! Matthew?"

"I'm up," he croaked, trying to surface completely. Showering and dressing quickly, he ran downstairs. Everyone, including Will, was seated at the dining room table.

"Hurry up," Ed grumbled. "I'm starving."

"Sorry." He slid into his place next to Pearl.

As John asked the blessing over the meal, Matthew peeked at Will. The youth had steadfastly refused to pray but had learned to maintain a respectful silence while others prayed. Matthew was surprised to see Will's eyes closed and his head half-bowed. They made quick work of Pearl's chicken and rice casserole and Carolyn's home-frozen peas. Will refused the latter with several disparaging remarks which brought a rebuke from Ed.

"Sorry," Will mumbled to the table at large. "But they really are gross!" he insisted under his breath.

John said, "I remember going through about a ten-year phase where I thought the only good thing that was green was money."

Will laughed, nodding. "So what's for dessert?"

"Gingerbread with whipped cream," Pearl responded.

"Cool!"

"Then I'm sure you'll be glad to clear the table," the old woman said.

"Yes, ma'am." Not even Will would try her.

Matthew let the easy conversation flow over him like a warm southerly breeze. He ate a couple of peas for virtue's sake and hid the rest of them under his uneaten rice. He drank the milk Pearl had set in front of him.

"I saw that," Pearl said, "and you will eat the gingerbread." She traded his dinner plate for a small bowl.

"Yes, ma'am." He observed she had poured milk instead of whipped cream over his small serving of gingerbread. He began to break up the gingerbread into small pieces which quickly turned to mush. He stirred it idly.

"Eat it," Pearl said firmly. "I remembered you like to mush up your cookies that way. Now get that mess inside you where it will do some good."

When they had finished, Pearl instructed, "Now go sit in the other room for a while and digest. We women will do the dishes."

Ed guffawed and made a snide remark about "women's work" which earned him a stint with a dishtowel. "Ain't you guys gonna rescue me?" he begged.

"Not a chance!" John laughed. "It's frontier justice, Ed, and Pearl's a hanging judge."

The three remaining men headed into the living room without a backward glance. John sank down into his chair and picked up the Sunday paper. He handed Will the comics and Will dropped into Carolyn's chair.

"Want part of this, Matthew?"

Matthew sat down on the couch and thought about it for a minute. "No, thanks."

The room was quiet except for the occasional sound of pages turning. Will traded the comics for the arts and entertainment section; John studied the editorial page. Matthew practiced indifference. He heard arrhythmic scratches as John began the crossword puzzle.

"I need a six-letter word for 'a tropical American rodent' - begins with 'a,'" John said, looking at Matthew.

"Agouti," Will replied without looking up from his paper. "A -g-o-u-t-i."

"Yep, it fits. Thanks! How did you know?"

Will looked up then. "I dunno. Musta studied it for a spelling test or something."

"Well," John yawned, "so much for the puzzle, and so much for me. I'm going upstairs and take a nap."

"See ya," Will said. Matthew nodded absently.

Will became antsy from sitting still and quiet. He twisted in the chair to hang his legs over the arm, then sat up straight, then sprawled. At last he sat up half-way and tossed the paper carelessly over the side of the chair. The pages came apart in an untidy heap.

"Shoot!" Will reached over to straighten the paper. As he fished some pages out from under the chair, his hand encountered something. "Hey! What - ?" Will drew his hand out holding an object Matthew recognized. He recalled tossing it down; it must have rolled under the chair.

"It's that head from the bookshelf," Will exclaimed. "How'd it get under the chair?"

Although he knew, Matthew didn't answer. Will held the figure in one hand and declaimed in a phony British accent: "'Alas, poor Yorick! I knew him, Horatio!'" He grinned at Matthew. "Think I've got a future playing Hamlet?"

Matthew shook his head slowly. Seeing Will clowning with his carving made him vaguely uneasy. "Put it back, okay?"

"Yeah, in a minute. I never looked at it close before. Man, this thing is ugly!" He examined the face from several angles and suddenly stared at Matthew.

"What?" asked Matthew nervously.

"This dude looks like you!"

Matthew's entire body prickled with fire and ice. "No! Not me!"

"Yeah, he does. Older, a little, and - I dunno - sick? sad? - but a lot like you." Will continued to examine the carving closely. "I bet some guy made a lotta money on this. But, man, it's so ugly! It's depressing. Why would Carolyn want something like this? It's not her style at all."

"It's not Carolyn's. It's John's. He - he got it for Christmas a couple of years ago. You know who it is?"

"Not a clue, if it's not you."

"It's Jesus."

Will stared at the carving, then at Matthew. "Wow. You look like Jesus, Matt. Cool. I guess he was bummed, too, huh?" He tossed the figure up and caught it a couple of times before replacing it on the bookshelf. He sauntered out, repeating, "Cool!"

Fifty-Five

Although looking at the golden corn kernels piled high above the edges like pirates' treasure gave him nearly a miser's satisfaction, Matthew didn't like hauling the wobbly red grain wagons. He didn't like the grain elevator. He didn't like the pudgy man in bib overalls who ran the grain elevator. He didn't like the greasy sweat which kept beading on his upper lip and trickling at the small of his back.

Home at last, he stood in the yard coughing, stamping, brushing the golden haze of grain-dust from his hair and clothes. The dusty-sweet smell hung in his nostrils, making him sneeze.

Seeing him from the barn, Ed ambled over. "You having some kind of fit?"

"Dust," Matthew said, sneezing again. "I hate that place!" He wiped his nose on the back of his hand.

"Here!" Ed shoved a blue bandana into Matthew's hand. "I swear you're worse than a kid for never having a handkerchief."

Matthew blew his nose and stuffed the bandana into his back pocket. "Thanks. Listen, I really mean it, I hate that place. Can we swap something and you haul the rest?"

"Reckon so, if the boss don't care." They began to walk together toward the barn. Ed asked, "What's it about the elevator?"

"I don't know. I don't remember feeling this way last year, or the year before... I've never liked hauling the wagons, though. Too easy to lose your load."

"Did you, ever?"

"No..."

"Y'know, Matthew, you're a great one for borrowing trouble." Ed went over to the milking machines, where he had been tinkering with something. Turning away from Matthew to resume his task, he commented casually, "Maybe you ought to quit trying so hard to analyze everything and just let God be God for a while." He began to whistle softly between his teeth.

As Matthew headed toward the house, the school bus stopped at the end of the driveway, belching out Will and a cloud of exhaust at the same time. The youth loped up the drive, a stack of books under his arm. Matthew waited for Will to catch up and followed him into the kitchen. Carolyn stood by the table pouring a large glass of milk. Seeing Matthew, she took another glass from the cupboard.

"No, thanks," Matthew said.

"I'll eat his," Will offered. "Only a fool would pass up milk and the world's best oatmeal-raisin-chocolate chip cookies!" Will flashed a cocky grin at Carolyn and stuffed most of one cookie into his mouth before he even sat down.

Carolyn's warm smile played over both of them. She put the second, smaller glass of milk at Matthew's place and jerked her head toward it. "You can't possibly insult me by refusing now, can you?"

"Guess not." He sat and sipped the milk. Will pushed the plate of cookies to the middle of the table and Matthew took the smallest one.

Carolyn sat next to Will. "You're certainly in a good mood today! No homework?"

"Math," Will mumbled around his third cookie. He swallowed. "History test." He grinned again.

Matthew picked a chocolate chip out of his cookie and let it melt over his tongue. He sipped the milk again and wished they had a dog to dispose of the cookie while Carolyn was distracted.

" - name's Tracy," Will was saying. "Blond, with these pale green eyes - kinda reminds me of Celeste."

Matthew burst into a laugh which sputtered his milk all over the table. Wiping his face and the table with a paper napkin, he chuckled, "You sure won't win any points if she knows you're comparing her to an old barn-cat!"

"Yeah, well, maybe not. But I just meant she's little and graceful and her face - her eyes - like Catwoman, you know? Besides, she says

I'm cool." Embarrassed, Will fell silent and demolished the rest of the cookies.

Carolyn looked at Matthew and sighed. "Can't even tempt your appetite with the best cookies in the whole world, huh?"

"If I felt like eating anything," he said regretfully, "this would be it. I guess I had too much dinner."

"You had an apple and half a grilled cheese sandwich." Her voice was accusing. "You can't go on like this! You'll get sick."

"Matt?" Will said suddenly.

"Yeah?"

"Did you know I tried to kill myself when I was in jail?"

Carolyn gasped. Matthew looked at Will. "Yeah. The p.o. told us."

"I tried three times. It seemed like things were so bad - like they might get worse, but they'd never get better - I was real serious that last time. I was real mad when they stopped me, and I swore when I got out I'd do it."

Matthew nodded, understanding better than he had before.

"Only, when I got out... I dunno... I came here, and things - well, they keep getting better. If I'd killed myself then, I'd have missed it." Apparently embarrassed by his sudden outburst of feelings, Will grabbed the last cookie and fled. Matthew gazed after him, too surprised to say anything.

"He really cares about you under all that snarling," Carolyn said behind him. "He's terrified you're going to die and leave him." Her voice fell almost to a whisper. "So am I."

Matthew turned to face her, noted tears in her eyes, deepening the blue, noted the way her small fingers twisted around each other. He tried to smile for her, just a little. "Y'know, Doc Hanna sort of threatened to do me harm if I made you cry, and he's a lot bigger and tougher than I am."

Carolyn sniffed and wiped her eyes with her wrist. "I've been so scared, Matthew. I don't understand what's going on with you - I don't know how to help - You're family now, really you are, and –" her lips trembled and her eyes filled again - "I just can't stand to lose any more of my family!" She turned away and sobbed into her hands.

Horrified, Matthew jumped up and put his arms around her. "Please don't!" he begged. "I'd *rather* have Doc Hanna beat me up than have you cry over me. Please!" He patted her awkwardly, but her sobs continued. Over Carolyn's shoulder, he saw John in the yard and pounded on the window.

John looked up to see Matthew beckoning frantically. He was across the yard, up the steps and through the door in seconds. "What? What's the matter?"

Matthew looked panicky. "She won't stop crying!"

John took his wife into his arms. "Honey? What's the matter? What happened?"

"Matthew - " she sobbed.

John turned a terrible glare on Matthew. "What did you do to her?"

"Nothing!"

The truth of his denial was plain on Matthew's face. John relaxed and tried again with his wife. She finally managed to choke out, "He won't p-promise me - "

"Won't promise you what, honey?"

"Not to k-k-kill himself!" she wailed.

"I didn't know that's what she wanted! Carolyn, it's okay. I promise!"

"Really?" she asked in a small, muffled voice, her face still buried in John's shirt front.

"Yes, really. I promise. Please don't cry."

Gradually her tears ceased and she mopped up her face with a handful of tissues. Matthew recapped for John the conversation with Will and what had followed. Carolyn nodded her agreement.

"I did think about it," Matthew said quietly. "At first, after I treated Will that way, it was almost all I could think about. Suicide just seemed like - like what you'd do to a big, mean dog if it attacked a kid. You know - put it down for the common good." Ashamed, guilty still, he looked at his feet. "I guess I'm a coward, though, as well as a bully, because I didn't do it. And now - well, like Will said, Carolyn, it's - it's getting better. I guess."

Carolyn came back to Matthew and hugged him, hard. "Thank you," she whispered. He patted her again and watched in bemusement as she began to prepare supper as if nothing had happened.

John smiled at Matthew behind Carolyn's back and asked her, "How'd I do?"

"Do what?"

"When you were crying."

"Oh!" She laughed gently. "Much better, dear. You didn't say 'Don't cry' even once."

PART FOUR

REDEMPTION

NOVEMBER, 1996 – MARCH, 1997

I have called you by name;

you are Mine.

Isaiah 43:1

Fifty-Six

The first Sunday in November did not dawn. The black sky under which they had trudged to the barn at four-thirty was scarcely lighter two hours later. A raw wind began to spill hard, small white flakes over the backs of their necks as they headed in to breakfast. By the time they left for church, the ground was white, the flakes larger and wetter. The snow came fast, cutting visibility and making the road slick. The car's heater didn't seem to reach the back seat, where Matthew huddled into his heavy coat. His knee twinged.

"I'll drop you two," John said as he eased into the church driveway. "Go on in and save me a seat."

Carolyn and Matthew stepped out onto the clear walk under the portico and gasped as the wind attacked. He took her arm just in case and hustled her into the building. Ed and Will caught up with them, soon followed by John.

Will looked remarkably out-of-place and uncomfortable in his jeans and black tee-shirt. His eyes darted furtively over everything and everyone; his hands fisted in his pockets. Matthew observed how close Will stood to Ed, almost touching. *He's really scared*, Matthew realized. *Wonder why he came?*

"Let's get seated," John said, leading his little group up to the smiling usher. They followed him like ducklings, Will sandwiched between Ed and Matthew, who brought up the rear. The usher greeted each of them with a handshake and a bulletin. Will ducked his head and mumbled something, taking the bulletin, avoiding the outstretched hand. They followed John up the center aisle until they were only a couple of pews from the front. Matthew could feel Will's panic building pew by pew.

"John," Matthew said urgently.

"Yes?"

"I'm not going to sit up here today. I need to sit in back."

"Come on, Matthew. We always sit up here."

"No, I can't. Maybe Will could sit with me, okay?"

Will turned quickly to follow Matthew. They hurried down the aisle all the way to the back wall, where a row of padded folding chairs waited for latecomers. "Here," Matthew said. "Backs to the wall, okay?"

"Yeah, sure," said Will with elaborate unconcern, "if it makes you feel better." He sank into the aisle seat and slouched into a nonchalant posture.

"What made you decide to come today?" Matthew asked. "You never have before."

"Nothing better to do." Will stretched casually and looked around the sanctuary.

"I remember the first few times I came here, I was scared. Too many strangers, didn't know how to behave, didn't know how weird 'those people' would get - "

"How weird do they get?"

"Not very. Nobody falls down in the aisles or anything. They sing a lot. Pastor Corrigan talks a lot."

"Oh, great," Will grumbled. His darting eyes continued to assess everything.

"He's a good guy," Matthew defended. "I didn't say he talks too much, just a lot. He's pretty good at helping to sort things out, too."

"Whatever." Will fidgeted. "When do they get this show on the road?"

"Just about now," Matthew replied as the choir entered and assembled on the platform. The thirty or so men and women wore natural linen robes with gold satin around the necks and down the fronts; they carried black music folders. Their director was a small, skinny woman who had to stand on a box to direct them.

Will began to laugh at the little woman waving her arms about like a grasshopper; but he fell abruptly silent as the piano crashed and the voices rose in loud, brilliant, soaring notes. The obscenity he whispered was nearly as reverent as an "amen."

On the way home, Carolyn asked, "Did Will feel better sitting in back?"

The heat of embarrassment tingled across Matthew's ears and cheekbones. "You knew?"

John laughed. "You fooled me this time, but you didn't fool her for a minute. So, what did he think?"

"Well... I know he liked the choir. He said the praise music was 'lame.' He looked around a lot during the prayers."

"He say anything about the sermon?" John asked.

"He was up and out of there as soon as it was over, even before Miles and Penny made it to the back door to shake hands with people. I did find out why he came, though."

"Tell!" Carolyn pressed.

Matthew laughed. "Tracy. The 'Catwoman' girl from school. He described her just right. And she does think he's cool. She cooed and giggled and batted her eyelashes at him - "

"Whatever works," John said. "Maybe she goes to youth group, too."

The car suddenly shimmied across a patch of ice hidden beneath drifting snow. The back windows were fogging. Carolyn prayed aloud, but Matthew closed his eyes and day-dreamed about summer in Kentucky, all hot, yellow sun and smells of tobacco, earth and flowers.

Nearly three inches of snow mounded on the truck and obscured the porch steps. Huge, wet flakes continued to drive down from the dark sky on a hard north wind.

"Stay in the car and let me clear a path," Matthew offered. "Carolyn's shoes'll be ruined." He slithered from the car to the porch and found the snow shovel. The snow was dense and heavy, reluctant to give up its claim, leaving behind a slick film. Matthew cleared the path and continued on toward the barn as John escorted his wife up the treacherous steps.

At the barn, Matthew cleared the doors and paused to wipe a light sweat from his face. His feet in their dress shoes were wet and numb, his knee twinged a little. He turned to look at his work and saw millions of snowflakes competing to fill in the path he had just opened. Leaning the shovel against the barn wall, Matthew entered the barn. Celeste lazed over but left quickly when she saw it was not yet milking time. Matthew made sure the patient Jerseys had fodder and water and could come in if they chose. He took feed to the ducks and chickens and made sure their water wasn't frozen. By the time he retrieved the shovel and slogged back to the house, the path was gone.

Carolyn met him on the enclosed porch with a towel. "You must be frozen! You're soaked! Whatever possessed you to stay out there in your good clothes?"

Kicking off his wet, snowy shoes, Matthew shrugged out of his coat and hung it on a hook to drip. "I don't know. Just seemed like a good idea to keep going. Then when I saw how fast the path was disappearing, I figured I'd check the stock before things got worse."

"Dinner's ready, but we'll wait while you change your clothes. You're soaked!"

"I believe you mentioned that already," he teased. Applying the towel vigorously to his hair, Matthew squished upstairs in his wet socks. His teeth began to chatter and he thought longingly of a hot shower, but he settled for a brisk rubdown with yet another towel. His feet, white and numb, turned bright red and burned enough to bring tears to his eyes as he rubbed circulation back into them. He added heavy socks and a sweater to his dry jeans and tee-shirt before hurrying downstairs to see what Carolyn had made for dinner.

"Hurry up, Matt!" Will insisted from his place at the table. "Just because you're never hungry doesn't mean the rest of us aren't."

"I'm sorry. You should have gone ahead." He slid into his chair. "Where's Pearl?"

"She decided to stay home because of the weather," Carolyn answered. "She doesn't like to drive much any more, even when it's clear."

As John asked the blessing, Matthew closed his eyes and felt peace flow into him. He opened them again, slowly, as John began to carve thick slices of ham. Matthew accepted half a slice of ham and surrounded it with dabs of whipped sweet potatoes, succotash, hot biscuits, carrot and celery sticks.

"Man, you'll never eat all that!" Will exclaimed.

"I got to see this!" Ed agreed.

"Want to bet?" He attacked his food with enthusiasm.

"You should shovel snow more often," Carolyn said. "No - don't pick the lima beans out of the succotash."

"Drat," he said mildly. "Please pass the applesauce."

"We need to talk about Pearl," John said. They all looked at him. "She's well over eighty now," he continued, "although she won't say exactly." They laughed. "I don't like thinking of her all alone in that apartment."

"You think we should bring her here," Carolyn said.

"I do."

"Where you gonna put her?" Will asked.

"Well – for now she could have David's room. I think she can still handle the stairs."

"David's room?" Carolyn whispered.

Matthew forced a bite of ham past the sudden lump in his throat.

"Let's start with whether we agree we'd like to bring her here."

"Suits me," Ed replied promptly.

"Sure," Matthew agreed.

Carolyn nodded.

"Will?"

The youth jerked around to look at John, blue eyes wide with surprise. "Me?"

"Everybody's vote counts," John said. "You're part of the family, too."

"No - kidding!" He quickly masked the look of delight. "Yeah, I think she oughta come. She's a good cook."

"I'm not?" Carolyn teased.

"No - I mean, sure you are! I just meant - like, there'd be two of you."

"I know," she replied gently.

"Maybe me and Will could double up and give her Will's room," Ed suggested.

Will paled and swallowed hard. "Sure. Then she wouldn't have to climb any stairs."

Carolyn took a deep breath. "Or Will could have David's room," she said. "Just until spring. Then, if she wants, we can add on over here."

Matthew watched the fragile moment balance like a soap bubble on a pin. Will was torn between leaving Ed and helping Pearl. Carolyn was poised at the next step away from her grief. The family was changing right in front of him. He closed his eyes.

"What if she doesn't want to come?" Will asked, popping the bubble.

"Then we'll just have to persuade her," John said decisively.

"Me and Will will talk, right, boy?" said Ed. "See how we want to do things."

"Right," Will agreed, giving his attention to separating lima beans from corn.

A few minutes later, Will and Matthew began to clear the table, encouraging Carolyn to take the rest of the meal off. The profusion of dishes required quite a few trips back and forth, especially after Carolyn made clear to Will that he could not develop a circus balancing act with her good china.

Matthew was placing a piece of hot cherry pie topped with melting vanilla ice cream in front of Ed when John remarked, "How's your knee?"

"Huh?" Matthew frowned, puzzled. "It's fine. Why?"

"You don't seem to be limping. It's raw, snowy weather and you shoveled a lot of snow. I thought you'd be hurting pretty bad."

Matthew considered. "Nope. I felt a twinge or two earlier, that's all."

John persisted. "Doesn't it usually hurt a lot in cold weather?"

"Yeah, it always has." Matthew sat down with his own pie and ever so slowly sank his fork into it. The glazed lattice of the top crust broke away translucent layer by layer and a thin, creamy trickle of melted ice cream ran across the rosy filling. He conveyed the bite to his mouth and chewed slowly, savoring hot and cold, tart and sweet, all on his tongue at once.

"Does it seem odd to you that your knee doesn't hurt today?" John asked, ignoring his own pie.

Matthew noticed he had closed his eyes to appreciate the pie and opened them to look at John. "I hadn't thought about it. Why the big interest in my knee?"

Frozen in fascination, Ed and Carolyn watched the two men. Only Will seemed oblivious, steadily forking pie and ice cream into his mouth. Matthew himself was fascinated, waiting for John's answer.

"Remember the day Miles came over here and prayed for you? You'd been sitting by the pond in the cold for a long time, and your knee was so painful you had to put ice on it."

"Yeah. I was reading in bed with an ice-bag on my knee and he came up to my room."

"And after he prayed?"

"He left."

"No, your knee."

"Oh. I don't know. The aspirin kicked in by then, I guess. It was okay. Why?"

"Has it bothered you since then?"

Matthew considered. "No. Just a twinge here and there, like today. I've been lucky. What *is* this, for Pete's sake?"

"When Miles came downstairs, he kept looking at his hands. I asked him what was the matter, and he showed them to me. One palm was a lot redder and hotter than the other one, like he'd laid it on a hot stove. He said, 'I had my hand on Matthew's knee while I was praying for him.' Do you remember?"

"Yeah. He put his hand under the ice-bag, on top of my jeans. And I remember my knee got hot. I figured it was the contrast between the ice and body warmth."

"Praise the Lord!" Ed burst out, a wide grin taking over his face. "You been healed, boy!"

Will's fork clattered onto his plate and his head snapped up. Matthew blinked like a swimmer trying to clear the chlorine from his eyes. "Why?" he asked.

"What?" Ed spluttered. "Why? How about 'thank you, Lord!'?"

"I didn't ask for any favors. Please may I be excused?" Matthew stalked away from the table, his knee working perfectly, leaving the others in stunned silence behind him.

Will pushed his unfinished dessert away and rose clumsily. "This is too weird!" he said loudly and bolted from the room.

"Habakkuk and Haggai!" Ed blurted. "You'd think folks would be grateful for a miracle!"

Fifty-Seven

Will tracked Matthew to ground in his room, where he stood in the near-dark gazing out into the snow.

"Can I come in?"

Matthew turned from the window. "If you mean are you able, yes, you are. If you mean may you, as in have permission, no, you may not." He turned back to the window.

"Who elected you the grammar police?" Will snapped. "Come on, Matt, let me come in. I gotta talk to you."

Matthew slumped and beckoned Will without turning from his post. Will joined him and tried to see through the whirling snow.

"Is this a blizzard?" Will asked.

"I don't know. It's a lot of snow, a lot of wind. Could take out the electricity."

"What then?"

"Then we're in trouble. No water, no heat, no refrigeration, no milking machines. I really don't want to milk all those cows by hand or fill buckets from the pond to flush the toilets."

"Yuck! We'd go to a motel, right?"

Matthew laughed. "Farm families can't do that, Will, 'cause we can't leave the animals. Cows have to be milked twice a day, no matter what."

Will began to pace back and forth. "Maybe you'd better pray or something, huh?"

Matthew turned to observe Will closely; the look he received in return was totally sincere. "Hey, Will, I'm holding out on you. John has a huge gasoline generator and Ed lives to keep the thing in perfect running order. We have fuel tanks, so we could go a long time on backup power."

Will eased appreciably at this information. "So a real bad storm is, like, no big deal, right? Except I'd get outa going to school for a few days."

"I guess that's about the size of it."

"Cool! So you don't hafta pray about it."

"I wasn't going to." Matthew renewed his inspection of the weather, rocking back and forth on his heels, sighing heavily.

"Can I sit down?" Will asked uncertainly.

Matthew sighed again. "It's 'may I?'"

"May I sit down?"

"Yes, all right! Sit! Lie down! Do whatever you want."

"Skip it." Will edged toward the door. "I'll get outa your hair. I just needed somebody to talk to."

"No, wait a minute!" Matthew quickly drew the shade and walked over to the table to switch on the lamp. Mellow light filled the room, making it seem warmer. Will hovered in the doorway, trying to gauge Matthew's temper.

"You've got nothing to be sorry for, Will; it's my fault again. I didn't mean to be rude or to scare you." Matthew plopped onto the foot of the bed. "When you came up, I was looking at the snow and feeling - trapped. If the truck were mine, I'd take it and go someplace - anyplace away from here - for a while. But I can't take a chance with John's truck, so I'm stuck. And I don't like it."

"Why do you want to get away so bad?"

"Shoot, I don't know! I was alone a long time. I guess sometimes I just don't like having to answer to other people." Matthew grinned up at Will ruefully. "Sound familiar?"

Will eased over to the chair and perched on the edge. "Yeah, no kidding! But you're supposed to be too old for adolescent rebellion."

"Guess I'm not, though." Matthew stretched out on the bed. "What did you want to talk about?"

"Well – um - " Will suddenly became very busy with a ragged cuticle. "This church thing - this pastor guy - "

Matthew waited, his best pastor imitation.

"So what did he do to your knee? What did Ed mean, and why

did it make you mad?"

"The Bible has lots of stories about people being healed. Jesus healed blind men, lepers, cripples. He gave his followers the power to do it, too. Some people think God still heals through certain people, even today."

"You believe that?"

"Yeah... In theory."

"So, your knee. Did that pastor guy do some kinda hocus-pocus about hot hands and praying over you?"

Matthew stood and stretched, flexing his knee. "He was praying for me, right here by the bed. He did put his hand on my knee, and it did get hot."

"And did he, like, shout 'devil spirits come out!' like on TV?"

"No!" Matthew sat on the edge of the bed, grinning at Will. "Not even close! Honestly, I don't even remember him saying anything about my knee."

"So was it a miracle?"

"I don't know. The Bible says there used to be miracles..."

"Yeah, the Bible. Tracy said she can't go out with me because the Bible says I'm going to hell if I don't 'get saved,' whatever *that* is. So I figured, okay, I can go to church like you do, do whatever I have to do - but that guy talked about some weird stuff, man!"

"Why don't you ask Ed this stuff? Or John?"

"Aw, come on, Matt! John's Mr. Religion, and Ed's almost as bad."

"I got the impression you like Ed."

Will bit at his cuticle. "I do. He'd have made a cool dad. He's real patient and he teaches me stuff and he doesn't make a rule for everything - but I hear him, every night. He prays about you. And he - he prays about me."

"On his knees, too," Matthew teased. "And naked, in the shower."

"No way!"

"Oh, yeah. He told me so himself. So what, though? You know we're all 'those people.'"

"I don't want to hurt Ed's feelings by telling him he's full of it."

"But you don't care if you hurt mine?"

"It's not the same. You're not really coming from the same place they do."

Ouch! Matthew thought. *So much for being a good example.* He sat up and reached for his Bible. "You sure you want to go into this? Find out what I believe?"

"Yeah..." Will squirmed on the chair.

"I gotta start with a confession," Matthew said nervously. "I've never done this before, and I'll probably screw it up."

"Like I'll know the difference," Will joked.

"Okay." Matthew took a deep breath. *Lord, help me! Not because I deserve it, but because Will does.* "Here goes." He held up the Bible. "I believe what it says in this Book. And it says there is a God, Who made everything and controls everything. And He made us. And when we screwed up, He made a plan to bring us back to Himself. He made His son Jesus into a human being, to live like us, to feel everything we feel, only never to give in to temptation because He's God, too..."

"What's your point?"

"Well - uh - Jesus had to really understand how bad we can get, so He'd really understand what He was dying for. Because He, uh, He volunteered - this is hard - "

"He volunteered to what?"

"To be tortured to death for us. To hang on the cross in agony, feeling every sin every person in the world had ever done or would ever do, all at the same time. To feel completely separated from God, His Father, because that sin was all over Him like slime. And to feel all that and finally die and even go into hell so that when He rose again God could accept His own Son's blood as payment for our sins. So God could forgive us and take us to be with Him instead of sending us to hell when we die."

"You believe that."

"I do. It's in here - " he gestured again with the Bible - "in John 3:16: 'For God so loved the world that He gave His one and only Son, that whoever believes in Him shall not perish but have eternal life.'"

"So why didn't God figure out some other way, if He loved His Son so much?"

"I don't know."

Will warmed to his argument. "If God is so all-powerful, how come He doesn't just make everybody be good and believe in Him and be happy and live forever?"

Matthew felt sweat breaking out all over him. "I don't know. It says somewhere in here that His ways are not our ways and His thoughts are above our thoughts."

"Well, that's pretty convenient!" Will's mouth twisted in disgust. "How can you believe that crap?"

Wiping a damp hand on his jeans, then over his face, Matthew looked helplessly at the angry teenager. "I told you I wouldn't be good at this."

"Yeah, well, you were right. You're as weird as the rest of them."

"Probably." Matthew felt cold and tired. What was the use?

"So why were you mad at Ed?"

"I wasn't mad at Ed. I guess I'm mad at God."

"What for?"

"I don't know," Matthew whispered, feeling tears pressing against his eyelids.

"Are you gonna get all depressed again?" Will asked anxiously, alarm and embarrassment shading his voice and furrowing his brow.

"No. I just - don't know. I don't know how to answer your questions, I don't know how to explain salvation, I don't know what God's doing to me - "

"Wow!" Will said softly. "All circuits totally blown!" He stood, stepped to the door, turned back. "Thanks for trying, anyway. Even if it is all crap."

"You're welcome." Matthew kept his eyes on his hands, clenched around the Bible.

"Hey, Matt?"

"Hmm?"

"Could I maybe borrow that book for a couple of days?"

Matthew looked up into the guileless face, the bottomless eyes so like his own. "Borrow my Bible?"

"Yeah. I mean, since Tracy thinks it's such a big deal, maybe I can impress her."

"Sure, why not? It's a great read, even if you don't believe it." Matthew extended the Book and gave it into Will's hand. "Enjoy!"

"I'll take good care of it."

"I know you will."

"Uh - any ideas about where I should start?"

"Well, in the Old Testament, the first half of the Book, the Psalms are poetry. You'd like them. And John started me in the book of John in the New Testament. There's an index in front."

"You quoted from John a while ago, right?"

"Yeah. Third chapter, sixteenth verse."

"So maybe I'll start there." Will clattered away down the stairs, whistling between his teeth.

Matthew stretched out on the bed again and stared at a long crack in the ceiling. *Well, I'm sure not Philip the Evangelist. Will doesn't even think I'm a real Christian. Maybe because I haven't been acting like one. You gonna 'zap' me? Are You even listening? Do You even care?*

"Yeah, that's what I thought," he said bitterly into the silence.

Fifty-Eight

By late afternoon the snow was over a foot deep and still falling. Matthew heard from his room the rumble and scrape which told him Ed was plowing. As he lay there listening, Carolyn came to the door carrying an oil lamp and a small box of matches.

"I've brought these just in case," she said, placing them on the table. "John thinks the power will go before morning."

"Thanks. I think he's right." Matthew sat up. "I guess I'll go do the milking before that happens."

"John will help you. Ed's beginning his annual love/hate relationship with the snow-blade."

They went downstairs together and were joined in the utility room by John, who climbed into his warm, brown coverall and began to pull on heavy, insulated boots.

"You look like twins, all bundled up," Carolyn teased. "Do you have your sleds and mittens?"

"Women never take these guy things seriously," John said to Matthew

Carolyn responded with a brief kiss for her husband and a quick pat on Matthew's heavily covered shoulder. "Be careful, guys, and look out for Ed."

The snow on the way to the barn drifted over the tops of their boots and blew down their necks. By the time they were safely inside, their faces were red and their noses running. The gentle little Jerseys were quite willing to enter their stanchions, safe inside from the biting wind.

"You had a long talk with Will," John began almost at once. "Must have gone pretty well, because he left whistling. Was that your Bible he was carrying?"

"Yeah, he asked to borrow it to impress Tracy. He did ask where to start, though."

"Like I said before," laughed John, "whatever works. You didn't read it as God's word at first, either."

"No, I didn't."

"While he's got yours, though," John continued, "you'll need another one. We have a couple more on the bookshelf."

"Yeah, thanks." Matthew studied the machinery to avoid eye-contact, and John studied Matthew.

"Then, again, maybe you won't miss it, since you haven't been reading it much."

"How'd you know that?" Matthew asked sharply.

"Dust. Also, you haven't asked any questions in a long time. I didn't figure you know it all quite yet. And you've been miserable. Other than that, I have no idea."

Matthew took off his coat and hung it on a nail. "Can we talk?"

"Sure. Let's sit." John hung his coat over Matthew's and unzipped the neck of his coverall. He plopped down on the straw bales.

Matthew began to pace back and forth in front of John. "Will wanted to know about the 'church stuff' and about what I believe."

"That's great!"

"Not really. I did a lousy job trying to explain. I couldn't answer his questions and he said he asked me instead of you or Ed because I'm not - not really into it the way you are, so he wouldn't hurt my feelings."

"Oh."

"That's it? 'Oh' ?"

"What did you want me to say?"

"I don't know. How about, 'Matthew, you're such a loser. You never do anything right and you never will!'" Matthew turned abruptly and felt a sharp twinge in his left knee. "How about, 'You screw up everything you try and you'll never amount to anything!'" He turned back and felt the pain again.

"Matthew - "

"Or how about, 'The whole world would be better off if you'd never been born!'"

John rose quickly and put his hands on Matthew's shoulders. "Stop! Stop it."

"Or - "

"No, Matthew! Stop it!" John's fingers bit into Matthew's shoulders even through the coverall. He shook Matthew gently. "Come on, sit down."

They sank onto the straw and Matthew began to rub his knee. Slowly his breathing returned to normal. Embarrassed, he hung his head. "I'm sorry. I don't know where all that came from."

"Don't you?"

"Yeah, I do," Matthew whispered. "That was my father's voice." He shuddered and rubbed harder at the ache in his knee.

"Whose voice do you suppose your dad heard when he said those things to you?"

"What?"

"Did you know your father's father, your other grandfather?"

"No. He died before I was born. He was in the army in World War II. Then he was a Baltimore cop, like my dad."

"Did your dad ever say what kind of a dad your grandfather was?"

Matthew looked at John oddly. "He used to say - when he'd hit me - that he'd make a man out of me the way his dad made a man out of him."

John put his hand on Matthew's knee. "It's never an excuse, but can you see why your father would think hitting was the right way?"

Matthew leaned back against the wall and closed his eyes. He felt a chill as John removed his hand, and the ache in his knee intensified. Behind his eyelids Matthew saw his father, beer bottle in one hand, belt in the other, towering over Matthew's own slight, cowering little self, ranting about making a man of him, cursing, swinging - and then he saw his little self turn into another little boy, darker, larger-boned, cowering before a man who looked like the old photo of Matthew's father's father, a little boy crying, "No, Daddy! Please don't hit me!"

"Oh, Daddy!" Matthew whispered. "Oh, poor Daddy!"

Fifty-Nine

Matthew raised brimming eyes to meet John's. "I saw him," he whispered, "my father. Little, like I was. Getting hit - being scared, like I was."

"I thought it might have been like that."

"He couldn't help it, could he? It probably went back in our family for generations."

"That seems to be the case in a lot of families," John agreed.

Matthew dropped his gaze to his hands again. "I guess it's a real good thing I won't have any more kids. As long as I never do, if Will stays away from me, it stops here."

"No. Whether you have children or not, it stops here. Because you've changed, you're a new creation in Christ, like Paul says. You've been shaped by your past, Matthew, but you're not bound by it."

"But - "

"No buts. If God can save your soul and heal your knee, don't you think He can change your behavior? He says He makes all things new."

Deep inside him, where the permafrost never melted, Matthew felt something green stretch and push a little under the surface.

As they finished milking and wallowed back to the house through knee-high drifts, Matthew waited for his knee to hurt. Climbing the stairs to bed, he waited for it. Waking cold at two a.m., he waited. The pain never came.

Wrapping himself in the puffy white comforter, Matthew walked to the window across floorboards so cold they burned hot against his bare feet. The yard-light feebly illuminated snow still falling, whipped by a heavy wind. The trees bent and groaned, the wires billowed and sagged like ship's rigging, until, as he watched, the lights went out and the roar of the furnace stopped abruptly.

In sudden black velvet darkness, Matthew's feet remembered their way back to the bed one shuffling step at a time. As he dropped the comforter, shivering, to fumble for the lamp and matches, he heard John's grumbles across the hall, a sudden yelp, a poorly stifled giggle. Striking a match, he removed the lamp chimney and raised the wick before the flame singed his fingers. On the second match he was able to light the lamp. As he lowered the flame and set the chimney, he heard a light knock at his door.

"Come in."

"Thought you might be awake," John said. "I'm headed for the generator - hoped you'd lend a hand."

"Sure. Just give me a minute to put on some clothes. Or maybe all the clothes I own; I'm freezing!" Matthew dragged on layers over his pajamas, continuing to shiver. "One of the best things about being married has to be sleeping warm in the winter."

John laughed. "Yeah, but it works the other way in summer. I tried to call Ed, but the phone's out. We've got ourselves a real blizzard."

Matthew pulled on a second pair of thick wool socks. "Will's gonna love it; no school." He stood. "Shall I bring the lamp?"

"No, thanks. I've got this - " John indicated a flashlight - "and we have lanterns in the utility room."

They made their way down the eerily dark stairway and through the dark, silent house. "Feels like we should whisper," Matthew whispered.

John laughed again, quietly. "I really like it like this," he said in a hushed voice, "with no sound but the wind. It must have been like this when my granddad lived here."

They pulled on coveralls, struggled to cram their heavily covered feet into insulated boots. John tightened the drawstring hood of his coat; Matthew pulled a red wool hat down over his ears and fitted the knit cuffs of his coat over the wrists of his gloves. "Snowsuits," he grinned.

"We're going to need them. I about wish I'd strung a rope from the house to the barn like my granddad used to do." John handed Matthew two battery-operated lanterns and a huge hand-flashlight.

"I'm going to leave a lantern in the window to light us back - I hope."

"You worried?" Matthew asked, surprised.

"No... just cautious. You know no farmer ever takes weather lightly, especially not something like this. Honestly, I'm just not as well-prepared for this one as I should be. But Ed is - the plow and the generator - so, let's go!"

The wind struck Matthew in the throat like a heavyweight's fist, taking his breath, forcing tears from his eyes. He clung to the lantern and tucked his chin, following close on John's heels. The heavy swirl of snowflakes in the feeble light, surrounded by shrieking wind, gave him vertigo, as if he were spinning down a steep, narrow tunnel. The journey to the barn seemed endless, timeless, until they nearly fell into the dry, still darkness and slammed the door behind them.

"Okay?" John asked.

"Yeah, sure," Matthew replied. *Except for being scared and disoriented and dizzy and frozen.*

With remarkable speed and grace of language, John got the generator running, while Matthew held the lanterns and prayed silently. "There!" John said with evident satisfaction. "Now we have heat and water." He put his gloves back on and took a lantern. "Ready to head back?"

"I don't suppose we could wait it out in here?"

"You can. But only if you want to wait alone. I want to go back to bed."

They wrestled the door open and plunged again into the vortex. *I wonder,* Matthew thought as he floundered in John's wake, unable to see, *I wonder if this is what Frost meant about the world ending by ice. God promised no more floods, but He didn't say anything about blizzards. They probably don't have snow in the places those Bible writers came from. Well, they could have my share!*

The light in the window was invisible until their last few steps.

§ § §

As he made hot chocolate on the gas stove, struggling to see the lines on the measuring cup by oil-lamp-light, Matthew noticed the time. "It's three-thirty. We're going to have to go right back out to milk."

"Relax. We can let 'em go until six and then go back to bed. Thanks," John added, taking a blue goose mug between chilled fingers. "I think my feet are beginning to thaw. How's your knee?"

Matthew sat across from John, cupping his own mug. He sipped quickly, burning his tongue. "John?"

"Hmm?"

"Do you think - my knee. Did Miles really heal it?"

John blew gently across the surface of his chocolate, thinking. "It doesn't hurt any more, does it?"

"Not really. It hurt a couple of times when I was talking about my dad... Those have been the only times - when I was thinking about him, angry about him-"

"How do you feel about him now?"

Matthew studied a tiny bubble at the rim of his mug. "I guess I feel sorry for him. I know how scared he must have been as a kid. And - and maybe - maybe he was scared as a grown-up, too. I know he didn't know how to love, or how to be loved, either." He popped the little bubble with his spoon.

"Do you forgive him, Matthew?"

Matthew's head jerked up, eyes wide with surprise. Confusion settled over his features, a delicate frown that reminded John of David for a moment. "Uh - "

John held his breath.

The faint frown smoothed into a tentative smile. "I guess I do."

John exhaled quietly.

"But what does that have to do with my knee?"

"Okay: first, I do believe your knee is healed, but Miles didn't do it – God did. He just used Miles as a – well, as a conduit. He answered Miles's prayer."

"Oh."

"And I believe the Lord healed your knee as a symbol for the healing He wanted to do in your heart, in your spirit, about your father."

"Oh."

John noticed he was holding his breath again. Forcing himself to breathe normally, he tested the chocolate and found it cool enough to drink. After a few swallows, he decided to venture back out onto thin ice. "How does it feel, forgiving your father?"

Matthew pondered. "Good. It feels good. Light – like putting down a really heavy backpack after a long hike." He smiled. "I'm – free."

"Almost," John said, wondering whether he heard a faint cracking in the ice.

"What do you mean, almost?"

"For a while, you were angry with everyone, including yourself. We forgave you because we love you and we could see you were struggling with things. And after – well, you seem to have forgiven us, too."

"Yeah. None of it was your fault, anyway. I'm sorry I was such a jerk." Matthew bent over his mug to avoid John's eyes.

"You're not a jerk. You need to forgive yourself."

Matthew laughed lightly. "Will asked me one time why, if God forgave me, I didn't forgive myself."

"Good question. What did you tell him?"

"Nothing. He dropped it and split."

"Do you forgive yourself?"

"I'm working on it." Matthew drank deeply from the cooling mug. "So when I forgive myself, then I'm free?"

Oh, Lord, help me! John prayed. "No, not yet."

"What else *is* there?"

"There's God."

"God?"

John heard the ice crack behind him. "Matthew, you blame God for your problems, for your father, maybe for his problem. You're angry with God. If you want to be free, to be happy, to be everything you're meant to be, you're going to have to forgive God, too."

"Bull." Matthew shoved back his chair, rose jerkily and stomped out as loudly as his stocking-feet would allow.

Marooned, feeling the ice he sat on floating out to sea, John laid his head on his hands and prayed.

§ § §

Upstairs, unmindful of the wreckage in the kitchen, Matthew peeled back down to his pajamas and climbed into bed. He left the tiny flame of the oil-lamp to dance its shadows across the ceiling and watched them until he heard Carolyn go downstairs at six. Then he dressed again and met John in the barn to do the milking.

They emerged later to a still, white world drifted into fantasy shapes gleaming in pale sunlight.

"Storm's over," John offered, his first words since they had begun the milking.

Matthew's silence was suddenly overrun by the approaching roar of a snowmobile. The shiny black shell raced to the back door and stopped abruptly in a spray of snow. Two bundled figures, presumably Ed and Will, dismounted and met them mid-yard.

"Pretty cool!" Will exclaimed. "Woulda been even cooler if he let me drive!"

"I ain't got a death wish," Ed teased. "Generator working okay?"

"Fine," John answered. "I'm running the barn, the chicken house, the pump and the appliances. Phone's out."

The four headed for the house. Will tried to make a snowball, but the snow didn't pack well. "Save yourself, boy," Ed warned. "Don't go looking for trouble. I been known to pitch a mean snowball myself."

"You, old man?" Will taunted, trying another handful.

"Y'know those milk cans nobody can ever knock over at carnivals?" John asked. "Ed never misses. You have to accurate and throw *real* hard to take those down. 'Nuff said?"

Will grinned, dropped the snow and dusted off his bare hands. "Too cold anyway."

The kitchen welcomed them with fragrance of coffee and oatmeal and cinnamon. As soon as they were seated, Carolyn plunked huge bowls of the hot cereal in front of them, along with brown sugar, heavy cream and buttered toast.

"Pray fast!" Matthew admonished.

As they shoveled in oatmeal and toast faster than Carolyn could supply them, Ed remarked, "I'm going to get the drive plowed out this morning. Road ought to get cleared sometime today."

"Good," John said, "because we need to get Pearl."

"Surely someone in town will be checking up on her," Carolyn exclaimed. "Their phones are probably out, too, but won't someone think to go over?"

"Probably. But this is just what we were talking about before, having her here with us." John finished his orange juice in a long swallow and turned to Will. "Did you two figure out the housing problem?"

Will and Ed exchanged a long look. "Yep," Ed nodded. "Sure did.

Figured to put Will over here with you folks until summer and give his room to Pearl. Tell 'em, boy."

Will's eyes darted nervously from one to another. "Well, uh – I'd rather – but if you're not ready to – uh – change David's room, I'll – " he took a deep breath – "I'll move in with Matt."

"That's up to Carolyn," John said quietly.

She studied her plate for a tense moment while the others waited, suspended. "Matthew," she asked, her voice breaking, "will you help me pack David's things?"

"What if she doesn't want to come?" Matthew asked. "We never asked her."

"Tell her we're worried about her," Ed advised.

"Tell her we want to help," Carolyn offered.

"Kidnap her!" Will proclaimed.

"Let's tell her we love her and we need her," Matthew said. "Because she's family."

Sixty

"Well," Carolyn said cheerfully, sinking her hands into the bubbles, "at least the dishwasher isn't electric."

"Neither is the dish dryer," Matthew muttered, dishtowel poised. "I think this ought to be beneath my dignity."

Carolyn's laughter floated up like the bubbles. "Spare me!" she begged. "You've been spending too much time with Ed."

Secretly, Matthew rejoiced that she was laughing. He dreaded the moment when the dishes would be dried and put away, the tables and counters clean, and they would go upstairs together to David's room.

"It's going to be all right," Carolyn said, as if she could read his mind. "No matter how much it hurts, it's time for this step. I'll probably cry, but don't you worry about it."

Matthew slammed the silverware drawer. "Right."

"No, really. I mean it. Crying is good – you know that. And just think how much David would love to share his room with Will." She dumped the dishwater and chased the bubbles down the drain with the sprayer. "Let's go."

"Let me just sweep the floor first."

"Matthew! Come on. Bring a box of trash bags."

He froze, horrified. "You're going to throw out David's things?"

"No, of course not. We'll just pack them away in the attic with Johnny's things. I suppose someday I'll have to – but not yet. Not yet."

Despite her bravado, Carolyn stood motionless in the middle of

David's room for several minutes. At last she confessed, "I don't know where to start."

Matthew stared helplessly back at her, then turned to the bright blue shelves.

"All right," she said. "You pack toys and I'll do the closet."

At first Matthew was absorbed by the pain of touching David's trucks and blocks and coloring books, the pain of watching these few pitiful reminders disappear one at a time into anonymous black plastic. Then he began to hear hangers rattling and the bag crinkling in the closet. And then, silence.

Matthew moved quietly to the closet. Carolyn stood inside, the full bag at her feet, her face buried in the last tiny shirt. She didn't move or make a sound until suddenly she looked up, holding out the soft flannel. "It smells like him," she whispered, tears running slowly down her cheeks.

Bringing the shirt to his face, Matthew inhaled deeply. She was right. The fragrance of David rose in his nostrils, bringing back the image of David, the blue of his eyes deepened by the shirt, running toward Matthew from the school bus. His fists closed unconsciously on the flannel, crumpling it against his chest.

Gently Carolyn retrieved and refolded the shirt, placed it in the bag, tied the bag shut. "I'll do the dresser now." She stepped over to it and snapped open a new bag.

Placing a case of tiny steel cars into his bag, Matthew remembered David playing with them. Seeing Carolyn draw a little pair of red swimming trunks from a drawer, he remembered teaching David to swim. Carolyn's tears ran steadily, slowly, and from time to time she wiped her nose on her wrist. And at the same time, Matthew thought she was smiling. The waves of his own grief were rolling in higher and faster, carrying a vicious riptide of anger beneath them.

"How can you smile?" he asked tightly.

"Why, Matthew, I love him so much – and this makes him so real to me. Look at all these unpaired socks. I'll bet no two of them match. I remember David said the clothes chute ate his socks, so it wasn't his fault if he had to wear a blue one and a white one."

"It's not fair!"

"No, of course it isn't."

"Then, how can you be so – so okay with it? Aren't you even a little bit mad?"

Carolyn dumped the socks into the bag and moved on to under-wear, hands transferring tiny superhero briefs to the bag as she talked. "I was very angry a year ago, but not any more."

"Were you mad at God?"

"I was mad at God and everybody!" Carolyn laughed. "'Everybody' was John and the doctors and the pastor and every well-meaning Christian who said anything even faintly scriptural to comfort me – and every woman whose children were living."

"How did you get over it?"

"I cried so much, I guess I washed away a lot of it. I'm not a natu-rally angry person, you know. It's hard for me to stay mad."

"I used to think that about myself," Matthew reflected. "What about God? How can you forgive Him?"

Carolyn smiled at him, and Matthew tried to return it. "Time has helped that, too," she told him. "I was sitting in the living room one day, all alone, looking at your carving on the bookcase, and I was just so moved – I thought, how could a God who loves us enough to die for us like that possibly kill our innocent children? He couldn't! And then I thought, 'God didn't kill my son; leukemia did. My son didn't suffer as much as God's Son. And I got to hold his hand; I got to bury him...'"

Weeping overtook her at last. Locking a terrible sob inside his chest, Matthew gathered her into his arms and waited out her tears. He was surprised at how quickly they passed. As she swiped at her nose, he proffered a clean but crumpled bandana from his back pock-et.

"You really are spending too much time with Ed," Carolyn said with a watery smile, mopping her face. "Will you please take down the curtains?"

"Even the curtains?"

"Don't you think Will is too old for dinosaurs?"

"Yeah, but I – " His voice broke as the tears he had swallowed rose to choke him. Carolyn held him for a moment and returned the blue bandana. "I'm sorry," he said, wiping his eyes.

"I'm glad. I remember when Johnny died – it comes back like this for years. But the times in between get longer, the crying times get shorter, I promise."

Lifting down the curtain rod, Matthew nodded assent.

"I know this has been the hardest thing in a long time," Carolyn ventured as she folded the curtains and bedspread into a bag. "That's why I kept putting it off. It seems so – final."

"Yeah."

"Thank you for doing it with me, Matthew. I couldn't have done it alone. No, don't brush it off," she insisted as Matthew raised a hand to stop her. "I know it's about as hard for you as it is for me. And – and please forgive me for being so selfish – but I knew you could handle it better than John."

Matthew carried the four huge bags up to the attic and stowed them in the corner farthest from the Christmas ornaments, next to a dismantled baby crib and an ancient wooden high chair. *She put those up here to save for her grandchildren*, Matthew thought, *grandchildren she'll never have.*

By the time he came downstairs, Carolyn had worked a transformation in the room. Navy blue curtains were gracefully tied back to reveal the white shade and a navy pillowcase sat in sharp contrast to crisp white sheets. The red and blue quilt from John and Carolyn's room was folded at the foot of the bed. Carolyn grinned at him smugly.

"How'd you do this?"

"I pinned the blue sheets over the curtain rod and tied them back with the belt from John's robe. Of course, I had to cut it in half..."

An answering grin formed on Matthew's lips. "I'll never tell!" The grin faded as his wandering gaze crossed the desk. The three-masted schooner was still dry-docked there. "What about the boat?"

"I'm not sure. We could put it on the bookshelf in the living room. I've come in here sometimes to look at it, but I won't be able to do that any more. And it wouldn't mean anything to Will, anyway, even if he did appreciate the workmanship." She studied Matthew for a moment. "Would you like to have it?"

"I – " He truly did not know.

"Of course, you would have to promise not to sink it."

Color flooded his face. "No, never again. I promise."

"Then why don't you just try it in your room for a while?" Carolyn said, placing the ship into his hands.

Matthew gently carried the little ship to his room and placed it in the center of his empty dresser top. The wood gleamed and the sails shone.

"You did a good job."

Matthew whirled around at the sound of John's voice. "Thanks."

"Thanks for doing David's room. I didn't want to. I would have, but..."

"It's okay. I didn't mind too much."

"The county came by and cleared the road. I'm going pretty soon to kidnap Pearl."

"What do you want me to do?"

"Help Will settle in, I guess. I'm taking Carolyn over to Ed's. She seems to think their place won't be fit for Pearl unless she has a go at it."

"Will's stuff?"

"Ed let him drive the snowmobile home to start packing. Ed'll take the truck over and bring him and his stuff back. How much stuff can one kid accumulate in a few months, anyway?"

§ § §

A lot! Matthew thought later, helping Will haul most of it up the stairs. He watched the youth investigate, evaluate the changes in the room.

"Like it?" he asked.

"It'll do," Will said, dumping an armload of clothes onto the bed.

What did I expect? Matthew asked himself, plopping a box of books onto the desk. "You want help with this stuff?"

"No, thanks. I'd rather do it. No offense - "

"None taken." Matthew smiled. "I'll be in my room if you want me."

Sitting on the edge of his bed, Matthew pulled out the old pillowcase from under the bed and laid out his carving tools and some wood scraps. Taking a small piece of pine, he searched it for a moment, turning it in his hands to find the figure in it. Satisfied, he began to whittle.

A while later, a shadow fell across the emerging creature. "What are you doing this time?" Will asked.

Matthew held out the unfinished work. "Mouse."

"Jeez, Matt! How many does this make?"

"I don't know - a dozen, maybe?"

Will wandered over to the bookshelf and began to count. "There's already thirteen!" He picked up the pretty little dragon and straightened its tiny crown. "Why don't you quit on the mice and make some more of these? Dragons are cool."

"There's only one of her," Matthew said quietly.

"Yeah? Well, anyhow - if you ever get tired of making mice - well, maybe you'd like to make something bigger?" Will kept his back to Matthew, but the line of his shoulders telegraphed tension.

"Have anything in particular in mind?"

"Oh, I dunno. Just - like - maybe my room could use a shelf like this. I mean, you know, if you wanted to. If you ever had time."

"Would you like to help me?"

"Help?" Will turned around. "How?"

"Measure the space, measure the wood - oh, I don't know - use the saw, sand, varnish - whatever."

"So, if I do all that, what're you going to do?"

"Supervise!" Matthew returned promptly and was rewarded with a laugh. "Seriously, I thought you might like to learn to work with wood."

Will considered, inspecting the tools laid out on the bed. "Maybe. I'll let you know." He sauntered out and clattered away down the stairs.

Matthew's fingers continued to draw the little mouse out of the wood as his mind sorted boards and considered shelf designs. It was turning out to be a tall, skinny, suspicious mouse, its gaze canted sideways, a tiny book in its paws. He knew where it would probably live when it was finished.

Sixty-One

"Such a lot of fuss!" Pearl exclaimed, settling onto the couch after supper. She drew her heavy black cardigan closer against the faint chill which persisted at any distance from the fireplace.

"My fault!" Will said cheerfully, flopping down at the other end of the couch.

"And how is that?"

"Oh, I just told 'em I'm bored with the same old cookies all the time - and maybe I need a grandmother."

"Young man, if you think for one minute - John thinks I'm too old to live by myself any more, that's all. It's just been a while since he took in a stray - " Her wrinkled lips quivered just once before settling into a firm line.

"Hey, wait!" Will sat up straight and leaned toward the old woman. "Yeah, maybe you are too old, like I'm too young. So we both need some looking after. At least you can set your own bedtime! But, honest, Pearl, everybody wants you here. We took a vote, like you all did for me." He looked down at his hands, picking at his cuticles as he continued, "See, the thing is, they - uh - you know - love you."

Staring at his fingers, Will missed both the tears and the gleam in her dark eyes. "And what about you, boy?" Pearl asked briskly.

"Well, I – uh - " Will swallowed audibly. Then he met her eyes. "Ma'am, I never did have a grandmother. I really could use one."

"I suppose you'll be wanting to call me 'Grandma' or some such foolishness."

"Yes, ma'am."

"And expecting me to bake cookies."

"Yes, ma'am!"

"Anything else, boy?"

"Just one thing - " Will hesitated, plunged in again. "Could you please get rid of that black sweater? I heard Matthew and Ed - it reminds them of when David died."

Pearl looked down at herself in mild amazement, then up at Will. "Why in the world didn't they say something sooner? I'll put it in a bag for the church first thing tomorrow."

"Thanks - Grandma!" Will bounced across the cushions to hug his newest relative, who threw up her hands against his chest before he could follow with a kiss.

"Behave yourself, boy! No need to get sloppy." She patted his shoulder for a moment. "Now go tell Ed I'm ready to go - home. It's been an exhausting day."

Will headed for the kitchen, where the rest of the family clustered at the table.

"Well?" John demanded.

"Well, what? What are you guys doing in here, anyway?"

"We're waiting to find out if it's safe to come into the living room." Ed was more than half-serious.

"Why wouldn't it be?" Will was genuinely perplexed. "Ed, Pearl wants you to take her over to the house now. She's tired."

Ed rose quickly. "Right away. I'll warm up the truck for a couple of minutes."

"Is she mad?" Matthew asked in a low voice.

"Nah. She figured it out, made a pretty snide remark about John taking in strays. But - like - we worked it out."

"Quite the diplomat, aren't you?" John teased.

Will preened and favored John with a smug grin. "Must be. She says I can call her 'Grandma.'"

The three adults exchanged incredulous looks. "Huh!" Matthew said. "She never asked me to call her 'Grandma.'"

"Oh, you know," Will rubbed it in. "You've either got it - or you don't."

"It's good," John said. "It's a commitment to the youngest one of us. That gives her a reason to keep going for a long time."

Will blushed and bit his thumbnail. Abruptly he wheeled around;

they could hear him clomping up the stairs to his room.

"Quite a day," John remarked quietly, looking hard at Matthew. "What are you thinking, Matthew?"

Startled, Matthew froze for a moment. "What Pearl said about strays - Ed, me, Will, now Pearl - are we just throwaways you feel sorry for?"

Carolyn came to put her arms around Matthew from behind as he sat hunched over his coffee. "How many ways can we tell you? What's going to make you understand?"

"You're none of you 'strays'," John agreed. "You're family. You're relatives from out of town who finally came home to stay. You're the pieces that have been missing in our family puzzle. We need you."

Matthew's finger traced the line of geese around his coffee mug over and over. He watched their stylized shapes nodding to one another against the sky-blue china. "Sometimes," he said, watching the geese, "this all feels so right - so real - belonging, being loved - " He paused, felt Carolyn's breath ruffling his hair, her small hands kneading his shoulders.

"And other times..." John prompted.

"It's crazy. Nobody just loves everybody like that, no strings - not without some ulterior motive."

John smiled. "What was your ulterior motive in fighting so hard to get us to take Will?"

"He needed us!"

"So what? Will wasn't our problem. He had a place to stay."

"Oh, sure! Two old people hardly making it themselves - couldn't even feed him right - "

"Not our problem. The state has foster homes for kids like those."

"No! He needs a family, not to be stuffed away with some people who just do it for the money, who might abuse him again, who don't I-"

"Who don't... ?"

"All right! Who don't love him." Matthew slumped back in the chair and Carolyn ran her hand over his hair, smoothing it back from his forehead.

"So your ulterior motive for taking on Will is wanting to help him and love him."

"Yeah, I guess so. And he is my – son." He unconsciously leaned his head back into Carolyn's hand. She smiled down on him, then at her husband.

"Love's a funny thing," Carolyn mused. "It just crops up all by itself, doesn't it? You disliked Will so much - so did Ed – You didn't want to be his father, but you felt led to take care of him from that first day you brought him to the house to get his hands tended. And you brought him to me, I suspect, because you trusted me to be kind to him." She began to clear the coffee mugs away.

"Love's the great commandment," John said, rising and stretching slowly. "Seems like the better we understand God's love, that unconditional Abba-Daddy love, the easier it is to love other people. And the people we love aren't strays, they're family, blood or not."

Matthew wandered away from the conversation, to the porch for his snow-gear, to the barn to check the Jerseys. Celeste met him, curling around his ankles, meowing insistently. Although there was still dry food in her dish and water in her bowl, Matthew managed to snitch enough milk from an agreeable cow to fill an old tuna-fish can.

"Here," he told the little cat, setting the warm milk beside her water, "don't say I never gave you anything."

Celeste daintily sampled her loyal subject's offering, then dispatched it with remarkable speed and economy of motion. Grooming her whiskers, she acknowledged Matthew's tribute with a sort of "Mmmrrph!" sound.

"Matthew snorted. "I heard somebody on TV call that 'cupboard love'," he told the cat. "We know what your ulterior motives are!"

Celeste did not disagree. Seeing that Matthew had no more milk, she stalked away from him without a backward glance.

Sixty-Two

They passed through Thanksgiving on a tide of sage and cinnamon, buoyed by the steady good humor of Ted and Olivia, distracted by the suddenly publicly upset stomach of the youngest Seibenek, Greg, who blamed it on Teddy and Andrew for sitting on him.

While Ted cleaned the carpet and Livvie cleaned up the child, Pearl entertained Teddy, Andrew, Steve - and Will - by playing "Over the River and Through the Woods" on the sadly out-of-tune piano. The little boys sang in lusty, off-key, piping voices, and Matthew slipped away to his room to avoid the memory.

Cradling David's boat in his hands, he tried not to hear the faint music rising through the floor register. Grief took him prisoner once again; but the shackles were lighter, the sentence much shorter. In half an hour he could go downstairs again.

"I hear tell you've been using Uncle David's woodcarving tools," Ted greeted Matthew's return. "Hear you're pretty good, too."

Matthew blushed. "It's just - Christmas presents." He sat next to Pearl on the couch and studied his sneakers.

"Way I heard it," Ted argued, his big frame dominating John's chair and the conversation, "you've created a menagerie. Gonna show us?"

"No!" Matthew's blush faded to white. "I mean, there's nothin' to see. Y'all wouldn't be interested - "

"'Y'all'?" Livvie asked from her perch on the hearth.

"Don't tease, Livvie," Carolyn warned. "You know sometimes you can hear the Kentucky in Matthew's voice. Don't pester."

"Oh. Well, I'm sorry, Matthew. We didn't mean to put you on the spot, did we, Ted?"

"Sure we did," Ted laughed. "We just didn't mean to get called on it."

The big man's good humor was relaxing, contagious. Matthew surprised himself by thinking, *He'd make a good friend. I'd like to see him more often than just holidays.*

Sixty-Three

Full sun on his face woke Matthew hours after the alarm should have gone off. Scrambling into his clothes, giving a lick and a promise to his teeth and hair, Matthew raced down the stairs and screeched to a halt in the dining room, where John was working on the farm accounts.

"I'm sorry!"

"Blame me," John smiled up at him. "You didn't answer when I called, so I came in and turned off the alarm. You never even moved. Ed and I handled things all right without you."

"Thanks. I won't do it again."

"Sure you will," John laughed. He stood and gave a stretch which crackled all along his spine. "How about letting me join you for coffee while you get some breakfast?"

Rather than endure a lecture, Matthew fried himself a couple of eggs and toasted a slice of Pearl's rye bread. As he was adding glasses of milk and juice to his place, Carolyn came in with an armful of sheets and towels stiff from the clothesline. "Why didn't you call me?" she chided.

"I didn't want to bother you for a couple of eggs. I can cook, see? They're just a little crispy on the edges. Hey, where's Will?"

"I think," Carolyn said, taking Matthew's plate away from him and tipping the eggs into the disposal, "he must have gone to visit Tracy. He asked Ed for a ride into town. I've been thinking," she continued. "Will's going to be sixteen in February. He's going to want to take driver's ed and get his license." She set a dollop of butter into a clean skillet to melt on a front burner.

"Will the court let him drive?" John asked.

Matthew considered. "I don't know. I guess we'd better ask."

Carolyn broke two fresh eggs into the sizzling butter. "You should do that, Matthew. When you talk to them about taking permanent custody of Will."

Matthew froze, toast half-way to his mouth. "What are you talking about?"

"It's time," she told him, sliding the eggs onto a clean plate and setting it before him. "You've managed to accept that you're his father, and I think you've come to love him in spite of yourself. At least you give a good imitation. And he cares about you, about what you think. It's time to be Will's father – while there still *is* time. He's probably wondering why you don't say something, do something."

"But – I can't – you know - "

"Eat your eggs before they get cold," Carolyn said, turning her attention to the dirty dishes in the sink.

John gave Matthew a sympathetic half-smile. "Just chew on it for a while – the eggs, too. I'm headed for the accounts, so I'll see you at lunch."

Pearl brushed by John in the doorway. "Carolyn, I thought I'd bake some – well, Matthew, what are you doing sitting there with your breakfast getting cold? Eat, boy!" She patted his shoulder as she passed him.

Matthew's appetite had fled with the conversation, but he knew Pearl could be like Chinese water torture. He forked slippery bites of egg into his mouth and swallowed as fast as he could without chewing. The buttery mass sat uneasily in his stomach. The toast wouldn't go down. He fled, leaving his dishes on the table.

Back in his room, gulping down saliva and struggling not to be sick, he replayed the whole conversation. *Carolyn can't be right. She can't! Will doesn't want me to be his father any more than I want him to be my son. He feels more like Ed's his father. How can they think I can have custody of a kid? I know what John said about the abuse stopping here, but- Lord, the fact is, I don't believe it. John doesn't know me as well as he thinks he does. And maybe he doesn't know You as well as he thinks he does, because You let all this happen, time after time. You could have stopped it generations ago, and You just ignored it. Well, I'm not going to be Will's daddy and run the risk of hurting him again.*

I won't do it. Never. Surrendering, he vomited until nothing else would come up, knowing it was his own disgust for himself making him sick.

Sixty-Four

The next day during the morning milking, Ed turned to Matthew as if he were going to say something – but just stood there.

"What?" Matthew asked. Fascinated, he watched a faint flush climb up Ed's neck above the collar of his coat. "What's going on?"

"Uh - " Ed turned away and rubbed his hands over his face. "It's Will."

Matthew stilled. "What about him?"

"He come to me last night before bed and asked would I teach him to drive and help him get his license." Ed rubbed the back of his neck, still turned away from Matthew.

"Oh." *Why didn't he ask me?*

Ed finally turned to face Matthew. "I don't know why he done that. I told him he should ask you."

"And what did he say?"

Ed turned away again. "He said he don't think you'll want to be bothered."

"Is that all?"

"Aw, Matthew, don't make me - "

"Spit it out, Ed," Matthew snapped. "You're not going to say anything I haven't thought."

"He said he don't want you trying to act like his dad, telling him what to do. He said you don't care about him, and you never did. I'm sorry. It was hard talk." Ed moved tentatively toward the door.

"Hey, don't run out on me!"

Ed turned back once more. "Figured maybe you'd want some time to think it over."

"What's to think? Kid makes himself pretty clear." Matthew went to the cows and began checking their teats for irritation before turning them out into the alleyway to the lot. "John thinks I should apply for permanent custody." He laughed bitterly. "Fat chance he'd want that. He hates me. Can't say I blame him."

"Nah," Ed countered, "he don't hate you. He's just mad. Hasn't learned how to forgive people for being human and making mistakes. Too young to see beyond black 'n' white."

Matthew laughed again. "I wonder how old you have to be to get all that. I sure don't." He nudged the last, smallest Jersey out into the alleyway. "So what did you tell him?"

"Told him the big decisions is always family decisions. Said we'd talk it over before his birthday. Let's go get breakfast if you don't want to think."

§ § §

After dinner that evening, Pearl dragooned Will to help with the dishes. From the living room the others could hear him talking in a grumbling tone, suddenly cut short by a sharp retort from Pearl. John smothered a laugh with his hand.

"Never took that boy for a slow learner before," Ed snickered. Taking advantage of Will's preoccupation, Ed quickly outlined the driving issue.

"He needs to drive," Carolyn said. "Every boy around here has been driving since he was ten or twelve. I was driving Dad's tractor when I was that age."

"That's true," John agreed. "But farm kids are responsible, mostly. They grow up knowing about safety and hard work. I don't see Will really developing much of a sense of responsibility – do you, Matthew?"

"Well, he's better than he was... He works for the money, though, not for a sense of accomplishment. And he always blames something or somebody else if he makes a mistake."

"He ain't that bad," Ed insisted. "And I agree with Carolyn that he needs to drive. Could be powerful motivation, too, if he keeps liking Tracy."

"That's all we need!" Matthew exclaimed, clasping his hands across the sinking sensation in his middle. 'Will and Tracy in a car!

One generation of that mistake is enough!"

"Oh, Matthew," Carolyn began, but he interrupted.

"No, listen. There's no way that kid's ready to be a father – and I'm *sure* not ready to be a grandfather!"

"Pull yourself together and stop borrowing trouble," John said. "They're finished in there. I vote to help him get his license. That's three of us. Matthew?"

"Yeah, sure."

As the words left Matthew's mouth, Pearl and Will entered the living room companionably and Pearl seated herself in the rocker.

"Have a seat," John offered Will, gesturing to the spot on the couch between Ed and Matthew.

Will contemplated his options and plunked himself down on the floor at Carolyn's feet.

Smart, Matthew thought. *Knows a patsy when he sees one.*

"We been talking about you driving," Ed began.

Will's eyes widened slightly and his spine straightened. He looked from face to face.

"If Pearl agrees," John continued, "we think you should learn."

Will looked at Pearl, pleading with his eyes while trying to look indifferent.

"Of course you need to learn to drive," the old woman responded. "Do you understand that driving is a privilege, not a right?"

"Huh?" Will's perplexed expression provoked smiles all around the room.

"Means learning don't mean you'll get the keys any time you want," Ed explained, his tone more gruff by far than the look on his face.

"Matthew does," Will countered.

Matthew gritted his teeth; Ed laid a hand briefly on his arm.

"Don't be foolish," Pearl said. "Do you want to do this or not?"

Will looked down and fiddled with his shoe-string. "Yes, ma'am, I do."

"Matthew will pick you up after school tomorrow if Dan approves it," John said, "and take you to the DMV for your learner's packet. I'm not sure what the rules are now, but I think you have to take a driving course."

Glaring at Matthew, Will nodded and stood. "I have homework. Thanks for dinner." He left the room, and in a moment they heard the slam of his bedroom door.

"Well, that went pretty well, didn't it?" Carolyn said.

Matthew nodded, smiling to himself as he realized that she really meant it.

§ § §

The next afternoon Will climbed into the truck, dumping his backpack on the floor and buckling his seat belt.

Hi," Matthew offered as he pulled away from the curb and merged into post-school traffic.

"Hurry up," Will demanded. "I don't wanta be stuck behind a bus all the way to town." He turned on the radio and switched from NPR to the local hard-rock station.

"Do *not* crank that up," Matthew warned.

"Hey, it's supposed to be loud!"

"Driver gets to choose the station, kid, so the compromise is: I let you have your station if you let me have my volume."

"Man!" Will muttered, but he settled back in his seat for the rest of the ride.

On the way home, Matthew switched the station to one which played contemporary Christian music. Will groaned and made faces, but soon his foot was keeping time and his hands were wielding imaginary drumsticks.

"That's the kind of stuff the youth band plays at church," Matthew said, his voice carefully uninflected. "I think Tracy sings with them."

"Yeah," Will agreed, "she's into that whole show choir thing at school, too."

It was the first thing Will had ever volunteered to Matthew about the girl, and Matthew was a bit uncomfortable with how grateful he felt. Encouraged by Will's openness, he ventured, "Tomorrow I'll call about the driving course for you."

"Ed will do it," Will said. "No need to put yourself out."

Couldn't you at least try? I'm trying. "I don't mind. I have as much time as Ed."

"Don't worry about it. Ed's gonna take care of everything." Will turned his head to stare out the window for the rest of the trip, leaving Matthew to pray for patience.

Sixty-Five

Will turned sixteen on February second and passed his driver's test the next day. He had achieved more than his fifty hours by driving Ed and Carolyn everywhere they wanted to go and driving the family to church on Sundays. His favorite birthday present was a key-ring Ed gave him, with a note that said, "Keys to follow – when you show how good you can follow the rules."

"Never seen a boy so excited to drive," Ed laughed. "It's that Tracy, I know it is."

"So," Will said offhandedly on Thursday, "I need to borrow the El Camino tomorrow night."

"That so?" Ed grinned. "Got a hot date with Tracy?"

Will grinned back at him. "I hope so. She said she'd go to a movie with me." He sauntered off, whistling between his teeth.

"Bad idea," Matthew said.

"Now, calm down, son," Ed said. "He's been doing everything we asked him to do, driving real careful when he gets the chance, got all A's on his report – no reason not to let him have a little fun."

"Ed, his idea of 'a little fun' is different from yours. I know how it is."

"Come on, Matthew. Think I don't remember? But he's been reading your Bible, going to church... Tracy's a good girl. He ain't going to try anything with her. We gotta trust him!"

"You can trust him if you want to, but I don't. You may be the father he wants, but I'm the father he has, and he's just like I was."

Ed nodded. "I hear you. But I don't believe Will's going to repeat your mistakes. God don't want that boy to be lost – He wants him to be saved. I can feel it – he's that close. Needs to be encouraged, not stomped on."

"Ed, please don't trust him!"

Ed slapped his hand on the side of the milk-tank. "Chronicles and Kings, Matthew! Back off it! Court says he can drive, he's been behaving, it's my truck – and I reckon it's my decision. You want the say, you know what you got to do."

Will left after dinner Friday night, clean-scrubbed and clean-shaven (although Matthew couldn't see that the latter made much difference), smelling of cologne and some kind of hair gel which made the top of his head resemble a blond porcupine. Ed grinned from ear to ear as he handed over the keys; Pearl admonished him to behave; John and Carolyn smiled and waved. Matthew watched in silence, waiting for Will to look at him, even for a moment, but Will never did.

Pearl and Ed went home before nine; not long after, Matthew saw the lights go out in their house. John and Carolyn went to bed at ten. Matthew turned off the t.v. and sat in the dark in Carolyn's chair, from which he could see Ed's driveway in the white beam of the yard light.

Lord, please keep him safe. And Tracy. Keep her safe, too. Please.

At ten forty-five, Matthew saw the El Camino pull in across the road. He waited a moment to watch Will get out and begin to trudge across the road, then ran quickly upstairs to be in his room with the door closed before Will could reach the second floor.

§ § §

The next day Will attacked his chores with fury, snarling at anyone who attempted conversation. On Sunday he refused to go to church, gaining a strong tongue-lashing from Ed for a remark to Pearl.

"Shall I stay home with him?" Matthew asked as the angry youth stamped up the stairs to his room.

"Nah," Ed said, pretending indifference. "He's gonna be fine. You'll see – by the time we get back, he'll be asking what's for dinner."

In fact, Will's return to equilibrium took until Tuesday, but at last he was no more surly than usual.

"He wants something," Matthew warned. "He's getting ready for something – I know it." He finished filling the John Deere's gas tank and set about knocking mud off his boots with unnecessary vigor.

"Then we'd better pray harder," John said. He stifled a yawn. "And we'd better get back to those fields before the rain comes."

Disking the black soil, which would hold corn instead of wheat this year, Matthew had plenty of time to worry – and to wonder why he worried. He even prayed a little. Rained out of the fields by that afternoon, the men turned their attention to other things. Ed drew Will in with him after school to tinker with the engines of various huge pieces of equipment. John caught up on his paperwork, and Matthew began carving a tall, skinny mouse at the wheel of a low-slung sports car.

Sixty-Six

Friday after supper Will approached Ed again. "May I borrow the El Camino for a while tonight? I don't have any homework – well, not much, and I'll have plenty of time to do it before Monday."

"Where you want to go on a rainy night? If you got a date, you left this wait a long time."

"Uh, it was sorta – if I could get the ride..."

Matthew noticed that Will wasn't making eye-contact with Ed, but he held his tongue.

"Sure, why not?" Ed said, fishing the keys out of his pocket. "Home by eleven-thirty."

Will grimaced but nodded as he took the keys.

"Don't forget your jacket," Carolyn warned. "It's cold out there!"

"Yeah, yeah," Will teased, smiling at her. He ducked onto the back porch to retrieve his jean jacket, then exited by the front door. Matthew watched him sprint to the El Camino, parked close to the house for Pearl's convenience.

"Let's hurry with those dishes," Pearl said. "I could use a good game of Scrabble before bed."

Matthew helped with the dishes and went down in ignominious defeat at Scrabble. He flinched every time the thunder rolled and lightning flashed across the black sky, landing in the fields near the house. He wondered why he seemed to be the only one worried about Will.

At nine-thirty the phone rang, freezing everyone in position.

"I'll get it," John said, heading to the kitchen.

They all waited, hearing the sound of John's voice but not his words. Then from the kitchen doorway he said, "That was Tracy."

The frozen silence fractured as everyone exclaimed at once. "I thought she was with Will," Ed said.

"Apparently not," Pearl said.

"She called looking for Will," John explained. "It seems they had a big fight last Friday night and he hasn't spoken to her since. I guess she really likes him, because she wants to make up."

"Nice girl," Pearl said. "Now, who's for another round of Scrabble? We can't talk to Will until he gets home."

§ § §

Unable to find any takers, Pearl let Ed drive her home in John's car. John and Carolyn turned in early, leaving Matthew to his own devices. Surfing through the television channels, he rapidly despaired of entertainment there. He sat in John's chair, leg jiggling, putting his hand on John's Bible and drawing it back several times before he finally let himself pick up the book and let it fall open. John had a bookmark at Matthew, chapter seven:

> *Do not judge, or you too will be judged.*
> *For in the same way you judge others,*
> *you will be judged.*

Oh, Lord, I don't want to read that! He turned the page to find a familiar heading, "Ask, Seek, Knock." Quickly he skimmed through to verse nine, where his attention caught:

> *Which of you, if his son asks for bread, will give him a stone? Or if he asks for a fish, will give him a snake? If you, then, though you are evil, know how to give good gifts to your children, how much more will your Father in heaven give good gifts to those who ask him!*

Matthew closed the Bible and put it back.

Which of you, if his son asks for bread, will give him a stone? Will I?

For the first time in months, Matthew went upstairs and dragged the old pillowcase out from under the bed. He began to carve a tiny mouse from a pine-scrap. His fingers moved automatically, almost as if he were blind, guided only by touch. When cramp forced him to lay aside his work, Matthew looked at the clock. Midnight. Will wasn't home, and he wasn't with Tracy.

Unable to see Ed's house from his room, Matthew tiptoed downstairs to look through the front window. No lights showed except the yard light. Ed was sleeping. The rain still fell steadily, but without the pyrotechnics of earlier in the evening.

Matthew's mind began to offer up a smorgasbord of possibilities. *Where would he go? Who would he be with? He doesn't hang with the boys from the accident any more... Accident! He's not experienced at driving in the rain. If he went off the road maybe no one would see him...Or what if he knows some girl like Dinah, some girl who –*

Matthew wheeled and ran into the kitchen to grab the truck keys. In seconds he was splashing across the yard to the truck, heedless of the cold rain plastering his tee-shirt to his body and flattening his hair into his eyes.

§ § §

Easing the truck down the long gravel driveway, Matthew tried to decide which way to turn when he reached the road. *Lord, show me where to go, please. I have no idea.*

A right turn headed him toward town. *This doesn't make sense. Why would he go to town? Lord, are you going to give me an address? I guess You could...*

No street address forthcoming, he drove randomly up one street and down another, looking for the El Camino. *This is stupid. You're just wasting gas.* He came to a cul-de-sac on the east side of town and recognized the entrance to a small park. *No*, he thought, but he turned in anyway.

About two hundred yards in, under a small stand of elderly maples, sat the El Camino.

Thank You, Lord! Matthew turned off his headlights and pulled up parallel to the El Camino. As he got out into the rain, he observed that the windows were fogged and the vehicle was rocking.

"Stop it!" Matthew roared, ripping open the passenger-side door.

In the faint glow of the dome-light, he saw two dark heads snap toward him, two startled faces blanch white, two mouths drop open in shock. He took in a glimpse of breasts before Will grabbed the edges of the girl's shirt and pulled them closed. The white of the girl's face rapidly flushed red with embarrassment and she began to fumble with her buttons.

"Is that your dad?" she asked in a tiny voice.

Will levered himself back into the driver's seat. Matthew was grateful to see that the boy's clothing was intact. He turned his attention to the girl.

"Yes, I am Will's father, Matthew Ryersen. Who are you?"

"Jessie Miller. Listen, we were just - "

The girl shifted uneasily and Matthew heard clinking glass at her feet. Looking down, he saw three empty beer bottles. "Jessie Miller," Matthew said in an unnaturally soft voice, "I want you to go get in my truck over there so I can take you back to your mama. If you have a cell phone, call and tell her Mr. Ryersen's bringing you home." He stepped back to let the girl exit the El Camino, but she hesitated.

"Is this guy safe?" she asked Will.

"For you, he is," Will replied, affecting more nonchalance than his flushed cheekbones and clenched jaw suggested. "He's probably going to kill me."

Jessie slithered past Matthew and climbed up into the truck.

Matthew headed around the front of the El Camino and pounded on the closed driver's door. "Open it!"

Will complied. "What're you doing here?" he asked angrily.

"You're late. You didn't come home or call. Of course, now I know why."

Will snorted. "It's none of your business. Thanks for ruining a good thing."

It was too much. Matthew grabbed Will's arm and hauled him out of the vehicle, slamming him up against the fender and holding him there. This time no fear widened Will's eyes; he glared at the taller, stronger man.

"You just don't learn, do you! Drinkin' and drivin' after what you've been through – after what you put us through – and who is that girl? What'd you think you were doing? Haven't you figured out yet that one dumb mistake can ruin a whole bunch of lives?" He shook Will, hard.

"Yeah, I get it," Will yelled back. "You've said it often enough. And no, I don't want a kid any more than you do. That's why I've got one of these." He dragged a small foil packet out of the front pocket of his jeans. "Now let go of me so I can take Jessie home. I figure you've killed the mood."

Matthew held on, snarling, "No! I know better than that. You head home and go to bed. We'll talk more about this in the morning."

Will snatched his arm away. "Shut up, will you! I don't have to talk to you about any of this. I don't care what some paper says, I don't care how much I look like you, you're not my father and you never will be! You wish I'd never been born? Well, so do I! I hate you!" He jumped into the El Camino, slammed the door in Matthew's face and gunned the engine. Matthew stepped back to let him drive off.

Jessie Miller, clearly frightened by the furious man and all the shouting, clung to the passenger door of the truck as if she might jump out at any moment.

"I'm not goin' to hurt you, Jessie," Matthew said gently, easing into the driver's seat and heading the truck back onto the road. "Give me your address so I can take you home."

Voice just above a whisper, she named an old trailer park on the west edge of town. When they got there, Matthew stopped just inside the gate to ask which was her trailer.

"I'll just get out here," Jessie said, reaching for the handle.

"Wait a minute. It's pourin' down rain. I'll take you to your door. I'd like to explain to your folks..."

"Listen, Mr. Boone, or whatever your name is, if my dad sees me in your car or hears I was with Will, he won't believe nothing happened. If he's been drinking, he'll think I did it with both of you." She flung the door open. "Thanks for the ride. You oughta be nicer to Will. Maybe he wouldn't turn out so bad if he had a dad who cared." She disappeared into the rain.

Sixty-Seven

The rain began to ease as Matthew pulled into the driveway. Only a few huge, renegade drops assaulted him before he made the safety of the back porch. Prominently displayed on the kitchen table lay a note: "Wake me if you need me. John."

He must have heard the truck leave – or Will come in.

Matthew left his shoes in the kitchen to go more quietly up the stairs. At the top, he turned toward Will's room. No light shone beneath the door, so he very gently eased it open. As his eyes adjusted to the darkness, Matthew saw the empty bed.

Adrenaline making him shake, Matthew fled down the stairs again to stare across the road at Ed's driveway. He could see John's car parked close to the front steps; beyond it was only empty driveway and yard.

Little weasel! He took off!

"I've heard running up and down stairs is a great work-out," came John's voice from behind him, causing Matthew's heart to give a huge thump, "but I wish you'd pick some other time for doing it." John laughed lightly. "Sorry I startled you." He turned on a light. "What's up?"

Matthew turned from the window, blowing out a huge sigh of relief. "You almost got your revenge on me there for waking you again. Will's gone." Briefly he recounted what had happened.

"Are you worried?" John asked, sitting down in his chair.

"Are you kidding? Of course I'm worried!"

"Most kids, I'd figure they'd show up by morning, after they got it out of their system. I'd just pray and wait."

"You really think Will's like that?"

"Well," John said carefully, "he might be. You hit him pretty hard - "

"No!" Matthew protested, "I *didn't* hit him! I swear I didn't!" His eyes filled with tears.

"Shh. I know you didn't hit him. What I meant was, you really embarrassed him in front of the girl and left him feeling pretty raw, pretty frustrated."

Matthew dropped into Carolyn's chair but jumped up immediately as he realized how wet he was. "Will's not like most kids, though, is he?"

"I don't think so," John said. "But he surprises me time to time." He stood and walked over to Matthew. "So let's pray and wait until after milking in the morning to figure out what to do. Ed has to be in on it, too."

Laying a hand on Matthew's shoulder, John prayed. Matthew did what he had heard an older woman at church call "the do-wops," mm-hmming and agreeing as John prayed. He added his own post-script this time, too, although not aloud.

Will did not return over night.

Ed noticed the absence of his beloved El Camino and demanded an explanation before the cows were even coupled. Matthew told the story again, hoping John had told Carolyn.

For the first time since they had met, Ed seemed to Matthew to be panicked and unable to cope. He couldn't say anything but "Oh, no!"

"Come on, Ed, relax. Calm down. It'll be okay."

Ed gave Matthew an anguished look. "Don't you get it? He stole the truck. If the cops catch him, they'll put him in jail. If he's gone, we have to report him to Dan, and he'll be in violation of his parole. He's going down again and they're going to throw away the key!" Ed's hands shook as he applied a blue bandana to his eyes and nose.

"Ed, come on! The El Camino's only stolen if you say it is. You gave him permission to drive it."

Ed nodded. Then the other problem resurfaced. "But the parole thing - "

"We can take some time," John said as he walked into the barn. "Carolyn and I prayed just now, and I have a real peace that we're going to bring him home."

"God speak to you, boss?" Ed asked, already visibly calmer.

"I believe He did."

"It's okay, then," Ed nodded, proceeding about his chores from there on as if he hadn't been on the edge of collapse minutes before.

"How long is 'some time?'" Matthew asked.

John sighed. "I don't know. Unless Dan calls sooner, I think we could wait until tomorrow afternoon."

"That's not long."

"Long enough for Will to cool off and run out of money. Then he'll call."

John seemed confident, but Matthew was not. He remembered that long bus-ride which had ended by a wheatfield outside Bucklin, Kansas. *I would have kept on going, because I didn't know – I couldn't believe they would want me back.*

§ § §

The next day, Sunday, came with no phone call. "I'm staying home from church," Ed declared, "for when Will calls."

And Ed's face told it all when they came home.

"Guess we got to call Dan," he told the family over dinner. His plate looked much like Matthew's, small blobs of ham and sweet potatoes and green beans, muddled but untasted.

"You're right," Pearl said. "He needs to know so he can do something. There's nothing more we can do but keep praying. Did you talk with Pastor Miles?" she asked John.

"Yes, I told him everything. We prayed about it with Carolyn and Penny."

"Good. We'll do that, too." To Matthew's surprise, she pushed her beans into her potatoes and set down her fork.

Legally responsible, Ed made the call, John and the others clustered around him in support – and curiosity. They heard him give his name and both his and the Abbott's phone numbers. "He ain't in," Ed explained. "Said to leave a message unless it's an emergency. So I'm saying it ain't an emergency."

§ § §

The rain began again on Monday, and the temperature dropped

into the high thirties. Ed and Matthew were shivering over second cups of coffee and the remains of breakfast when the phone rang. They looked at it, and at one another.

"I'll get it," Ed sighed.

Dan said he would come over and asked that anyone who might have input be present.

"I think that's the two of you," John told Ed and Matthew. "I'll be around if you need me."

Dan stood in the doorway shaking the rain from his jacket and military-cut hair. His hazel eyes, his whole face, had a hang-dog expression.

"Come in and sit down," Matthew said, leading the way into the living room.

"I'm wet," Dan said. "I better stand." As Ed and Matthew related the events of Friday night, Dan paced back and forth in front of the fireplace. At the end he plopped down on the couch, wet or not. He uttered one short, unprofessional word.

"It's my fault," Ed said. "I should of asked where he was going, and was it with Tracy."

"No, it's my fault," Matthew said. "I should have minded my own business."

"Will *is* your business," Dan replied. "The two of you have been dancing around this ever since last summer, haven't you?"

Matthew shrugged, but Ed nodded.

"You know I'm gonna have to report him to the court, don't you?" Dan continued. "We'll put out an APB on the stolen car."

"It ain't stolen! I loaned it to him."

"Sticking with that?" Dan asked. Ed nodded. "Okay, then. Word goes out on a runaway. Won't be quite as bad in court." He stood with a faint groan, as if he had aged beyond his years while sitting there. "Call me if you hear anything, and I'll be in touch, too."

Dan made it to the doorway, then turned back. "Mr. Yoder, for what it's worth, you've been a great foster-father. Will respects you and likes you a lot." He looked at Matthew. "And I think he'd really like to have his real dad. He tries to hate you for abandoning him, but the need's there and the hope keeps sneaking back. Remember that if he calls."

§ § §

On Tuesday the sound of the unrelenting rain began to pound inside Matthew's head, giving him a headache which didn't respond well to aspirin.

"It might have to do with not sleeping," Carolyn suggested, rubbing his temples with something mentholated as he sat at the kitchen table.

"How'd you know I'm not sleeping – unless you're not sleeping? Thanks; that feels – interesting."

"I'm not sleeping well," she agreed, washing her hands at the sink. "At least, not as well as usual. John, either. I'm so worried about Will. I thought the highway patrol would have found him by now!"

"We don't know how much money he had or which way he went – he could be in Kentucky or New York or – or Kansas by now."

"Or he could be - " Carolyn crumpled into tears.

Pearl, coming in through the back door to avoid tracking mud into the front hall, moved forward to envelop Carolyn in a rare hug. "Shhh," she admonished. "God will take care of the boy. He's smart and resourceful." She patted Carolyn's shoulder, looking across it at Matthew.

"Uh – yeah. Sure he is," Matthew responded, hoping he was giving Pearl what she expected. In his own heart, a terrible despair was growing.

Someone stayed near the phone at all times, but it didn't ring.

§ § §

Shortly after dinner on Wednesday, they heard the unmistakable sound of Dan's rough engine and the slam of his car door. Matthew flung open the door before Dan had cleared the porch. He took Dan's wet overcoat and hung it on the antique oak hall tree.

"Come on in."

"Thanks." Dan saw the entire family gathered at the living room doorway. "Maybe – uh – could we all sit down?"

Dumbly they arranged themselves, John on the couch with Carolyn and Pearl, Ed in the rocker, moving it rapidly back and forth. Dan took John's chair, where he had sat before, leaving Carolyn's chair for Matthew. Remembering Will sprawled in that chair, Matthew went to perch on the arm of the couch next to Pearl.

Dan cleared his throat and cracked his knuckles.

"Get it over with!" Ed exploded.

"I'm sorry, Mr. Yoder. I don't have a lot to tell you, but – well – the Illinois State Police found your vehicle in a ditch off the toll road, just over the Indiana line. They've had ice over there while we've been having rain. The vehicle apparently was going too fast for road conditions and went into a skid. It went through a guard rail and must have flipped over a couple of times."

Carolyn was weeping, getting louder despite efforts to stifle the sound.

"Ma'am – Mrs. Abbott – please! Listen! The vehicle is mashed like a pancake, but – no, listen! – there was nobody in it. God knows how, but Will must have walked away."

"What!" "How?" "Where is he?" They all spoke at once.

Dan held up his hand. "I don't know. The State Police conducted a huge search – under the vehicle, up and down the ditch, out into the field, up and down the road – nothing. No Will, no blood, nothing. He walked away."

"Then where did he go?" Carolyn wailed from John's arms.

"I'm d-arned if I know!" Dan rubbed his hand over his crew-cut. "But we'll find him now. His picture's out to every law enforcement department between here and Milwaukee." He sighed and slumped back in the chair. "It just may take some more time."

Ed blew his nose loudly into his blue bandana. "What if he's in trouble out there? He's just a boy. You got to find him before somebody kills him!"

"Ed, stop it!" Matthew warned. "You're scaring people."

"Fact is," John said, "we have to keep on trusting God. Maybe some very nice people have taken him in."

"Then why ain't they called us?"

John threw up his hands. "I don't know! Maybe he lied about who he is because he's still mad. Maybe they don't watch t.v., or it's not on the news. You know what we need to do."

"I need to be on my way," Dan said. He looked, to Matthew, grateful for an excuse to get away.

"Thanks for coming," Matthew said, leading the way to the door.

He helped Dan on with his wet coat and asked in a low voice, "Do you really think you'll find him?"

"Yes," Dan said, meeting Matthew's troubled eyes. "But I can't promise what shape he'll be in. I'm sorry."

"You think he's dead."

"No. Not yet. But anything can happen out there. You know how he is, and what his history is." Dan pulled gloves out of his pockets and shoved his big hands into them. "You folks just keep praying; that's what I'm going to do."

Sixty-Eight

When the phone finally rang on Thursday, late in the afternoon, Matthew happened to be standing close, a half-empty mug of coffee in his hand. The sudden, shrill ring made him startle and drop the mug, which shattered at his feet.

"Hello?"

"Matt? Is that you?"

"Will! Where are you? Are you all right?"

"I'm in Chicago. Matt, I wrecked Ed's El Camino. Some guy brought me here and - "

The boy was crying too hard to go on.

Matthew's gut cramped with panic. "Will, talk to me! Where in Chicago? What's going on?"

"I'm sorry. I'm sorry! Please, Matt, I want to come home!"

Matthew demanded that his body obey his mind. Taking a deep breath, he calmed his voice as much as he could. "We want you to come home, son. If you just tell me where you are, I'll come get you right now. I promise."

"I don't know where I am! These people, they - "

After some mumbling at Will's end of the line, a light male voice said, "This is Carl Wilson. I'm an outreach worker at The Night Ministry in downtown Chicago. Is this Will's father?"

"Yeah. Matthew Ryersen. What's happening to Will?"

"He's all right, Mr. Ryersen, just tired and scared. The Night Ministry reaches out to homeless people, including teens; and, when we can, we help them get off the streets. I found Will last night in a pretty unsafe place and brought him here. We don't keep anyone under eighteen for more than twenty-four hours unless we contact their parents. Will was going to tough it out and leave, but something seems to have changed his mind."

"Thank you for takin' him in. Are you sure he's okay?" Matthew dragged the phone over to the table and sat down, too wobbly to keep standing.

"He has a few bruises from the accident, but he says nobody touched him."

"Touched him! You mean some man - "

"I know what you're thinking," Carl Wilson said quietly, "and I could see that's what he's afraid of, but he kept himself safe, even though he ended up on Belmont."

"What's that?"

"Homeless kids sometimes turn to survival sex in exchange for a bed to sleep in, Mr. Ryersen, boys as well as girls. Belmont Avenue is one of those places."

Matthew felt bile and coffee rising in his throat and tears rising in his eyes as he envisioned Will back in the midst of his worst nightmares. "Oh, God!"

"He's *okay*, Mr. Ryersen. And he wants to come home. Does he have a home to come to?"

The tears spilled down Matthew's cheeks. "Of course he has! We've all been worried sick about him. Just tell me where you are so I can get started!"

When he had scribbled directions on the refrigerator white board, the magnet for which a blue goose held in its beak, Matthew dropped the phone and sank to his knees. John and Ed came in moments later to find the receiver dangling by its cord and the man sobbing incoherently into his hands.

"Will!" Ed gasped.

"Talk to us," John commanded, dragging Matthew to his feet. Looking at Matthew's face, he also commanded, "Ed, give him your bandana."

Mopping his eyes and nose, Matthew managed to say, "He's all right. He wants to come home. I have to go get him."

John summoned the women to hear the story, which Matthew recounted quickly, leaving out the Belmont Avenue details.

"I thought he must be dead, the way you was bawling," Ed said.

Matthew flushed. "I was so relieved, and so grateful – I was praising God. Carolyn, will you fix me a thermos of coffee? John, may I borrow the truck?"

"I should go," Ed insisted. "I'm the legal - "

"No," John said, "Matthew should go." He gave Ed a knowing look which caused the farmhand to nod immediately.

Preparations for the trip, including a paper copy of the directions in Pearl's elegant Palmer script, took less than ten minutes. They prayed in a tight circle and then Matthew headed west into the gathering dark.

Lord, help me. Help me to get there safely; I've never driven in a big city before. Help me to say the right things to Will. Help me to act like a real father to my boy.

§ § §

By the time he reached the address Carl Wilson had given him, less than four hours after he had left home, Matthew had sweated through his shirt and his hands had gripped the wheel so hard he almost had to pry his fingers free. He found a parking place a couple of buildings down and stepped onto the sidewalk. Standing in a circle of street-light, he surveyed the turn-of-the-century brick and stone buildings, most of them three stories high, noting neon lights down the street advertizing bars or restaurants. In between the pools of light from street-lamps, the street seemed dark and forbidding. For the first time in a long time, he locked the truck and pocketed the keys.

He hurried to the building with its porch lights on and pushed the buzzer.

Finally, a tinny voice asked him his name and business. The door opened. "Please lemme see your driver license," asked a large black man in a Chicago Bears hoodie, extending a hand the size of a catcher's mitt. Matthew complied quickly. "Now please come in," the man said, standing aside.

Another man, about Matthew's height and build, with very pale skin and dark hair and eyes, came forward, hand extended. Matthew notice that his ears had been pierced multiple times, and the main holes in his lobes were as big as dimes.

"I'm Carl Wilson," the man smiled, shaking Matthew's hand. "It's good that you came. Will told me a lot about his history, including his relationship with you. I was afraid you wouldn't come."

Matthew was stung, although he knew the fairness of the remark. "I was wrong, Mr. Wilson, and I've been tryin' to figure a way to make it right for some time. Way I see it, God's givin' me a second chance to be Will's father – if he'll let me."

Carl Wilson smiled, a kind, happy smile. "Oh, I think he'll let you. Come with me. Will's asleep on the couch in the office."

Curled on his side in an almost-fetal position, hair every which-a-way and mouth slightly open in deep sleep, Will looked to Matthew almost exactly as he had the day they met – little, young and innocent.

"I'll be in the hall if you need me," Carl Wilson whispered, patting Matthew's shoulder as he left the room.

Matthew crouched down beside the faded couch to drink in the sight of the sleeping boy. Will's clothes were filthy and reeked of sweat and some other bad thing, the same thing he had smelled in the hallway. A large bruise was fading on Will's forehead. His fingernails would never have passed Pearl's inspection, although dark rings around his wrists suggested he had recently washed his hands. He twitched and whimpered in his sleep.

Oh, Will, I could never give you stones instead of bread.

Will muttered something and rolled onto his back. Still more asleep than awake, he opened his eyes and looked at Matthew. Hope and uncertainty mingled on his face and in his voice as he whispered:

"Daddy?"

Sixty-Nine

Before Matthew could gather Will into his arms, the boy had returned to full awareness. He sat up and carefully blanked his face.

"Hey, Matt."

"Hey, Will." Matthew stood carefully, knees cracking. "How are you?"

"Fine. I want to go home."

No more effort was required to leave The Night Ministry than to enter. Matthew signed some kind of release without reading it, and they were on their way. Carl Wilson shook Matthew's hand, then Will's. "Be safe," he told the boy.

As they made their way down the steps, onto the street, Matthew saw Will turning his head side to side, constantly watching everything around him. As fast as Matthew unlocked the truck, Will clambered in and relocked his door.

"You know how to get outa here?" Will asked.

"Yeah. I went over the return directions with Carl Wilson. He seems like a nice guy."

"Yeah."

No conversation, huh? Oh well. Guess I should concentrate on my driving anyway.

Will turned the heater up as high as it would go and huddled in his seat. Matthew drove and prayed. Not even the radio pierced the uneasy silence.

Somewhere around Gary, Indiana, Will said, "Carl Wilson's gay."

"Oh." *What am I supposed to say to that!*

"His family kicked him out when he told them. They pretended he doesn't exist, except his sister. He goes out there on Belmont and helps kids now, because a lot of them had homes like his. He says, you know, nobody should have to be out there on the street, if people would just, you know, take them in or not throw them out in the first place."

"Yeah, I know. I never ended up any place like Belmont Avenue but I got kicked out of my home and I met some real bad guys on the road. Then I found a family to take me in. Or, really, God sent me there. I didn't have that much to do with it."

"I didn't think about where I lived that much until that guy dropped me off near Belmont. I mean, the farm was better than DYS, but it was just another foster home."

"We don't see it that way."

"Yeah, maybe." Will turned back to the window and slumped into silence again.

Matthew concentrated on his driving as they headed east into the rain. Traffic was light on the turnpike except for huge semis which drove waves of water over the truck's windshield as they passed. Matthew finally pulled into an oasis, parking as close to the door as he could.

Will snapped awake. "What!"

"Relax. Just takin' a break. I'm sleepy; it's past my bedtime."

"Oh."

"You want to come in? Men's room, food, anything?"

"Okay." Will dashed ahead of Matthew but waited just inside the door. Not making eye-contact, he said, "You – uh – going in there?" He gestured vaguely toward the men's room.

"Heck, yeah!" Matthew laughed. "Coffee in, coffee out. Come on." He didn't miss how closely Will followed him, or how thoroughly Will cased the room before stepping up to the urinal.

"Want anything to eat?" Mathew asked as they passed the fast-food places.

"Yeah! I - " Will looked down at himself. "No, that's okay."

"Hey, come on. I'm good for it."

"I can't go in there like this." Shame colored Will's downcast face.

"Oh. Okay. Here's the keys. Tell me what you want and go wait in the truck."

"You kidding me?" Will gave Matthew the suspicious look he had used so often in the beginning.

"Since *you* called *me*, I figure we're going to the same place," Matthew said, placing the keys in Will's hand. "What do you want to eat?"

Will kept his eyes on the keys. "I guess – just a Coke, please."

No stones for bread, Matthew told himself, *and no snakes for fish. I guess a double cheeseburger will do for a fatted calf.* "Supersize every-thing," he told the waitress.

Will stared at the bags in Matthew's hands and swallowed audi-bly. "What'd you do!"

"Brought you some dinner, even if it is the middle of the night. All those days you were gone, I didn't like thinkin' about you bein' hungry. Go ahead; eat all you want."

Matthew filled the gas tank and the windshield washer fluid res-ervoir while Will inhaled a cheeseburger and fries and unwrapped another burger. As Matthew climbed back in, Will asked, mouth poised to take a bite, "Is this really all for me?"

"Just for you," Matthew affirmed, pulling smoothly back onto the turnpike.

"Thank you," Will mumbled around a huge mouthful. He ate as if he were starving, and Matthew's heart ached.

§ § §

Just across the Ohio border, Matthew realized that Will was cry-ing. Wordlessly he handed the boy the clean blue bandana Carolyn had stuffed into the pocket of his jacket. Will clutched the bandana, but his shoulders continued to shake.

Matthew kept driving, but he slowed below the speed limit. There was almost no traffic now that they were off the turnpike. He took a deep breath.

"When I'd been with the Abbotts a couple of years, I took off one time. I was just – I dunno – fed up, feelin' trapped – maybe runnin' from the pain of bein' my father's son, or from God – I dunno. I bought a bus ticket as far as my money would take me and ended up on the side of the road in Bucklin, Kansas.

"I didn't know what else to do, so I started hitchin' like I used to, and this truck pulled up to give me a ride."

Will's sobs had stopped; he was listening.

"Well, it really was '*this* truck,' and John was drivin'. I asked him, 'What are you doin' here?' and he said, 'I've come to give you a ride home.' Then he told me no matter how many times I ran away, they'd always come after me and take me back, because I'm family – and they love me."

"I didn't think anybody'd come," Will said, his raw voice barely audible about the hiss of the tires, the pounding of the rain and the noise of the old engine. "I figured the cops would get me and send me back. I figured everybody would be so mad you'd all just say, 'Good riddance.'" He began to cry again.

Matthew pulled over onto the berm next to some farmer's wheatfield and turned off the engine. He pulled off his jean jacket and draped it around Will's heaving shoulders. Will pulled the jacket close around himself.

"I lied to you, I stole Ed's truck – and wrecked it. How can you want me back?"

Matthew gave in to the impulse he had been fighting since Chicago and pulled the boy close. He felt tears prickling behind his own eyelids. "I think I've wanted you back ever since I sent you away. But I was afraid, and maybe I still didn't believe a father can love his son and forgive him no matter what he does." He smoothed Will's wild hair. "But when you were gone and we didn't know whether you were alive or dead, all I could think was that I didn't care what you'd done. I just wanted you home safe so I could - "

"Could what?"

"Could try to be a real father to you. I know I don't deserve a chance, but I want to try." His own tears dripped into Will's hair as he held the boy close. "I love you, Will, and God loves you, even more than I can. Please forgive me for abandoning you. It wasn't your fault. It wasn't *ever* your fault."

Will relaxed against Matthew and his breathing steadied. Outside, the incessant rain battered the old truck but inside, peace descended. Matthew felt himself wrapped in a warm embrace, one he had felt before. "Abba," he whispered.

"What?" Will whispered back.

"Abba," Matthew repeated softly. "Daddy. God Who loves us

like a real daddy should." He ran his hand over Will's hair again and cupped the back of his head the way he had once held David. "Abba, I'm sorry. Forgive me for being angry with You – and Dinah, and Will – and for not trusting You. Thank you for bringing Will back to me and for bringing me back to You."

After a few minutes the presence lifted and Matthew eased Will back into his seat. "Time to go home."

"Matt? Was that - ? Did God just - ?"

"Yeah, He did."

"Did you – hear anything?"

"Not this time. I felt His arms around me, holding me like I was holding you."

"Maybe I'm, like, crazy," Will said with a shaky laugh, "but ever since the El Camino went into that skid – aw, never mind."

Matthew glanced briefly at Will before returning his eyes to the road. "Has He been talking to you?"

"Well, somebody has!"

"What did He say?"

"The first time, in the truck – this voice said, 'Trust me – take your hands off the wheel.'"

"Did you?"

"I don't remember. I don't remember getting out of the wreck, or out of the ditch. I was standing on the edge of the road, soaked in ice-water, and it said, 'Put out your thumb. The green car is safe.' So I did, and it was."

"Was that all?"

"All? Isn't that enough?"

Matthew stifled a laugh. The conversation was so familiar.

"Then Carl Wilson found me, and he kept telling me to call home. But I wasn't going back there to be yelled at and rejected and sent back to jail. Then I was eating a peanut butter and jelly sandwich and that voice said to me, 'Trust me. Call your father.' I told it no. I told it to shut up and leave me alone. I told it you didn't want me. And then it said, 'Trust me. Your father loves you.'"

"We're almost home," Matthew said, turning onto their road. "Your father does love you, Will, even if it took me a while to get there. And your heavenly Father loves you. He wants us to come home to Him. He's calling you the way He called me." He turned the truck onto the driveway. "See how just about every light in the house is on? They're waiting up for us. Abba-God is waiting up for you." He parked the truck and turned off the engine.

"Wait!" Will's voice held an edge of panic.

"What?"

"What if – I mean, maybe Ed's all mad and John'll say I can't stay any more, and - "

"Will. Hush. That's not goin' to happen. But if it did, I would go with you and find us a place of our own. I know you don't have much reason to trust me yet, but I promise: I won't leave you again. And God's promise is, 'I will never leave you or forsake you.' You can trust Him even if you can't trust me."

Before they could exit the truck, the front door burst open, spilling light and people across the porch and down the steps. Will found himself dragged from the truck into one embrace after another, patted, stroked, welcomed at a pace he wasn't ready for. Matthew's jacket slipped from his shoulders, exposing him to the freezing rain.

"Let's take this inside," John said, smiling and turning the group toward the porch.

Will dug in his heels, looking around. He snatched up Matthew's jacket and clutched it to himself, oblivious to the mud. He fought against the pull of Ed's big hand on his arm.

"Daddy?"

Everything in the world seemed to stand still, waiting for the reply to that call.

"I'm here, son," Matthew said, coming to Will's side. "Welcome home." With an arm around Will's shoulders, Matthew led him into the house.

About the Author

Mary Mueller loves her God, her family and friends, her life and her books. A graduate of the University of Dayton, she has been writing since she was nine and has previously published poems, short stories and devotions. When not working on her next novel, she keeps out of trouble by taking singing lessons, volunteering, directing (and sometimes writing and acting in) skits and dramatic musical productions for her church.

Also by Mary Mueller

Stargazer: The Story of Mary

Stargazer is a first century masterpiece of the life of Mary, mother of Jesus. In retelling the biblical story, we follow Mary from a young girl, through her betrothal to Joseph, the birth of Christ, his childhood, his ministry, and his eventual crucifixion and resurrection. This heartwarming story will help you better understand the biblical story of Mary and the culture she lived in, as well as bring you to a new understanding of the humanity of Christ.